M000202179

Property of the
Sutten Mountain Book Exchange.

If found please return to

_____

Rewrite OUR STORY

KAT SINGLETON

For all my besties who prefer their book boyfriend to have a backwards hat, a pair of cowboy boots, and a filthy mouth. I hope you have the ride of your life with Cade Jennings.

Playlist

'Tis The Damn Season - Taylor Swift
Love Of My Life - Harry Styles
Right Person Right Time - Rachel Grae
Drunk Text - Henry Moodie
Another Go - Logan Michael
Always Been You - Shawn Mendes
Maroon - Taylor Swift
The Exit - Conan Gray
Something In The Orange - Zach Bryan
Evergreen - Christian French
Blame's On Me - Alexander Stewart
Marigold - Phillip LaRue
Hung Up By Now - Page Mackenzie and Garrett Biggs
Excuse The Mess - Austin Snell
Hate This Hometown - Erin Kinsey
Next To You - John Vincent III
Put Me In My Place - Muscadine Bloodline

Prologue
MARE *age 10*

Her frail hand is cold and shaky as she moves blonde ringlets from my forehead. She looks so tired as she glances down at me sadly. "Momma's gonna leave tonight, honey," she tells me, her voice not quite sounding the way I know it should.

"Where are you going, Momma?" I ask, nuzzling deeper into her chest. I'm as gentle as possible, careful not to hurt her. Daddy's always reminding me that Momma is fragile now. I have to watch my movements around her so I don't make her feel any pain.

Momma sighs. It's long and drawn out. One of those big sighs I only ever hear from grown-ups. Suddenly, her body begins to shake underneath mine. I look up to see her eyes full of tears.

"Don't cry, Momma," I beg, carefully pushing off the bed to wipe away her tears. "I'll go with you so you don't have to go alone."

Her eyes close as water streams down her pale cheeks. I miss the color they used to be before she got sick—tan with a tinge of pink from the sun from when she'd forget to wear a hat while we rode down the trails on our horses.

"I'm afraid where I'm going I have to go alone, Marigold," she answers sadly.

Tears form in my eyes, even though I try to fight them.

Daddy always tells me Momma doesn't like to see me cry. I try to make them stop, but Momma's tears increase, and it's no use controlling mine either.

"I don't want you to go anywhere I can't go," I beg.

Her frail fingers work through my hair. "With everything in me, I wish I didn't have to go. But sometimes we aren't the ones to make these choices. You understand me?"

I nod my head even though I don't understand at all. Both Momma and Daddy have been telling me that she would be leaving soon, and I won't be able to see her again, but it doesn't make sense to me. It goes over my head, even though I'm trying hard to understand their words.

Why does Momma have to go somewhere I can't go?

"You might not see me anymore, my dear Marigold, but I know—I *swear*—you'll still feel me." I look up at Momma through blurry, tear-filled eyes.

"How?"

She places her cold palm against my chest, right above the princess on my nightgown. "You'll feel me right here. Forever. Until we're together again."

I sniffle. "I'll see you again?"

Momma pulls me into her, burying her face into my hair as I hide mine against her bony chest. "You'll see me again. When it's time, I'll meet you in a field of marigolds. Just like the one you were named after."

I'm trying to be strong for Momma, but I can't keep it up any longer. I sob; the thought just now occurring to me that I may never see my momma again. Not for a long, long time.

"I'll be waiting for you, my soft, sweet, Marigold. But I don't want to see you there for a while. You hear me? You live your life, honey. Take your time meeting me there."

"Don't go, Momma," I plead, clutching her nightgown.

She wipes my tears away, her eyes moving over my face. "I'll always be with you. This is not a goodbye. Not truly. Anytime you need me, I'll be here."

"How will I know?"

She purses her lips and takes a deep breath, her eyes closing for a moment before she opens them again.

She looks so tired.

"I'll make sure you know."

I nod because I don't know what else to do. I hug my momma tight until Daddy comes in and tells me it's time to go to bed. I don't tell him that Momma told me she was leaving. I know my momma. She'll want to be the one to tell him herself.

So I cling to her for a few more seconds, squeezing her tight, even knowing I was supposed to be gentle with her.

And then I leave, trying to hide the tears as Daddy helps me get ready for bed.

I knew I wouldn't sleep at all. I won't be able to sleep knowing Momma might not be here in the morning.

I don't know how long I've been staring at the snowflakes falling from the sky when I hear Daddy's first cry. I shake my head, trying to get the sound to go away. With each added snowflake on the ground, Daddy's cries get louder. They turn into something more, too. Almost like a screaming-cry. They get so loud that I hold my hands over my ears because I know what's happened.

Momma had been right. She left. She'd gone somewhere Daddy and I can't follow.

My feet take off on their own. One moment I was sitting on the little seat in front of my window that overlooked the trees and the stables, the next I'm running through the snow in a pair of socks and my nightgown, my eyes set on the large home at the top of the hill.

I'm careful as I sneak through the backdoor, knowing the Jennings family never locks it. They don't have to. There isn't anyone around for miles.

There's an ache in my chest as I tip-toe down the familiar hallway, being extra careful to avoid the old floorboards that creak underneath the lightest of pressure. The moon shining through the expansive windows at the front of the house is the only thing guiding my way. I'm careful to not make any noise as I come to a stop in front of a cherry-wood door. Posters of football players and rodeo stars are messily taped to it in a way that makes the wood almost invisible underneath it all.

My shoulders shake violently as I try to take a calming breath. It's something momma taught me to do. *In through the nose, out through the mouth.* I repeat the motion a few times before my small, shaking hand reaches up to grasp the doorknob. It's cold against the inside of my palm, causing the hairs on my arm to raise. I pause, waiting to turn it as I peek down at my clothes.

Momma would be horrified if she knew I was running around in my nightgown with a cold bite in the air.

Too bad Momma isn't here anymore.

I stare at the door, my mind racing with how much things are going to change with Momma gone. Deep down, I know I should turn in the hallway and slip into the room where my best friend sleeps. Pippa could sleep through anything. She probably wouldn't even wake up if I crawled into bed with her. I could pretend, just for a little while longer, that Momma hasn't left us.

It wasn't Pippa I wanted—or needed. At the same time, I knew it was wrong to open *his* door and slip inside his room. With a sad sigh, I turn, my wet socks making a quiet slapping sound on the hardwood as I take a few steps toward Pippa's door.

"Goldie?" a familiar voice calls out from behind me.

I freeze, knowing I've been caught. Slowly, I turn to face the voice behind me.

Cade Jennings.

My best friend's big brother. The boy I've had a crush on for as long as I can remember.

His eyes widen when he takes me in. His pajamas have superheroes all over them. I remember Pippa making fun of them at breakfast a couple of weeks ago.

I thought you weren't supposed to like superheroes anymore now that you're a teenager?

Cade hadn't batted an eye when he looked down at the heroes. He didn't care what she thought.

He gently tugs on my arm, pulling me into his room and shutting the door behind him.

"How'd you know I was out here?" I'd asked, trying to wipe away the tears on my cheeks.

Cade doesn't answer me at first. He pulls me toward his bed and softly pushes me down to sit. "Cade?" I repeated, for some reason focusing on how he knew I was out there.

Bending down, he pulls the wet socks off my feet. He throws them toward his laundry basket that has clothes spilling from it in every direction. Immediately, he walks to his dresser and pulls out a pair of wool socks. They're too big for my feet but he slides them on anyway. I don't care about the size. They're comfy. They're *his*.

He looks at me with something I don't quite understand filling his eyes, and his hands rest on his hips in a serious position. I think he might've learned it from his mom. It's something she does all the time.

"I don't know, Goldie," he whispers. "I woke up and just felt like you were there. That you needed me. And then—"

"Then?" I whisper, clinging to every single one of his words. Maybe if I focus hard enough on him, I won't remember the sound of Daddy's cries echoing throughout the small cabin.

"Then you were there." He pauses, taking in my appearance. "Why are you wet?" he asks before noticing the tears coating my cheeks. "And why are you crying?"

He throws a blanket over my shoulders and pulls me into his scrawny body.

His question opens my heart. All of my feelings come pouring out, and I start crying right there on the edge of Cade's bed.

"Oh shit," Cade mumbles into my hair as he awkwardly wraps me in a hug.

"That's a bad word." My voice shakes as I struggle to get the words out between my sobs.

Cade pulls his blue comforter around us. Without words, he nudges me up the bed. "Not sure what you expect from me when you're crying like this, Goldie. Pops always says we can use bad words if the timing is right."

I let him help me get comfortable under the sheets. There's a warm spot where his body must've been before I interrupted his sleep. Cade scoots closer to me. Carefully, he pushes a stray, wet piece of hair from my face. It reminds me of the gesture my momma just did a few hours ago. Hours before I lost her forever.

At least until we meet again like she promised.

In a field of marigolds.

His copper eyes take in my face. "I don't like seeing you cry, Goldie."

Cade Jennings is never soft. Even at thirteen, he's rough around the edges. Our mommas always joked about how wild and untamed he was. Like the mustangs us kids love to observe from afar. I've never quite seen Cade's eyes go soft the way they are right now.

Time seems to stop as he reaches over and wipes the tears off my cheeks. He looks at the water that's now on the tip of his thumb. "What do you need?" he whispers into the dark. "How can I take away the pain?"

"Momma," I croak, closing my eyes, hoping maybe if I squeeze them tight enough the world will disappear and I'll never have to remember the way Daddy sounded when his heart broke—how he sounded when my momma left us. "She's gone."

His arms wrap around me and pull me into his chest before I can get any other words out. In the next breath he's dragging his soft comforter over our heads, blocking the rest of the world out.

I don't know how long he holds me as I cry. The thing I've always liked about Cade is that he doesn't feel the need to fill the silence. He's so much quieter than I am. He prefers to observe rather than to interject. Right now, I'm grateful. I'm glad he doesn't try to fill the room with words that don't mean a thing in these circumstances.

"I'm sorry if I woke you up." I sniffle against his chest, wishing we could stay underneath the protection of his comforter for forever.

"Wake me up anytime you need."

I look at him through blurry eyes. I must look like a mess, but Cade doesn't seem to care. "You mean that?"

He nods. His mouth opens like he wants to say something, but he must think better of it because he quickly closes it. It seems like forever until he finally opens his mouth to talk again. "I mean it, Goldie."

Cade Jennings did mean it. He was there for me night after night. When I was a sad child mourning the loss of her mother— her world—he was the one to help me through it. He never asked questions when I'd show up at his door throughout the years. He always had some sort of sixth sense, always somehow knowing when I needed him. He'd open the door to find me standing there, needing him for one reason or another. I knew Cade would always be in there in the dark confines of the four walls of his bedroom.

Cade Jennings was always there for me when I needed him— until he wasn't.

Chapter 1
MARE
fourteen years later

WHAT IS it about airplanes that make people forget about all semblance of personal space?

We've only just landed on the tarmac when every person next to me stands up, despite the fact we're at the back of the plane. We won't deplane for another ten minutes at the very least, yet I've got all three passengers from the row behind me leaning over my seat and breathing on me as if huffing and puffing down some stranger's neck will help everyone else move faster.

I'd had to book the flight in the middle of the night after my best friend, Pippa, called me sobbing. There weren't many choices of seats for a flight at seven the very next morning. I'd had the wonderful luxury of sitting in a middle seat between two strangers; neither adhered to the armrest rules—AKA the person in the middle gets at least one armrest. It's just human decency in my own little humble opinion.

The phone vibrating in my lap snaps me from my thoughts. I look down at it, holding it close to me so the hoverer in the window seat next to me doesn't read my texts.

PIPPA

> I checked the app and saw you just landed. I can't wait to see you!

MARE

> I'll text you as soon as I'm through baggage claim. You know how it is here. I'll probably be awhile.

PIPPA

> Sounds good. Love you, Mare. Thank you for coming.

MARE

> I wouldn't be anywhere else.

My chest constricts as I recall the reason I'm here. Pippa's mom, Linda, suddenly passed away two days ago, taking everybody by surprise. She'd been in perfect health—or so we'd thought. Turns out, her heart wasn't in good condition. The night before last she went to bed and just never woke up.

Pippa had been in shambles when she'd called me with the news. I was in the midst of a writing retreat when I received the call. I'd been desperately trying to finish the book that was due to my publisher but I dropped everything to be here. I hadn't been lying to Pippa when I'd said I couldn't imagine myself being anywhere else. Even though I left the small town of Sutten Mountain for college, it'd always be my home. Linda was a mother to me. She picked up where my own mother left off when she passed away, and she filled the void in my heart effortlessly.

Linda Jennings was a ray of sunshine in my often dark life. Dad was never the same after Mom passed. He did what he could, but he was mourning the love of his life. He didn't have it in him to realize how much I was grieving not having a mom. That's where Linda stepped in. For years, she was my rock—my mother figure. She never let me forget my own mother, though. Linda made sure she passed the memories she shared with my mom down to me. She always said she admired how I was as sweet as honey with a little bit of tang and sass.

As the man with the window seat next to me attempts to squeeze between my knees and the back of the seat in front of me, that sass comes out. I push my knees farther in front of me, preventing the man from inching his way even more into my personal space.

The guy glares down at me. "Excuse me." He coughs, making me grimace because that may have just been his spit that landed on my cheek.

I plaster on a fake smile. "Sorry sir, I just don't think it's our turn yet." My eyes flick to the rows of people in front of us that are still waiting to grab their bags from the overhead compartments.

The man on the other side of me snickers. Even though he's an armrest thief and stood up entirely too early, he seems to be on my side in this case. "Are you trying to catch a connecting flight?" he pipes up, looking over my head at the window guy.

Window guy furrows his eyebrows. "Yes. I've got a flight in two hours to catch."

I try my best to fight the smile on my lips. This guy has more than enough time to cross the small airport before his next flight begins boarding.

Aisle guy clears his throat. "I think you'll make it."

I don't continue a conversation with either of the men. As soon as it's actually our turn to leave our seats, I grab my bag from the overhead bin and anxiously deplane.

The pit in my stomach gets bigger as I wait at baggage claim and prepare for what's to come. Linda was the glue that held the Jennings family together. Her husband, Jasper, is probably beside himself. They had been together since middle school. She loved to tell the story of how he stole her pencil and she instantly fell in love with him.

And then there's Linda's pride and joy—her kids. I'm all too familiar with the pain that comes from losing a mother. Cade and Pippa have to be absolutely devastated. The pit in my stomach sours with a feeling of regret. I should've come back home more after I left for college. Linda had asked me to come home around every holiday and every birthday. She was always encouraging me to come back to the Jennings Family's Ranch and see them. I always found some excuse to avoid going back to the place that held so many happy—and so many terrible—memories.

The truth is, I never really intended to return home. Not really. At least not until my broken heart had mended. I'd loved Cade for so long, and when I finally came to the catastrophic realization that he'd never loved me in the way I wanted him to, I was gutted.

The sight of my dented black suitcase looping around the luggage carousel brings me back to the present. A few unlady-like grunting noises leave my body as I try to heave the suitcase off the lip of the conveyor belt. With a few more tugs, the suit-case falls to the ground with a loud *thump*. Taking a deep breath, I push the blonde curls out of my face and grab the handles of both my bags.

Pippa had only asked me to stay until after the funeral, but I knew my best friend would need me longer than that. It's the reason I told Rudy, my agent, that I'll be finishing up the book in Sutten. It isn't ideal, and he didn't seem thrilled about the sudden change of plans, but there isn't much I can do. We both know how behind I am on this book. I had so many people supporting me when I wrote my debut novel—the first book in this duet—and I don't want to let the people who took a chance on me down with the conclusion to this couple's love story.

Before leaving baggage claim, I text Pippa that I'm heading out and slide my phone back in my pocket so I can have use of both my hands. My phone vibrates in my back pocket as I wheel my suitcases toward the exit. I'm guessing it's Pippa texting me back, but I don't have a free hand to check it. If she's texting me that she's here, I'll find out soon enough when I see her truck outside.

The sun coming up over the mountains is blinding, and I have to squint to search for Pippa. I frown, not seeing her anywhere. I'm seconds away from pulling my phone out when I hear a familiar voice.

"Goldie." My stomach plummets from the way the nickname sounds coming out of *his* mouth. The two syllables coming from his lips still make my stomach twist, even years later. It used to be in anticipation. Only now it's in distress. Maybe it has something to do with the menacing way he pronounces the name he's called me for as long as I can remember.

I stare at my feet, afraid to look him in the eye. I knew I'd have to come face to face with Cade again. It's just that...I thought I'd have time to prepare myself. I thought I had the two hours it took from the airport to the ranch to get my shit together and to goad Pippa for information on how Cade is doing—on what I could expect from him.

A pair of cowboy boots come into view. I don't have to look up to know who they belong to. Just like Cade always felt me when I'd shown up at his bedroom door late at night, I can feel him. In any room, any place, I can feel him. Just like right now.

Taking a deep breath, I look up and into the eyes of the boy who broke my heart. Except, it's no longer a boy that looks back at me. It's a man, and he looks better than I could've ever imagined.

Chapter 2
CADE
present

MY EYES FLICK down Mare's body as she gawks at me in what looks like disbelief. Her gloss-coated lips part as she stares a hole right through my head.

I'm not sure I blame her. The last time we saw each other—the last time she saw me—we were standing at this very airport. She'd offered to give me everything she had to give but I denied her. I walked away from her.

It seems she hasn't forgotten how we left things.

I haven't either.

"Did that big city steal your voice?" I ask, pulling one of her blonde curls. Her hair is much longer than the last time I saw her. I loathe how much more tamed it looks now that she's all grown up. Maybe it's the fact that the carefully styled locks are just another reminder that she left our small town and didn't look back once. She adapted to city life like it was made for her.

Like her place wasn't at the ranch where mine would always be.

Mare scrunches her nose at me. If it's an attempt at a snarl, she epically fails. It's much cuter, and far less intimidating than I think she intends it to be. "I was expecting Pippa," she says. Her words have a bite to them that I'm not entirely surprised by. She refuses to look at me as she pulls her phone from the back pocket

Even her jeans don't look the way they should. They're not worn in the slightest. There isn't a single hole or fray on them. I *hate* it. Mare always had a way of wearing jeans until they were so destroyed; Mom would scold her until she got a new pair.

My heart twinges from the memory of Mom.

I wait as Mare stares down at her phone. Pippa said it'd be best if Mare didn't know I was going to be the one to pick her up. At first, Pippa had intended to do it. But the funeral director had questions for Dad, and he didn't have it in him to answer what kind of casket or what flowers she preferred, so he delegated it to Pippa. I don't exactly have an eye for details—not in the way Pippa does—so she was the easy option.

Staring at the woman in front of me, I almost wish I was the one going over the funeral details. At least I wouldn't be spending the next two hours in a car with a woman who clearly hasn't forgotten the scars of our past.

"Couldn't Pippa have sent someone else?" Mare questions. When I try to take one of her suitcases, she slaps my hand away in defiance.

I fight a grin. There's something about the way Mare–the girl I nicknamed *Goldie*—attempts to look intimidating; it soothes the ache in my heart.

Despite her attempts to push me away, I grab her larger suitcase and head toward my parked truck. "And who would you suggest?"

Mare reluctantly follows me, and her eyes narrow when they focus on the tailgate I pull down. "I don't know, one of the stable hands."

I shake my head at her. "They have jobs. Trail maintenance in the morning and then we've got a full schedule of trail rides today."

"Oh," she says under her breath,

"Is there anything you didn't pack?" I heave the larger suitcase in the truck bed. It's heavier than I was expecting. "How much did you pack?"

"I wasn't sure how long I'd be staying…"

I scowl, turning around to face her. "Hopefully not long."

She anxiously chews on her lip as I tear the other suitcase from her grip and gently toss it in the bed of the truck.

Turning to face her, I look at the space surrounding her for more bags. "Anything else?"

She shakes her head. "That's all I brought."

"I meant did you have any other questions, but that's good to know," I quip sarcastically.

"I see you're just as peachy as ever."

"Since when has anyone called me *peachy*?"

Mare rolls her blue eyes at me. "It's a figure of speech, Cade. Trust me, if anyone knows how much of a dick you are, it's me."

Damn. She's going there already. Apparently living the big city life has strengthened her backbone. The Marigold that left for college and the Marigold glaring back at me right now are two very different people. This new version of her has way more bite, it seems.

It shouldn't excite me. Yet, it does.

I prop my arm against my truck. I don't bother hiding the lingering look I give her as I observe her from head to toe.

Marigold Evans.

My Goldie.

Fuck has she changed since the last time I saw her. She was nineteen and eager to see what else the big world had to offer. She had freckles on her face and a slight sunburn on her forehead. Now, she stands in front of me with pain in her eyes and skin shades lighter than back then.

She's different now in so many ways, yet she's somehow exactly the same. My gaze is drawn to her lips first. They're still puffy, the bottom one plumper than the top. If she were to smile at me, she'd no doubt have the deep dimples on either side of her face that had, at one time in my life, driven me wild.

Her hair isn't as light as it used to be. Probably because the sun isn't beating down on it during long trail rides like it used to. It's sad to see her typical golden locks not shining like they used to.

"Are you going to keep staring?" Mare asks, interrupting my thoughts. It's probably for the best.

I slap the truck, smirking at her as I shake my head. Pippa's always scolding me about how I need to smile more, especially when it comes to customers. I've told her countless times that my face wasn't meant to smile. Yet, I've been in the presence of Mare for five minutes, and I've already caught myself smiling more than usual.

Maybe it's the familiarity. For all the bad between Mare and I, there's still a lot of good too. She and Pippa were glued at the hip growing up, which meant I was also always around her. I never admitted it, but I liked it. She and Pippa were the only kids on the ranch. We had to wait for school days or for customers to see anyone else. It's only natural how close we all used to be.

"Get in the truck." I round the hood, opening the door and loving the fresh scent of new leather. I saved up for ages to get my own truck; one that didn't have the Jennings Ranch brand on it. As much as I love the work trucks, and I still mostly drive those as I prepare to take over the family business, I wanted something that was my own.

Apparently, Mare doesn't seem to have the same sentiment. In fact, she seems peeved that I'm not driving the same old truck she remembers from five years ago. People walk behind her, all going about their own lives, while she stares daggers at my pride and joy.

"I'll call an Uber."

I fix the baseball cap on my head, flipping it backward so I can slide a pair of sunglasses on. "Marigold," I chide. "I know it's been a long time since you've been home, but you know how it is. It's off-season. You could be waiting for a car for hours."

Her hands find her narrow hips. "I guess I'll wait."

A frustrated growl falls from my lips. "If I don't return home with you, Pippa will kill me. You know that. I know that. So get in the damn truck."

Her feet stay planted.

My head falls backward with a defeated sigh. I don't have the energy to do this with her. I turn to face her, taking a long, slow breath. "Get in...*please*."

Her eyes soften. When she takes a step toward the truck, I get a glimpse of the girl I used to know. For a few short moments, she doesn't look angry with me anymore. In fact, she looks at me the way she used to. She watches me like she thinks I hung the moon. Like I can do no wrong. Sometimes I wish we could go back to old times. A time before I let her down.

Just when I think she might do as she's asked, she raises her chin defiantly and looks me square in the eye. "No."

"No?"

"I don't want to get in the truck with you, Cade."

"I don't remember asking what you wanted."

"Well that makes sense because you *never* cared about what I wanted."

Her words are like a kick in the gut. Years ago, we were in almost this exact same spot when she begged me to listen to her and what she wanted. We stare angrily at each other for a few more seconds before I let out a long sigh.

"Get in the damn truck or I'll put you in there myself. Either way, I'm not fucking leaving without you."

She looks me up and down, as if she's trying to see if I'm bluffing.

I'm sure as hell not. The past few days have been shitty. Adding in the fact that I have to see her again, where we ended things of all places, means my patience is non-existent.

To prove a point, I step closer to her.

Her hands instantly come between us in an attempt to keep me at a distance. "Fine!" she yells, taking a step away from me. "I'll get in the truck."

She's silent as she slides into the seat and closes the door. I get in, yanking my door closed.

My fingers tap against the steering wheel. With both of us in the truck, I know I should just shift into *drive* and go, but something stops me. I feel like there's more I need to say to her, but I just can't get a grasp on what I should say.

She beats me to it. With a long sigh, she slides her hand across the leather between us and carefully places it on my thigh. "I'm so sorry about Linda, Cade." Her voice shakes as she squeezes my leg. My hand falls to hers instinctively. For a few moments, the rest of the world fades away, and it's just Goldie and me again. Things aren't complicated. It's just her hand in mine and the feeling of immense comfort. The angry tension is gone, at least for the moment. For a few short seconds, I remember why I gave her the nickname Goldie in the first place. Aside from it being a shortened version of her name, she always reminded me of the sun. She brought light into my life. And for right now, even if it's only for a brief moment, she brings a little bit of light into a darkness.

My thumb brushes over the top of her hand once before she pulls away, and the connection is broken. I swallow through the lump of emotion stuck in my throat.

I was the one who found my mom in my parents' bed. It should seem real that she's gone, but somehow it still hasn't hit me that we're never going to see her again. Before I can say anything else, I throw the truck into drive and pull away from the curb, embarking on what might be the two longest hours of my life.

Chapter 3
MARE
present

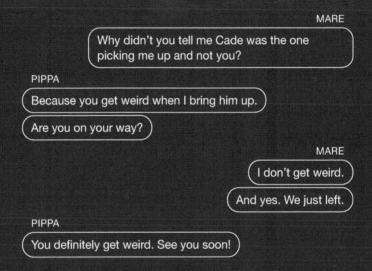

MARE

MARE

Why didn't you tell me Cade was the one picking me up and not you?

PIPPA

Because you get weird when I bring him up.

Are you on your way?

MARE

I don't get weird.

And yes. We just left.

PIPPA

You definitely get weird. See you soon!

I TUCK my phone back into my lap. I'd love to scroll aimlessly on one of my social media accounts, or at least catch up on the emails piling up in my inbox, but I do neither. Soon we'll be driving through the mountains and overpasses. If I stare down at my lap too much, I'll get car sick. The last thing I plan on doing in the excruciating two hours I'm stuck with Cade is throwing up the complimentary snacks from the flight.

I brave a peek at him from the corner of my eye. He's only gotten better looking with age. Why can't he look silly in a backward cap? He's closer to thirty than he is twenty. He shouldn't look so damn hot in something he wore as a teenager. I don't even want to take the time to really get to know the new, defined muscles that line his arms. I wish it wasn't off season and the weather wasn't so nice. Then I'd see him in his usual flannel shirt or weathered sweatshirt, both options keeping his improved physique a secret.

I have no such luck. His Jennings Ranch T-shirt fits him too perfectly. It hugs the bulging muscles that weren't as pronounced when I last saw him—back when he was twenty-two.

"How's your dad?" I ask, leaning back in the seat to get more comfortable.

Cade whistles under his breath. "Terrible. I've never seen him like this. It's like he's *there* but not *there*, you know?"

I nod, staring at the mountains coming into view through the windshield. There's snow on the very top, greens and grays covering the rest. "Yeah, I do," I whisper. My mind flashes to the years after Momma died. Daddy was never the same after she passed. He rarely laughed. Most of the time he didn't even realize that another human was sharing that little cabin in the woods with him. He buried himself in work…but I found a way to not be lonely. I found a second home with Cade and Pippa's family. Every single one of them were there for me when I was a lonely child. But it still made me sad for my dad. He didn't have a new family like I did. He didn't want one.

Cade's knuckles hit the dashboard. "Shit, I'm sorry. If anyone knows what this is like, it's you."

I swallow, trying to keep my emotions at bay. Truthfully, the hardest part about losing Momma was seeing Daddy's reaction to it.

The day he told me he was moving from Sutten and getting a fresh start somewhere else was the first moment I felt hope for him. When he told me he met a woman, and when he ended up privately marrying his now wife, Suzie, four years ago, I'd never felt such relief. I know Momma will always hold a place in his heart, but the absence does get easier with time. Or at least more bearable. I want to tell Cade this, but I hold my tongue.

Sometimes when you're grieving you don't want to be told things will get better. You just want to feel the pain without people making false promises. With death nothing gets better. They're still gone. Things just get more tolerable to deal with.

"There's nothing to be sorry about. I asked because I wanted to know. Because I care."

Cade briefly glances over at me. His dark eyebrows bunch together on his forehead like he's deep in thought. I rest my head against the cold glass window. There was a time where he'd openly tell me what was on his mind. I wonder if he'd tell me what he's thinking about if I were to ask him.

Because I'm a masochist—and apparently enjoy being hurt when it comes to him—I decide to ask. "What's on your mind?"

The muscles running along his sharp jawline flex. He works his jaw back and forth, like he's fighting the urge to say whatever he wants to say.

"Cade?" I prod. My heartbeat picks up inside my chest. If he gives me a one word answer, or worse, tells me nothing, I'll have to accept that he's a much different person than the one I grew up with. I might have to unfortunately accept that he may not open up to me the way he used to.

Time may not have healed all wounds when it comes to us. There still might be too many hard memories between us for things to go back to the way they used to be—before he broke my heart.

Unlike the Cade I used to know, music isn't pouring from the speakers of his truck. It makes the silence between us even more deafening. I'm moments away from telling him to forget about it when he lets out a loud sigh.

"I was just thinking how much she'd love to know that

you're back. If it were under different circumstances, that is." His voice is low and much more hoarse than it was before. There's still a hint of anger to it, but it's a soft kind of angry. His words cut deep. I should've come back more. It was just too hard. I was too afraid to face the man seated next to me. I was naïve enough to think one day it wouldn't hurt to come back. And that I'd have countless more years with Linda. I was wrong about both.

"I should've come back more."

He nods, fixing the ball cap on his head. "Yeah. You should've."

I have to look away from him, turning to face the window as I try to rein in my emotions. When Cade reaches in front of him and turns on the radio, I let out a sigh of relief. The truth is, I don't have a good enough excuse to explain my absence. At the time, I thought it was the only excuse needed. My heart was broken, and I couldn't face the man who broke it. I thought because Pippa came to college with me, and I saw Linda and Jasper when they came up to visit, that everything was fine. Pippa went back to Sutten when we graduated, and I told her I couldn't go with her.

I'd secured a major book deal, on the first book I wrote, shortly after moving to Chicago. Life got busy, my heart didn't heal, and I never got the nerve to return to Sutten.

But I should have.

Every time Linda called to catch up, I could tell she wanted me to come home. If I wasn't so selfish, I would have. Deep down, I knew I'd always feel hurt, no matter how much time passed. If I would've pushed past it I wouldn't be living with the deep regret I am now, knowing my time with her was cut short.

It takes everything in me to keep the tears welling up in my eyes at bay. Cade just lost his mom. He has every right to be angry with me for not coming home to see her. *I'm* not the one who should be crying. I don't deserve to feel this sad when I never made the effort to come home.

If he notices the war I'm having with my emotions, he

doesn't say anything. In fact, he turns the music up. The old song floating through the speakers takes me back to a memory many years ago.

Chapter 4
MARE
age sixteen

I GROAN as I try for what feels like the millionth time to wake up my best friend. The tip of my finger jabs into Pippa's side. Any other person would wake up howling from the pressure. *Not Pippa*. She lets out the faintest of growls in her sleep and nuzzles even deeper into her pillowcase.

"Pippa, you promised." Grabbing her hand, I pull with all my might. It's no use. She sleeps like the dead.

With an aggravated sigh, I let her hand drop to the mattress with a *thud*. When I told her how I wanted to spend the night I turned sixteen, she'd swore she'd stay awake long enough to execute said plans with me.

Pippa is a *liar*.

Like always, she fell asleep and now I'm left having to decide if I want to cancel how I wanted to spend tonight or if I want to spend it alone.

I stomp to her door, roughly pulling it closed behind me. It's mostly to make myself feel better. If my pokes and prods for ten minutes didn't wake her up, then the slam of the door won't either.

During the entire walk to the stables I plan all the things I'm going to say to Pippa when she wakes up tomorrow morning. I should've known better than to trust she'd stay up, but I had hope. When the clock strikes midnight, it'll be my birthday. My sixteenth. It's a *big* deal. And she'll be sleeping right through it.

I'm so busy being angry with my best friend that I don't notice the body coming out of the tack room. I barrel right into him, almost knocking the saddle in his hands to the ground.

"Woah!" Cade calls, balancing the saddle in one hand and using the other to steady me. "You talking to yourself again, Goldie?"

I look up at him, eyes wide when I notice the open button up T-shirt he wears. And what he *doesn't* wear underneath it.

God, why does he have to have perfect abs? And why do I want to memorize the feel of them?

"I don't know what you're talking about," I argue, putting my arms over my chest defensively.

His lips twitch as he attempts to fight a smile. It doesn't work for long. He shows off his perfectly white teeth as he shakes his head at me. "You talk a lot. It's probably a talent how much you can talk when nobody is listening."

He takes off, walking out the barn doors. Cade doesn't leave me many options. I can stand here and go about my night alone, or I can follow him and continue our conversation. It's really not a decision at all. I'll take advantage of any extra second I can have with him; especially if it means we're alone, which doesn't happen often.

"I really don't talk that much." I scurry out the doors, coming to a halt when I notice the two horses tied to the hitching post. My head tilts in confusion. "Are you going for a ride?"

Music blares from the stereo in the tack room. I recognize it as one of Cade's current favorites. He's been playing it non-stop. It's become one of my favorites right along with his.

Cade places the saddle on Tonka's back. *Weird.* He normally rides Ranger. Reaching under Tonka's belly, he fastens the girth before answering me. "No. But I figured you and Pip were for your birthday. I just got back from checking the trails for the night. Figured I'd get the horses ready for your birthday ride."

My heart flutters. It's no use fighting it. I know his action doesn't mean anything. But to me, it means *everything*.

He remembered.

The high only lasts for a few moments before I let out a defeated sigh. "We were supposed to go for one. But she's asleep. I figured I'd go alone."

Cade watches me carefully from over Tonka. Normally Pippa rides Tonka and I ride Dolly, which makes sense because those are the two horses he has tied to the post. The only problem is the fact that Pippa is fast asleep in her bed.

"You aren't riding alone," he sternly says.

I frown. There's no way I'm missing this ride. I'm going whether he likes it or not.

"You're not the boss of me, Cade Jennings."

"Who else is going to tell you when you're doing something stupid?" he counters.

"I could ride these trails in my sleep and you know it. I'll be fine. It's summer. The snow has melted. It hasn't rained in ages. Again. I'll. Be. Fine."

"You'll be fine because you're not going alone." Cade loops the reins around Tonka's saddle horn. He looks to Dolly, who is already tacked up and patiently waiting to go out.

"Yeah?" I argue, placing my hands on my hips. "And who's going to go with me? Because I'm not missing it. It's *my* birthday after all."

"You won't be going alone because I'm going with you."

This makes my mouth snap shut. I glance down at my boots. The black leather is dirty, in desperate need of a cleaning but I've been too lazy recently. I think through what I want to say in response to him before looking back up.

When our eyes connect again, he's buttoning up his shirt, his focus solely on me.

I flex my fingers anxiously, wondering if this is too good to be true. "Don't you have somewhere else to be?"

"Nowhere that's more important than celebrating your birthday," he answers. The rasp in his voice sends tingles down my spine.

Last week when Parker Prewitt asked to take me to Pop's Ice Cream Parlor for a date, I hadn't felt the same shivers as I do now. And this isn't even a date. But it's alone time with *Cade*. The boy whose name I've doodled in every notebook. The one I always hoped to land on in every MASH game. And he's offering to spend the night of my birthday with me.

No birthday wish could be better than this.

"You don't have to," I argue weakly. I want to spend this time with him with every part of me. But I'm in this weird limbo of no longer being the little girl who didn't care if it bothered Cade when Pippa and I tagged along with him. Cade isn't young anymore and I'm not either. I don't want him to feel like he has to spend tonight with me because he feels bad Pippa isn't. "I'm fine being alone."

He rolls his eyes. "You *hate* being alone."

I fight my own eye roll. *Damn Cade*. He knows me too well.

"I hate feeling like a responsibility even more." I walk up to Dolly, running a hand down her gray-speckled body. She whinnies in excitement when I pull a peppermint from the pocket of my cutoff jean shorts and hold my hand flat for her to lap it up.

The candy crushes between her teeth. I smile at her, loving how she nuzzles into my hand as she searches for another treat.

"You aren't a responsibility. Now, let's go."

I turn my focus from Dolly to Cade. He stands next to Tonka, his fingers scratching at the horse's favorite spot. Tonka lets out a pleased sound, turning his head to get Cade's hand in the optimal position.

The two of us engage in a silent stare off. I pay close attention to his every move, trying to decipher if he means it or not. He isn't typically the kind of person to lie to make someone feel better. He just won't say anything at all. But for some reason, I can't shake the feeling that he's only doing this as a favor to his sister—or maybe for his parents. It could even be a favor to me.

None of those answers are the reason I want him to be doing this.

The crush that I haven't been able to shake has me believing that maybe, just *maybe*, he actually wants to spend his evening with me.

Dolly lets out a loud neigh, making me jump.

Cade laughs. "You tell her, Dolly. I thought we were going to go for a ride, but Goldie seems to be happy just checking me out."

I slide my foot in and heave myself over, adjusting my position in the saddle. "Stop fooling yourself," I chide. "I wasn't checking you out."

Cade repeats my same motion, throwing one leg over Tonka's back until he's seated in the saddle. "You were definitely checking me out." He clicks his tongue, coaxing Tonka away from the hitching post. "Let's go."

Before I can argue that all the girls that have started flocking to him in town have gotten to his head, he's digging his heels into Tonka's belly, propelling the horse forward.

He leaves me no choice but to guide Dolly right after him.

Chapter 5
MARE
present

I'VE BARELY HAD the chance to open the passenger door of Cade's truck when a body comes crashing into mine. My back digs into the frame of the truck as Pippa envelops me in a bear hug.

"Mare," she breathes into my hair, squeezing me tightly. "I'm so glad you came."

I pull my best friend into my body, clutching her as tight as I can manage. "Of course I came," I mumble into her hair, getting a mouthful of her straight, brown locks.

Silence unfolds as we hold each other. It's only been three months since Pippa came up and visited me in Chicago. We had the time of our lives as I showed her every tourist attraction possible in the seven days she spent with me. Neither one of us could've imagined the reason we'd be reunited again.

Pulling away, Pippa hooks her arm through mine. "I really don't know if we'd be able to do this without you."

With her mention of *we*, my eyes flick to Cade. He still sits in the driver's seat, his attention on Pippa and me. There's an unreadable look in his eyes as he stares back at me.

I don't tell Pippa that I'm fairly certain Cade doesn't want me here. Looking away from him, I let her pull me toward the stone path that leads to the front door.

My heart sinks when I notice the rocking chairs that are perched on the large front porch. One of Linda's favorite things to do after dinner was to rock in the chair and look out on the land. She'd make tea, sweetened with way too much honey, and talk your ear off sitting on that porch. I hadn't realized how much I missed those evening chats until it dawns on me that they'll never happen again.

I look to Pippa at my side. Her eyes are red, free of makeup as she keeps her gaze pinned on the front door. I wonder if her mind is wandering to the same place mine was. Looking over my shoulder, I notice Cade pulling down the tailgate of his truck.

"I should probably get my bags."

Pippa shakes her head, keeping a tight grip on me. She clings to me for dear life. As if now that I'm here, she can't stand to let me go. "Cade can do it," she states, the tone of her voice leaving no room for discussion. Pippa is as head-strong as they come. Whatever she says, goes.

Proving her point, Cade pulls both my suitcases from the truck bed. His fingers wrap around each handle as he follows far behind Pippa and me.

I tear my gaze from him, not wanting to be caught staring at the bulging biceps fighting against the sleeves of his shirt. "What do you need from me?" I ask Pippa, following her through the large wood front doors.

Pippa takes a deep breath, leading me to the expansive kitchen. She points to a counter full of photos, papers, and catalogs for different packages from the funeral home. "I need a *lot*, honestly. But most importantly, I was wondering if you'd maybe speak at the service?"

Blood drains from my face as I think about having to stand in front of the entire town. I had to do it once before—for my mother's funeral. I was too young to stand up there, but my dad wouldn't say anything and so many people from the town were looking at us. I thanked them for coming and tried to use words to describe what Momma meant to all of us. It wasn't something any ten year old should have to do. Linda had been there to save the day. She'd left her seat and said some words to the crowd on behalf of our family.

Pippa must notice the color leaving my face because she chews on her lip nervously. She looks away from me and focuses on the photos of her mom laid out on the table. "You just have this way with words that no one else has."

"*Written* words. I don't know if I'm good at the whole *saying it aloud* thing."

Pippa's shoulders slump as her eyes focus on a picture of her mom holding baby Cade. "Will you at least help me write something that I can read?"

As terrifying as it is to stand up at one of those podiums again and address a crowd full of people, I don't want Pippa to have to go through it since it's clearly something she isn't comfortable with. "I'll write and read it," I assure her, squeezing her shoulder. "But will you read it once I'm done to make sure I'm saying what you want me to say?"

Pippa's eyes fill with tears. She wipes at them immediately, not wanting me to see them. That's Pippa. She's headstrong and extremely confident. She'd much rather people not know her emotions, to not see her falter, even if it's in the instance of something as tragic as this. She and Cade are more similar than they'd care to admit.

"I'm sure anything you write will be perfect, but of course I'll read it."

I swallow, ignoring the sound behind me as Cade brings my suitcases through the front door. I'm already terrified of having to write a eulogy for Linda. How are you supposed to encapsulate all the good and wonderful things someone did in their life in a few short paragraphs? It's unfair, to reduce something as incredible as Linda's life to a few short moments in time.

"Where should I take the bags?" Cade's interruption has Pippa and me turning to face him.

"I can stay at my old place," I offer, not wanting to get in the way of them. They're all grieving, the last thing I want to do is to be a bother to them.

Cade and Pippa share a look.

"Cade is staying there now," Pippa explains nervously. "We kept it for you for a while after your daddy left, but something had to be done with it and you didn't come back. Then we uh, kind of rebuilt it. The wood was bad and we wanted to add extra rooms and bunks for staff to sleep. But it's been Cade's place while he finishes up with his own house. We've both been staying in the main house anyway, just so Dad isn't here alone."

"Duh," I breathe, swatting the air. "I don't know what I was thinking. I'm good with any of the guest rooms." I look at Cade. Will it ever be easy to look into his deep copper eyes? Or will I always feel an ache in my stomach when our gazes collide? "Just pick one for me," I add. Cade's parents' house is massive. While it was built ages ago by Cade's great-grandfather, it's been kept in pristine condition throughout the years. Different things have been expanded over time, adding to the luxury of a house they all still call a cabin despite it being more like a mansion instead.

He nods and grabs my suitcases without saying a word before heading up the stairs.

Pippa watches her brother with concern. Despite being a few years apart, the two of them are closer than most siblings. I remember the fights they got into when we were kids. Even though they fought a lot, their arguments never lasted long. Cade always ended up letting Pippa win. He'd apologize, even when it was typically her that was supposed to be the one apologizing.

"How's he doing?" I ask, unable to help myself. Despite Cade always working closely with their father so he can take over the ranch one day, he was still a momma's boy. He was sweet to her. If anyone could pull him out of a bad mood it was his mom. He's got to be hurting. But in typical Cade fashion, you'd never know it.

"You know Cade," she answers sadly, picking up a picture of

Cade and Linda from when he was a baby. "He won't really show—or tell us—how he's feeling. But I know it's not good. All he's been doing is working."

"That doesn't surprise me."

"He was the one to find her."

My head whips in her direction as dread settles deep in my bones. "What?" I croak as sadness washes over me. The trauma Cade must be dealing with is overwhelming.

Pippa begins to place the photos in different piles. I want to ask her what she needs me to do to help sort them, but right now I'm too stunned. "I was at work, and Dad was on the trails. Cade stopped by for a morning coffee with Mom. It's something they'd been doing for a few years. She'd been on him for working too much. One of the paramedics, someone who stops by the bakery often, told me Cade had given CPR on his own for at least thirty minutes until they arrived. Since then he's just been...quiet."

"I can't even imagine." I help her straighten a pile of photographs just to give myself something to do, my mind focusing on the pain Cade must be going through.

My eyes travel to the stairs again, shocked to see Cade leaning against the wood bannister. His expression is unreadable. I wonder how long he's been listening to our conversation. He hadn't been there when I looked not too long ago. He's the only person I know who can walk so quietly in a pair of heavy cowboy boots. I rip my gaze away from him, not wanting to look at him longer than necessary.

"So what are we doing with the photos?"

When Pippa tells me we're searching for ones to include in a slideshow for Linda's memorial, I dive into the task. Hours pass as we sit at the large kitchen table, sorting through pictures that span decades.

Chapter 6
CADE
present

I BOTH HATE and am strangely comforted by having her back in this house. It's contradicting. I can't imagine having to go through all of these arrangements without her. She was like a second daughter to my mother. But I also hate being in her presence—of being reminded of the past.

Mostly, I hate how different she is. I used to know Mare almost as well as I knew myself. Now it feels like I know nothing about her. I know everything about who she used to be and nothing about who she is now.

Coming to terms with that realization might be the reason I sit at the opposite end of the table from Mare and Pippa, a scowl on my face as I try to hide how closely I've been watching her. The pair sort through another box of photographs. They had to take a break earlier to pick out an outfit for mom to be laid to rest in, but it's after dinner and they're back to it.

At least they convinced Dad to join them. He sits in a chair next to Pippa, laughing under his breath at a photo Mare holds up of Pippa and me dressed as clowns for Halloween.

Mare wipes under her eyes, tears forming from how hard she was laughing. "Oh my god," she wheezes, waving the photo in the air. "How have I never seen this photo before?" She looks at Pippa. My sister smiles wide back at her. It's nice, for a brief moment, to see the pain softened on my sister and father's faces.

They both smile at Mare. At least that hasn't changed about her. She still has the natural ability to make people laugh, even in the midst of the most intense grief imaginable.

"Probably because Mom knew how terrifying those costumes were," Pippa remarks, shaking her head.

Dad clicks his tongue. "No, she was fiercely proud of those costumes. It was the last year the two of you let her coordinate what you were for Halloween." His eyes find mine. It might be the first time my dad has actually looked at me and realized I'm here since mom died. Every look before this he was incredibly distant. He's been a shell of himself. "The next year you insisted on being a cowboy. I'd tried telling you that you'd be that for the rest of your life and to choose something different. But you *insisted*."

I shrug. "You want what you want. I was what, *five*?"

Pip flips the photo over, reading the date in mom's loopy handwriting. "Well, we were creepy clowns when I was one and you were four. So you're right."

Marigold pulls a photo from the pile, smiling softly at whatever she's looking at. I can't see it from the other side of the long dining table. Whatever it is also catches Pippa's attention.

"I remember that day perfectly," Pippa muses, resting her cheek against Mare's shoulder.

"That was the meanest pony." Mare laughs, flipping the picture around so I can see it.

Pippa isn't the only one that remembers that day. We'd gone to the auction to get some ponies. Pippa and Mare had been begging for their own ponies. They both had their own quarter horses at the time, but it wasn't enough. Every little girl wants a pony and the two of them were no different.

"You insisted on bringing it home, even though it snapped at you every time you tried to put your hand near its muzzle." Pippa gives Mare a look. Probably because even at eight years old, Mare was determined to take home that mean old pony, despite all the other younger, nicer ponies that were also there.

"I felt bad," Mare explains, running a finger over the picture of the three of us standing in front of the pony. The pony, one she later named Bits, looked pissed, while she looks at him lovingly. Pippa watches Bits with an anxious expression. I don't stare too long at myself in the photo. Eleven year old me has his hand out, watching Mare carefully to make sure Bits didn't try to bite her. "If I hadn't brought him home, who would've loved him?"

"No one probably," my dad pipes up. "That thing was mean as hell to everyone but you, Marigold."

Mare places the picture in the pile of photographs we won't be using for Mom's memorial. A sad look crosses her face when she looks up. "He liked sugar cubes. The extra-large ones. Linda always remembered to keep those stocked for him."

"I think she secretly liked that old horse," Dad says. "I always found her sneaking him extra food."

We all share a laugh. Reminiscing on the past—on Mom—hurts like a bitch. But it's comforting to know we have memories of her. One day, it'll feel better to sit around the table and talk about her. But right now, with her visitation and funeral so close, it really hurts to think back on the memories knowing we can't make any new ones.

Dad sighs, his eyes roaming over the photographs. It's quiet at the table until he stands up and looks around at us. "I think I'm going to get some air." The grief washes back over his face again, making his wrinkles more pronounced. There's no hint of a smile left, only devastation written on his face.

Pippa hops out of her chair. "I'll go with you." Turning to Mare, she wraps her arms around her. "You okay with that?"

Mare nods. "I think I might get cleaned up and go to bed."

"Understandable," Pippa answers. "I'll see you in the morning." It's silent as they embrace for a few beats longer before they pull apart.

Pippa and Dad walk toward the door, leaving Mare and I alone once again.

Our eyes meet from across the oak table. She stands. I stay

sitting. Time around us seems to come to a pause as our gazes lock.

"Why do you look at me like you're mad at me?" she whispers. Her knuckles turn white from how hard she grasps the back of the chair she stands behind.

"That's a loaded question."

Two tiny lines appear on her forehead as she frowns. I fight the urge to close the distance between us and smooth out the skin with the tips of my thumbs. "I didn't mean it to be," she presses.

My knuckles tap against the table in front of me. With a large exhale, I stand up. My feet get closer to her on their own accord.

"You don't know me anymore." I know my words come out harsh, but I can't help it with her. I *am* angry at her. There are so many reasons for me to be upset. The biggest one being I hate that after all these years apart, I still feel an intense pull toward her. "You don't know what my looks mean. Maybe that's just how I always look."

"Cade," she says with an exhale. *Fuck*. I hate my name coming from her lips. I want to demand that she never says it again. That way I never have to hear the sweet and sultry way it sounds coming off her tongue, even when it's laced with a disappointed tone.

Unable to resist, I pick up a strand of her hair, rubbing the end of the long tendril between my thumb and index finger. "I hate that you're here. It's *you*—but it's *not* really you," I answer hoarsely.

"I'm still me, Cade."

I shake my head, focusing on the darker strands of hair. She's all big city and no longer small town. The city doesn't fit her. Not the way the small town does. "No. You aren't. You're not Goldie. I don't know who you are anymore, but it isn't the same girl that left. Not the one I—" I cut myself off before I say something I'll come to regret. Dwelling on the past does nothing for either of us. It won't change things.

For the slightest moment, my knuckle runs over her exposed collarbone. It's over as quick as it began. She swats my hand away, her narrow fingers wrapping around my wrist to keep me away. "Years have gone by. I'm not a teenage girl anymore. Of course I've changed in that regard." Her blue eyes stare into mine. "But deep down, it's still *me*."

I take a step back, needing to get away from her. My boots are loud against the hardwood as I put distance between us. My eyes quickly look her up and down. With a disapproving sigh, I shake my head. "I think it'd hurt worse if you came back the same person. The Goldie I knew would've come back, would've visited. Maybe I'm relieved you're not the girl I used to know."

Her eyes go wide. She blinks, trying to keep her emotion at bay. She's terrible at it. She's never been able to hide her feelings. I guess that's still the same about her. Her bottom lip trembles. Her mouth opens like she wants to say something, but she must decide against it. Quickly, she turns around and rushes up the large staircase, leaving me standing alone in the kitchen.

We both know my words were harsh. The hidden meaning behind them was clear. She should've been home more. It broke my mom's heart that she never came back to visit. It was low of me to bring attention to it, but it needed to be said.

Really, I'm just angry with her because not only did she leave this place and leave Pippa and my mom behind—but she left me, too. And even though I told her to go all those years ago, I never could've imagined she'd take me so seriously.

Chapter 7
MARE
age sixteen

I LOVE A COLORADO WINTER, but there's something about a Colorado summer that makes it so I can't imagine ever living anywhere else. With the sun no longer in the sky, the air that kisses my skin is cool and refreshing. The only thing that lights up the trees in the clearing around us is the full moon above us.

One of the horses whinnies behind us. Cade looks over to where they munch on grass not too far from where we sit. Looking away from the horses, his focus turns to me. Even with the chill in the night air, I feel hot under his heated stare.

"You're quiet." He pulls his hat from his head, tossing it into the grass next to him. It gives me the opportunity to take in the shaggy mess that is his chestnut hair. His momma keeps telling him to cut it, but he always finds an excuse not to. There's a slight indent around it from the cap. He runs a hand through the strands, tousling it. His movement brings me back to attention.

"Maybe I'm just tired."

Cade stretches his legs in front of him, leaning back on his elbows. He'd offered to lay a blanket down, but I'd declined. I liked the feeling of the grass against my skin. It makes me feel free but nothing could make me feel more free except the smirking boy right next to me.

"You look forward to your birthday all year. Something tells me you feel more awake than ever."

I mimic his position, except instead of propping myself on my elbows, I lay all the way down. Blades of grass tickle my neck as I move my hair out from underneath me. My hands fold over my belly as I get comfortable.

"Am I wrong about that?" he presses.

My gaze moves from the bright, blue moon and turns to look at him. He watches me intently, his hair almost covering his eyes from its shaggy length. "Maybe you know me better than I thought."

I stop myself from admitting that the reason I feel more alive —more awake—than ever right now isn't because we're minutes away from my birthday. It's because I'm out here with *him*. This clearing has always been one of my favorite places in the world. I picture it as the same clearing Momma used to tell me about. The one with the field of marigolds that resulted in my namesake.

Every one of my nerve endings are awake, my brain the most alert it's ever been, because of the way the air feels different around us. I rub my lips together in an attempt to hide the wide grin that threatens to overtake my face.

"Of course I know you, Goldie," he responds, his tone offended. "Did you expect something different?"

I shrug, turning my attention back to the moon high above us. The stars are putting on a show tonight. They twinkle, as if they're as excited as I am for what the late night will bring. "You just haven't been around much lately."

Things seemed to shift right after he graduated high school. Truly, things may have already been changing before that. Regardless, him graduating really changed things. For starters, I no longer spent every weekday morning in his truck, singing along to whatever new song he'd found the night before. I hadn't realized how much I cherished those early mornings with Cade, Pippa, and me until they were gone. Even summer mornings are different. He's awake before all of us, already out helping his dad around the ranch by the time we make it downstairs for breakfast.

"You know I've got to work," he answers, his elbow bumping into mine as he lays all the way down next to me.

I bite my tongue. He does have to work. It isn't the workday that has me missing his presence. It's the time between work and bedtime that we used to see him more. Now, he quickly showers and leaves the ranch to hang out with his friends. I don't always know what he's up to or where he is, all that matters is that he isn't home like he used to be.

Not that I have the right to admit that I wish he'd be home more. He's nineteen and works his days away. He deserves to go out and have fun. I'm just jealous that I'm not part of that.

Cade sighs, the sound loud and dramatic compared to the quietness of the clearing. "Say whatever you're thinking. You've got your lips pressed so thin I know you're dying to say something."

Damn. Maybe he does know me well. I don't want to prove him right. Mostly, I don't want him to know how much it bothers me that he's gone. I'm left lying in bed every night wondering if he's off with Rhiannon. Or maybe some other girl from our town. He could even be with a tourist, someone visiting for the summer.

"*Mare.*" My name is said as a warning.

"It'd just be nice to see you more. That's all." I turn toward him, propping my body up using my elbow as my hand cradles my cheek.

He watches me carefully. His eyes travel over my hairline, down my cheeks, and pauses for the slightest moment on my lips before he makes eye contact once again. "You're seeing me right now." His voice is low and husky. I don't know why it's said so quietly with no one else around.

Heat flushes in my cheeks. "Yeah, but you're only here because you feel bad for me."

A dark look passes over his features. In one swift motion, he sits up, leaning closer to me with a serious look on his face. My body freezes when he reaches into the space between us and tucks a piece of hair behind my ear. It's something he's done before as an innocent act. *Your hair is always in your eyes, Goldie. One of these days you're going to take a horse right into a ditch because your hair is in the way.* His constant gripes about my hair rush through my mind.

It doesn't seem as innocent right now. Maybe it's because, for the slightest moment, his fingers paused against my cheek before his hand fell back into his lap. His breath tickles the tip of my nose when he exhales. "You're giving me more credit than I deserve. I'm not that nice. If I didn't want to be here, I wouldn't be here."

My heart lurches in excitement. It's like it wants to jump out of my chest and prove to Cade right here and right now that it's completely his after one simple sentence.

"Understood?" Even with the boyish haircut, I'm realizing how much Cade is no longer a boy and now *every* bit a man. He's grown into his wide shoulders. Dark stubble now peppers his cheeks. Even the tone of his voice is more commanding. It's deeper and seems to wrap around me and caress different parts of me.

All I can do is nod. Words don't come to me. I'm too locked in on what's happening between Cade and me in this clearing.

He taps my thigh, a slight smile on his lips. "Get up real quick."

I do as he says, but stare at him, confused. I watch his moves closely, wondering where he's going with this. Maintaining eye contact, he reaches into the pocket of his worn Levi's. He pulls out a black lighter. The air around us becomes thick as he inches across the grass until his knees bump against mine.

His full lips tilt up ever so lightly. He holds the lighter between us. "If Pippa had been awake she no doubt would've brought some homemade birthday treat for you, but I'm shit at baking, and wasn't exactly prepared for tonight."

"I don't need anything," I interrupt. What I don't say is that no matter how much I love Pippa, tonight with him, is a better way to spend the night I turn sixteen than what I'd originally planned. A dessert isn't needed. The alone time with him is more than enough. It's all I could've ever wanted.

Cade slides his phone out of his pocket, looking down at the lit screen. It's one minute until midnight. One minute until it's my birthday. "It's your birthday, Goldie. Everyone deserves to make a wish on their birthday."

He flicks the lighter, a flame illuminating the space between us. He leans in closer, his breath hitting my cheek as he breathes out. Lifting his hand, he cradles the flame to protect it from the breeze around us.

My breath catches in my chest when he looks up at me. The moon reflects off the flecks in his copper eyes. I'm so close that if I dared, I could reach out and feel his sharp jawline. I might even feel the soft prickle of facial hair that dusts his skin. I don't dare to move, afraid if I moved even a fraction of an inch that I'd ruin the moment between us.

His eyes flick to the phone on the grass in front of us. We both watch it as it turns to midnight. Cade looks back at me and smiles.

I've never been more sure I'm in love with him. This isn't just a crush. It's the soul crushing kind of feeling, one I'm not sure I'll ever be able to recover from. His lip twitches before he speaks. "Happy birthday, Goldie. Make a wish."

Leaning forward, I move my hair to my back so it isn't in the way. I close my eyes, already knowing what my wish is going to be.

I've never wasted a wish on Cade because it felt silly to wish for something that I couldn't have. But the way his eyes lingered on my lips as my eyes fluttered shut had me thinking *what-if*.

With a smile on my lips, I make my wish.

I wish for Cade Jennings. I wish for him three times, hoping maybe the extra two times will be the reason it comes true. When

REWRITE OUR STORY   37

my eyes slowly open, I find him watching me with hooded lids. My lips pucker before I blow out the flame.

Cade lowers his hand, tucking the lighter back in his pocket, never once looking away from my lips. "What'd you wish for?"

My tongue peeks out to wet my lips. I can't help but wonder what he tastes like. Will he taste like the peppermints he's always sucking on? Will he taste like something different? More manly? At seven I told him to kiss me on a dare, telling everyone he was my first kiss and I was his because I was afraid he'd kiss someone else. Since then, I've shared soft kisses with a few other boys in my grade.

But deep down, the only boy I've ever wanted to kiss was the one staring at me like he might do just that—kiss me.

"If I tell you my wish, it won't come true."

"That must be one special wish."

I laugh. If only he knew. "Only the most special."

Everything around us fades to black as he leans in closer. Heat washes over my body in anticipation.

I think Cade Jennings wants to kiss me. And I'm desperate for him to.

My eyelids flutter shut, my lips parting slightly, eagerly waiting for him. One second ticks by, and then another and another. When I don't feel him press his lips against mine, I open my eyes, to find him farther away than he was.

His expression has hardened once again.

My heart sinks. Maybe my wish was silly. His body language says everything. He isn't going to kiss me. But for a moment, it really felt like he wanted to.

Cade plucks a blade of grass from the ground, bringing it closer to his face. "We shouldn't be out here."

Annoyed, I bring my knees to my chest and wrap my arms around them. "And why is that?"

"You know *exactly* why."

"Don't be vague with me, Cade." I'm shocked by the bluntness of my words. My head spins from the back and forth of the last few minutes with him.

His features soften. As if he's trying to drive me crazy, Cade pops off the ground. Before I can ask him what he's doing, he's bounding down a hill, only his head visible.

I'm about to get up when he returns, his hands behind his back.

I raise an eyebrow. "What could you have possibly found out here?"

One side of his mouth upturns. "A birthday present."

I stand up, wiping dirt and grass from the backs of my thighs. "For *me*?"

Cade looks around us. "No. For Tonka. Is it his birthday?"

I smack his stomach. His muscles are hard underneath my skin. He grunts, having to take the hit because his hands are still tucked behind his back. "You don't have to be an ass."

"Close your eyes."

Mine narrow on him. He tucks his chin, gesturing for me to do as he says.

He doesn't know I'd do anything and everything he told me to. Even with the rollercoaster ride of an evening with him, it's the most excitement I've had in a long time.

Doing as I'm told, I close my eyes, eager to see what he found. My eyes don't have to be opened to know he's gotten closer. I can just feel him—sense him.

"Open." His voice is much closer.

My eyes flutter open, focusing on what he holds in his hands.

"A marigold," I whisper, marveling at the vibrant flower clutched tenderly between his thumb and pointer finger.

I look at him, silently asking if I can take it. He nods, handing the flower over to me. "I didn't know we had any here."

He shrugs. "I guess we do now."

My eyes take in the vibrant yellow and orange colors of the petals. They're so bright. The colors remind me of the flame of his lighter. "It's beautiful," I marvel, twirling the flower between my fingers.

"That's the thing about marigolds. They're all beautiful."

My eyes immediately find his. He just called me beautiful. Right?

"Cade."

He softly takes the flower from between my fingers. I don't protest. I can't. Not after what he just said. Not with the butterflies fluttering in my stomach.

His rough fingertips brush the tender skin of my cheek. He pushes all my hair behind my ear before he tucks the flower right behind it. He must feel the thump of my racing pulse against his fingertips as he cups my cheek. There's the rough scratch of a callus from his thumb when he lets it brush over my cheekbone.

"Thank you for spending your birthday with me, Goldie."

Cade Jennings may not have kissed me tonight, but even without the press of his lips to mine, I feel like he's said so much without really saying anything at all.

I don't think I'm the only one who has felt the shift between us, but I just might be the only person who wants to act on it.

Chapter 8
MARE
present

I STARE at my reflection in the mirror, trying not to grimace at the absence of color on my face. The bags under my eyes are dark and pronounced from staying up until the early morning hours. I'd spent all night obsessing over the eulogy I'd written for Linda. Pippa had approved my first version of it, but it hadn't felt perfect. So I'd stayed up all night making sure I made it as flawless as I possibly could.

Her visitation was brutal. Everyone wanted to stop and talk. Some people even used the time to tell me they enjoyed my book and they're anxiously awaiting the next one, which was wildly inappropriate. My father made sure to tell them so. He and his wife had three delayed flights, but they showed up to the visitation just in time. I'd been comforted by his presence next to me. We'd grown closer in the years since he moved away from Sutten. I think he needed to heal a bit more from Momma to be able to be a father again. I'll never get back the time he was absent during my childhood and teenage years, but if Linda's death has taught me anything, it's to not dwell on the past. Dad and I have an unspoken agreement, we just don't really talk about Sutten.

Speaking of the past, mine appears in the doorway of the guest room. I hadn't tried to think too much into it when Cade had put my bags in the room farthest from his. His distance from the moment I arrived has told me enough. He's mad at me. He has a right to be upset, but deep down, I'm still mad at him, too.

Cade holds a black tie in his hand, a sheepish look on his face. "Pippa told me I had to wear a tie to this thing but I keep fucking it up and I can't find her to help me. I didn't want to have to ask you, but you're my only option."

I swallow and ignore his jab. "I'll help."

"You will?"

"Always," I whisper, taking a step away from the mirror. The two of us meet in the middle, stopping in front of the four-poster bed of the guest room.

He smells like the same body wash he used years ago. It smells like clove and pine. He usually smells like fresh air and leather from being outside most of the day, but not today. He's all cleaned up for Linda's funeral.

Even the facial hair he'd been sporting when he picked me up at the airport isn't as grown out as it was. There's still a hint of it, but it's trimmed and neater than it was a few days ago.

The biggest physical difference about the Cade I grew up with and the Cade standing in front of me is his hair. It used to be overgrown and shaggy. Now it's buzzed on the sides and only slightly longer at the top. I fight the urge to run my fingers through the dark tendrils. I wonder if they're long enough for me to hold on to or if my fingers would just slip through the locks.

Cade hands me the tie, pinning his stare above my head. I try not to focus on the veins on the tops of his hands. I want to trace them, feel them, and remember what it felt like to feel the rough skin of his fingertips against my skin.

Any other day I might be offended at his reluctance to meet my eyes, but I can't imagine what he's going through right now. Funerals aren't for the dead, and they aren't for the people closest to the dead. They're for the people on the fringe, the ones who feel the need to give their condolences even though they mean nothing. They'll never bring the person back.

The skirt of my long, black dress brushes over the tips of his shoes as I take a step closer to him. They aren't the pointed tips of his typical cowboy boots. They're nice dress shoes. Something I didn't even think he owned.

I loop the tie around his neck, pulling one side longer than the other. Neither of us say a word as I begin a Windsor knot at his neck. I'm finishing it up when he looks down at my work.

"Look at that." He scoffs. "You're even more city than I thought. You've got that down to a science."

I roll my eyes. "It's a tie, Cade. It doesn't define anything about me."

He sighs his disapproval. I should step away, but I'm not going to back down from him. He's upset because it's his mother's funeral today. If he needs someone to take his hurt out on, then I'll be that person for him. "Have you been tying a lot of ties? Let me guess. You were with a lawyer. Or no—an investor? That seems like your type."

My teeth grind against each other as I try to keep my mouth shut. I'd been casually seeing a doctor, but we'd ended things before I left for my writing retreat. I was supposed to be locked away finishing a book, I didn't need a distraction. Matt took it well because we'd only been casual. Cade doesn't need to know any of this. I know he's hurting. He has the right to hurt. I just wasn't expecting for him to come in and declare war with me before I've even had time to finish getting ready.

"Are we really doing this?" I seethe, meeting his angry stare.

His eyes bore into mine. There's so much I see in them. The biggest thing is pain. The bags under his eyes are darker than my own, making me think he isn't getting much sleep either. His cheekbones look slightly more hollow, like he's forgotten to eat the last few days. The corner of his eyes soften slightly as a resigned sigh passes through his lips. "No. Don't tell me how many. I can't take it. Not today."

God. Even when he's being a dick, he has a way of keeping a grip on my aching heart.

"I learned it on YouTube three months ago," I admit. "When I was doing research for a scene I was writing." I don't tell him that I didn't need to learn to tie a tie with Matt. He mostly left my apartment in the mornings wearing his white coat or a pair of scrubs.

His jaw flexes as his shoulders fall slightly. It's like his whole body was tense and my words eased some of it. "I can tie any knot with rope and somehow I'm fucking up a goddamn tie."

"The other knots are far more impressive," I joke, trying to lighten the moment. I know nothing will be able to completely take the pain from his features, but I can try my best.

The slight twitch of his lips tells me maybe it's working. "There she is."

I crane my neck to look up at him. "What?"

"I got a glimpse of the old Goldie. The one I was so—"

"You ready?"

Cade and I both jump, taking steps away from one another like we'd been caught doing something we weren't supposed to.

Pippa narrows her eyebrows looking between the two of us. Whatever she's thinking, she doesn't say it out loud. "Well, I guess I have one less room to stop by," she mutters. "Are we ready to go?"

Cade clears his throat. "I am. I just needed help with the tie. You were nowhere to be found."

Pippa frowns. "Sorry, I was checking in on Dad. But he's ready to go. I figured we could all ride together? Cade, you'll drive us?"

He nods, walking toward the door. He doesn't even look back at me as he crosses the space and leaves the room. Pippa watches him leave, her eyebrows still pulled together as if she's thinking deeply about something.

I run my hands down my dress. "I just need a minute to finish up and I'll be down."

Before she walks out, I stop her. "Hey, Pip?"

She turns to face me. The pain in her eyes has me bee-lining across the room and wrapping my arms around her. "I love you," I say into her thick hair. "I love you so much and I'm here for you. You got that?"

She nods, her body shaking in my embrace. "Whatever you need today, I'm there. If you need a minute, just leave. You owe nobody an explanation for how you feel today."

I let her sob into my shoulder. Pippa has been trying to keep it together for everyone, but eventually she was going to break. I didn't want her to be alone when it happened.

Maybe the same could be said for Cade.

I hold her until she pulls away and wipes under her eyes. She sighs, regaining composure. "Thanks for that, Mare. I needed it."

Chapter 9
CADE
present

I'VE NEVER ENJOYED BEING the center of attention. I would much rather fade into the background of everything. When you're in the background, people don't have expectations for you. You get to go on about your life with no one judging you.

I'm not given that luxury today. We're sitting in the front pews of the church like animals on display as people stop to give their condolences before the funeral even starts.

It's been hard to look anywhere but the coffin at the front of the church. I'm sick to my stomach over what it represents—the death of my mother. I shouldn't have to help pick out my mother's casket at twenty-seven. There's still so much she was supposed to be there for in my life.

My wedding.

Coming home with grandkids.

Dad fully retiring so they could travel more.

She wasn't supposed to go so early.

I wasn't ready to let her go.

I'm too busy cursing how cruel life has become to realize that Mare left her spot next to Pippa and is already standing at the wood podium at the front of the church. She's got her hair pulled back, away from her face, and she doesn't have even a lick of makeup on. She's cried so much that her nose is red.

She shuffles the papers on the podium. Her shoulders rise

and fall as she takes a deep breath. I don't know why Pippa asked her to do this. I know it must be hard. I'll never forget having to watch her speak at her own mother's funeral when she was just ten years old. It was agonizing watching her do it back then. And it isn't any easier now.

Mare fixes the microphone so it lines up with her mouth. "I think we can all agree that this is not the way Linda would've wanted to see us gathered here today." She pauses, letting everyone laugh in an attempt to briefly lighten the solemn mood. "Linda loved an excuse to have a party and she'd hate to see all the misty eyes in this church."

Everyone nods. This room is where everyone in the town gathers every Sunday. There's no other choice. If you don't show up, the town talks. Momma loved Sundays. She loved coming into town and socializing with everyone. Everyone in this room adored her.

"I don't have to stand up here and tell you all how incredible of a woman Linda Jennings was." She takes a breath. "*Was*," she emphasizes. Shaking her head, her eyes roam over the crowd. "What a terrible way to talk about someone you loved with every fiber of your being. You never want to talk about someone you love in the past tense." For a fraction of a second, her eyes land on me as the church stays silent. As soon as it happens, she's moving on, keeping her composure as she continues to give the speech.

"With everything in me, I know all of you already know that we lost one of the best humans to walk this Earth. She'll be terribly missed, and I think it'll be a long time until it really sinks in that she isn't here anymore. I don't want to stand up here and go on and on about how we will move on from this because truthfully—I don't know how we will."

Mare's eyes meet mine again, and it feels like we're the only two people in this room. I'm captivated by her. By the composure she keeps. I only know she's nervous because I can see the slight tremble of her hands. "How does one move on from knowing somebody so incredible? The answer is pretty simple, actually—you don't."

Pippa reaches across my lap and grabs my hand. Her hand is hot and clammy as she squeezes mine tightly. I squeeze hers back, hoping the counter pressure will help her get through this.

"I'm not here to get over the death of Linda. Instead, I'm here to talk about the *life* of Linda. Because one thing I'm sure of when it comes to Linda Jennings is that she'd much rather be known for her life than for her death. I want to talk about that life a little today. If that's okay with you all," she adds nervously.

I might be angry with her for leaving this town behind, but the people who all watched her grow up don't seem to hold the same grudge. They watch her with soft smiles and admiration on their faces as they wait for her to continue.

"I sat on these church stairs years ago when I lost my momma. I'd tried to escape from the crowd. It was all too much for me at the time. Linda came looking for me as soon as I ran off during the service. I'd snapped at her, too hurt to allow someone to comfort me at the time. I'd told her I wanted to be alone. Linda had nodded, but I can tell you what she didn't do. She didn't leave me alone. She brushed her hands down her finest black dress and took a seat right next to me, even though the stairs were dirty and ice-cold. Now that I think about it, I think they may have even had snow on them. She didn't seem to care. I remember her words clear as day. She said, 'That's fine if you don't want to talk, Marigold. But one thing I'm not going to do is let you feel such big feelings alone.'"

I hear the hitch in her voice. For a moment, Mare's eyes flutter shut as she tries to keep the tears at bay. "And from that day forward, she kept her word. She never left me alone—even when at times"—her eyes found mine once again—"I deserved to be left alone and didn't deserve her love."

I feel a stab of hurt. I know Mare is referencing her leaving, and how my mom was relentless in keeping in touch with her even if she was hundreds of miles away. I only opened that wound when I pointed out to Mare how she'd never come home to visit my mom.

"But she gave it to me anyway. That day, when I'd finished crying and needed someone there, she wrapped her arms around me and pulled me into her lap. She wiped my tears and braided my unkempt hair. She told me, 'I'll never try to replace your momma, Marigold. But I'll be whatever you need. Every little girl deserves a momma, and if you'll let me, I'll do my best.' And that's what she did. Her best. She became the only mother-figure I knew, even though she didn't have to."

She reaches up and wipes underneath her eyes. Her hand covers her mouth for a moment as she tries to keep herself together. My fingers twitch. I want to stand up and comfort her. To do something to stop the tears from falling.

"Linda Jennings taught me a lot about what a mother's love feels like. And I think if all of you here were to think about her, you'd have a story to add that encompassed how deep her love ran for those she cared about. For a moment, I want everyone to close their eyes and think of a favorite memory you have with Linda."

She nods her head. "Please," she encourages. "Close your eyes and think about a time that you felt that love. I know that's what she'd want to be remembered for."

As if to lead by example, she pinches her eyes shut. I look to my sides, noticing how the people I've grown up with all close their eyes. Sniffles are heard through the room as Mare gives everyone a chance to follow her direction.

Even though it hurts to think of happy times, I find my eyes closing. My chest feels too heavy as I think about the times I took for granted…

At the times my mom was here and we were happy.

Chapter 10
CADE
age twenty-one

"I THOUGHT you were going out tonight?" My mom's voice breaks me from my wallowing. I shove my spoon into my bowl of cereal, taking an angry bite as my mom steps into view.

I chew, swallowing the sugary cereal before answering her. "I'd planned on it," I clip.

She nods slowly, giving me a look of concern that can only come from a mother. "What changed?"

I shrug, looking back down at my bowl until she can read my frustration all over my face. "Just didn't feel like it, I guess."

Cups clink against each other as she probably searches the dishwasher for her favorite mug. "It's not often that you're home on the weekends," she notes. "Actually, none of you are here. Now that the girls are in their senior year and having the time of their lives, I feel like everyone has vanished."

I grunt. Not wanting to talk about the girls. More specifically —Marigold.

I'm all too aware of her plans. She seems to have them all the time now. Every boy in this town has been wanting to occupy her time.

My mind flashes to a little over two years ago, when Goldie accused me of not spending much time at home. It's a little ironic school, friends, fuck…maybe even a boyfriend. I try not to pay attention to it.

The problem is, Marigold Evans takes up way too much goddamn space in my mind. She's my little sister's best friend. Fuck, she's pretty much *my* best friend. She's in all of my earliest memories. It's not weird for me to think about her, but it should be weird just how *much* I've been thinking about her.

"Honey?" My mom's voice breaks me from my thoughts. I look up, finding her holding a piping hot mug of tea.

I must've been spacing out longer than I thought. I move to get another spoonful of cereal, but it has become soggy in the meantime. Pushing the bowl away from me, I try to soften my features as I focus on my mom. "Sorry, I don't know where my head was at."

I know *exactly* where my head was. I just don't want to admit that to her.

My mom gestures to the front door. "Sit on the porch with me?"

I nod. She heads outside as I walk to the sink and rinse my bowl out before leaving it in the basin. Opening up the cabinets, I pull out a mug and pour some tea from the kettle on the stove for myself.

When I step outside, we get hit with the chill of the fall air. It's unseasonably nice for this time of year, and Mom's been trying to take advantage of every moment of being able to sit in her rocking chair before winter seeps in.

"Did you know the girls are going to Bucky's tonight?"

This catches my attention as I take a seat in the rocker next to hers. "They're barely even old enough to go there," I snap, maybe a little too harshly.

It's confirmed my words may have come out sounding a bit too harsh by the rise of my mother's eyebrows. "You know they've been dying to go there since your sister turned eighteen." She takes a sip of her tea. "Marigold has been nice enough to wait to go until Pip was old enough. I'm shocked they didn't go last week for your sister's actual birthday."

I decide it's best I take a sip of my hot tea instead of responding hastily. Marigold is old for her grade. She started her senior year of high school already eighteen. It was something our parents did on purpose so Pippa and her could be in the same grade.

I swallow. "It's really not that great of a place. It smells like smoke and the music is terrible and always played way too loud."

My mom laughs. "Honey, that's kind of the point. It's an old bar and pool hall. There's not much else to it."

"Well, they'll be let down. They can't even drink. Buck won't serve anyone underage."

"Something tells me they'll still have a blast—and probably get into some sort of trouble. I thought you'd be there to keep an eye on them, if we're being honest. You love that place."

I snort. The last thing I want to do is monitor them. I'm not their chaperone. While I spend most of my weekends at Bucky's, I might have to find somewhere else to hang out if that's going to be their new spot to linger.

"I heard Marigold tell Pippa that your friend Brendan asked her on a date."

"Brendan is too old for her," I bite. If he touches her, he's as good as dead. Even if he's one of my oldest and closest friends. He needs to look at girls his own age, not focus on girls still in high school. He's always asked far too many questions about her. Now it makes sense—he'd been interested in her.

"Maybe you should stop by there and check in," my mom offers softly.

The last fucking thing I want to do is show up to Bucky's and find Brendan hot on Mare. I'll rip him right from the dancefloor if he even thinks about putting his hands on her. I don't give a damn if it embarrasses Mare or not.

"It's best I don't," I clip, keeping my ass planted in the chair.

Just as Brendan has no right to Marigold—I don't either. I'd no doubt cause trouble by showing up, and I'm not trying to ruin my sister's birthday celebration. She'd never let me forget it.

"Cade?" Mom says my name cautiously, catching my attention enough to look in her direction.

"Yeah?"

"It's okay to feel something for her."

My stomach plummets. Mom has always been observant, I just didn't think my mixed feelings when it comes to Marigold had become so obvious.

I shake my head. "It's not like that." Even as the words fall from my mouth, I don't know if that's quite the truth or not. The simple answer is my feelings toward Mare aren't—and never have been—simple.

Mom hums under her breath. "Whatever you say, honey. Just know I'm here if you ever need someone to talk about it with."

Relieving me from having to respond, my mom reaches toward the table next to her. With a click of a button, she turns on the old stereo that Dad used to keep in the barn.

We sit in silence for a bit, both of us sipping our teas as we stare at the stars in the sky.

Eventually, one of Mom's favorite songs comes through the speakers. She hums along as her chair squeaks from the rocking motion.

I set my tea down and stand up to face her. "Dance with me?"

She looks shocked. "Oh honey, you don't have to do that."

We both know that it's an unspoken rule in the house that when this song plays on the radio, Dad is supposed to stop whatever he's doing and dance with her.

He's at an auction a few towns over, not here to keep up with his end of the deal. So I decided to take his place.

"Mom," I say with a smirk. "This is your favorite song. Let's dance."

She doesn't argue any further. She places her mug next to

mine and stands up. Mom steps into my arms. I grab her hand and guide her around the porch as the music spills through the speakers.

Mom smiles widely up at me, her hand squeezing mine tight. "I remember when you were so small that you had to stand on my feet to dance with me."

"It was probably better then. At least I didn't step on your toes."

She sighs, shaking her head. "You're an excellent dancer."

I spin her, my jealousy from earlier disappearing at the bright smile on her face. And even as the song fades into another, we don't stop.

After a few more songs, we both take a seat in the chairs on the porch. "Thanks for that, honey."

"Happy to drop everything and dance with you anytime," I say, picking up an old beer bottle cap from the table and spinning it between my fingers.

For the next hour, Mom and I sit on the porch and talk about life. It's a reminder that even though I still live at home, I need to do better at spending time with her.

We sit on the porch long enough for Pippa and Marigold to return home.

"How was the night?" Mom prods, putting an arm over Pippa's shoulders.

Pippa shrugs. "It was fine, but not as fun as I'd always imagined it to be. Right, Mare?"

Mare wrinkles her nose, quickly pulling her eyes away from mine. "Not sure I see the appeal," she answers honestly.

And when the girls rush inside, talking about how they might sweet-talk Buck into giving them a beer next time they go, my mom follows behind them.

Before Mom goes inside, she lays a hand on my shoulder and squeezes. "I love you, honey. Thank you for making this a night to remember. It's always the ones you weren't expecting that end up being the best."

Chapter 11
MARE
present

My feet drag across the driveway as I follow Pippa into the house. Before we walk through the door, she intertwines our arms and rests her cheek on my shoulder. "Thank you again for the speech, Mare. It was beautiful."

I squeeze her hand, pressing my cheek into her hair. "Anything for you, Pip."

The day has totally drained me. Too many people wanted to talk and catch up on my life. Or wanted to comment on the eulogy I gave for Linda. The last thing I wanted to do was speak with any of them. Any other day, I'd be happy to see the people I hadn't seen in years, but not today.

Today my heart hurts. I want to make sure everyone in the house has what they need for the night and then I want to crawl into bed and forget that Linda isn't here anymore.

Pippa focuses on the setting sun as she lets out a slow breath. "Maybe one of these mornings we'll wake up and find out this is all one terrible dream."

"I wish it worked like that," I answer sadly.

Boots scratch against the pavement behind us, catching both our attention. We turn to find Cade walking in our direction, his arms full of different casserole and Tupperware dishes. He tucks his chin over one of the dishes to keep the stack of food from falling. "I think we have enough food to last a lifetime," he says.

I rush to pull the door open for him. Their dad comes into view behind Cade, his arms full of bags with what I assume is even more food.

Cade walks past, not saying a word to me. In fact, he hasn't said a word to me since this morning in my room. It should upset me, but he's hurting. I try to keep reminding myself of that. Linda was his entire world. He was such a momma's boy, and I'm sure he's really going through it. I just wish I could do something for him, but his angry, lingering stares tell me all I need to know.

He's still upset with me for leaving Sutten behind. If he wants to be left alone with his grief, then I'll leave him alone. Even if being back here brings back all the memories—all the *feelings*—from a time when he was my everything. To be able to get through this, to be around him, I need to forget everything that's transpired between us and just be there for him and his family.

I'm the last one into the kitchen, all of them already busy stuffing food in the fridge and stocking the pantry. My eyes travel over the array of food spread over the kitchen island. I whistle. "Why is it when somebody dies everyone suddenly thinks you want to eat casserole?"

Pippa scrunches her nose, pulling the lid off one of the containers. "Why does it all look the same?"

"The town's just trying to help," Jasper comments, stacking food in the fridge.

"A salad or something would be nice," I joke.

Pippa moves the foil from one of the disposable containers. "Well, this one looks unique at least."

Cade leans in, inspecting the food in front of Pippa. "Let's pop that one in the oven then. I like that this one isn't a weird brown color."

"Smells like buffalo chicken," Pippa adds.

Dinner is pretty quiet as we all get swept up in our thoughts as we get food into our systems. You can tell no one actually *feels* hungry, but we all know we need to eat. It was such a busy day that we really didn't have time to feed ourselves.

Pippa pushes her plate out from in front of her as she sits back in her chair. "I think I'm going to go up to the bakery and make us some things to have here. We can't live off casseroles—but we *can* live off pastries."

This gets her dad to let out a small chuckle. "Something about that logic doesn't make sense."

She lets out a dramatic huff as she stands up and throws away her paper plate. "Basically, I need to go bake. I need to do something to forget any of this is happening. So, baking it is."

He nods in understanding. "Yeah, I'm going to take a ride around the land to do the same thing, sweetie. Do what you need to do."

Cade doesn't say anything. I want to ask him what he's doing to process his mother's death, but I keep the question to myself. Standing up, I throw my plate away and clean the small mess we made in the kitchen while preparing dinner. The mess takes no time to clean up. When I finish, I find Cade staring at me from his spot at the table.

Turning the sink off and wiping my hands, I give him a hesitant smile. "Need anything?"

His cheeks hollow out as he sucks in a large breath. "Another loaded question."

I fold the hand towel to give myself something to do. "It doesn't have to be."

His knuckles tap against the wood table. He watches me closely. There's an entire island between us, but it feels like I'm standing right under his gaze. I'd give anything to climb into that head of his and really figure out what he's thinking.

I just want to know he's going to be okay.

Cade stares back at me. Neither one of us bother to hide the fact we're assessing the other. It's like we're both trying to find the person we used to be close with within each other's eyes.

His broad shoulders heave up and down. He stands up, breaking eye contact.

I sigh in relief. I don't like looking back at him and realizing how much I don't know the man who I used to have memorized.

"I think I just need to be alone."

I nod. That should've been the answer I was expecting, but part of me hoped he'd maybe open up a bit.

Before I showed up in Sutten, I would've never wanted to have a deep conversation with him. I would've wanted to avoid him as much as possible. But being in his presence has done something to me. I want things to go back to the way they were, but without me still being hopelessly in love with him. I want my best friend back without the ache in my chest of wanting him as much as I want my next breath.

"Okay," I whisper.

Cade stares at me for a few more drawn out moments before he sighs and heads toward the stairs. I watch his every move, fascinated in all the ways he's changed from the last time I saw him.

His shoulders are much wider, his legs thicker. There's so much more muscle to him than there was before. It's all obvious, even underneath the formal attire he wore to the funeral. I don't know which Cade I liked better. This more rugged, toned, closed off version of him that I barely know or the leaner, softer side of him that treated me like I hung the moon.

Cade doesn't look back at me once and I have to accept the fact that it hurts, even when I know it shouldn't.

Chapter 12
CADE
present

SLEEP DOESN'T FIND ME. It feels like I haven't really slept since Mom died. Every time I shut my eyes, I imagine what she looked like. I have so many amazing memories to remember my mother, and the only one that seems to stick is the tragic last one I have of her in her bed.

It doesn't seem fair to her to remember her that way. I try to remind myself of that each time I close my eyes, but it doesn't seem to work. Trying to remember every happy memory of her only results in me reliving the memory of the worst one—the one of me screaming and pleading for her to wake up despite not feeling a pulse or any warmth coming from her body.

I angrily toss a pillow off the bed. As if blaming the pillow for my lack of sleep will solve things. Scrubbing my hands down my face, I groan.

After I realized trying to think of good times with mom won't help anything, I tried not thinking about her at all. But then thoughts of my mom drifted to Mare, and the images of her didn't help me fall asleep either.

I don't know how much longer I toss and turn before my frustrations finally get the best of me. Shooting up out of the bed, I pace to try and put my mind at ease. The more time that passes, the more I realize I think I'm finally falling apart.

I've tried so long to keep my shit together. For Dad. For

Pippa. Hell, for myself. I'd hoped that maybe if I stayed busy and kept my head down my emotions wouldn't ever hit all at once.

I was fucking wrong.

My throat feels like it's closing. I can't fucking take a breath. My vision goes blurry, and I wonder if this is what it feels like to have a panic attack.

Without even thinking about it, I almost rip my door off the hinges as I burst into the hallway. When I'd first picked out Mare's room, I'd put her in the room farthest from mine on purpose. Now I hate it.

There's only one person I want to see right now. Only one person I need.

And it's her.

Despite our past and lack of a future, in the present, as I fucking lose control because my mom is gone forever, she's the only person I need. I forget how angry I am with her. I don't remember how much she's hurt me. All I know is that I can't breathe, and I don't think I will until I'm near her.

I stop in front of her door. I'd been too busy trying to sleep, then fighting a breakdown, that I never thought to check the time. I know it's late, I just don't know how late—or maybe, early—it is.

I pause, wondering if I should just lose my shit on my own. I don't deserve her help. Fuck, with how I've treated her, she probably doesn't even *want* to help me.

I've been a dick to her. It's a coping mechanism.

Now, I don't know how to fucking cope with the fact Mom is dead. And I'm going to have to live with the fact that my last memory of her is of her lifeless body. The only thing I can think to do to cope with it is by being in the presence of the woman asleep on the other side of this door.

At least, I thought she was asleep.

But just as I turn to go back to my room and figure this shit out on my own, the door is pulled open.

Mare stands on the other side of the door. Her eyes are heavy, like she'd just woken up, but they widen when she takes me in.

"Cade?" she says, her voice groggy with sleep.

"Where were you going?" I manage to get out.

Her head tilts to the side in confusion. "What? Nowhere. Why?"

"You opened the door."

She grasps the door a little tighter, her eyes focusing on my bare chest. It's only now that I realize that I hadn't taken the time to put on a hoodie in the peak of losing my shit. She stares at my body for a few more seconds before she meets my eyes once again.

"I don't know. I just felt something. It just felt like you nee—"

"Like I needed you?" I finish for her.

She nods, taking a step back into her room. I follow her silent invitation. I know with every part of me that I shouldn't be step- ping into this room alone with her but it doesn't stop me from doing it.

She's always been my kryptonite, my favorite drug and sobriety was never an option. But the problem is—I'd rather deal with the addiction to her than the suffocating realization that my mom is gone forever.

I've dealt with losing Mare before. I know I could do it again. What I can't do is come to terms with my mother's sudden death. At least not tonight.

"How did you know?" she asks.

The door shuts behind me. "Because it's the same feeling I used to get with you."

Her lips part in shock. She runs her hands down her pajama pants with nerves. "Yeah?"

I nod. I'm brave enough to take a few steps closer to her. She surprisingly lets me crowd her space.

"I know there's still so much fucking baggage between us, Goldie. And I know that I've been shitty to you since you showed up, but I really need you right now."

I wish I had the right to pull her against me and get reacquainted with the way her body feels pressed against mine. As if she can read my mind, she closes the small space between us and wraps her arms around me.

The moment she presses her cheek to my chest I feel like, for the first time since my mom died, I might be able to get through this. At least as long as she's here.

"Anything for you, Cade. Always," she says against my chest. Her breath is hot against my bare skin.

"Always?"

She squeezes tighter, nodding her head. "Always," she responds with conviction.

I allow myself to believe her, even though deep down I don't know if she means it. If she did, she wouldn't have left. If she'd do anything for me—she would've stayed. She wouldn't have listened to me when I stupidly pushed her away because I thought I was doing what was best for her.

Mare pulls away just enough to look up at me. My hands itch to cradle her face, to run my fingers across the places where her freckles used to be.

Her eyes bounce to the bed a few feet away from us. "Like old times?" She doesn't have to say much else for me to understand what she's asking.

There were so many nights throughout the years she lived here that she'd crawl into bed with me. It was innocent. She needed comfort, and I didn't have it in me to ever deny her. Even when I knew I should have.

Mare holds eye contact with me as she backs up toward the bed. As soon as the backs of her thighs hit the mattress, she turns and crawls into the sheets. She yanks on the comforter, remembering that I hate having it tucked in at the end.

Knowing this idea is terrible, but already feeling comforted by it, I follow her. The room is dark, only softly illuminated from the glow of an alarm clock on the nightstand.

We're both silent as we lie down and get comfortable. Mare

tucks her hands underneath her cheeks, her eyes watching me carefully.

I shift underneath the blankets, bringing my body slightly closer to hers. My heart beats wildly against my chest. I don't know if it's from the breakdown earlier or because I'm so close to her again.

"Talk to me," she whispers. Timidly, she reaches across both our pillows. Her hand rests outstretched in front of me. A silent invitation.

I gladly take it, needing contact with her. My hand effortlessly wraps around hers. "I don't even know what to say," I confess.

"The truth. Someone needs to know how you're feeling, Cade. Let someone be there for you." She pulls her hand from mine and tenderly brushes her thumb across my jaw. "Let *me* be there for you."

Tomorrow I'll have to go back to being angry with her in an effort to protect my heart. But tonight, I'm going to let her do exactly that. I'm going to let her be there for me. Because I need her more than ever before.

Chapter 13
MARE
present

CADE IS BROKEN.

I respect him for how long he tried to keep it together, but as he stares blankly back at me, I know that he's far from being okay. He seems to be moments away from completely breaking down, or maybe he already has.

When I opened the door to find him on the other side, he had a look of pure agony in his eyes. His whole body had shook as he'd walked into the room after me. It only stopped shaking after I took his hand in mine and tried to give him a physical reminder that he isn't alone.

"I can't get it out of my head," he admits hoarsely. He squeezes his eyes shut, like he's trying to remove the memory of his mom from his mind. "All I can see when I close my eyes is… her. In a way that no child should have to remember their parent."

I want to cry at the brutal honesty of his words. My mom had prepared me for her passing. I knew she was going to leave, and still I'd felt an unbearable pain. I can't imagine losing someone so suddenly—and being the one to discover something so tragic.

"The only time I really ever slept was when I'd escape here to see you," I confess. Even as a child, something about Cade's presence made me feel safe. When he was next to me, the bad thoughts couldn't follow me into my dreams. I could get some rest. But only when I was with him.

"Take the pain away," he pleads, his voice breaking. There's no more anger in his face, it's all pain.

My heart breaks right along with him.

I can't see him like this. I'd rather have the angry Cade than the broken one. I can take him being angry, but I can't handle him being this devastated.

"I don't know how." My voice shakes.

My breath hitches when he reaches across the mattress and tucks a piece of hair behind my ear. "By just being you, Goldie. By just being here."

His knuckles brush my cheek softly. My eyes flutter closed. Why does one little brush of his knuckles against my skin blow every other touch by a man out of the water?

"I'm here."

He cups my cheek, his fingers splaying across my neck. His thumb rests against my racing pulse. I wonder if he feels it. If he's aware of the effect he has on me even all these years later.

"For how long?"

His question makes my stomach sink. It's vulnerable. Something I know he hates being.

I search his face for anger. But it doesn't seem like he wants the question to come off like he's upset. I think he genuinely wants to know how long I'll be here.

"For however long it takes."

"However long what takes?"

I place my palm against his heart. It's been years since I've felt his bare skin against mine. His muscles are hard against my touch. "However long it takes for this to heal."

He shakes his head, his hand coming to rest on top of mine. He applies pressure, pressing my hand deeper against his chest, right on top of his racing heart. "Oh Goldie, you'd be here forever. It was broken way before this happened. I don't think it'll ever heal."

I hate that for the briefest of moments, I wonder if being back here forever would really be so bad.

Before I can get out a response, he grabs my hips and pulls my body flush against him. I breathe him in, my face pressed to his heart. His warmth envelops me immediately. My ear presses to his chest. I can hear his heartbeat. It thumps in a fast-paced rhythm that has me nuzzling deeper against his skin.

His fingers slip into my hair. He begins to run them through the long strands, his fingertips tenderly massaging my scalp. It's what he used to do when I'd find myself in his bed. I'd tell him he doesn't have to do it, but his breathing has become lighter. He doesn't suck in air like he's about to choke anymore. If giving his hands something to do takes his mind off his pain, I'll lie here all night and let him do it.

The tension in the air between us changes. It gets thick and charged. When his fingertips brush over my neck, I try to hide the shiver that runs through my body.

It's a completely inappropriate time for my body to feel so electrified from his touch.

But I can't help it.

I've dreamed of feeling his touch again for years. Now that his scent surrounds me, his body engulfs me, and his touch destroys me, I'm lost in him all over again.

His fingers untangle from my hair, taking my breath away as his fingertips flutter over the back of my neck.

I hold still as Cade's fingers travel down my back. They drift over the small amount of exposed skin between the waistband of my pajama pants and my shirt.

He watches me intently, his eyes full of heat. They're still sad, but the sadness seems different. It isn't pure agonizing pain staring back at me. It's something more captivating.

He lets his fingers drift underneath my shirt. I sigh, reveling in feeling his skin against mine.

He pushes the fabric up, exposing my midriff.

His eyes rip from my gaze as he looks at the skin he just

bared to him, longing in his eyes. "Goldie," he breathes, his voice restrained.

His fingers slightly shake as he cautiously runs his hands up my sides. His fingertips push in slightly harder at my hips as he tries to bring us even closer together.

"God, I'm so fucked up." His voice shakes as he runs his nose down my cheek. "Why can't I think of anything other than you right now?"

I can't give him a response. Something that feels so wrong shouldn't feel so right. He's right. He is fucked up. He's clearly still dealing with the death of his mom. It isn't a good idea for us to be doing this. But for the first time since he showed up at my door, I'm not afraid of him breaking down in front of me.

And Cade Jennings has always been my weakness. If making this mistake even helps ease the pain for him for a few moments, then I can't help but give him that.

His hands squeeze the narrow of my hips. Leaning down, he buries his face in the crook of my neck, taking in a deep inhale.

I cradle his face to mine, loving the feel of his weight on me. "Let me take the pain away, Cade." My tone comes out more begging than I'd meant it to.

My words make him pause. Pulling his head away, he stares down at me with an unreadable look in his eyes. Sighing, he turns my body and pulls my back to his front. I still fit against his body perfectly, a realization that causes a wash of pain.

We could've been so perfect.

"I wish it was that simple."

I grab his hand and pull it over me so our intertwined hands rest against my middle. "Me too, Cade," I answer sadly.

He presses the softest kiss right below my ear. "This right here." He completely molds his body to mine. "This takes the pain away—at least for tonight."

His thumb brushes over mine for a few minutes before it slows and stops all together. When his breathing evens out, I know that he's finally fallen asleep.

I'd do anything to help heal his heart. Even if it means breaking mine again in the process.

Chapter 14
MARE
age nineteen

"I think this might be the best idea I've ever had," Pippa muses, squeezing icing onto a cupcake.

I dip my finger into a bowl of orange frosting. "It might go down as one of my favorite birthdays," I agree before popping my finger in my mouth and licking the icing off.

Pippa looks up and glares at me. "Get away from the icing! If you eat too much of it I won't have enough to finish icing your cupcakes."

I raise my eyebrows at her, my eyes roaming over the various different bowls of icing lining the island. "Something tells me you have enough, Pip."

The door is pushed open, Cade bounding through. He wears a Jennings Ranch T-shirt that fits him way too well. I swear each summer he gets more and more toned, only fueling the intense crush I've had on him for years.

"Enough of what?" he asks, coming to a stop next to me.

I point to the countless bowls of icing. "Pippa got mad at me for taste testing the icing. She's worried she doesn't have enough."

He laughs, fixing the hat on his head. He gives his sister a look. "You definitely have enough to go around." He looks at the orange bowl I'd just dipped my finger in. "I want a taste."

Pippa pins him with one of her *Pippa Stares*. I think it's meant to be terrifying, but Cade and I have received it too many times over the years for it to be intimidating. "Cade. Don't even think about dipping your muddy finger into my icing." Her words are leveled and full of venom, but her eyes stay trained on the intricate piping details she's adding to my cupcake.

Cade looks at me, a mischievous gleam to his eyes. It's like him and I are on the same wavelength.

"I promise I won't dip my finger in the icing," he promises, doing a mock salute. "But Goldie didn't make any promises."

His eyes go dark. Pippa's curses go completely unnoticed as Cade takes me by surprise. He wraps his fingers around my wrist and guides my hand into the tub of icing. He forces me to scoop the icing onto my fingertip before he brings the icing to his mouth. My finger is enveloped in Cade's warm mouth. His tongue runs along my skin as his cheeks hollow out.

Our eyes stay locked together. This kitchen feels way too hot, despite the open windows letting in the cool, mountain breeze. I attempt to slip my finger out of his mouth, my skin now void of any leftover icing, but he stops me. His front teeth dig into my skin as he keeps me trapped in this moment with him.

His tongue circles the finger before he lets me pull it out. I'm hot and bothered, hormones running rampant through me. He only fuels the burning desire I have for him when his face breaks out in a wide smile—something unusual for him. "The icing is *delicious*."

He winks at me and I think I fall in love with him all over again. If Pippa wasn't in the room, I might do something stupid like kiss him.

Pippa groans, tossing her piping bag to the counter. "Ew, Cade, stop looking at my best friend like that!"

The smile disappears as quickly as it came, but I have it burned in my mind to remember forever. There's still the glint of humor in his eyes as he walks to the sink and uses the back of his hand to turn on the sink.

"Tell me, Pip, how was I looking at Goldie?"

Pippa begins to carefully place the cupcakes she'd iced in a white box. "Like you wanted to eat her or something. I don't know. Don't let it happen again."

Cade's eyes find mine for a fraction of a second. He shrugs, acting nonchalant. "Had to have a taste for myself."

Using the same finger that's covered in his saliva, I take another swipe of icing and pop it into my mouth. "And what'd you think?" I ask.

His words are said to Pippa, but his eyes stay locked on me. "I think that's your best batch yet, Pip."

I feel his words *everywhere*. I tell myself there's a hidden meaning in it. The thought is confirmed when his gaze lingers on me longer than necessary.

"I tried out a new recipe," Pippa announces, wiping her hands on her neon pink apron, completely unaware of the moment happening between her brother and me.

Which is probably for the best. She made her feelings clear on how Cade was looking at me.

At least she saw it too.

At least I know my mind wasn't playing tricks on me.

I'd stupidly wished that things would change between Cade and me three years ago on my sixteenth birthday. I'd been so confident that something would happen between the two of us after that night.

Nothing ever did.

But something seems different this summer. He doesn't seem afraid to look at me a little longer. To find ways to talk to me alone.

I'm wondering—*hoping*—that maybe Cade is finally coming to terms with the inevitable.

There's something between us.

I've known about it since my sixteenth birthday. I've just been waiting for him to play catch up.

He didn't on my sixteenth, seventeenth, or eighteenth birthday. But today is my nineteenth birthday, and maybe this one will be the one that really changes things.

Or maybe it won't.

Pippa and I are off to college in the fall. This summer kind of feels like the last summer for me to find out if everything with Cade is all in my head or not. It's another year under my belt and the last year I'm silently holding out for him. I'm about to be in a big city where I'll be around a bunch of guys who won't make me guess where we stand. This is the last summer for anything to happen.

During the day, Cade and I seem like friends that maybe look at each other a little too long.

But at night, when life seems to get a little too hard, it seems like there's no way Cade and I could ever just be friends. He holds me too tightly, caresses me too tenderly for there not to be something more.

Pippa bumps her hip against mine. "Mare," she sing-songs, dragging my name out into two syllables instead of one. "Why aren't you listening to me?"

I plaster on a fake smile and look up from the bowl of icing. "Sorry. I spaced out for a moment. What's up?"

Pippa narrows her dark eyebrows at me. "Did you lie to me?"

I take the cupcake she hands to me. It's always been a rule that I get to eat what she calls her reject cupcakes. "What do you mean?"

Cade opens the fridge on the other side of the kitchen. I try not to stare too long as he pulls out a water bottle and eavesdrops on our conversation.

"Were you up past midnight to celebrate your birthday? I would've hung out with you."

I chew on my lip as I avoid looking at Cade again.

I'm a terrible friend. Pippa had offered to stay up and help celebrate my birthday the moment it turned midnight, but I'd told her I was tired.

"No. I went to bed," I lie. I'd gone out to the barn, hoping Cade would be there waiting for me like he had the years before. Both my seventeenth and eighteenth birthday we'd gone out to the clearing just the two of us. I'd blown out a stupid candle lighter and it'd felt like the best gift in the world. But we never told Pippa that. It was our secret. I liked having a secret with Cade, something that was just shared between him and me.

Cade wasn't there last night.

I'd come up with a million excuses as to why he wasn't there, but it still hurt. We'd never talked about going out for a ride for my birthday, but it seemed like a tradition after the years before. Like an unspoken rule. It seemed obvious that he'd be there waiting for me.

He wasn't.

It broke my heart a little.

But my heart only stayed broken for a moment. When I woke up to him waiting at my bedroom door hours later, an apologetic look on his face for missing it, I had to forgive him.

He slept all night in my bed, the first time he'd ever been in mine instead of me being in his. We've never kissed, it's always been very PG, but PG has never felt so right.

Now that we're going on an overnight camping trip with our friends to celebrate my birthday, I think this is the time to change things.

I might be brave enough to confront Cade about what's happening between us. I can't guess any longer.

"Do you think you need a nap before leaving?" Pippa looks at the clock on the stove. We've still got about two hours before we need to head out.

I nod, a nap sounding amazing. Once Cade had slid underneath my covers, I hadn't slept very well. I didn't want to sleep and waste committing him in my bed to memory. I wanted to be awake in his arms, to feel his breaths against my back.

I'm paying for it today. A nap would help me rest and get ready for my birthday celebration.

Because my birthday wish is the same as it's been since my sixteenth birthday. I want him. But this year, I'm going to take matters into my own hands.

Tonight will be the night I kiss Cade Jennings.

Chapter 15
MARE
age nineteen

"Pippa!" I scream, wiping mud from my helmet. I push down on the throttle of the ATV, racing after my best friend.

Her squeal of laughter rings through the air as I try to close in on her. She cuts through another mud pit to avoid me, knowing I won't follow her into it. She loves to get filthy in the mud when we go riding, I don't mind it, but I won't do it on purpose either.

Cade's friend, Brendan, pulls up next to me and we both come to a stop. He flips the visor up on his helmet. "Not going to follow her in?"

The ATV rumbles between my thighs as I shake my head at him. "If she wants to get dirty, that's her choice. I'd prefer to not spend the next hour soaked and muddy as we get to the campsite."

He laughs. His eyes focus on me a little too long, looking up and down my body. It feels good to be appreciated by him. It just feels better with Cade. "How about you and I veer off on our own trail?"

I'm quiet for a moment, content that he can't see my face through the helmet as I think about his offer. Cade has barely looked at me since that incident in the kitchen a few hours ago. He pretty much pretended like I didn't exist as we packed.

He's giving all sorts of mixed signals, and the last thing I want to do on my birthday is spend the day trying to decipher every one of them. If he wants to act on it, he can do something about it. I wouldn't even mind making the first move if he would even bother to look my way.

I stand up, stretching my legs out for a second. "Only if you can catch me," I yell.

Before he can respond, I push down on the throttle and leave him staring behind me. I hear his ATV fire back up a few seconds later, but by the time it does I've already cut down a different path than the one the rest of the group took.

I know these trails like the back of my hand. I can find my way around the mountain just fine.

My T-shirt rides up in the wind as I navigate the terrain. It doesn't take long for Brendan to pull up next to me. I like that he doesn't try to pass me or pretend that he's more familiar with this mountain than me. Brendan, Cade, and all their friends come out here sometimes, but I still know it better than any of them do. I like that Brendan's not like other guys who have to be in control at all times; like Cade, who is a control freak. There's no way his overprotective personality would've let me take the lead.

Once we reach an open stretch of land, I slow down before coming to a complete stop. Pulling off my helmet, I turn to find Brendan stopping next to me. He follows my lead, pulling his helmet off and showing off his clear blue eyes.

"You're a wild one, Marigold Evans," he says, hanging his helmet off the handlebar.

"Yeah?" I counter. "And why's that?"

He tilts his head backward and his blond hair falls into his eyes. "Because I have guy friends who wouldn't dare go through tight trees like that at the speed you did."

I shrug. "I didn't even realize how fast I was going." It probably wouldn't be a bad idea to take it a little more easy to stay safe.

"That's why I called you wild."

He gets off his ATV and stops next to mine. His elbow rests

on my handlebar. I love his body language. It feels good to have a clear picture of what he wants.

I pull on the hair in my ponytail. "Normally Pippa is called the wild one."

His eyes flick to my lips. "Maybe she's got some competition."

When he leans in a little closer, I wonder if he's going to kiss me. If he wants to, will I let him?

I'm not given the chance to make the decision.

The sound of an engine racing toward us catches our attention. I narrow my eyes on Cade. His T-shirt flips up in the wind, showing off his toned abdomen as he hauls ass right at us.

He jerks his handlebars to the side, narrowly missing crashing right into both Brendan and me. Mud sprays from his tires, coating both of us.

"Cade!" I scream.

"What the *fuck*, man," Brendan says right after me, wiping mud from his cheeks.

Cade angrily rips his helmet off. His chest heaves up and down as he stares daggers at me. It's like Brendan isn't even here. It's just Cade and me.

"Just what the fuck do you think you're doing?" he grits out.

I angrily wipe mud from my eyes, wondering why the hell he's mad when he's the one who just barged in on my moment. "What am I doing?" I shriek. "What are *you* doing? You could've killed us!"

He scoffs, ripping his eyes from mine to look at his friend. "What are you thinking breaking away from the group like that?"

Brendan doesn't seem fazed by his friend's outburst. "I'm thinking that Mare is fully capable of handling things out here herself. I trusted her to know where she was going."

"Something could've happened," Cade bites.

Brendan looks at me, giving me a questioning look. He

shrugs. "Something could happen whether we're in the group or not. What's your problem, Jennings?"

"Right now, *you*," Cade fires back.

Oh my god, is he *jealous*?

I roll my eyes. "You're overreacting. I've been out here alone with Pippa. Alone with you," I say under my breath. If Brendan catches the added comment, he doesn't say anything. "We're fine. You can go now."

"Oh, I'll be going. So will you."

"I've got her," Brendan interjects.

Cade gives him a scathing look. His jaw clenches so hard I wonder if it hurts his teeth. They have to be grinding against one another. "Like hell you do. I'd love to see you try and find your way to the campsite from here." He hooks a thumb over his shoulder. "Go for it."

Brendan looks uneasily at me. He's probably just as confused at Cade's terrible mood like I am.

"Stop being a dick," I scold. "You know he doesn't know where to go. But I do, so we're fine."

Cade revs his engine for theatrics. This man is going to drive me fucking insane.

"We'll all go," he states. He holds eye contact with me for a few beats before he shoves his helmet back on, keeping his visor open so I can still see his eyes. "Let's go."

I decide to try and wait him out. Maybe he'll take off angry and leave me and Brendan to it.

He does no such thing. We're in a battle of wits, and poor Brendan is just a spectator.

"Now," Cade snaps. The tone of his voice has Brendan leaving my side and getting back on his ATV.

I walk up to Cade's ATV, leaning over it to bring my face close to his. "You had no right. We'll talk about this later."

He laughs. It's dark and twisted, the sound doing funny things to me. "*He* has no right being alone with you."

Rage courses through my body. "You don't get to decide that."

Cade's eyes darken. They flick to my lips for a moment before he looks over to Brendan waiting at the ATV. "You know what," he says mockingly, "it kind of looks like I do."

Letting out an annoyed sigh, I pull my helmet back on. There's no point in arguing if Brendan is going to listen to Cade.

But I'll make sure to say something about it later. He's not getting off this easily. If he's going to be a jealous asshole, then I'm going to give him even more of a reason to be.

Chapter 16
MARE
age nineteen

A SLIGHT RUSTLING sound outside the tent pulls me from my sleep. I look to see if maybe it was just Pippa coming to bed for the night. I find her fast asleep on the other side of the tent, her forearm covering her eyes.

I pull the blanket up to my chin. I'd gone to bed early, too upset with Cade to enjoy what was supposed to be my birthday celebration. After he'd ruined the moment between Brendan and me, he'd gone right back to not talking to me.

He stopped ignoring me at least. He didn't grace me with another word, but he did glare at me the entire night. Even when his on and off again girlfriend, Rhiannon, tried to get his attention, he'd barely looked at her. He'd barely looked at anything but me or the labels he kept tearing off his beer bottles. The only time he pretended that I existed was when I tried to spend alone time with Brendan. If I even *looked* in Brendan's direction, Cade would find a way to stop it like a damn guard dog.

I let him scowl and throw a temper tantrum. I was throwing one of my own. Words spun through my head all night as I'd planned what I'd say to him the first time we were alone. He can't ignore me until he sees me try to give my attention to somebody else. It was a shame we're in the presence of our friend group for tonight. I didn't want to hash it out for all of them to see.

I'd still gone to bed angry. Pippa had been shocked I'd wanted to go to bed so early, but I told her I'd be ready to keep up with the celebrations tomorrow.

When another rustling sound comes from outside the tent, I figure people must still be up and having fun. At least someone on this little trip is having a good time for my birthday.

The tent zipper moving and getting pulled open catches my attention. I sit up immediately, watching it warily. At first I panic thinking it's a bear, or a serial killer, but when Cade's face pops through the opening, I let out a sigh of relief.

For a second.

Then anger courses through my veins at what he pulled earlier.

I open my mouth to tell him exactly how I feel, even with Pippa sleeping soundly right next to me. Before any sound comes out, he puts a finger to his lips.

"Come here," he mouths.

I narrow my eyes at him. My mouthed "no" in response is clear as day.

"Goldie," he responds silently.

I shake my head at him.

He doesn't get to ignore me, get mad at me for spending time with someone else, refuse to speak to me, and then wake me up because he feels like it.

His eyes soften. "Please," he mouths.

I'm so fucked. One simple word and the anger dissipates enough from my body to have me crawling out of my sleeping bag and leaving the tent.

I say nothing as Cade quietly zips the tent back up as I shove on my boots.

"What do you want?" I whisper, stepping away from the group of tents so no one hears us.

Cade fixes a backpack on his back. What does he need that for?

"To celebrate your birthday."

"You already had that chance."

He shoves his hands into the pockets of his jeans. A small worry line forms on his forehead. "I'm asking for another."

I let out a resigned sigh. "I'm tired of this, Cade."

"Tired of what?"

I start walking even farther from the group of tents. When I'd envisioned talking to Cade tonight, I thought it'd be me convincing him to finally give in and kiss me. Instead, I'm now convincing him to just leave me alone and stop pretending like he wants me if he doesn't.

Once I feel like we're far enough away from everyone, I spin to speak with him. "I'm tired of this back and forth with us. I'm tired of guessing how you feel. Really, I'm just tired of *you*."

Cade's lip twitches, which only annoys me further. "I'm done," I say exhausted, already turning my body toward the tent.

I'm going to go to bed and wake up tomorrow and pretend that my heart never wanted him so desperately. He clearly doesn't deserve it.

A strong hand grabs me by the wrist. "Goldie, wait." Cade pulls, spinning me so I'm looking at him once again.

Why does he have to look so good under the moonlight?

I feel like so many of our encounters, some of my favorite moments with him, all take place in the dark. It's like the moon is the only thing to know anything about us. It's a sad thought. Maybe I want him to acknowledge me in the sun, too.

"I'm tired of that nickname, too," I point out. If he ever stopped calling me that, I think my heart would break, but he doesn't have to know that.

Cade's thumb brushes the inside of my wrist. He keeps it there, looking down at where our skin touches. I look down, too. At the spot where my pulse gets stronger and stronger with the connection of our skin.

"I'm tired, too," he confesses. He looks up at me, and I forget every shitty thing he's done when I see the vulnerability in his eyes.

"What do you have to be tired about?" I've given him every clear signal in the world. He doesn't get to be tired.

"I'm tired of fighting myself over how much I think about you. I'm tired of telling myself that I shouldn't look at my little sister's best friend the way I look at you. I'm really just tired of pretending that my entire head isn't full of you and only you."

I'm too stunned to say anything. I hadn't expected him to be so honest—to be so vulnerable.

"I'm tired of pretending that my day doesn't begin and end with thoughts of you," he admits, his chest heaving up and down.

His fingers caress against mine as he watches me closely.

"Cade." My voice shakes as I try to figure out if I'm hearing him correctly.

He reaches out and grabs me by the waist, pulling me against his warm body. "I know I haven't acted like it. Truthfully, I've tried fighting it for as long as I can. There are so many reasons I shouldn't be saying this, beginning with Pippa and ending with the fact you're leaving in a few months, but I don't care anymore."

His hands move from my waist to cup my face. His callouses scratch my cheeks. It's the best feeling in the world. "Forgive me for not being able to fight it any longer."

I want to make a career out of putting words to paper. I've always been one to find the right words, but right now—I can't think of anything to say back to him. So I do what I've been dreaming about for years.

Standing on my tiptoes, I press my lips against his.

As soon as our lips collide, it feels like everything in the world has fallen into place. Kissing him is familiar but exhilarating. It's like seeing your home through a whole new lens.

I may be the one to start the kiss, but Cade takes control immediately. His fingers weave through my hair as he tilts my head, giving his tongue access to slip between my lips. He tastes like the peppermints he's always stealing from the stable.

I've waited so long to kiss him like this that it almost feels like it really isn't happening. It feels too perfect—too right—for this to be real life.

We both gasp for air as we refuse to even pause long enough to breathe. Peppermint has never tasted so good as his tongue caresses mine. I don't even like peppermint, but I can see myself becoming a fan.

"Cade," I whisper as he feathers kisses along my jaw. My heart threatens to erratically beat right out of my chest at the rush of adrenaline that comes from finally kissing the man I've been in love with for years.

Our foreheads press against each other's as we both catch our breath. My fingers press against my lips in disbelief.

I finally got to kiss the boy I've loved for as long as I can remember. And he kissed me back with a matched passion and desperation.

Cade's fingers wrap around my wrist as he pulls my hand toward him, pressing it to his sharp cheekbones. "If I'm being honest, Goldie, I've always loved the beautiful words you write, but I might like how your body speaks to me even more."

The mountain breeze tickles my cheek as I shyly smile up at him. "What's it saying?"

He quickly presses another kiss to my lips, taking me by surprise. I like the hastiness of it. I'm comforted by the idea that he's as desperate to taste me as I am him.

"It's saying that you've been thinking about that kiss just as much as I have." His knuckles brush against my arm right before he joins our hands together. He tugs on our linked hands, pulling me down a narrow path.

"I've probably thought about it more." I don't ask where he's taking us. It doesn't matter. I'd follow him anywhere. I'm still riding the high of kissing him. The destination where he's taking us makes no difference to me. It's just about the journey of going on it with him.

Cade looks over at me, the moon reflecting in his eyes. "I don't think so. It seems like more and more recently, my mind is full of nothing but thoughts of you."

His words steal any kind of response. I'm trying to wrap my mind around what's happening between us. I'd gone to bed swearing that by the time I woke up the next morning, I'd never pine after my best friend's brother again. When sleep finally took me, I'd been chanting over and over again how he was nothing to me anymore.

My, how things have changed.

Cade lifts a large evergreen branch over his head, giving me room to cross underneath it. I keep walking, wondering where he's leading us to. There's no longer a clear path, and we seem to be somewhere we haven't visited before. Well, at least I haven't. With the way Cade effortlessly steps through the tall grass, his eyes trained in front of him as his thumb brushes my knuckles, I wonder if he's taking me somewhere familiar to him.

I'm about to ask him where he's leading us to when there's a break in the trees. He pulls us through it and I'm met with one of the most stunning views I've ever seen.

My feet stop, my body too stunned by the sheer beauty of the scene in front of me.

"Oh my god," I whisper, taken aback by what I see.

Cade comes to a stop next to me, his shoulder brushing against mine. "I know it's not our typical birthday spot for you, but I was hoping this scene might make up for it."

From our spot on the mountain, you can see down to a stunning valley, a body of water tucked in between the trees below us. The moon reflects off the water in a way so stunning that it takes my breath away. If you look far enough into the distance, you can see another looming mountain where the highest peak still has snow at the top.

"Is it Mare approved?" he asks. I know him well enough to

know there's a hesitant edge to his voice. I don't know why he'd ever think that this wouldn't be one of my favorite scenes in the world.

I turn to him, my eyes burning with the tears of happiness that are threatening to spill over. "I didn't know this spot existed," I manage to get out. "It's the most beautiful thing I've ever seen."

Cade cocks his head, a lopsided smirk appearing on his face. "I could think of something even more beautiful."

My heart leaps in my chest at his words because Cade isn't staring out at the scenery. He's staring at me.

He doesn't give me time to form any kind of response. His rough hands grab either side of my face, his thumbs brushing over my sunburnt cheeks. "I think this might be my favorite birthday night of yours."

"I think this might be my favorite night out of all the days I've lived—not just my birthdays."

He pulls me into him, like now that we've both addressed the shift in feelings between us he can't handle losing any kind of contact between our bodies. "Mine too," he says with a large exhale.

We carefully walk down the slope of the mountain until we're steps away from the pond.

Cade pulls the backpack off his back. Reaching inside, he pulls out one of the nice blankets Linda keeps in the house. She'd kill him if she knew he brought it tonight. I can vividly imagine how angry she'd be at the sight of him spreading it over the damp grass next to the water.

He points to the blanket. "Sit."

I follow his direction, sitting down and pulling my knees against my chest. I tuck my chin against my knees, staring out at the captivating scenery in front of me. "I'm not over this view."

His side presses against mine. I like how adamant he's being about keeping our bodies touching in some way. He sets his backpack in front of him, reaching in to grab something else from the sleek, black bag.

He pulls out a few marigolds. They're a little smashed, maybe from the contents of whatever else he has in the bag. It doesn't take away from their beauty. If anything, that in combination with the sheepish smile on his face makes me prefer them the way they are right now. "I found these this morning before we left. I wanted to give them to you before we headed out, but you were with Pippa."

I take the marigolds from him delicately, not wanting to do anything to jeopardize the petals falling from the stems.

His breath tickles the back of my neck as he leans over me. "They're probably not the best birthday present now that they're all messed up."

I clutch them to my chest, angling my head so I stare into his chestnut eyes. "I love them."

"So your birthday isn't ruined?" he jokes.

"I thought it was earlier when you were being a dick."

Cade swallows, a muscle rippling along his jaw. "I'm not sorry for acting that way. Seeing you with Brendan made me…" His words trail off as he stares out at the pond in front of us.

"Jealous?"

His eyes find mine. "So fucking jealous, Goldie." He traces my bottom lip with his thumb, watching my lips intently. "The thought of another man touching you, tasting you, is enough to drive me fucking mad."

"Even if they tried, I'd still be thinking of you."

He traps my mouth with his. His kiss is dangerous and possessive, something I hadn't seen from him until today.

When he finally pulls away, both of us are breathless. "Don't think I won't act like that again," he warns, his eyes traveling my face.

"There's nothing for you to worry about. For me, it's always been you."

He seems to accept my answer. He leans back, pulling me along with him.

It feels like second nature when he wraps his arm around me and tucks my head against his chest. Maybe it's because we've spent so many nights in bed with some sort of contact. In fact, all the times I found myself in his bed, I never woke up without some part of us touching.

It always felt meaningful with him—but this feels like so much more. We've kissed. He's admitted that I'm not the only one whose head is spinning from the feelings between us. The contact of our bodies feels like so much more now. Something I didn't even know was possible.

"Look at the stars with me, Goldie," Cade whispers.

As I adjust my body, getting comfortable in his warm embrace, I fight the urge to tell him I'd lie here with him forever. I'd count every star to infinity to stay locked in this moment with him.

Chapter 17
MARE
present

LIGHT POURS through the window of my room, stirring me from dreams of the past. I reach across the bed, expecting to find warmth from Cade's body.

There's no warmth. My hand brushes over cold, empty sheets. I don't know why I'd expected to find him here with me this morning. It shouldn't be a surprise that he's gone.

He'd even told me he only needed help taking the pain away in the night. I'm not what he needs to help in the daylight.

It's the same thing from all those years ago when he took the pain away from me in the night and was responsible for the pain and longing in my heart during the day.

I sigh, turning in the bed to stare up at the ceiling. The orange glow filtering through the drawn curtains tells me that it's still pretty early in the morning. I always used to be an early riser until after I got my first publishing deal. After that, I learned that my words flow better in the silence of the night. I'd spent many nights in front of my laptop and many days in bed, catching up on just enough sleep to write through the night again.

My phone vibrates on the nightstand. I ignore it. Or at least I try to. When it rings from the second call, I groan and reach across the bed to grab it.

Just as I expected, I find my agent's name on the screen.

Swiping to answer, I mentally prepare myself for a slew of questions on the current state of my manuscript.

"Hi Rudy," I say with a sigh.

"Good morning," he responds cheerfully. He always sounds so cheerful for someone who is constantly giving me lectures. I can't be too upset with him. He risked taking me on when I was a young debut author. "I was calling to check in on you."

"On me or the manuscript?"

He scoffs on the other line. "I'm not that cold, Marigold. I know the funeral was yesterday. I wanted to see how you were doing."

I'm not good or bad. I'm just numb. I've felt so many emotions recently that I don't want to feel anything at all. I hold my tongue and don't tell him that, though. Rudy is my agent, not my therapist. Although sometimes I may use him as both.

"About as expected," I comment, running my hand over the spot Cade vacated. Linda's death hit hard. But so has being back in the presence of the only man I've ever loved.

"Whatever you need from me, you just tell me. Your team is here if you need us."

I'd already turned over all my social media accounts to my publicist before my writing retreat, wanting to focus solely on finishing the manuscript that was so beyond late. Not that I was really active on my accounts even before my last ditch effort to finish this book. I preferred to stay off social media, not wanting to see the posts of people from the past.

When I left Sutten, I told myself I had to really quit it. I couldn't be half in and half out. That's why I never returned until now. That included using my socials to keep in touch with people from school.

The biggest thing was that I didn't want to see anything that had to do with Cade. I didn't want to know who he was dating, or what he was doing. Pippa didn't really mention him and neither did Linda. I think they always knew something was off, even though I never quite told them what'd happened between Cade and me.

"Marigold? Are you still there?"

I jump, totally forgetting that I'd been on the phone with Rudy. "Yeah. Sorry, I think the service might be spotty here."

"Since I've got you…" he begins, his words trailing off.

I let out a pent up breath, knowing exactly where he's going. "I haven't had time to write anything," I interrupt.

"Understandable." I know him well enough to know there's a hint of disappointment in his voice. I hate it. The last thing I want to do is let down him and the publishing house that took a risk on me.

"Things shouldn't be so hectic now. I should have more time to write."

"Do you know how it's going to end?" he asks.

I chew on my lip. "Maybe," I lie. When we'd sold the duet to the publishing house, I'd expected a different outcome for the two characters. When I'd plotted and released the first book, I had this vivid plan on how the second book—and the characters' love story—would end. But now that I'm writing the conclusion to their love story, nothing feels right. I hadn't quite admitted that to him yet. If it were up to me and if I wasn't under such immense pressure, I'd scrap the story completely and start all over.

"That's what I like to hear," he says enthusiastically. "Can't wait to read it."

That makes two of us.

Now I just need to write it…

He runs over a few more business things with me before he ends the call. I actually didn't mind starting the morning doing a bit of work with him. It gives me an excuse to not go downstairs. I don't know what it's going to look like seeing Cade. Will he finally acknowledge I'm here and actually forgive me? *Unlikely.* Will he pretend that he didn't spend all night clutching me to his body like he was afraid I was going to disappear? *Probably.*

I'm halfway into putting my hair up when the door is pushed open and a sleepy-eyed Pippa stands in the doorway. It's clear she hadn't spent much time getting herself ready. Her hair is braided, but it looks like maybe she'd slept in it from the tendrils that messily spill out of the woven hair.

She stifles a yawn as she crosses my room and belly flops onto the bed. "I think I hibernated last night," she says, her voice muffled as she speaks against the comforter.

I pull an elastic from my wrist and twist it around the pile of hair on top of my head, forming a messy bun. "That's good, Pip. You needed to sleep."

"I don't think I woke up once."

"I'm actually shocked you're up this early. I figured you'd sleep the day away."

She turns on the bed, catching my eyes through the mirror as I dab some blush onto my cheeks to give myself some form of color. "I thought about it," she answers sadly.

I turn in my seat, looking her in the eye. "No one would blame you if you did."

She takes a deep breath, trying to keep her emotions at bay. That's the thing about Pippa. She's always had such big emotions, it's hard for her to hide them. It works out when she's happy because her happiness is infectious. But when she's sad, she can't hide it, no matter how much she wants to. It's hard not to be upset right along with her.

"I know," she finally gets out. "But I don't want to just stay in bed. The way I see it is that I could lie in bed and be sad, or I could be sad and actually be productive. I'm choosing to be productive. At least that way I get out of my head a little."

"If that's what you want to do." I get up and cross the room before plopping down on the bed next to her. I hadn't got around to making it quite yet, and the side I lie on smells just like Cade. She must be so caught up in her own head that she doesn't notice.

I grab Pippa's hand, giving it a comforting squeeze. "I'm here for whatever you need. If you're wanting to go into the bakery, how about I join you? I can sit in a corner and write until you need help with something."

"You don't have to do that. You can work here if you want."

And risk seeing Cade alone? *No thank you.* I'm not emotionally ready for him to pretend like we didn't share a moment last night. If I learned anything as a teenager, it's that Cade Jennings is good at pretending I don't exist, even if he was crawling into my bed at night. My heart isn't calloused the way it used to be at him ignoring me but I'm not ready to face him.

I can't even be mad at him if he does end up acting like nothing happened. How can I be mad at him when his mom just died? The answer is I can't.

So instead, I'll avoid being alone with him at all costs. And if that means following Pippa to the conjoined bakery and coffee shop she owns, then so be it.

I fly off the bed and head toward my open suitcase, searching for something to wear. "I want to go with you. Plus, I've never seen the shop. It's time we change that."

Pippa rolls over on the bed, her feet kicking the air. "I invited you to the opening. You didn't show."

A twinge of guilt rattles through me. There were so many things I missed out on because I was too chicken to face Cade—my best friend opening her dream bakery and coffee shop being one of them. I strip out of my pajamas and slide a pair of worn jeans up my legs. "Shittiest best friend award goes to me," I say, only half-joking.

She purses her lips. "You were busy becoming famous and all. Me opening the shop wasn't as cool."

I smack her butt with my sweatshirt before pulling it onto my body. "Shut up. I'm hardly famous. You're known more around here than I am thanks to your kickass cupcakes."

Pippa rolls her eyes at me. "You were on like five morning talk shows because your book was sold out everywhere. Admit it, Mare, you're famous."

I go back to finishing my makeup, coating my lashes in mascara before we go out in public.

"You were on the news, too. Your mom sent me the link to watch it," I counter.

Pippa crawls off the bed once she realizes that I'm almost ready for the day. All I need to do is make sure I have my notebook, laptop, and charger to take to the cafe.

"The *local* news," she corrects.

"The video online had tons of views."

Her dark eyebrows raise on her forehead. "Only because with a name like *Wake and Bake Cafe*, people thought we were selling weed."

I laugh. "Hey, if you ever want to dive into that area, you've got the name for it."

She rolls her eyes. "The wake is the caffeine, the bake for, you know—the bakes. There's no weed to be seen there. At least that I know of," she adds at the last minute.

We continue to laugh about all the attention she got when she opened—due to the name of her shop—as we make our way downstairs. I stop dead in my tracks when I find Cade sitting at the counter, an open computer in front of him as he holds a mug of coffee to his lips.

Pippa stops at the counter in front of him. She grabs the mug right from his hands, taking a drink of his coffee without even asking.

He gives her an annoyed look, carefully pulling the steaming cup from her grasp. "Pippa," he argues. "Get your own coffee."

Pippa gives him an unbothered smile. She shrugs. "Just wanted to make sure you weren't being a traitor and drinking any other blend than Wake and Bake's."

He refuses to look over at me, despite me stopping in the kitchen to join them. "I think you've thrown away all evidence of any other coffee beans in the house except the ones that have come from you."

"As it should be," she says proudly. Pippa focuses on me,

turning her back to her brother. "Are you fine with waiting on coffee until we get to the cafe? I've got an idea I want you to try."

I look away from Cade, willing him to look at me instead so I can get an idea of how it's going to be between us. I meet Pippa's eyes. "That's perfect for me. I'm ready when you are."

Pippa grabs her keys from the bowl on the island, focusing on her brother once again. "We'll be at Wake and Bake if you need us."

"Goodbye Pip," he says, taking another sip of his coffee.

I'm shocked by him flat out ignoring me after us spending all night together, but I still follow closely behind Pippa. I'm barely out of earshot when I hear him say. "Bye, Marigold."

The use of my full name—and the icy tone in his voice—tells me two things. He isn't going to flat out ignore me. He's just going to act cold all over again.

Having him look at me with something other than anger was nice while it lasted.

Chapter 18
MARE
age nineteen

"Do you ever wonder what the stars look like in other places in the world?"

Cade and I lie on his mom's nice blanket, both of our faces turned to the stars. I don't know how long we've been here. Long enough for my breathing to go completely calm from stillness. Cade's fingers brush through my hair, combing through the waves as we sometimes talk and sometimes sit in silence as we take in the beauty of the stars above us.

Cade shifts from underneath me, his fingers skirting along my hairline. "Not really. I don't think there's anywhere else in this world that has a better view than I do right now."

I push off him so I can look him in the eye. My eyes narrow. "Surely you think there's somewhere else, anywhere else, that has a better view than here in Sutten."

He shakes his head, tucking a piece of hair behind my ear. "I've never wanted to leave. I don't care about the other views." His eyes rake over me in a way that has shivers running down my spine. "Not when I have this one."

His words strike something deep in me. My throat feels clogged while my body hums with desire. My head and heart are at war. I've always envisioned leaving this town and seeing what else the world has to offer. But Cade is convincing. Maybe I've been wanting to get out of this town for so long that I haven't appreciated it for what it is. It's *home*. And maybe sometimes home has the best view of them all.

Right now, I can't imagine anything being better than the view of him lying next to me. The sky could be the clearest it's ever been, reflecting over the ocean or desert or some other mountain far away from here, and I don't know if the stars would seem as beautiful as they do right now.

His thumb brushes tenderly over my cheekbone. I lean into his touch. Sadness settles deep in my bones at the thought of leaving him after I've finally got him like this. "What about you?" His voice is deep and gravelly. Almost like it pained him to even get the words out.

"I don't know," I whisper, wanting to keep this moment between us forever. "I've always imagined that anywhere would be better than here. But now..."

"Now?"

I lean closer to him until my hair creates a barrier around us. "Now I can't imagine myself being anywhere else but here... with you."

His lips twitch, hinting at a smile. "Prove it."

I don't waste another second without feeling his lips pressed against mine. I want to memorize the way he kisses, I never want to forget how he lets me feel like I'm in the lead right before he tilts my head and takes what he wants from me.

Before I know it, I'm straddling him, my hands clinging to different parts of him to get him as close to me as possible. I rock against him, desperate to feel as much as I can with the kiss.

His hands are warm as they drift underneath my T-shirt. It's the first time I've felt his skin against mine like this. The touch sets my entire body on fire.

Cade takes his time running his hands along my skin, as if he's memorizing the way I feel against his fingertips. They dig into my tender skin as he rips his mouth from mine, his broad shoulders rising and falling in deep breaths. "This is too much," he says against my neck.

"No such thing," I beg, rocking myself against him. I've never done anything with anyone else. I've never had the desire to. Every fantasy of mine has always been filled with him and only him.

But now, I'm ready to find out what it feels like when Cade touches me in places I've only touched myself. I've waited so long for it. Now I'm ready to know what it feels like to come apart underneath his touch.

His breath is hot against my chest and he lets out a groan. "I don't want to move this fast with you, Goldie," he counters, meeting my eyes. There's so much vulnerability in them. They say everything his mouth isn't.

"I feel like I've waited my whole life for this," I argue, cupping his face between my hands. "How could that be too fast?"

"I don't want you to think I took you out here to just…"

I press my fingertips to his lips. "That isn't what I think at all."

His hands press into the skin above my hips. I don't know if he's about to push me off him or bring me closer. I hope it's the latter.

"I just don't want to rush things," he answers softly. His eyes focus on my lips for a moment. "I feel like I just got you."

I laugh, shaking my head at him. "You've always had me. You just weren't paying attention."

He swallows. Somehow the air becomes even more electrified around us. "I am now."

With three words, I fall even more in love with him. I didn't know it was possible. I thought after all these years of loving him, that I couldn't love him more. I was so wrong.

I smile, stealing a kiss from him. "About time."

He playfully nips at the finger I run over his bottom lip. "I know it's technically past your birthday, but I still want you to make a wish."

Cade reaches between us, his knuckles brushing against my

inner thigh as he reaches into his pocket. He brings out the same lighter from a few years ago. "It's not a proper birthday unless you make a wish and blow out the candles."

"I made a wish earlier. You were there. The cupcakes, remember?"

He'd been busy sulking in a corner, pinning me with an angry glare as I'd made a wish for my heart to get over him. What a silly thought. My heart has always been Cade's. One simple little birthday wish wasn't going to change that.

"It doesn't count."

"And why's that?"

"Because it wasn't just us when you made it."

I'd always wondered what my birthday celebrations meant to Cade. Since my sixteenth birthday, they'd meant everything to me, but I couldn't help but wonder if they meant anything to him. Part of me wondered if he was just doing it to be nice.

Now, I know they *did* mean something to him.

"Do you have your wish?"

I nod. It's the same thing I've wished before on the flame of his lighter. I'll wish for him, to keep whatever has started tonight. Even after I go off to college in a few months, I want to find a way to keep this up.

Maybe I just won't leave at all. Maybe I should wish to find something to do here. Books can be written from anywhere, right?

A flame lights between us, the reflection of it dancing against his amber colored eyes. "Make sure you make it a good one."

I smile, closing my eyes right before I make my wish.

I wish that Cade and I can figure this out together. I wish for this to be the best summer of my life. My biggest wish is that I get to keep him once this summer ends.

Chapter 19
CADE
present

"CAN'T WE CHANGE THE SONG?" Pippa begs from the passenger seat of my truck. "This music isn't getting me in the mood. Right, Mare?"

She turns in her seat to look at Mare in the backseat. Mare looks out the window, clearly lost in her thoughts and not as worried about getting in the mood to party like my sister. "I like the song," she answers, shrugging.

Of course she does. It's a song we used to listen to all the time. I still use the same CDs she burnt for me when we were teenagers.

Pippa frowns in disappointment. "Traitor," she tells Mare. "We need party music, Cade. It's our first night out in forever. We need to get in the mood."

I switch the setting over in the truck so she can connect her phone to the speakers. I'm not sure she'll deem any of the CDs I have in the glove box worthy to pregame for a night out.

Truthfully, I didn't want to go out tonight to begin with. It's almost been a month since Mom passed. I don't know how much time needs to pass before I'll feel like hanging out at Slopes and drinking with the guys again. The only reason I'm here is because Pippa begged me to and I couldn't say no. If she needs a night out after the month we've had, then that's what I'll give her.

It doesn't mean I have to enjoy it. I'm going to try my best to just forget the hell the last few weeks have been. I've buried myself in work, barely coming up for air unless I had to eat or sleep. Even though sleep doesn't come as well as it should.

I slept great the night of Mom's funeral because I spent it with Mare. Since then, not so much. If she had showed up at my door, I would've let her in. I can't say no when it comes to Mare. But she never showed up.

Last week, I moved back to the cabin and out of the main house. Dad was doing better, and he was insistent that he spent enough time with me during the day, he was done with me hovering over him at night. I couldn't help it. I needed to know he was okay.

Maybe part of me wanted to be in Mare's presence, even if I didn't want to admit it. I've been a dick to her because if I don't put up some kind of wall between us, I'm going to end up the same way I was when she left this town, and I can't do that again. Not without Mom here to pull me out of it.

Even though I'm not sleeping in the main house anymore, most nights I still opened the cabin door to check and see if she was on the other side. If we did have the sixth sense to feel each other, it seemed to be broken. She couldn't feel how broken I was. She didn't know how much I begged her to be on the other side of my door when I pulled it open in the middle of each night, how much I needed her and how much I hated it.

Pippa sings along to a Nash Pierce song that's been severely overplayed. I don't know how she likes anything he releases, but she and Mare have been obsessed with him since they were teenagers, and he was still part of some silly boy band.

"You're about to go to a country bar and *this* is what you listen to?" I sneak a glance over at Pip, giving her a look of disapproval.

Pippa belts out the lyrics even louder, having no shame. "We'll get all the country in the world when we show up to Slopes."

I laugh. Slopes is the tourist bar in town, but it's Saturday and dance nights are something Pippa can't resist. I'm more of a Bucky's guy. It's so dingy that tourists barely show up there. It's perfect. Luckily, we're in the off-season. Slopes will no doubt be busy with people who visit for the summer, but it'll be nothing compared to what it's like during ski season.

"If only people knew you were jamming to this shit before going line dancing. You'd be kicked out of the place."

This elicits a small giggle from Mare in the backseat. I fight the urge to find her eyes through the rearview mirror.

Pippa is completely unbothered by my comment. If anything, it only further fuels her to sing louder. She turns up the song and uses her phone as a pretend microphone as she screams the lyrics from the passenger seat.

For the rest of the car ride, we don't say anything. Pippa sings, Mare looks out the window, and I stay lost in my thoughts, wondering if maybe I shouldn't have volunteered myself as a DD. Mare's thighs are hanging out of a pair of cutoff jeans in a way that's driving me wild. She looks more like the Mare I used to know, looking more country than city girl.

Men will fall at her feet tonight. Something I don't think I'm capable of witnessing—especially sober.

As soon as I put the truck in park, Pippa is swinging her door open and squealing in delight. It's clear she needs this night out, and she's actually excited about something. I'll find a way to deal just to see her not crying over Mom or burying herself in work and pretending like nothing happened.

Pippa pretty much pulls Mare out of the backseat, immediately looping her arm through hers as she pulls her body toward the entrance. Music pours out of the open garage doors as we make our way toward it. Mare and Pippa walk ahead of me as I follow a few steps behind. We had to get a spot toward the back of the parking lot, the party already in full-swing at Slopes.

I follow the two of them as Pippa hunts down the rest of the group she'd invited. She finds them, all of our friends piled into a circular booth close to the dancefloor.

Everyone greets us. I hate that there's pity in all of their eyes as they look at the three of us. It's hard to get over the death of someone when everyone around you reminds you of the pain you're feeling with the pity in their eyes.

Brendan slides out of the booth, pulling me into a half hug. "It's good to see you, Jennings." At least he doesn't look at me with as much pity as some of the other's do. Brendan's eyes light up slightly as he looks to my right, his focus solely on Mare.

Jealousy jolts through me when she smiles at him.

What the fuck. She hasn't even smiled at me like that since she's been back. Not that I've done much to get one from her since I've been such a dick.

"Evans," Brendan says right before letting out a whistle. "Miss *bestselling author* in the flesh. It's been too damn long."

She shakes her head at him, anxiously tucking her hands in the back pockets of her shorts that are too fucking short. "Stop," she pleads, embarrassed. "You make me sound cooler than I am."

He wraps her in a tight embrace, and her cowboy boots come off the floor as he lifts her in the air.

I have to tear my eyes away from them for a moment before I act like a jealous, raging, asshole and rip her right from his arms.

"Are you kidding me? You're the coolest fucking person this town has known, Evans. Your book sat proudly in every store when it was released. All the women in town had a book club for it." His voice gets a little lower when he risks a glance at me. "Linda hosted it," he finishes sadly.

"All the paperback sales make sense now," Mare teases, finally stepping out of Brendan's grasp.

Thank fuck.

I stare at the spot where Brendan and Mare still touch at the arms. "It's good to have you back in Sutten." He isn't bashful when he looks her up and down. "Country looks good on you, girl."

Pippa wraps up whatever conversation she was having with our friends. She stops next to Mare. "We need to go get a drink. I might need one or two before I feel loose enough to go out to the floor."

Brendan smiles. He finally breaks contact with Mare and walks up to the table. He pulls out three opened bottles of beers. He hands one to Pippa, then me, before he focuses back on Mare.

I'm certain he still wants her by the look in his eyes, even all these years later. He lays it on thick when he hands the beer over to Mare. "Will you still drink cheap beer or are you more of a martini girl now?"

Mare rolls her eyes, pressing the tip of the bottle to her lips and taking a long gulp. Pippa's eyebrows raise, impressed. Mare gulps down more than half of the bottle before she pulls it from her lips and wipes some drops away with the back of her hand.

She looks at me for a split second before looking back at Brendan. "Please," she begins. "I'm more of a white wine *woman* than a martini woman." She lifts the beer in the air, knocking it against the one in Pippa's hand in a cheers. "But there's nothing that goes better with Slopes than some ice-cold, cheap beer."

Brendan beams as he pulls her arm downward, nudging her to sit next to him in the booth. "That's my girl," he states proudly.

Like fuck she's your girl. I bite my tongue, knowing I have no right to say that even though it's exactly how I feel.

If Mare is going to be anyone's in Sutten, she'd be mine. The problem was, Mare didn't want anyone in Sutten. She wanted the big city dream. Brendan and I don't stand a chance against the trust-fund city boys.

If I thought she'd end up with someone in this small town, I'd make damn sure it was me.

Before Pippa can beat me to it, I slide into the booth after

Mare. If she's going to be pushed against Brendan, then I'm going to make my presence known on the other side.

Her knee brushes against mine as Pippa slides into the booth, making everyone scoot a little bit closer to one another.

"Sorry," Mare mumbles under her breath, totally ignoring whatever Brendan is saying to her.

I should do the whole gentleman thing and scoot into the empty space on my other side. At least that'd make it so we weren't pressed up against one another. But if she's going to be that close to Brendan, she's going to be stuck with being that close to me.

So I keep my jean-clad thigh against her bare one.

The entire time our friends talk, everyone catches up and the night gets more normal the more it carries on. After two beers, I ask the server for water and stick with that for a bit.

Pippa sets her bottle on the table loudly. She looks across the table at Mare, shimmying dramatically in place with a wide smile. "Let's get on that dance floor, Mare!"

My sister looks over at Chase. She steals the cowboy hat off his head with a proud smirk. "I'm ready to shake my ass."

"I'm not sure line dancing counts as shaking your ass, Pip," Mare comments. Her body has become more relaxed with the three beers she's sipped on while we've all been sitting around the table. "You might have picked the wrong bar."

Pippa swats the air, scooting out of the booth. She bounces on the balls of her feet as she looks past me at Mare. "I'll do whatever I want. And so will *you*." She hits me in the stomach. "Now move, brother. Mare and I are going to shake our asses however we damn well please."

"Now that I'd love to see," Brendan quips next to me. I'm unable to resist the death glare I aim his way at the remark.

He puts his hands up defensively as I slide from the booth. I don't move that far away from the exit, making Mare press her body against mine to get out.

I've never claimed to be a good man.

"Didn't mean to talk about your sister that way," Brendan teases.

I grunt. It wasn't because he talked about Pippa like that. Pippa can hold her own. If she didn't love the attention, she'd say so.

It's because he made that comment about *my* Goldie.

Mare looks at me over her shoulder, her blonde hair billowing down her back as Pippa pulls her to the dance floor.

The moment Goldie's little hips start moving to the beat, I know coming tonight was a horrible fucking idea.

There's no way I can sit here and watch her move like that and not do something about it.

Chapter 20
MARE
present

MY FEET ACHE. I'm four beers and two shots deep into the night. Shockingly, I'm having the best time. It feels good to let go for a bit. Life doesn't feel as heavy here. Not right now. Not in this moment.

Pippa and I laugh freely as I miss so many of the steps; my line dancing skills are a bit rusty from the years I've been absent. With every drink and every new song, I get more comfortable. The steps come back to me, and I'm reminded of all the nights Pippa and I spent here before we went off to college.

Pippa and I almost keel over in a laughing fit when we bump into one another by accident. The impact was so abrupt that we almost topple over.

A hand grasps my arm, steadying me before I can get too off-balance. Looking up, I find a smiling Brendan looking down at me. I'm reminded of how much I appreciated him at nineteen. I liked that I was never guessing if he was interested in me or not —unlike with Cade. Even now, it seems like the interest is still there. He hasn't bothered hiding it tonight. It's nice to look a man in the eyes and not question where I stand.

Right now, it's nice to look a man in the eyes and not see pain, hurt, and anger staring back at you.

I'm nowhere near looking for anything serious, but I could

look for fun. Brendan just might be the kind of fun distraction I need.

When he runs his hands down the sides of my arms, I lean into him slightly. I look up at Pippa, who is now dancing with Chase. I attempt to hide a smile when she winks at me.

It turns out maybe we both need the fun.

Another song starts up. Brendan grabs my hand, falling in step next to me as we move to the music. Our bodies brush against each other with the beat.

For a few songs, Pippa, Brendan, Chase, and I just laugh and have fun. Eventually, the tone changes. Our bodies get closer. My back presses to Brendan's front as we move to the music. His hands bravely drift, lowering on my sides, coming to a stop right over the waistband of my shorts.

We rock back and forth before he spins me around. When he pulls me against him, there's a wide smile on his face. "I like seeing you like this, Evans," he says, his voice low. His breath tickles my cheek with each one of his words. It doesn't feel the same way it did with Cade. But it doesn't feel bad either.

"Like what?" I ask, intertwining our hands as both our bodies circle each other, copying the same movement as the other dancers on the floor.

"Happy," he responds instantly.

I can't help but smile right back at him. I do feel happy. At least for right now. I'd dreaded going out tonight. But it's turning out to be exactly what I needed. "Me too."

We dance to a few more songs before I decide I need water—and maybe another drink—immediately. I pull away from Brendan, watching him say something to Chase and Pippa.

"I'm going to go grab us some drinks," I announce.

"I'll go with you," Brendan offers.

I shake my head. "I've got it. You keep having fun."

He looks like he wants to say something else, but I don't give him the chance. I slip through a narrow opening between two dancing bodies, disappearing into the crowd of people.

It takes longer than I expected to navigate through the dancing bodies, but eventually I make it to the outskirts of the dance floor.

Taking a deep breath, I look toward the bar to see how busy it is. I'm taking a step toward it when an arm snakes around my waist and pulls me into a hard body.

"What the h—"

"Shh." A hand gently slips over my mouth at the same time a familiar scent washes over me. My body instantly recognizes the scent and the feel of his body pressed against mine. "It's just me, Goldie."

I'm relieved that a stranger isn't trying to grope me. But it still doesn't change the fact that I'm angry he thinks he can just pull me against him in the middle of all these dancing people after he hasn't said a word to me all night.

"What do you want, Cade?" I ask, trying to step away from him. He doesn't allow it. Instead, he pulls me against him—hard —as he takes a few steps backward. His steps lead us into the middle of a group of people, the rest of the bar disappearing around us as we get lost in a sea of bodies.

His hand travels down my back, resting right at the curve of my waist as he holds me tightly against him. There's fire in his eyes when he goes from looking over my head to looking me in the eye. "What do I want?" He scoffs. "The answer is pretty fucking simple, actually. I want to not have to sit here and watch you dance with my friend all goddamn night."

He roughly turns me, gluing his front to my back. I try to pull away, but it's no use. I'm pinned against him. He begins to rock his body left and right, pulling me with him. I hate how my body breaks out in goose bumps, despite the heat from the surrounding bodies, at the way our bodies brush up against one another.

"I don't know why it bothers you," I snap, giving up and letting my body relax. There's no way I can overpower him, even if I wanted to. And the sad fact is I don't want to. Deep down, I don't want to get away from him.

I'm extremely turned on by the jealousy that was heating his stare. My skin lights up with desire feeling his body against mine once again.

His body shakes with a sarcastic laugh. Cade leans over me, talking right next to my ear. "You don't know why it bothers me?" His fingertips tease the top of my waistband, making my breath catch in my chest.

Why can't it feel like this with anyone else? It's tragic to want a man you can't have.

My head shakes back and forth, falling against his chest as he inches deeper into the fabric. His fingertips scratch my tender skin in a way that lights up my entire body.

"It bothers me because he can't fucking have you, Goldie. He couldn't have you then, and he can't have you now."

I'm essentially panting as his fingertips slip into the fabric of my panties. We know way too many people in this town for us to be doing this on the dance floor, but all sense of reason has left my mind at the feeling of him getting so close to the wetness pooling between my thighs.

"That shouldn't bother you." I moan when one of his fingers slides against my sensitive core. Everyone around us seems to be swept up in their own movements, but it doesn't make him touching me so intimately any less inappropriate. We go to church on Sundays with some of these people, yet here we are as he brushes up against my clit in the middle of a crowded dance floor.

Cade takes me by surprise when his lips tenderly brush along the top of my exposed shoulder. "It wouldn't bother you to see me on the dance floor with another woman's body hanging onto mine?" His fingers slip out of my shorts, and I don't know if I'm upset or relieved by the loss of touch. "It wouldn't bother you to see someone else's hips moving against me like this?" His hands find my hips. He rubs them against his obvious erection.

I swallow, desire running thick through my veins from feeling him against me. This is so wrong, but it feels way too right. I feel power in knowing the effect I have on him. But with power comes the anger at the constant back and forth that comes with Cade.

"It wouldn't bother me," I lie. I'm sick at the thought of all the times that exact scenario has probably played out here in the years I've been gone.

Cade roughly spins me around, forcing me to look him in the eye. "You're lying."

There's too much emotion in his eyes, so many mixed-signals considering he's done everything in his power to ignore me since his mom's funeral. Since the night I thought *maybe* he and I were turning over a new leaf. Frustrated, I rip out of his grip and throw myself into the bodies surrounding us.

"Goldie!" he angrily yells behind me.

Ignoring him, I force people out of my way as I try to get away. I haven't had enough to drink to erase all the pain he's caused me. I can't do this with him. I can't let him get under my skin—into my heart—again. I barely survived the first time I let him in my bed and heart. I'd be incredibly naive to let it happen again.

I refuse to look at anything but toward the back exit as I rush through the crowded bar. If Pippa were to see me right now, she'd immediately know something was wrong. She's having the time of her life tonight. The last thing I want to do is bother her with my problems with her brother. I have to make sure she doesn't catch me. She can think I've been held up waiting for drinks or something.

The moment fresh air hits my face as I push open the back door, I take in a relieved breath. I hadn't realized how stifling the air was inside Slopes until I'm met with the air from outside.

Gravel crunches underneath my feet as I race to the edge of the back parking lot. I look at the mountaintops in the distance, their peaks lit by the moon as I continue to try and suck air into my lungs.

My entire body freezes when the door opens behind me.

Chapter 21
CADE
present

EVEN WITH THE cold air hitting my cheeks, my entire body feels heated with rage. With each minute that's ticked by tonight, I've had to watch Brendan touch all of the places on Mare that I've only dreamed about for years—and it has my blood boiling.

I've got no fucking right to chase her out of the bar like this, to have any say on who she does something with. But it doesn't stop me from crossing the parking lot with rage until I'm standing right behind her.

Her body stills. She doesn't turn around, but I know without a doubt that she knows exactly who is standing behind her. There's not a single movement from her body except for the blowing strands of her hair in the wind.

"I wasn't done talking to you." There's not a hint of softness to my voice. I know exactly how my tone comes off—like an asshole. I swallow, trying to figure out how to get her to turn around and look at me without forcing her to.

I've already dug myself a deep enough hole tonight. I don't know if I should make it worse or not. The problem is, I'm not sure I really care. She can hate me all she wants. I need the answer to my question. Desperately.

Finally, she moves. Her shoulders rise as she sucks air into her lungs. Her exhale is loud, even over the sound of the thumping bass that radiates from the building behind us. Slowly, Mare turns around to face me.

Her face is filled with so many contradicting emotions. The look in her eyes confirms how upset she is. There's a defiant set to her jaw as she stares back at me. All of that is a stark comparison to the tears running down her pink cheeks.

"I can't do this with you, Cade," she whispers. It feels like someone has reached inside my chest and ripped my heart out after hearing her voice breaking saying my name.

"I can't *not* do this with you, Goldie," I answer, ashamed of myself for putting us through this. I wish I was a better man. If I was, I'd turn around and give her the space from me she deserves. I'd go back to the bar or wait in the truck so she can enjoy the rest of her night with Brendan without me jealously watching on.

But I'm not a better man. My feet don't take me farther away from her. Instead, I take a step closer to her, crowding her space.

She shakes her head as she attempts to wipe the tears from her cheeks. "Why do you care if I'm lying or telling the truth? It shouldn't matter. *I* shouldn't matter to you."

"Some days I'm fucking terrified because it feels like you're the only thing that really matters."

Her eyes go wide. She watches me with apprehension. Like she has no idea who I am, or if she can believe a thing that comes from my mouth.

It's not like I blame her. I've done enough in the past that I can't fault her for second-guessing every single one of my words.

Her tears fall even more freely now. They coat her lips, collecting for a moment in her prominent cupid's bow before they continue their path down her face.

"You act like you hate me."

"Maybe I do hate you."

She sniffles. "Maybe I hate you, too."

"Maybe we hate that we feel so many things other than hate."

"I'm not lying." She changes the subject, and I let her. I know she's lying straight to my face by the way her voice shakes with every single syllable that comes from her mouth.

My jaw clenches in frustration. "Bullshit."

"Don't talk to me like that. You don't know me anymore, Cade. Don't pretend to know me well enough to know if I'm lying or telling the truth." She throws my words right back in my face.

"There you are lying straight through your teeth all over again."

She pushes her shoulders back in a defensive position. "What's that supposed to mean?"

"It means neither one of us can hide the fact that we know every single fucking thing there is to know about the other person. Time, miles, nothing will change that I know you, Goldie. I know you almost better than I know myself. And I know for a fucking fact that you're lying."

"How?"

"Because I know how much it fucking hurts my soul to see another man look at you the way I look at you. To see him touch you the way I want to touch you. And I know that after every fucking thing between us, even after you leaving me, that you feel the same."

"You told me to leave!" she shouts, her hands angrily thrashing through the air. "You told me to leave and that you wanted nothing to do with me once I did. So that's what I did, Cade. I left. Even though it broke my heart to leave things how we did." She gasps for air as she tries to keep a grip on her emotions. "You can't pretend like we know anything about each other now. You don't know me, and I don't know you."

"I do know you," I bite. So many things race through my head, but I don't know what to say and what to keep to myself.

This conversation is pointless anyway because it won't matter once she inevitably leaves again.

I might've broken her heart when I told her to chase her dreams and leave. But she fucking obliterated mine past the point of no return when she actually left and never came back.

"And you know me," I continue, braving reaching up and wiping at the tears coating her cheeks.

She shakes her head but makes no indication of trying to get away from my touch. "That's not true. I know nothing about you." Her voice trembles as she gets out each word. "I don't know what you've been doing in the years since I've left. I don't know your favorite movie anymore. Your favorite food or which one of Pippa's cupcakes is your favorite for the month." She pushes blonde strands from her face, some of them sticking to the wetness of her cheeks, in an attempt to keep herself busy. "I don't know what you like to do in your free time or how many times you've fallen in love since I left," she finishes, her voice resigned. "I don't know anything about you."

I close the distance between us, bringing her body flush against mine. "Working," I answer, my fingertips brushing over her forehead.

Her eyebrows narrow as she stares up at me in confusion. "What?"

"In the years since you've left, I've been working, drowning myself in it, really. I lost you partly because I wanted to keep the legacy of the ranch my great-grandfather created. I had to make damn sure I attempted to make my choice worth it."

Her lips part in shock. The pad of my thumb runs over her bottom lip. Before she can say anything else, I continue addressing the rest of her statements.

"My favorite movie is still *Good Will Hunting*, but you knew that already."

She laughs, probably remembering all the times I made her watch the movie with me. She cried every single time. I'd laughed at her, even though it made me choke up as well.

"I didn't appreciate it at the time, but my favorite food is definitely my mom's famous fried chicken and cheesy potatoes that half the town has begged her for the recipe of."

I let out a sigh of relief when she nudges deeper into the palm of my hand. For the moment, I have her. She isn't running. She isn't fighting me. She's looking at me the way she used to. The way I've missed every single day since she left.

"And right now my favorite cupcake flavor of Pip's is blueberry lemon."

"I had one of those this morning."

"They're fucking phenomenal." I pause for a moment. "And working some more."

"What?"

"That's what I do on the weekends. Sometimes I make it out, but most of the time I'm too tired so I end up playing card games with the ranch hands."

"Do you still suck at Poker?"

I laugh, wondering how I ever thought my feelings for her would dull. "They take all my fucking money. Just like you always did."

"You really need to get better at Poker."

It doesn't feel like I'm close enough to her, so I grab either side of her face and tilt her head to look up at me. "And zero."

A line creases on her forehead. "Zero?"

"I haven't fallen in love with anyone since you left. I'm not able to. You can't fall in love with someone if your heart still belongs to someone else."

"Cade," she mutters, her breath hitching.

I press my fingers against her lips to stop whatever she's about to say. I don't need her to ask me more questions, or for her to say something else that'll try and convince herself that I'm making things up. "If I ask you one more thing, do you swear to not lie to me again?"

She nods.

"Do you want to kiss me as bad as I want to kiss you?"

"No," she whispers, the one word feeling like a punch to the fucking gut. "I probably want to kiss you more."

Chapter 22
MARE
present

COULDN'T HANDLE STARING BACK at the hurt in Cade's eyes any longer. I could've lied and told him that I didn't want to kiss him, but it would've been the furthest thing from the truth. From the moment I saw him again, I couldn't help but wonder if he still tasted the same.

I need to know if he still tastes like mine.

Our lips crash against one another in a wild frenzy. We're all lips and teeth and tongues as we try to make up for all the lost time between us. He kisses me angrily, as if he's throwing all his pent up aggression into the kiss.

He still tastes the same. But better.

He must've recently had a peppermint because that's all I can taste when his tongue caresses against mine. My mouth opens wider for him when he pulls on the hair that runs down my back, angling my head in a way that makes the kiss even deeper.

I forget that we're in the middle of a back parking lot, making out like a bunch of teenagers even though anybody could find us.

It doesn't matter. I'd kiss him anywhere—in front of anyone —just to experience what it's like to kiss Cade Jennings again.

I knew I'd missed him. I knew no other man I've kissed since leaving Sutten could even compete with the way Cade kisses. Now I'm reminded just how much the others didn't compare.

Nothing has ever compared to how it feels with him. I'm willing to bet nothing ever will, either.

As if the kiss doesn't already have me falling in love with him all over again, what he does after breaking our kiss is enough to have me falling fast and hard once again.

He presses a kiss to my hairline. It's so tender compared to the way he sucked and bit my lips with our previous ones. Before I can try to kiss him all over again, he's wrapping his arms around my body and pulling me into his chest.

I breathe him in, wishing I could bottle up the scent of pine that clings to everything of his and keep it forever. He presses his cheek to the top of my head. I feel his deep breath as he inhales and exhales. It's like he's just allowing himself to relax.

Maybe my touch brings him just as much comfort as his brings me.

The music from the bar wafts around us as we stay clutched in an embrace. If anyone has walked out to find us in this position, I wouldn't know. I keep my face pressed against the person who's still able to bring me comfort all these years later.

His hands move up and down my back in a soothing motion. "I missed this, Goldie," he admits, his voice deep and gravelly.

I nuzzle deeper into his chest, trying to forget about all the reasons this moment can't last forever and instead doing my best to make it last as long as possible.

"Me too," I respond, my voice muffled as I talk against his chest.

"There's one more question I wanted to—"

He pushes away from me when the door to the bar creaks open, the music now loud thanks to the open door.

We both look at the open doorway. I think we both let out a sigh of relief when we don't find Pippa staring back at us.

Everything is complicated between the two of us. I don't want to have to explain that to Pippa. I've always wondered if she knew something happened in the past between Cade and me. She hasn't ever really questioned me about it. It's one of the reasons I love her. She's good at minding her own business, even if it may kill her natural curiosity to do so.

A man I don't recognize, who has clearly had too much to drink by the way he stumbles around, goes to lean against the building. He pulls out a cigarette, not paying attention to Cade and me.

When I look from the man back to him, I find Cade watching me. His eyes are wide, but I can't read what's behind them. I want to ask him what he was about to say, but I don't. Instead, I'm busy lecturing myself for falling right back into the trap that is him.

I spent *years* trying to get over him. Trying to mend the heart he broke when he pretended that what we shared was nothing to him. I gave in to him once again. Except this time, I only have myself to blame. I know what it's like to try and get over Cade. I'm well aware of how impossible it is to forget his taste, touch, and kiss. Yet all it took was a few sentences from him to get me right back to where I started.

Naively in love with a man who won't fight to keep me.

Although I can't tell what's written on Cade's face, I'm confident he can sure as hell see what's written on mine.

His eyebrows pull together as fear and fury flashes through his eyes. "Goldie, no," he whispers, reaching his hand out toward mine. "Don't do this."

"We can't do this," I correct, already walking to go back inside. "I can't handle it, Cade. Not again."

He tries to get me to stop, but his efforts are useless. I'm racing toward the door, needing to get away from him, desperate for space and desperate for a moment to get my head on straight.

I just kissed Cade again.

What's worse, I believed him when he told me he'd never fallen for anyone else.

At least for a moment.

Now as I shoulder my way through the crowd, looking for

the booth where I'm sure Pippa and the rest of the group are waiting for us, I'm wondering if he was actually lying to my face.

There's no way he hasn't loved someone else in five years. That's unrealistic. He can't really expect me to believe that. He never even told *me* that he loved me. I try to think back on his words, to think if I misheard him. It shouldn't matter anyway. He told me back then he didn't love me. That's what I have to believe.

I let out a sigh of relief when I see Pippa sitting at the table. She laughs at something Brendan says, her shoulders perking up when she spots me.

"Mare!" she shouts, her words slurring. "Where have you been?" She holds up a glass of beer. Apparently we've now switched from bottles to a pitcher of beer.

I feel him behind me, forcing my spine to go straight.

"We're not done," he hisses under his breath, his fingers running down my arm. I yank it from his reach, holding it close to my chest.

Pippa narrows her eyebrows, accusingly looking from Cade to me. Her head cocks to the side. "Why do I sense something is going on?"

"It's nothing," I hurriedly say, looking at Brendan apologetically. He also looks between Cade and I. Except where Pippa looks confused, he looks between us knowingly.

Cade's shoulder bumps against mine as he comes out from behind me and stops next to me. I feel his gaze hot on my cheek. "I don't know about that, Goldie," he says through gritted teeth. "I definitely feel like something is going on."

My head whips to look at him in disbelief. He was adamant we stayed a secret the summer before I left for college. Now he wants to hash out all the bad blood between us in front of a group of innocent bystanders that includes his sister and one of his ex-girlfriends.

I roll my eyes, appalled by his childish behavior. I train my eyes on Pippa. "I'm just not feeling that well. I think I drank too much or something."

Cade lets out a sarcastic laugh, not even bothering trying to hide how much of an ass he's being. "Or something," he clips.

Pippa frowns, her focus leaving Cade and staying on me. "You sure?" she asks slowly.

I nod. "Yeah." My eyes flick toward the front exit. "I think I'm going to get some air for a bit. Don't worry about me, though. Keep enjoying the night."

Pippa tries to scoot out of the booth, but I hold my hands up to stop her. "Really, Pip. I don't want to leave quite yet," I lie. I don't want to just leave Slopes, I want to leave Sutten. It was a stupid idea to think I could handle staying here long-term. "I just need air for a few minutes. When I come back, I want to see you back on that floor."

I don't give her time to argue. I don't meet anyone's eyes as I turn on my heel and race toward the doors. Pulling my phone from the back pocket of my shorts, I look to see if I can find a ride back to the ranch.

I lied in there. The last thing I want to do is stay here for a second longer. I especially don't want to be locked in a car with Cade and Pippa on the way home. Between the lingering tension with Cade and the questions Pippa is bound to ask, I'd like to wait until at least tomorrow to deal with either.

I'm not drunk enough to have that conversation but have had just enough to drink to know it's not the wisest idea to broach the topic of what just happened with either of them.

Plus, I need to work out my own feelings about what the hell has transpired in the last hour before having to spend time with either of them.

I'm ordering an Uber ride when rough fingers wrap around my bicep and begin to pull me deeper into the parking lot.

"Get off me," I screech, trying to yank my arm from the tight grip.

Cade stops, turning to face me. His eyes are ablaze with anger, all of that resentment aimed in my direction.

His fury doesn't bother me because my own anger rivals his. He acted like a child in there, not making the already confusing situation we've found ourselves in any better.

"Where in the hell do you think you're going?" he growls, his fingertips digging into my skin.

I wave my phone in the air, showing him my screen. "Getting a ride. I can't be near you for another second. Not after the stunt you just pulled in front of *everyone* in there."

His nostrils flare. "Like fuck you are. You've got a ride. *Me.*"

I roll my eyes, attempting to step out of his reach. He doesn't allow it. It takes little effort for him to tug on my arm and bring my body right in front of his once again. Briefly, I glance over my shoulder to make sure we don't have an audience. It was dumb for Cade to follow me out here in the first place after the suspicious looks that were pointed at us from all of our friends in the booth.

Pulling my phone to my face, I toss a glare in Cade's direction. "Sorry, Cade, hate to break it to you, but right now, you're the last person I want to be stuck in a car with."

"Does it look like I care?" he answers gruffly. He must trust that I won't go anywhere for the moment—or have confidence in his ability to catch me if I did try something—because he lets me out of his grip. I take a few steps backward, but don't make a run for it yet.

"Why don't you go back in there and enjoy your night?" I ask, basically pleading for him to leave me alone. Eventually, we're going to have to talk about how big of a mistake it was for us to kiss, but it's the last thing I want to do at the moment. I need time and space to think about what the fuck just happened.

His eyes widen slightly, like my words are completely ludicrous. "I can't," he answers through gritted teeth.

"Oh, so you're incapable of turning around and going inside?"

"If you aren't going with me, then yes."

I let out a frustrated groan. "Cade, just go," I beg. Looking down at my phone screen, I find the little car icon, showing me my ride will be here in eight minutes. "I've got a ride. We'll talk tomorrow or whenever, maybe never," I add under my breath.

"What the fuck happened?" he asks.

"I don't know what you're talking about."

Cade catches me off guard. I'd let my guard down for a fraction of a second, long enough for him to reach between us and pluck my phone from my grasp.

"Hey!" I yell, trying to swipe it back from him.

He holds it above his head, tapping the screen a few times before he slides my phone into the pocket of his jeans. "Looks like you no longer have a ride." He nods his head in the direction of his truck.

"What the hell, Cade!"

The smirk he aims my way is infuriating. He gives not a single indication that he's sorry for canceling my chance at getting some space from him. "Come on, Goldie. Time to go home so we can have the conversation you're so clearly trying to avoid."

"No."

He adjusts the hat on his head, pinning me with his stare. "Fine. You won't get in the car? We'll have it here." His arms cross over his chest. I have to stop myself from focusing on the ripple of the muscles on his forearms with the movement. I look at the noticeable vein that runs into the sleeve of his T-shirt, trying to remember the way it felt to have that arm draped over me the night of Linda's funeral.

If he notices me gawking at him, he doesn't say anything. Instead, he angrily kicks at a loose piece of gravel while he clears his throat. "Tell me what the fuck happened earlier. What changed?"

Looking into Cade's eyes, one word comes to mind as he stares back at me. Betrayal. I don't know if he feels betrayed by himself for giving into the tension between us, or if he feels betrayed by me for stopping what we should've never begun. "It's not about what has changed, it's about what hasn't."

"The fact that there's no use fighting our feelings for each other? I agree. We couldn't fight them years ago, and I've given up on fighting them now. So good point, nothing's changed. We can hate each other all we want. It doesn't make denying one another any easier."

I shake my head at him. "You know that's not what I meant." Before I can say anything else, the breeze picks up around us. My body shivers. I hadn't expected to be out in the cold for long tonight so I hadn't brought a coat. Now I regret it as goose-bumps rise on my skin.

Cade uses the opportunity to grab me by the hand and roughly begins to pull me toward his truck. "You're going to get in the damn truck so you stop shivering, and then we're going to finish this conversation."

I attempt to push the heels of my boots into the pavement, but it doesn't work. He's pulling too hard. I'm afraid if I pull against him too much that I'll fall flat on my ass. He'd probably let me and find it hilarious if the rage in his eyes was any indication on his feelings toward me right now.

I slap at him with my free hand. "You can't just leave your sister here alone," I argue.

He grunts. "Leave her alone like you were going to? Pot fucking kettle, Goldie."

"*Technically*, I wasn't leaving her alone. I was leaving her with you as her ride. If you kidnap me now, she won't have any ride home."

Cade throws a dirty look over his shoulder when I pinch the skin on his forearm. "Well, it's good that at least one of us gave a shit enough to check in with her. She said she'll uh"—he coughs —"find a ride back to her place tonight."

My eyebrows raise in understanding. *Go Pippa*. At least someone is having a good time tonight.

Cade angrily rips open the door to his truck. Before I can protest, his large hands find my waist and he lifts me up until he's placing me in the passenger seat.

"I can do it on my own," I argue, pushing him away from me.

He smells too good. He smells too familiar. His warmth surrounds me, and I'm scared I'll give in all over again and yank him toward me so I can taste the peppermint once more.

Cade hovers above me. Even though he still looks angry, the slightest bit of humor lights his eyes. "Oh but I enjoy helping you," he says slowly. My whole body heats when he doesn't hide the way his eyes focus on my lips for a few moments longer than necessary.

Before I can attempt to shove him away again or do something stupid like pull him closer to me, he backs away from the truck and closes the door.

Like a child, I cross my arms over my chest and pout. If I'd known he'd be such a stubborn ass and follow me out, I would've just sat in the booth for the rest of the night.

At least then I wouldn't be alone with him right now.

The engine roars to life as he starts the truck. He doesn't say a single word to me the entire car ride.

He doesn't have to. Even with his silence, I know the conversation isn't over. He's just dragging it out, waiting until we get home to really battle this one out.

This night is nowhere near what I'd expected it to be. And it isn't even over yet.

I LEAN FORWARD in the passenger seat of Cade's truck, my eyes narrowing as I stare at the dirt path in front of me. "Where are we going?" I ask, not bothering to hide the exhaustion in my voice. I want to go to bed. I want a replay of the day, to forget that anything happened between him and I tonight. I want to keep pretending that I don't love him anymore.

I can't do any of that. Partly because of the stubborn man refusing to answer my question next to me.

"Cade," I push, trying to figure out where we were just by looking at the looming trees above us. "You said we were going home."

"I did."

I look at him, my mind reeling with what he's talking about. Just when I'm about to open my mouth and ask him if he'd had more beers than I'd thought, his headlights illuminate what appears to be a paved out driveway.

The truck lurches forward a bit when he puts it in park, his headlights now fully illuminating a framed out house up a hill a bit in front of us.

"What is this?" I ask, unable to stifle my curiosity. It seems like, during the years I grew up on the ranch, that I'd seen every mile the property has to offer. I've probably seen this exact spot at some point, but the framed out house wasn't here the last time I'd been here.

Cade leans back in his seat, staring in front of him thoughtfully. "This is home." He rubs at the stubble peppering his jaw. "At least this will be my home one day."

"You're building here?"

He continues to stare at the frame in front of him for a few more seconds until focusing on me. There's reservation in his features. Like he's unsure if he should've brought me here or not.

I'm not sure he should have. It seems personal. I don't want to get personal with Cade. I want to get over him.

"Don't act so shocked," he comments, opening his truck door. If I want him to answer any of my questions, I'm left with no choice but to open mine and step out to follow him.

"Why can't I be shocked?" I ask accusingly, staring at him from over the hood of the truck.

"Don't," Cade says, his voice slightly breaking at the end of the word. "Don't tell me you forgot."

I swallow. "Forgot what, Cade?"

He steps in front of the truck, the headlights illuminating his face perfectly. The yellow light shining on his face flawlessly captures the muscle angrily ticking on his jawline. Cade comes to a stop in front of me, his eyes searching my face for answers.

I wonder if he finds them or not. I hope not. Even after all the years we've known each other, I was hoping the time apart made it so he couldn't see past my poker face.

"Being a liar doesn't suit you, Goldie." His words are angry, so much bitterness laced in his tone. Surprisingly, the goose bumps starting to appear on my skin aren't from the cold. It's from the subtle rage burning in his eyes.

"Stop telling me I'm lying when you don't know what you're talking about," I fire back at him.

"You know exactly what this house is. What this spot is," he says, raising his voice. He points behind him. "We spent summer nights under the stars going over your favorite floor plans, what you wanted in a house. Right here. At this spot. You can't tell me you forgot that."

I shrug. I remember every fucking second of it. It's torture to recall a simpler time, a time where I thought love could overcome anything. It was a time that I thought Cade Jennings loved me the way I loved him.

I was so very, very wrong. And the fact that he remembers—and that he's carrying out with the plan—makes me want to break down right here in front of him. How dare he still make good on his promises when he's broken so many before.

Cade takes a step closer to me. Our chests brush against one another, our angry, deep inhales and exhales falling in sync. "You called me a coward when you left this town." He laughs sarcastically. "It's funny because the only fucking coward I see here is you. I'm trying to open up to you, to be honest with you —something I remember you begging for in the past—and here you are, lying to my fucking face. Do you really think that low of me, Goldie? Do you really think I wouldn't know when you're lying?"

My lip quivers as my head rocks back and forth. "I don't…" my voice breaks, "I don't remember."

He shakes his head at me in disbelief. I see the disappointment written all over his face.

I once had called him a coward. But the way he dismissed my love years ago made me into who I am today. He may hate it, but he made me this way. He made me afraid to feel anything. I felt everything with him. When we ended, I had to attempt to feel nothing at all.

"Let me remind you then," he declares, taking angry steps toward the wooden beams that'll eventually become a home— his home. The one we'd planned out in vivid detail when we were just two kids who didn't put much thought into what it really meant to be an adult.

I keep my feet planted by his truck. Maybe if I don't follow him, he'll stop throwing accusations my way. Maybe if I stay far enough away, he won't be able to see right through every lie I've cowardly uttered tonight.

He stops at the right side of the house, opening his arms wide. "We'd talked about how we loved the entryway at my parents' house. So this one is planned to be even bigger!" he yells, making sure I hear every word he says.

Cade takes a few steps closer to the center of the house. "You once said you loved the idea of a breakfast nook that overlooked the mountains, a space you could sit and write at. Well, right there is where the biggest nook my contractor has ever built is going in."

"Stop," I shout, my hands running through my hair. "I don't want to hear any more."

Pinching my eyes shut, I try to imagine myself anywhere else with him. I pretend that this isn't happening. That Cade isn't rocking my world all over again.

I'm supposed to be over him. I'd worked so hard to forget him. Yet here he is, breaking down every defense I've created in his name.

"I don't give a fuck what you want, Goldie!" he yells. I'm glad he's so far away. I don't want to get a front row seat to the hurt that overtakes his face. "You're going to listen. You're going to remember," he spits. "Since apparently you've *so conveniently* forgotten."

Cade steps in an opening between two wood beams. I can't see the bottom half of him. A very messed up part of me wants to follow him up the hill, to see the house he's building for himself up close. I keep my feet firmly planted.

I don't want to know what he has planned for the future. It doesn't matter. I won't be here to see it. I can't bear it. My stomach rolls at the thought of who he could share this house with one day. One thing is for certain, it won't be with me.

"Up those stairs they've framed out will be guest rooms,

maybe even a couple rooms for future children, as well as an office that will have a built-in bookshelf lining three of the walls."

My eyes flutter shut once again, remembering a night long ago when we'd planned the house he's describing perfectly.

Chapter 24
MARE
age nineteen

"GOT ANY PLANS TONIGHT, GOLDIE?"

I smile at Cade, admiring the way his arms look in his current position. He has them hiked over his head, holding on to the top of the entrance to Dolly's stall. He leans forward a bit, his shirt straining against his growing muscles with the position.

My hand drifts over Dolly's mane before I run a comb through it. "It depends," I answer, my voice lowered. I think all of the stable hands have gone home for the night, but you can never be too sure. Pippa is gone for the weekend, at some workshop in Denver for aspiring pastry chefs, so at least I'm confident that she won't hear the conversation between her brother and me.

Cade clutches his chest, his lips turning down in a dramatic frown. "Depends on what?" he asks carefully.

I shake my head. I like this slightly playful side of him. The more time we spend together this summer, the more I'm learning that even though I thought I knew everything there was to know about Cade, I didn't.

There's so much I've learned about him this summer. Which makes the move-in date for college freshmen that's right around the corner even harder to face.

Cade's arms wrap around my middle, pulling me tight

against his body. He nips at my neck. "Be very careful with your answer, Goldie."

Leaning into his touch, I continue to brush Dolly. She happily chews on the sugar cubes I'd given her when I started. "It depends on your plans," I respond.

I turn around, wrapping my arms around his neck and pulling his head down until his forehead rests against mine. The whisper of a smile on Cade's lips makes me feel giddy all over.

I know he doesn't smile for just anything. Even the hint of one is a win, a reminder that I'm no longer the only one lost in the feelings between us. "Good answer," he says before pressing a kiss against the tip of my nose.

My nose scrunches. "Why are you always doing that?"

He squeezes my hips before taking a step back. He grabs Dolly's water bucket and sets it in the opening of the stall. Reaching over the stall-door, he grabs the hose. Cade's eyes find mine as he puts fresh water in Dolly's bucket. "Why am I always doing what?"

"Kissing the tip of my nose. You're doing it more and more often recently."

This time he actually does smile. It's sheepish and sweet, something I don't see often from Cade. "Oh, that's an easy answer. I'm kissing your new freckles."

"What?"

Turning the hose off, he tosses it back over the top of the stall before returning Dolly's water bucket to its hook. He closes the distance between us, wiping his hands off on his jeans before his fingertips softly brush over my cheeks. "When I was a kid, I'd always thought about the new freckles that popped up on your face with each hour you spent outside. I'd always felt like they needed a proper welcome now that they were part of a face as beautiful as yours. So now that I can, I want to kiss them hello."

His words steal my breath, and the next one. The comb falls and lands with a soft thud as I leap into Cade's arms, totally trusting that he'll catch me. "You're something else, Cade

Jennings," I mumble into the crook of his neck. It's not exactly what I want to say. I want to tell him how much I love him, how much I've always loved him, but I hold my tongue.

The naive part of me is hoping that he'll be the first one to utter those words between us.

I inhale his scent that surrounds us. Even after being out on the trails all day, clearing the pathways after the big storm we got earlier this week, he still smells divine. It's the scent of his soap, the outdoors, and the scent of him that wraps together in something so manly. I'm intoxicated by it.

I'm intoxicated by *him*.

It's probably why I've already written countless chapters of a novel I hope I'm brave enough to release one day. A story whose characters are incredibly similar to Cade and me. Something I'd never admit to anyone but myself.

Cade gives me a squeeze, holding me as tightly as I hold him. It's wild that at the beginning of the summer I was still head over heels for him, and he'd still been pretending like he wanted nothing to do with me. So much has changed, except one thing. The fact that I'm supposed to leave soon.

My legs wrap around Cade's middle on instinct. I like the height the embrace of our bodies puts me at. It allows me to sneak in and kiss him anytime I want, not having to count on him leaning down to take what I want.

Cade's hands move up the backs of my thighs, his palms cupping my ass. It sends fire throughout my body. I've been desperate to experience what it's like to do more than kiss Cade, but he hasn't let it go that far.

If he wasn't so steadfast in how much he desires me, I might take it to heart. Why won't he be intimate with me when I've heard him talk with his friends about what he's done with other girls? But Cade has squashed any worries I could have about how bad he wants me. He says he just doesn't want to rush things.

I, on the other hand, am more than ready to speed things up.

I want to know what it's like to be consumed by Cade Jennings. He's already consumed my mind and soul, I'm ready for him to have my body as well.

Feeling bold, I slide my hips up and down, grinding against him. He sucks in a large gulp of air, his hands tightening on my ass. I love the feel of his fingertips biting into my tender skin. He grips me so tight, preventing me from being able to rock my hips again.

"Goldie," Cade says tightly, keeping me pinned against him.

Dolly lets out a noise behind us. If it weren't for the horse bearing witness to this, I'd try and push his buttons further, to see if finally he'll stop trying to be a good guy and actually touch me. Cade walks us a few feet until he places me on the top of the stall door.

"You're killing me," he says through gritted teeth. Even though he no longer holds my weight, he stays standing between my legs, his palms pressed to the tops of my thighs.

I steal the hat from his head, placing it on the top of mine. "I'm killing you? You're killing me. I just want to know what it's like to be touched by you."

Cade straightens the hat on my head, even though I know it probably bothers him he no longer wears it. If he's on the trail, he normally wears a cowboy hat, but whenever he's off the trails, he always wears the Jennings Ranch ball cap. I don't know which one I prefer. What I do know is he isn't typically found without one or the other on. "Fuck, all I want to do is touch you, Mare," he finally answers. The look in his eyes tells me that he means what he's saying, but there's about to be a *but* that follows that sentence.

I prepare myself for whatever excuse he'll give me this time when his lips part to say something else. "But I'm trying not to rush you. To rush this, or us." He seems like he wants to say something else, but he doesn't end up saying it.

"You can't be rushing me when I'm the one begging for it."

The corner of his mouth twitches. "I kind of like the idea of you begging, Goldie."

I gasp, playfully pushing his shoulder. "I repeat. You're something else, Cade Jennings."

"Want to know what else I am?" he asks, his tone getting more serious.

My boots kick against the stall door as he plucks the hat from my head. Traitor. He was distracting me with his intense, broody, copper eyes. "What?" I still ask, wanting to know what his answer will be.

"Yours," he answers simply. He traces half a heart over his chest.

Before I can tell him how much I am his, he's clapping his hands and changing the subject.

"Now back to the reason I tracked you down in the first place," he begins, lovingly scratching Dolly's chin for a moment. "How about we go for a ride tonight? I know a place," he teases.

I hop off the door, excitement coursing through my veins. "I'm ready when you are."

Chapter 25
CADE
age twenty-two

"I THINK I know what you mean about the stars," Mare announces, interrupting the comfortable silence between the two of us.

We stare up at the twinkling balls of light above us. High up in the mountains, it almost seems like we could reach out and touch some of them if we dared.

"And what's that, Goldie?" My fingers absentmindedly play with the hair that falls over her shoulder. I've never felt so at peace. This has been the best summer of my life, and there's still so much I have planned for the two of us.

She turns, resting her chin against my chest. With the moon behind me, it perfectly reflects in her large, blue eyes. Mare stares at me with so much adoration, it makes my chest feel tight. "That I don't think they shine any brighter than they do right here in Sutten."

I try not to let her words affect me. If only she really meant it. I can see why she could get swept up in the moment between us, for her to forget that her dream has always been to get out of this town where mine has always been to never leave it.

Mare stares at me expectantly. I let out a sad sigh. For the summer, I can pretend that deep down she actually means those words. "Tonight, I don't think there's anywhere else in the world they shine brighter," I tell her, knowing at least that's the truth.

They fight for attention from her. She's my Goldie. The sun. The stars fail in comparison to her, but they sure do put up a fight.

Her finger softly traces the emblem for the family ranch. She traces it three times before she meets my eyes again. "What if I didn't go?" she asks softly. I'm only able to hear her words because the night is quiet and still around us.

She must see the shock written on my face. I can't hide the raise to my brows or the way my body stills underneath her. "Would it really be so bad for me to stay here forever?" she continues, her voice timid and unsure. "To stay here forever... with you."

I bite my tongue. I don't want to tell her all I could ever want is for her to stay here forever with me. But I won't hold her back. I *can't* hold her back. Deep down, I know I can't be the reason Goldie stays. One day far from this night, I can't have her resent me because I asked her to stay when she always dreamed of going.

Mare rakes her top teeth over her lip, catching it between them as she watches me anxiously. She presses her palm into my chest. If she feels the way my heart ricochets against my sternum, she doesn't say anything.

"Say something, Cade," she pleads.

I'd give anything for you to want to stay, runs through my head. *I'd give anything for us to have more than just this summer.*

I can't live with knowing I held her back. I'm confident that if I asked Mare to stay, she would. But what good would that do us? Eventually her feelings for me would fade, and all that'd be left in their wake is resentment toward me for holding her back.

I swallow the lump in my throat. It pains me to speak up and not tell her how I'm feeling. But I do it anyway, because I'd do anything for her, even when it hurts me. "I think that I'm counting on you to find all the other beautiful places the stars shine bright in the world."

Her eyelids get heavy with sadness. She closes them for a few seconds, as if she's trying to get ahold of herself. I have to keep my jaw locked to not open my mouth and tell her the thing I want most in this world is for her to want to stay on this ranch forever. My teeth grind together so loudly I'm wondering if she can hear them.

It appears she's too lost in the hurt to realize the restraint it's taking me to ask her to stay. Finally, she opens her eyes. There's sadness in those beautiful blue eyes of hers. I'd rather see it now then later on when we're already too far gone.

My thumb brushes over her cheekbone. "Will you do that for me?"

She leans into my touch, locks of her hair brushing against my arm in the movement. "I can't imagine leaving you, Cade," she answers hoarsely. "I can't imagine losing this."

My head shakes. "Then don't imagine it." Leaning up, I pull her into my lap until she straddles me on both sides. "Don't think about it." Grabbing her wrist, I place her hand against my heartbeat. Once I'm confident she won't move her hand, I place a hand against her own heart, cherishing the way her heart seems to beat in the same rhythm as mine.

It's like our heartbeats have always beat in sync, like our hearts knew something we hadn't quite realized.

"Focus on our heartbeats, Goldie. Focus on us. Right now, in this moment."

She nods her head, her eyes fluttering shut. Her features soften, the sadness almost disappearing from her face. It doesn't completely go away. There's still a hint of it when she focuses on me.

I do the only thing I can. I lean in to kiss her, hoping that the connection of our bodies can clear the hurt from our hearts. At least for right now.

Mare clings to me, kissing me with everything she has. I meet her pace with the same desperate need for her. When her hips roll against mine, I can't fight how much I want to feel even closer to her.

Pulling my lips from hers, I kiss along her neck. When her

head falls back, letting out a loud moan as my teeth graze the tender skin of her neck, I know that if she pushed for us to take the next step tonight, I wouldn't be able to say no.

My lips hover over her collarbone, my eyes focusing on the small red mark I left on her neck from my teeth. I'm an ass for thinking it, but I want to keep that mark on her forever, so Brendan and any man brave enough to look at the girl that's always been mine knows that she's taken.

"Cade," Mare pants when my palm skirts over her breast.

My resolve breaks. I nip at her neck once again, my thumb brushing over her peaked nipple underneath her T-shirt. She moans, her hips bucking against me. There's no doubt in my mind that she feels my growing cock pressed against her center.

"This okay?" I ask, my voice breaking with lust.

She hurriedly nods. "More than okay," she rushes to get out. "This is what I've wanted for so long."

Her words encourage me. Slipping my hand beneath her cotton shirt, I marvel at the way her soft skin feels against my fingertips. Her stomach muscles tighten as my hand snakes up her shirt. When I make it to the edge of her cotton sports bra, she gasps in pleasure.

"You're so fucking beautiful," I mutter against her shoulder. My thumb slips underneath her bra, testing the feel of the swell of her breast against it.

Her back arches when I roughly swipe it over her nipple, my mind memorizing every sound and movement that comes from her.

"Can I see you?" I ask, my tone desperate with need. I want to see every part of Mare, to commit every curve and bare inch of her skin to memory.

Mare doesn't use words to answer. She separates her body just enough from mine to grab the bottom of her T-shirt. She hurriedly tugs it up and over her head, tossing it to the side. Keeping eye contact with me, she grabs the bottom of her sports bra. Slowly, she pulls the fabric up, taking her time revealing her perfect pink nipples to me.

"Is this what you wanted?" she whispers, watching me carefully.

I'm stunned by her beauty, by how perfect she is. Her breasts are heavy, her nipples peaked, and waiting for my attention. "Yes," I answer. "And this." Leaning in, I test the weight of her breast in my hand, loving how it fills my palm perfectly. My breath hits her sensitive flesh, causing her to let out a small sigh of pleasure.

The sigh turns into a loud moan when my tongue glosses over the peaked flesh. I take her nipple into my mouth, my tongue circling it as she pushes her hips against me. Her hands tug at my hair, encouraging me to keep going. My free hand plays with the other nipple, making sure they both get the attention they deserve.

Pulling away, I lay a kiss to Mare's lips, letting our tongues lazily push against one another like we have all the time in the world. With the stars seeming infinite above us, it really does feel like I can take my time exploring—tasting—every inch of her body.

"Don't stop," Mare begs when our lips part. "I want you to make me…" she doesn't finish, her words falling off as if she's embarrassed by what she wants.

I grip her face, forcing her to look at me. "You want me to make you what, Goldie?"

Color fills her cheeks. "You know what I want."

"Maybe." Quickly, I spin her body so she lays on the blanket, my body hovering over her. I trace over the skin right underneath the bottom of her full breast, the touch making her entire body break out in a shiver of pleasure. "But I want you to say it. Tell me what you want and I'll fucking do it."

"I want you to make me come, Cade. I want to know what it feels like when you do it."

My head rears back for a moment, jealousy flaring through my body. "When I do it? Opposed to someone else?"

She smiles at my words, reaching up to run her thumb over my bottom lip. "You're really hot when you're jealous."

"Mare, so help me god if another man has touched you—tasted you—" I say through gritted teeth—"then they're as good as fucking dead."

She playfully bites her lip, clearly amused by how fucking crazy she's made me at the thought of someone else intimately knowing what's mine.

"I've come before, Cade," she whispers. "But it was only with my own hand—from thoughts of *you*."

Fuck. My cock pulses in my jeans, begging to be touched by her. I'm so fucking hard from her words. At the look in her eyes as she watches me expectantly. At the thought of her coating my tongue. "It seems it's time for you to find out how much better it is when it's *me* making you come."

My knuckle brushes over her bare skin above her jeans. I draw out the moment, wanting to take my time with her, as I slowly undo her button and pull down on her zipper. As soon as her jeans are loose, she's lifting her hips off the blanket, guiding me to peel them off. My hands grab at the fabric on either side of her hips as I slowly pull them down the tops of her thighs. My patience wears thin as I pull the denim down her shins. I toss the jeans to the side, having no interest in needing them for a while.

"I can already see how needy you are for me," I announce, absentmindedly guiding my palm over my rock-hard cock. It's straining against my Levi's, desperate to break free and finally know what it feels like to be touched by Mare.

Mare must get the wrong idea for my brief pause. She tries to close her legs, but my palms press to the insides of her thighs stopping her. "What do you think you're doing?"

She worriedly chews her lip. "Stopping? I don't know," she whispers. "You stopped...I didn't know if that was a good thing."

My tongue runs over my lips. "Goldie," I say, lust laced in the huskiness of my voice. "It's the best thing in the fucking world to know how fucking ready you are for me. I love the idea of your pussy already dripping with need for me, and I haven't even tasted or touched you yet."

Her mouth pops open in shock. "Oh," she mutters.

"Spread those legs open and wide for me, baby. It's time for me to show you how much better my tongue is compared to your fingers."

Chapter 26
MARE
age nineteen

W‌ITH A SIMPLE BRUSH of his fingertip against my clit, I'm already fully confident that having Cade touch me is infinitely better than touching myself. His breath tickles the skin between my thighs, making me ache to feel his tongue touch the same spot his finger does.

He takes me by surprise by licking my inner thigh. "You're so wet it's coating the inside of your thighs," he muses, running his finger up and down my slit again. This time he applies more pressure, making my thighs quiver anticipating what's in store.

Cade slides the tip of his finger inside me, testing what it feels like. I moan. He only has one digit in and I can still feel him stretching me.

"God, you're so tight, Goldie." A sound comes deep from inside Cade's throat. "I fucking love that I'm the first one to do this. To feel you wrapped around me." He hooks his finger slightly. It feels so good that I don't even recognize myself by the loud moan that falls from my mouth.

"One day, it'll be my cock that pushes into you." I didn't know he had such a mouth on him. I *really* didn't know I'd be so turned on by his dirty words. "But by how fucking tight your pussy squeezes my finger, we're going to have to work our way up to that."

Cade pushes a second finger into me, stretching me even more. "Making you ready to take me will be fun." His fingers part slightly as he makes good on his words. My eyes squeeze shut as my legs begin to tremble with how good it feels to be stretched and touched by him.

"Time for me to taste that pretty pussy, baby," Cade says, his voice husky and sexy. "I want you to come all over my mouth. I want to taste you on my tongue for the rest of the fucking night."

Before I can think too much into the fact that he's about to put his mouth on somewhere so intimate, he's sealing his lips to me and I know I'll never get over the feeling of him kissing me like this—kissing me *there*.

I don't know if you can call it kissing. He licks and sucks, making it feel so much more different than a kiss. It's way more passionate. His tongue circles my clit at the same moment he pushes a finger inside me again. I'm feeling so many things at once. When my hips buck, trying to get away from the pressure that's building low in my core because it feels like too much, Cade uses his free hand to circle around my hips and pin me to the blanket.

He isn't done with me. I don't want him to be done with me, but *oh my god*, I think I'm going to come all over his face.

I attempt to push him off again, but his mouth seals even more to me, sucking my clit in the most delicious of ways.

"Cade, I think I'm going to come," I pant. My entire body feels flushed as tingles erupt all over my skin.

He slides another finger in me, his mouth leaving me for a second. "That's the point, baby. I want to make my girl come, and I want to taste every last drop when she does it."

The moan that comes from my mouth is so loud and wild that I barely recognize myself. I love it, the power I feel as the orgasm builds to something I've never felt before.

"Come for me, baby. You can scream if you want to. There's only me and the stars here to hear you."

When he licks me up and down, his tongue circling around

and around, up and down relentlessly, I can't help but let the waves of pleasure overtake my entire body. My shoulders come off the blanket as I yell his name over and over.

His tongue slows but doesn't stop. Cade makes sure I ride out every single second of the orgasm.

My eyes flutter open as my body relaxes from the best orgasm of my life. I'd given them to myself before, but I never knew what I was missing. I don't know how I'll be able to do it with just my fingers again, not after knowing what it felt like for him to give me one. Looking down, I find him watching me closely. He continues to lick me up and down, his eyes focused solely on me. We stay locked in the moment until my body goes limp from the pleasure.

He rises from his knees, his lips glistening with...*me*.

I focus on the wetness coating his mouth. I can't look away. Lust runs through me all over again at the sight of his lips covered with the proof of my arousal—of what he does to me.

Cade pulls his thumb to his mouth, wiping the corner and along his bottom lip. "You like seeing your cum all over my mouth, Goldie?"

Heat flares in my cheeks at the dirtiness to his words. I've never seen Cade like this, but I'll admit, he turns me on just by his filthy words. Cade pops his thumb into his mouth, licking it clean, all while his hooded eyes stay focused on me.

"Answer me," he demands, crawling up my body until he hovers over me. It's only just now occurring to me that he's fully dressed while I wear absolutely nothing.

All I can do is nod. I can't form words right now. My clit still throbs and my entire body feels spent by the intensity of the orgasm.

Cade's lips come to a stop an inch away from mine. With the position, the shaggy pieces of his hair cover his forehead, one piece falling in front of his eyes. I reach up to move it, not wanting anything in the way of the moment between us.

"Kiss me." My eyes fall to my cum still on his lips, not all of it fully wiped away by him yet. "I want you to taste yourself on my lips."

"Cade—"

He gets even closer. It would be easy for me to make one slight movement and do exactly as he says. "Do it, Goldie. Then maybe you'll understand why I'll never get enough of tasting that sweet little pussy of yours."

His words do me in. My fingers tangle in his hair as I yank him the rest of the distance, fusing our mouths together.

He doesn't taste like peppermint. He tastes like me.

And holy fuck, I'm so turned on by that realization that I feel wetness pool between my thighs all over again. I'd only been screaming his name from an orgasm moments ago, and it feels like it could happen all over again.

Cade brushes his tongue against mine, pushing more of the proof of my arousal into my mouth. My hips move against his. I don't mean to do it, but I need some sort of relief, some sort of friction to combat the pressure building again.

His hand runs down my stomach. He doesn't stop until his fingers are brushing against my clit. My body jerks feeling him there again. I'm still swollen and tender, still recovering from the way he made me feel.

"This time I want to make you come around my fingers while I steal every single one of your moans from your lips." His lips brush against mine with his words as he slides two fingers in right away.

I've never had two orgasms in a row. I've always just got myself off and went about my day. I didn't know it was possible to come so close together, but the way his fingers expertly rub and slide inside me, I know that it won't be long until another wave of euphoria rolls through my body.

When his thumb presses against my clit, I do as he says. I moan against his lips. He's ready to catch it, the fierceness of his kiss stealing it right from my lips.

The kiss is intense, the two of us pushing against one another to deepen it, all while his fingers work deftly at pulling another orgasm out of me.

He pushes deeper, pain and pleasure running through me. Cade makes sure I feel him everywhere. His weight pushes against me as his fingers move in and out of me with a punishing pace.

I yank and pull at his hair as my body shudders.

"God, you're getting so tight around me, baby," he mutters against my lips. His fingers move even faster inside me.

When the orgasm ricochets through my body, he tastes every one of my moans and mewls, his fingers staying buried deep inside me as I pulse around him.

Eventually, I come down from the high, but it still feels like I'm on top of the world when my eyes open and I find Cade looking down at me. The corner of his mouth lifts with a confident smirk. "You better watch out, Goldie." He softly brushes my hair from my face. It's tender and sweet. Totally different from the rough way he just ravaged me under the stars.

"Why?" I ask, snuggling against him. The air is cold against my bare skin, another reminder in the difference of our clothes— or lack thereof on my part.

"Because I don't think I can last long without making you come. The way you taste, the way you come apart from my touch, fuck…I never want to stop making you feel that way."

"So we'll do more of that?" I ask, feeling bashful as I tuck my face into the crook of his neck.

Cade sits up and pulls me against his body. Wrapping his arms around me, he envelopes me with a warm embrace. "Fuck yeah we will. You're going to come against my tongue every fucking day I have you here. Probably more than once."

I laugh, accepting my T-shirt as he hands it to me. There's a tender look in his eyes before he slides the fabric over my head and over my body. He forgot about the bra, but I don't complain. "Every day seems like a lot. How will we get away from Pippa that much?"

Cade doesn't seem to remember or care about me putting my jeans back on. He heaves me onto his lap, keeping me warm even without pants. My legs rest on either side of his hip. Our noses almost touch as we look at one another. "Trust me," he starts, playfully kissing my nose. "I'll find a way."

I shake my head at him, pushing at his shoulder. "If you insist."

"Oh I insist." He shifts my body a bit, aligning my core with the very noticeable outline of his cock.

"And by how warm you feel against me, I think that little pussy of yours insists as well."

"Cade Jasper Jennings you cannot keep saying things like that!" I screech, letting him pull us both down to the outstretched blanket.

"Keep saying things like what?" he asks, hooking a leg over mine.

"You know what."

He mischievously raises his eyebrows at me. "I can't say *pussy*?" he drags out the naughty word, making my body heat even more when he licks his lips.

I try to hide how much I love hearing that word fall from his lips, despite how filthy it is. I shake my head. "I never knew you could talk like that."

He ignores my comment at first, his lips traveling down my neck as he peppers kisses along my skin. Finally, he answers, his lips still hovering over the hollow of my throat. "That's because it's only with you. I lose my fucking mind around you, Goldie. I can't help how bad I want you."

His words are like a caress to something deep inside me. I love the satisfaction of knowing that he reserves his dirty words for me and only me.

I'm too overcome with emotion and I don't know what to say. So I kiss him. And we kiss under the stars for what seems like forever.

Eventually, I get dressed again before lying down next to him on the blanket. He pulls me into his body, placing my head on his chest. We both stare up at the stars, lost in our own thoughts.

I don't know how much time passes when Cade breaks the silence.

"If you were to look at these stars forever, tell me about the house you'd want to look at them from."

My heart warms at his words. I think about his question for a few moments. "Something right here. At our spot. Right where you found that very first marigold."

Chapter 27
CADE
present

I CLOSE the distance between us. I'm not going to give her the luxury of lying to me from afar. She knows exactly what this house means to me—what it once meant to *us*. It's hard to even look at her, I'm so fucking upset with her. I'm done with her pretending that she doesn't remember our past. It's so fucking ingrained in my mind, and in my heart, that I can't fucking fathom that she doesn't remember things that have haunted me for years.

I know damn well she remembers how we'd planned out everything she'd want in a house. It was the same night I tasted her for the first time. The first time I got to watch her fall apart under the stars.

And she's staring at me like she doesn't remember a fucking thing.

The tips of my boots stop right in front of her, almost touching the tips of hers with the proximity of our bodies. "Look me in the fucking eye and tell me you don't remember."

The tears running down her cheeks should bother me, but I don't give a damn about them. She can cry all she wants, at least the tears are proof that she remembers *something*. I want to hold her, to tell her how deep down I hate to see her cry. But right now I can't see through the anger—the hurt—of her pretending that for one summer, she and I weren't each other's world. For me, she stayed my world every day after.

Her bottom lip trembles. Her head rocks back and forth as she fights the sob that sounds from low in her throat.

A resigned sigh falls from my lips. I can't fucking do this. Not with my current mental state. Not with her making us seem like we were nothing.

I yank her chin, forcing her to look at me. Even with the fury coursing through my veins, I can't help but wipe the tears from her cheeks. I hate to see them, but I hate her lying more.

I'm so fucking mad at her.

I'm so fucking gone for her.

Always have been, always will be.

"I'm not going to waste my breath," I seethe. "If you're going to be a fucking coward, then be a coward, Goldie. But I don't want to be anywhere near you when you're reducing everything that's happened between us—past and present—to nothing."

My hands fall to my sides in defeat. Stepping away from her, I walk to the driver's side of my truck. I climb in, staring blankly ahead as I wait for her to get in the cab. It'll be an awkward few moments between us, but I can do it as long as I know that I'm close to escaping her presence.

My chest constricts at the memory of kissing her earlier. For a fleeting moment, it felt like she was mine again. The moment disappeared into thin air all too quickly. She's already slipped through my fingertips. I didn't have time to get a good grip, to find a way to keep her for a little longer.

After she silently slides into the seat next to mine, I angrily throw the truck into reverse and back out of the driveway.

Neither one of us utter a single word as I drive us to the house. The tension surrounding us is thick. Earlier it was with want and need. Now it's just with anger and pain.

I expect her to leave the moment I put the truck in park in the driveway. She doesn't. It's even worse, she stays and turns her body to face mine.

I don't look at her. I *can't* look at her. If I do, I might tell her she could keep on lying if it just meant I could have one more happy moment with her. If even for a few seconds we could pretend that shit hasn't gone up in flames between us.

"Cade," she whispers, my name coming out like a plea on her lips.

My hand brushes over my mouth as I still avoid looking at her. "What?" I bite.

"I'm sorry."

"You're going to have to elaborate on what."

"Forget I said anything," she responds, pushing the door open and hopping down onto the concrete.

I open the door, clearly unable to just fucking let things go with her. "Say what you want to say, Mare!" I yell.

She stops in the driveway, spinning on the heels of her cowboy boots to look at me. "I think I'd rather not. You just called me a coward and told me you didn't want to be near me. It was stupid of me to say anything after."

I lied. I do think she's being a coward, but I always want to be near her. That's the fucking problem. "What are you sorry for, Goldie?" I press.

There's a lot of distance between us, but when our eyes connect it feels like we're chest to chest. "I'm sorry for making things complicated for you," she finally answers.

Her words catch me off guard. They weren't what I was expecting. I figured she'd apologize for acting like she didn't remember, or maybe even for stopping our kiss. I wasn't expecting this. "Complicated?"

"Yes, complicated. I shouldn't have kissed you, Cade. It hasn't been long since your mom and god, I know I should've been strong and resisted you because the last thing you need is for me to make things more complicated for you. So I'm sorry."

I'm so stunned by her words that I don't speak. Her denying us is complicated. In fact, the only thing that is clear and makes sense in this fucked up world I'm living in right now is her.

But clearly she doesn't see it that way. And I'm not going to sit here and try to convince her otherwise. With a resigned sigh, I turn away, not wanting to exchange another single word with her.

I'm tired of speaking. I'm tired in general. And I know that crawling into my bed alone tonight will mean another sleepless night without her by my side.

Turning around, I angrily yank the hat off my head and shove it into her chest.

She looks at me confused, two tiny creases forming on her forehead. "Call us complicated all you fucking want if that's what makes you feel better. But stop pretending that, at times like this, we aren't exactly what we need for one another. It's always been that way."

I leave her standing there, my hat clutched to her chest as I get in my truck.

She knows how I feel. What I want. It's up to her to decide how to proceed.

Chapter 28
MARE
present

THE SUN PEEKS through my window, bringing attention to the fact that I spent almost all night writing. I slept for a few hours before waking up and feeling the need to keep writing.

Inspiration hit the moment I stepped into my bedroom and inspected the hat Cade handed me in the driveway. I was about to get rid of it somewhere when something caught my eye.

It was a photo tucked inside the seam of the ball cap.

I peek over at the photo and hat sitting next to me at my desk. They'd been next to me the entire night as words flew from my fingertips. Because of them, I suddenly felt inspired.

And it was Cade Jennings—even when he's furious with me —who was the inspiration for my words.

I pick up the photo, holding it out carefully in front of me.

It's a picture of me.

I'd forgotten all about the photo. He'd taken it one of the many nights we'd escaped to our special spot, and I never saw it again.

My thumb gently brushes over the photo as I try to figure out what it means that he still has it. Not only had he held on to it for so long, but he'd kept it tucked into his favorite hat. He's worn that hat every single day I've been here. Has it been there the whole time? Has he had it with him every day for years?

I can't think of any other explanation. None of it makes sense.

Maybe Cade was as rocked by the things that happened between us as I was. Maybe it killed him more than I thought to leave me standing there alone in that airport.

Maybe all this time, when I was thinking that Cade wanted to forget about the summer we shared, he was still here remembering every moment of it. He didn't have the luxury of leaving this place behind. Have the memories haunted him the way they've haunted me?

I longingly look down at the photo, wishing I could go back and prepare the girl that stares back at me. She was completely unaware of the devastating heartbreak she was about to experience. I look so carefree—so happy. Nineteen year old me didn't know the heartbreak the man on the other side of the camera would cause me.

Little did I know that heartbreak would change my life in many ways. It shaped who I am today, but it also shaped my career. Heartbroken and devastated, I wrote a book heavily inspired by Cade and me. It was cathartic to funnel all of my feelings into a love story that I could actually control. I never could've expected thousands and thousands of people to read it around the world.

The old version of me never could've expected how hard it would be to return to see the boy she thought she'd get to love forever. I focus on the marigold tucked into my hair. It'd been the reason Cade wanted to take the photo in the first place. My head rests against Dolly as I smile at Cade, the flower tucked right above my ear.

We found a marigold on our ride.

I need to take a photo with Marigold and her marigold.

I'd obliged because I'd do anything for him. Even if it made me uncomfortable to have photos taken of me. I'd secretly loved being the center of attention if it was *him* taking the photo.

I just loved being the center of his attention.

Tucking the picture back into the hat, I return my focus to the computer screen. I'd written four chapters overnight. I'd started an entire new manuscript. The characters were aged up a bit, and in my late night plotting session, I'd created an entire new ending for them. It wasn't the one we first pitched to my editor when selling the duet, but this one feels better. For the first time since I started writing the conclusion novel to a duet that changed my life, I feel hope. I feel like I'm finally giving these characters the happily ever after they deserve.

The words feel right. The story for these characters feels right.

Now if only I could figure out my real life. The things about me that aren't fiction. Starting with Cade and his intentions by giving me the hat. It's clear he isn't hiding the feelings he's harbored all these years. He's all but admitted that he wasn't over me. That he didn't feel like things were over between us.

Since the moment I arrived, I thought his anger toward me was for not coming back. But there's more to it. I think he's not just mad I didn't come back for Linda or Pippa—I think he's also upset I didn't come back for *him*.

If only he knew I would've been on the first flight home if he'd only asked me to be.

We're a mess and I don't know how to pick up the pieces between us. We're both so angry at each other for reasons I can't even keep track of anymore.

It's clear he still wants something to happen between us. He made that obvious by kissing me and being upset by me stopping it. He showed me the house that was clearly planned out with me in mind—with my comments all those years ago.

All this time I've thought Cade forgot everything we were but he was here living in those memories every day of his life. I want to believe every word he's telling me. I want to hope that things aren't really over between us, but I'm scared to have my heart broken again. When I left, I was vulnerable with him. I laid out every single one of my feelings, and he stomped on them. He crushed us. He crushed *me*. No matter what he says now, I can't get over the fear of ending up in the exact same position as last time.

I slam my laptop shut, probably a little too forcefully. I'd already sent the chapters to Rudy. He'll probably be calling me shortly, so I decide to leave my phone in the room before heading downstairs. I don't want to talk to him right now, not while I'm trying to sort through all the questions rushing through my mind.

I expect to find someone in the kitchen, but it's completely empty. There's not any hint that anyone was even up yet—except for the slight smell of coffee lingering in the air and an empty mug sitting next to the sink.

Yesterday Pippa asked me to help her prepare a last minute order for tomorrow, but I don't know when exactly she'll be coming to the house. I need to text her, but I don't know if she stayed at her own place last night or if she slept somewhere else. She looked like she was having a good time with Chase, so she could've ended up with him. Maybe I should've brought my phone down so I could check in on her. The top of the stables catches my eye from the kitchen window. I take a step closer, looking out at them. From the amount of cars parked in the lot near the stables, there must be a trail ride in session.

I get an idea. Before I know it, I'm pulling on a pair of Pippa's boots from the mud room and making my way outside.

There's somebody I haven't paid proper attention to since my arrival.

It's time I change that.

Chapter 29
CADE
present

I'M CURSING under my breath from the state some of our tour guides left the tack room when I stop in my tracks.

I sense her movements before I see her.

The stable is supposed to be *my* territory. It should be the one fucking place on this ranch that I can avoid the woman that haunted my sleepless thoughts last night.

I guess I don't get the luxury of avoiding Mare for long, because she's standing a few feet away from me, her focus pinned on Dolly.

I'm thinking about backing up and retreating out of the stable to leave her to it. At least with that option, I'd be able to avoid her a little longer. I'm still pissed about last night. I feel like a fool. It was hard to completely lay everything out for her, admitting to her that I want her so fucking bad, and I got nothing in return.

I'd laid in bed last night thinking maybe she'd see that picture of her in my hat and she'd come see me. I was dumb as fuck to think she'd crawl into my bed, and I'd wake up to her warm body next to mine again.

I was so fucking wrong. She didn't come see me.

She either didn't bother to notice the photo or just didn't give a fuck about it. I'm not sure which one of those choices I'd prefer.

Mare's attention is fully on Dolly, allowing me a few moments to figure out what I want to do. The horse happily nuzzles into Mare's palm. Mare laughs, looking at Dolly lovingly.

I can't walk away, even when I know I should. Even when I'm still upset with her and with how things are between us.

"Took you long enough to pay her a visit." My words catch Mare off guard. She jumps, her back straightening and going tight with the realization she isn't alone.

Dolly lets out a loud sigh, as if she's agreeing with my words. The horse was Mare's world before she left us. I can sympathize with how it feels to suddenly be dropped by Mare.

"How do you know I haven't already come to visit her?"

I stop a few feet away from her. "Have you?"

Rolling her eyes, she looks back at Dolly. Mare runs her hand down her neck, scratching behind the horse's ears. "No. I haven't."

I silently watch her and the horse get reacquainted with one another. Every now and then Dolly whinnies in excitement to have her favorite person back. Dolly isn't very picky about who she loves, but it was clear the horse always had a favorite —Mare.

"Looks like she missed you," I note, watching Mare press her forehead into Dolly's mane.

I missed you, I fight saying.

"Yeah. I should've visited," Mare mutters under her breath. I don't know if she means since she returned for the funeral, or if she just means in general.

I bite my tongue. It's no use trying to tell her she should've absolutely been back sooner. Been there, done that.

"She still have a mind of her own on the trails?" Mare changes the subject, avoiding eye contact.

I want her to look at me. I want to finish our conversation from last night now that we're both thinking with clear heads.

Mostly, I want to know what I can do to ease the tension

between us.

Or maybe I need to accept the fact that nothing will ever be the same between us.

I give her a few moments to see if she'll look at me. When she doesn't, I sigh, knowing I'll answer her anyway. "A huge mind of her own. The guests don't ever get her. Even though most try to pick her."

Mare lovingly scratches at Dolly's neck. "Because she's such a pretty girl."

"She's pretty until she takes you into a tree of fucking grasshoppers."

Finally, she looks at me. It hurts more than I thought it would. "She did that? To you?"

I fix the hat on my head. "She sure as hell did. I went to bed for weeks having nightmares of grasshoppers all over me."

Mare looks back to the horse. "What a good girl you are, Dolly."

My eyebrows narrow. So *that's* how it's going to be.

Mare looks over her shoulder, pointing to my head. "Nice hat," she says, her tone unreadable.

I cock my head to the side, wondering where she's going with this. At least she's not running. "My typical one hasn't been returned to me."

Mare clicks her tongue. "Don't give things away if you expect to get them back."

"It was an extreme circumstance," I say under my breath.

Mare pins her full attention on me. She kicks at the ground, brushing what I think is Pippa's boot along the floor. "Cade," Mare says breathlessly. "That picture."

My heart picks up speed at the same moment my stomach drops to my feet.

So she did see it.

I swallow slowly, trying my best not to look away from her angry but inquisitive eyes. "What about it?"

Mare uses petting Dolly as an excuse to collect her thoughts for a few moments. Eventually, she sighs. "Did you really have it? Every day?"

"Does my answer to that change anything?"

An annoyed breath fills the space between us as two creases form between her eyebrows. "Does it matter if it changes anything? I want to know how long you've had it."

I shake my head at her, turning to go back to the tack room. If she wants me to bear everything to her, she's going to have to give me something as well.

I'm not trying to fight with her. I am, however, tired of this push and pull between us. I'm exhausted by the back and forth. If things are going to be like this, I just want her to leave so I can go back to pretending my heart wasn't missing from the moment she left Sutten.

"Cade! Don't walk away from me!" Mare shouts. She must leave Dolly's side, because her angry footsteps can be heard behind me as I make my way back toward the tack room.

I laugh sarcastically. "Don't walk away from *you*? It's funny that it bothers you considering you've always been the one to walk away from me."

I hear her gasp. She follows me in, hot on my heels. She's silent as I angrily pick up the tack the seasonal hires lazily left on the ground.

These saddles cost thousands of dollars and they've treated them like nothing.

"Let me help your memory—"

I angrily turn around, my body coming to a stop in front of hers. "Help *my* memory?" My laugh bounces off the walls of the small room. "My memory tells me it wasn't me who pretended to forget the details of our history…that was all you, Goldie."

Her arms cross over her chest defensively. "You told me to go."

"You listened!"

Of course I told her to go. I don't understand how she doesn't realize that was really the only thing I could do at the time. If I'd asked her to stay, we would've ended up fighting—just like we are now. She would've hated me for keeping her from her dreams, for asking her to risk everything for me.

Mare's eyes are wide and untamed as she looks me up and down. It's like she doesn't recognize the man standing in front of her.

I can understand. Most of the time, I can barely recognize the woman that returned to this town.

Sometimes she's my Goldie, other times she's someone completely different.

"You can't hold a grudge against me for leaving when you're the one who told me to go."

My jaw tenses. I shouldn't have to explain this to her. "I absolutely can hold a grudge. It's not about you leaving. It's about the fact you never came back."

"I thought you'd want me to stay away!" she shouts. We're lucky that everyone on the ranch is currently away and busy or we'd have a full audience for the fight happening between us.

"Why the fuck would I want you to stay away when I was in love with you?"

Her mouth falls open. "What?" she asks, her voice breaking.

I let out a dejected sigh, anger and sadness coursing through my veins. I shake my head. "You knew that."

"No." She shakes her head back and forth, her eyes misting over. "I didn't know. I hoped. God, I wanted that more than anything. But I asked you if you loved me and you told me no. How can I trust you now?"

"You were my entire fucking world that summer. I wanted to spend every goddamn minute I could with you. How can you not trust me when I say I was madly in love with you?"

Her eyes go wide, her body jolts with my last words, as if I've stunned her. "After I left, I cried myself to sleep *so* many times, wondering where things went wrong. I obsessed over the idea of you being my world and I was nothing to you. You can't tell me years later that you loved me."

My nostrils flare. She's not getting out of this easily. I should've told her then, but I was scared if she knew how I felt, she'd never leave. She's older now. She's capable of knowing what she wants out of life. Mare doesn't get the same luxury of not knowing how I really felt—how I still feel.

"I can't keep it a secret any longer." I grab her arms, pulling her closer to my body. "I fell for you so hard and fast, it was almost like that love had always been there. I loved you, Goldie. I loved you so fucking much that it killed me to watch you leave."

Her eyes get wide as her bottom lip begins to tremble. She almost looks horrified by my words. "No, no, no," she chants. "There's no way. I would've known."

My fingers tighten around her skin. "I think you did."

Mare shoves against my chest. "No! I didn't. If I did, I wouldn't have left."

I pull her all the way against me. She pushes me away for a few moments before her body melts to mine. "You knew I loved you, Goldie. But you still fucking left. Worse, you knew and you never came back."

Fire rages in her eyes. She can be angry with me all she fucking wants. I'm done beating around the bush. I want her to know everything I kept quiet because I thought it was best for her.

When her gaze drops to my lips, I do something completely fucking stupid.

I grab her by either side of her face and pull her lips to mine. The kiss is angry and untamed. Mare's fists grab the fabric of my shirt as she yanks on it in an attempt to mold our bodies together.

We suck at using our words to communicate what we're feeling.

But the kiss says it all.

Mare and I are unfinished business.

Chapter 30
MARE
present

THERE'S a reason I haven't been able to wipe the feeling of Cade's kiss from my memories. A reason why nothing has ever felt even remotely comparable with anyone else like it does with him.

He kisses me like he owns me. I kiss him back in hopes that I own him.

Our lips are starved for one another, even though we just felt the press of them together last night.

This kiss feels heightened. It's like we're throwing our anger —our love—into it.

When Cade slides his hands underneath the sweatshirt I'd pulled on this morning, I let him. His fingertips brand my skin. He touches me like he's trying to memorize every single inch of my skin all over again.

My fingers brush over the exposed buzzed sides of his head underneath his hat. It feels so much more different than it used to. Before, his hair was long enough for my fingers to grip on to. Now I just guide my palm along the sides of his head and get used to the new feeling of the scratch of cropped hair against my skin.

Cade pulls his lips from mine. Before I can protest, he grips my hair and pulls, bearing my throat to him.

His teeth rake against the tender skin of my neck. "There's so many reasons I'm pissed at you."

My hands move to his shirt, fisting the fabric to keep myself steady. "I could say the same thing to you."

I'm so mad at him. There's so much he didn't tell me. I guess we're angry with each other. We were so young back then that a lot of hurt probably could've been avoided if we both had been more honest with each other.

We can't change it. All we can do is move on from it and try not to let the anger destroy any hope for a future between us.

Cade pulls away. The look in his eyes has me clenching my thighs together.

He grabs me by the chin, holding my head in place with the tight grip of his fingers. "Take that anger out on me, baby. Because I'm sure as hell about to take it out on you."

He's pissed, his fury only turns me on. I *want* him to take his anger out on me. I want to be punished, to feel everything I can from him. His hands aren't gentle as he grabs the bottom of the sweatshirt and pulls it up, ripping the fabric off my body.

I hadn't bothered with putting on anything underneath, giving him a full view of my breasts. They feel heavy, aching to feel his touch. Air hisses from between his teeth as he lets out a rush of air. "Goddamnit, Goldie," he marvels, lifting me by the hips and setting me on top of a saddle stand. "You're so fucking perfect," he growls.

I moan when he reaches up to palm my breast. I've ached to feel his touch against me. I've touched myself so many nights with thoughts of him. I'd never forgotten the feel of his callouses against me. The rough skin of his fingertips glide across my nipple. My back arches as I grab the hem of his shirt. He backs away from me for a second, only long enough to let me pull it off him.

Cade Jennings was part of every single one of my fantasies at nineteen.

But now...I have no words to describe how immaculate his body has filled out. He was defined and sculpted the first time I got to touch him however I pleased. But now he's so much more of a man. His muscles are bigger, the veins running down his arms are thick as his muscles strain.

Cade steps back between my legs, pulling me until we're chest to chest.

"You don't just have to look at me," he says, his voice low. Even the huskiness in his voice somehow caresses the most intimate parts of me. This man has such a hold on me. Always has, always will. "Don't just stare at me…if you like what you see, touch me."

My fingers tentatively reach between us, feeling the hardness of his chest. His muscles tighten underneath my touch. I let my hand drift down, marveling at the hard, sculpted, ridges of his stomach. It seems that all the work on the ranch over the years has done him well.

When my fingers play with the waistband of his jeans, he sucks in a breath. "Oh no." He clicks his tongue. "My turn first," he demands.

Cade takes me by surprise by leaning forward and taking my hardened nipple in his mouth. My back arches as his hands steady my hips.

We shouldn't be doing this where anybody could catch us. Hell, a customer could walk in—or worse, Pippa. It doesn't stop either of us. If he's aware of how risky it is for us to be in this position, he doesn't seem to care. He spins his tongue around my nipple with expert precision, making my clit throb with desire.

His teeth graze my sensitive nipple. He smirks, his mouth still partially around my flesh when I let out a loud moan.

"I missed how reactive you are to every touch," he mutters against my skin. He bites slightly harder, licking away the slight twinge of pain. "With every bite, suck, thrust…your body doesn't hide how needy it is for me."

This causes another moan from my lips. God. No one would know quiet, broody Cade would say such filthy things with so much confidence.

His hands grab the top of the tennis skirt I'd slipped on,

pulling at the fabric. "It's time I taste you—devour that pretty pussy of yours."

I nod in encouragement, hot and needy for him. I know this is wrong. I'm all too aware of all the baggage he and I share. There's so much we need to work out, but I can't say no to him. I can't say no to feeling him like this.

I've ached for his touch for years, touching myself so many lonely nights at the memory of him. Now I need to be reminded of how it really feels. I want to remember what it's like to be owned by him.

I reach behind me, holding on to the edge of the saddle to keep myself steady as he yanks at the fabric at my waist. I lift my hips, allowing him to pull the fabric off.

He rips my panties at both sides, stripping me until I'm only wearing a pair of cowgirl boots.

Cade's hands are warm as he pushes my thighs open. I rest my feet on the edges of other saddle stands, baring myself to him.

I could come at the sight of him licking his lips, his gaze is scorching as he watches me in anticipation.

"Your cunt is so fucking wet for me, Goldie," he states casually, like his words are part of everyday conversation and not ones that have my thighs quivering. "It's dripping, *begging* to be worshiped by me."

I moan, my head falling backward with pleasure. "Oh, god."

"*Cade*," he corrects. "That's what you'll be screaming by the time I'm done with you."

"Cade," I repeat, my tone coming out as a beg. "Please," I add. I need to feel him. I need him to touch me. My breasts feel so tight and heavy by the way he looks at me hungrily. My clit throbs so painfully I'm about to slide my fingers through my wetness just to give myself some release.

"Please what?"

"Please touch me."

He runs his fingers over the sensitive skin between my

thighs, just far enough from the spot I'm so desperate for him that I know he's trying to tease me. "Do you want me to touch you or taste you?"

His palms press into my thighs as he makes sure I keep my legs spread wide for him. He kneels to one knee and then the other, lining his mouth with my center.

"You going to answer me, Goldie?"

"Taste. Or touch. I don't really care. I just need you."

"Taste it is. I told you I'm going to worship that cunt of yours. I think my tongue knows how to do that best."

He brushes his finger over my clit, making my hips buck. His breath is hot against my skin as he teases me by nipping at the inside of my thigh. His tongue caresses the spot only inches away from where I really want him. At least his finger still slowly strokes me, giving me some sort of relief.

It isn't enough.

I need more. A frustrated moan comes from me when he draws the moment out.

"Frustrated are we?" he mutters against my skin.

The asshole laughs at my frustrated mewls.

"It fucking sucks waiting for something you want, doesn't it, Goldie?" His hot breath whispers against my clit as he pushes the tip of his finger inside me, but only going down to what I imagine is his knuckle.

"You said you were going to worship me."

His finger pushes in a little deeper, slightly hooking to brush right up against the spot he knows drives me wild, even all these years later. "Oh baby, I plan to. I'm on my knees, ready to do anything to worship and show my dedication to you—to your pussy—but I need to have a little fun first."

His voice is throaty, full of need as he continues to growl. "You've left me waiting here for so goddamn long. You didn't think you'd get away with that, did you? I feel the need to punish you. Even just a little."

I could combust when he pulls his finger from me, leaving

me desperate to feel him again. The only thing I can feel is the tickle of his breath against the inside of my thighs.

It's too much. I miss his touch. I need it. The desperation for him is so much that it has me speaking before thinking. "Punish me later," I hurriedly get out. "Worship me now, punish me later. Please."

Cade looks up at me from between my thighs. I don't know what it is but seeing his predatory smile while he's inches away from my clit, has me even more turned on.

He rakes his eyes over my face slowly. It feels like he's trying to see into my soul. "I guess we could play by your rules...but just for a moment."

Before I can say anything else, Cade runs his tongue down my slit and I'm so fucking gone.

I've spent all these years trying to forget Cade but feeling him claim me all over again only proves one thing. I can pretend all I want, but nothing has changed. He still owns me—every fucking part of me.

MARE DOESN'T KNOW this yet, but there's no way I'm letting us leave things the way we did last time.

I don't have it in me.

Not after tasting her like this again. Not after feeling the tremble of her thighs against my shoulders as I help her chase a release.

My cock strains in my jeans when a loud moan falls from her lips. Mare bucks her hips, shoving her perfect cunt against my face. She moves her hips so much, it's like she's riding my face without quite riding it.

I let her do whatever she needs as I lick and lap against her clit, doing whatever I can to keep the desperate moans coming from her lips.

When I can tell she's getting close, I push one finger, then another inside her. Her pussy clenches around my fingers, greedily taking me and keeping them in place. I pull them out before pushing them in, over and over again, until her moans are loud enough that someone might hear from a good distance away. I don't give a fuck if they do. I'd tried hiding us before, it ended up with both of us devastated and hurt. I don't intend to hide anything this time.

Her cunt clenches around me. She's so wet that my fingers

slip easily inside her. I have to slightly hook them to be able to hit the spot I know drives her fucking wild.

I lick her up and down, my tongue paying close attention to circling her swollen clit. "Remember when you come, you're going to scream my name, baby."

She answers by moaning unabashedly. I've always loved how reactive she is when I've got her laid out like this. She isn't shy about letting me know how fucking wild I drive her.

I continue to lap at her before one of her legs falls over my shoulder, the back of her boot pressing into my shoulder as she traps me against her. The movement isn't necessary. I'm not going to stop until she's screaming in ecstasy, telling me how good I did at worshiping her.

Her insistence on keeping my mouth to her clit turns me the hell on. My cock strains in my jeans. It throbs, needing to be touched by her.

"Cade," she yells in pleasure. "I'm going to come."

I nod, continuing my task. "I know," I say between licks. I press my thumb against the sensitive bud between her legs so she really feels me everywhere. "Your pussy is wrapping around my fingers so greedily, I can tell it's about to use them to get off. Do it, baby. Come for me."

I push my fingers in deeper, pulling her to the edge of her release. I know how much my words used to drive her wild and turn her on, so I get out one more thing before she's rocking against my mouth, taking what she needs to ride out the orgasm. "Show me how good I worshipped you. Come against my face."

She screams, her hips coming off the saddle as the orgasm overtakes her. Cum drips down her thighs and against my mouth, just begging to be tasted by me. I slide my finger over the drip of her cum, licking it clean from my fingertip.

Mare's chest heaves up and down. Her eyelids are hooded as we make eye contact. "Cade," she whispers. There's so much unsaid in the way she says my name.

Standing up, I pull her up so my lips hover above hers. Her gaze focuses on my lips—on the wetness of her all over me.

"Kiss me," I demand, grabbing her hair so I can guide her head the way I want. "Taste yourself on me before I fuck you until you're spent and punish you for all your lies."

Her lips part, her hands finding the back of my neck as she pulls me against her.

I love this wild side of Mare. The part that takes what she wants with no apologies or regrets. Our kiss is frantic and urgent, like we both know someone could stumble upon us at any time.

When Mare's little hands find the buckle of my belt, I let her undo it. My cock is hard as a fucking rock, aching for her touch.

Mare rushes at pulling my belt off and unbuttoning my jeans. She shoves the denim and my boxers down my thighs just enough to free my cock.

It springs to attention, the head already wet with pre-cum.

Her pink tongue comes out to wet her lips. My cock jerks at the close attention her eyes pay to it. She looks it up and down hungrily.

"You've made me wait so goddamn long, Goldie. It's time for me to feel you take my cock again."

She looks up from my cock to my eyes, a glint in her eyes. Rubbing her lips together, she tries to fight a smile. It breaks on her face anyway. "Want me to taste or touch it?"

Fuck. This is why I could never be anyone else's. No one else banters with me the way she does.

I grab my cock, wrapping my fingers around it and pumping up and down. It needs some kind of attention, my balls aching from being so fucking turned on by having her again. "While punishing that smart mouth of yours sounds like a great fucking time, it's going to have to wait for now."

My hand leaves my cock for a moment. Only long enough to grab her hand and guide it to me. She understands right away.

Her small hand wraps around my shaft. Her skin is so fucking soft wrapped around me. A loud growl rumbles from my chest.

"Fuck, Goldie." I grunt. It feels too fucking good. She strokes up and down with a perfect rhythm, driving me fucking wild already.

I allow her to have her fun for a few moments before I take control again.

She lets out a disappointed moan when I pull my cock from her grip.

I smirk, causing her eyes to narrow on me.

"Who said I was done?"

"You told me I could worship you, but we had a deal. You got worshiped, but then I get to punish you. It's time for you to hold up your end of the deal, baby."

She doesn't look scared by my words. In fact, she looks turned on and fucking thrilled at the thought of me punishing her.

Fuck. This woman will be my ruining.

"What did you have in mind?"

I roughly grab her by the hips and pull her off the saddle stand. Her boots hit the ground with a soft *thud*. She lets out a surprise squeal when I spin her, pressing her stomach into the saddle.

"This," I get out, answering her question. I kick her legs open, spreading her open from behind.

I'm way too fucking turned on by just the sight of her in a pair of cowgirl boots. Her ass is in the air, perfectly teasing me. Her pussy is pink and puffy, her cum still spread between her thighs.

My belt buckle jingles as I take a step closer to her, rubbing my cock along the seam of her ass.

She jumps, her hands gripping the sides of the stand to keep her balance.

"Cade," she pants, her tone unsure.

"Goldie." The tip of my cock plays with the wetness between

her legs. She's made such a mess, her cum splattering her inner thighs. It lubricates my cock perfectly. "Tell me you're on the pill."

She nods up and down, her hair falling off her shoulders with the movement. "I am."

"Can I fuck you? With nothing in between us?"

"Yes. *Please*."

Me too, Goldie. "I've been ready for years, having to fuck my hand night after night at the memory of you."

Now I get the real thing.

I lower to my haunches, running my fingers through her wetness. "Let's check to see if you're ready to take me," I note, spreading the wetness around and around. She jolts from the action, pushing her ass further into the air.

"I'm ready," she pants, moving her hips to get my fingers lined up with her entrance.

"Ready for what?" I ask, standing back up. I coat the head of my cock with her.

"Ready for you to fuck me."

"I'm not just going to fuck you, Goldie. I'm going to punish you for making me wait so"—I push a little deeper into her—"fucking"—another inch—"long,"—I'm halfway in and she's already gasping at the way I stretch her—"to get you back."

I'm not gentle when I push all the way inside her. She moans, her back arching as she holds onto the edges of the stand.

"Your cunt will be so raw by the time I'm done punishing you. It's the only way I can prove to you…"

"Prove what?"

Slowly I pull out of her before roughly pushing back in, my hips hitting the back of her thighs while hers rock against the stand. "That this pussy is still mine," I say through gritted teeth, the feeling of her wrapping around my cock so perfectly overwhelming me. "It's always been mine. It's time I remind you of that."

Mare tries to push against me to set her own pace, to take

what she wants. I don't allow it. I told her I was going to punish her and I meant it. She's already had my tongue worship that pretty little cunt of hers. Now it's time for her to pay for what she's done.

She'll come. Fuck, she might come a few times before I'm done with her, but I'm going to drag it out. Have my way with her.

"Cade," Mare whines, turning her head so her cheek presses into the saddle as she looks back at me. "I need more."

I stop, fully sheathed inside her as I feel her pussy clench around me. I know I'm stretching her, molding her to my cock perfectly. As it should be.

"I've needed more from you for years," I tell her, rocking my hips slightly. It still doesn't give her a lot of friction or really any relief. "But you didn't give that to me."

Mare tries to push herself off the saddle, no doubt to change her position. Before she can do anything, I push her back into it, making her lay flat against it. "You're not in control here, baby."

She groans, moving her hips against me to try and move my cock inside her. "Cade." My name is the sexiest fucking plea coming from her mouth. I almost give in to her, I almost pick up speed and give her what she wants.

Almost.

I don't. I want to punish her. I want her to make up for breaking my heart—for leaving me here desperate for her and only her.

"You agreed to let me punish you," I remind her. "You got to come already, baby."

"Not enough."

I pull out of her, my palm coming down with a smacking sound against her ass. It isn't enough to hurt for long, just enough to sting a little. She moans, her pussy holding me even tighter. "You don't get to choose how we do this," I tell her, my palm massaging the pink skin on her ass.

Lucky for her, my cock is desperate to pick up the pace. To pound into her. To punish her.

When we're done, I'll make damn sure she'll be feeling me long after she leaves this stable.

"Hold on tight, Goldie," I say, pressing my hand against the small of her back. "I don't plan on being gentle."

Chapter 32
MARE
present

CADE'S angry thrusts are just another reminder of how much he owns me.

There's been years between us, yet as he pushes in and out of me with such force my hip bones are almost rubbed raw from slamming into the saddle stand, it seems like we've never been apart.

It isn't just the way he thrusts into me that proves I had no chance of ever being anyone else's. It's in the way he possessively wraps his fingers in my hair, looping the strands around his palm to control the top half of my body. Even if I wanted to push off this stand and put us in a new position, I wouldn't be able to. Cade makes sure that even as he pounds into me from behind in a way that follows through on his promise to punish me, that he's the one in full control.

I let him have it.

I thrive with him having it.

My body comes alive underneath his dominating touch. It feels too fucking good, the pleasure mixed with his painful thrusts, something I excitedly welcome.

Cade pulls on my hair, forcing me to arch my back. The movement helps him push even deeper inside me—something I didn't know was possible. He's too deep, so deep that it hurts every time he fully seats himself inside me. His thighs slap against my ass with each thrust, his pace punishing.

I gladly take all of it—all of him. I'll take anything he'll give me, my body desperate to feel completely owned by him.

He said he was punishing me, but his possessive thrusts and growls still feel like he's worshiping me.

When the hand not in my hair drifts up my ribcage and plays with my exposed nipple, I moan. Tingles move from my breast all the way down to my clit. His hips are unforgiving as he pushes in and out of me angrily, but his fingers playing with my nipple are gentle. He caresses over it, teasing me.

"Cade." I moan again, it feels too good. It feels like too much. I know that another orgasm is building inside me. I fight telling him that I'm about to come, fearful that he'll stop as another way to take his anger out on me.

"What, baby?" His words come out strained. I feel power knowing that he's as unhinged as I am. I need it as proof that nothing has changed between us—at least when it comes to the way our bodies speak to one another.

My teeth clamp down on my lip as I fight the urge to tell him how close I am. I wouldn't put it past him to cut me off from coming just to spite me for last night—for the past five years.

His quick, deep thrusts make my toes curl in my cowgirl boots. I know I'm seconds away from coming, the feel of his cock stretching me and punishing me too much.

Right before I'm about to be sent over the edge, his thrusts slow.

I moan because I was so close but the change in tempo has the pressure building but not quite reaching the edge. It's the most euphoric form of torture, being on the brink of an orgasm but not quite reaching it.

"I feel your cunt hugging me tighter. Did I say it was time for you to come again?"

My head falls forward, hitting the leather saddle. He allows it, but his fingers stay firm in my hair.

He slowly pumps in and out. Tingles run all over my body as the orgasm threatens to overtake me. I know whenever I finally reach the release, it's going to be powerful.

"What if I wasn't done punishing you yet?"

"I'm sorry," I croak, pushing my hips against him to try and get him to speed up, to go deeper, something to push me past that last little bit.

Cade rests his chest against my back, his weight heavy on top of me as he aims his mouth right next to my ear. "It's not fun thinking you're going to get something only to have it taken away is it, Goldie?"

His lips brush against the side of my neck tenderly. He steals whatever answer I could give him from my mouth when he pulls out of me and turns my body. The movement is so fast I can't even process what's happening until he's got me seated on the saddle stand once again, my legs spread wide open as he steps between them.

Cade doesn't make me wait long, he pushes inside me, not allowing much time for our bodies to be separated.

One hand runs up my back and over my shoulders until he grabs my chin, forcing me to look at him.

"I'm done punishing you. It's time for you to come, but you're going to look at me while you do it." As soon as he utters the last syllable, he's slamming into me, my body coming off the saddle with the movement. He lowers both his hands to rest under my ass, keeping me upright as he takes out all the anger and frustration from all our years apart out on me.

I gladly take each punishing thrust of his body. It only takes a few before I'm finally pushed over the edge. I scream so loudly from the orgasm ricocheting through my body. Cade's lips crash against mine, stealing any further sounds of pleasure straight from my mouth.

My entire body shakes from the position I'm in combined with the effects of coming off the orgasm. Cade thrusts into me, taking everything he wants from me as he chases his own orgasm. It doesn't take long until he's groaning against my mouth, his muscles going tight. He gives one last thrust until I feel wetness between my thighs, our cum mixing together as he moans Goldie one final time.

For a few moments, the only sound in the tack room is the sound of our intense breathing. His chest presses into mine, sweat coating both our bodies after what just happened. It feels like I just went for a run, but instead it was just me getting railed by the one man on this planet I have no business getting involved with again.

Cade pulls out of me, his cock still hard as he takes a slight step back. He doesn't break our connection, his fingertips still digging into the flesh at my hips. I look away from his still-hard cock—it's skin glistening with me—and look into his eyes.

I find him staring right back at me. When our gazes lock, I know that something has shifted between us.

He pushed it to shift last night, I just wouldn't let him.

Now, I don't know if I have a choice.

"Even after all these years," he says, breaking the silence.

"What?"

He pushes hair from my face, lifting my chin up before he presses a kiss to my lips. "Even after all these years your pussy still fits me perfectly. Like it was made for me and *only* me."

"Cade," I mutter, not knowing what else there is to say. He was the first man I was ever with—the only one I've ever loved. I would've spent the rest of my life with only ever having him and only him. It was him that made the decision to ruin everything we could've been.

I should feel exposed sitting completely naked on the saddle. I should definitely be rushing to get dressed before someone stumbles upon us. But I don't move an inch.

I'm too focused on the way Cade looks at me. It's easy to tell that I won't get away with pretending this never happened. Not like I'd even want to.

The moment I saw that photo in his hat, every reason I was

denying him disappeared from my mind. He hurt me more than anyone has ever hurt me when he forced me to leave. But I'm learning that maybe we were too young to handle how strong our feelings were.

We're older—*wiser*—now. Maybe we can give in to each other, and it won't end in devastation.

All I know is that when Cade pulls me into his chest in a warm embrace, I'm not capable of being angry with him any longer.

We both let out a collective sigh of relief. It's as if he's coming to the same conclusion as I am.

He presses a kiss to my shoulder before pulling away. He grabs my sweatshirt from the ground. His movements are soft as he pulls it over my head. Once we're both dressed and cleaned up, he grabs my hand in the doorway of the stables.

"Goldie?" The nickname caresses deep parts of me. I forgot how much I'd missed the nickname, how much I still love it after all the time and hurt that's passed between us.

"Hm?"

"You're sleeping in my bed tonight. If I don't find you at my door, don't think I won't come and get you and put you where you belong."

"And where is that?"

He laughs. "For tonight? With me."

"Just tonight?" I ask hesitantly.

His eyes soften as he fixes a piece of my hair. Hurt flashes through his eyes briefly. He hides it as quickly as it came. "That's not my decision," he answers.

We stare at each other, neither one of us saying anything else.

It makes me wonder, not for the first time, what would happen if this time I didn't leave Sutten.

What if I stopped fighting the feelings between the two of us and actually gave things a chance?

I know one thing for sure. What Cade and I have is undeniable, no matter how much hurt we've caused each other—and how much hurt we'll cause each other if I do end up leaving Sutten again.

Chapter 33
MARE
age nineteen

BUTTERFLIES SOAR in my stomach as I utilize the mirror above my dresser to fix my hair. I've lost track of how many times I've changed my hairstyle and my clothes. I even changed the color of my nails twice because of nerves.

Luckily, my dad isn't here to watch me fuss over my appearance. Not that he really pays much attention these days anyway. He went with Jasper to go pick up some new horses from a few towns over, meaning I have the cabin all to myself.

Well, *almost* all to myself. I'd invited Cade to sneak away from the main house and come stay the night with me.

We'd shared the same bed hundreds of times. But tonight felt different. It was the reason I'd spent so long obsessing over what I looked like. I'd always snuck into Cade's bed with others in the rooms next to us. Tonight, no one will be around. It'll just be him and me. No distractions. No fear of being caught.

I want it to be the night we go all the way.

A knock rattles on the door, echoing through the halls of the small cabin. I rush down the stairs, not wanting to make Cade wait long. Stopping at the door, I take a deep breath. My heart beats wildly against my chest as I wonder if I'd picked the right outfit. Is it weird to have my hair down and straightened when we aren't going anywhere?

I puff out my cheeks, taking one last deep breath before pulling the door open.

The way Cade looks standing on the other side of the door disarms me. He stares at me, a whisper of a smile on his lips as our eyes meet.

"Goldie," he says, his voice low. The deepness of it feels like an intimate touch along my entire body.

"Cade," I answer back. I should step out of the doorway and let him in, but my feet don't move. I'm stuck staring at him—appreciating him—my tongue wetting my lips as I think about finally getting to touch all of the man standing in front of me.

A T-shirt with a zip-up jacket isn't supposed to look this good. I know Cade well enough to know that he probably didn't think long about what to wear, yet both pieces of clothing fit him so perfectly. He has the hood pulled over his head, for once missing a hat. He looks good with the sharp edges of his face shadowed in darkness.

The slim fit pair of joggers he's wearing also have no business molding to his perfect body so well. *God.* Cade Jennings looks hot as hell, but he'd be hotter if he'd finally let me strip him naked like he's stripped me numerous times before.

I only look back at his face when I hear him let out a low chuckle. My eyes snap to him, finding one corner of his lips lifting up in a smirk. "Are you going to leave me out here to freeze?"

Rolling my eyes, I grab his hand and pull him through the doorway. The moment I shut the door, he's pulling me into his arms. His lips press to my forehead as I tuck my hands between the fabric of his jacket and his t-shirt.

"Missed you, Goldie," he mutters against my skin.

"Missed you more."

He cups my face between his large hands, softly pulling my chin so our eyes meet. "Not possible."

I smile, lifting to my tiptoes so I can feel the press of his lips against mine. The kiss is tender and sweet. We aren't rushing to have an intimate moment like we usually do. It's hard to find a second alone together between our friends and family, so most of our kisses are late at night under the moonlight or in his bed. Sometimes we manage to sneak some in the stalls, or in one of the barns, or in the trees on a ride. But those kisses are rushed. This one isn't.

I love knowing that I'll have him all to myself for the night. There are so many things I want to do. The biggest thing? Finally having sex with him. There's no one else I'd rather take my virginity than the man I've been in love with for years.

Our lips pull apart, but the rest of us stay pressed against one another. "For the record"—I begin, nipping at his thumb brushing over my lip—"I definitely missed you more."

Cade lifts an eyebrow. "And what makes you think that?"

"Because I couldn't stop thinking about you. Even as Pippa and I went out to get milkshakes at Pop's, all I thought about was you."

"It took me twice as long to get the nightly chores done because I kept getting distracted with the anticipation of spending all night with you."

"You spend almost every night with me."

"Not quite like this. I get you all to myself. It's like a date."

I pull him toward the kitchen. I'd spent an hour trying to come up with something to make the two of us for dinner, but there weren't a lot of options. Most nights I eat dinner with Cade's family. Linda always sends something back with me to give Dad. But tonight, even though it's technically a late dinner, I wanted to make something, to pretend for a moment that we live together and I've made him a meal after a long day of work.

Pointing at the small table in the corner, I tell him to sit. He surprisingly follows my direction. Cade falls into the chair, his eyebrows raised as he watches me closely.

I pull out a pot from the cabinet next to the stove. "You know, if you want to take me on a real date, all you have to do is ask."

"I'd love nothing more than to take you on a real date."

I busy myself with filling the pot with water as my cheeks get warm. He answered so suddenly and so sure, something I wasn't expecting since he'd never mentioned taking me anywhere off this ranch.

"You would?"

"Of course."

"Then why haven't you?"

"Because no one knows about us, Goldie. We probably need to tell Pip before we do anything. You ready to do that?"

My mouth snaps shut. It's been hard keeping this a secret from my best friend. When you have a crush, you want to be able to talk about it with your best friend, and I haven't been able to do that. When we were getting ice cream tonight, I wanted to tell her I thought I was finally going to lose my virginity. I haven't been able to tell her all the things I want to because the boy I want to give everything to is her brother.

It'd be easier to tell her if I knew how she'd react. I know everything about her, yet I have no idea how she'd take the news about Cade and me. She might be totally fine with it, or she might feel completely betrayed knowing we've kept this secret from her for months.

"That's what I thought." Cade sighs, leaning back in the kitchen chair. It groans underneath his weight.

"How do you think she'll take it?" I carefully set the pot of water on the stove before flipping the burner to its highest setting.

"I think she'll be hurt we kept this from her."

That's what I'm afraid of. The last thing I want to do is go into living together with her upset with me. Our college move-in date is getting closer and closer. The closer it gets, the more hesitant I am to tell Pippa anything.

Why couldn't I fall in love with someone who wasn't my best friend's brother?

"You're leaving in a few weeks. It's probably best we don't tell her—or anyone. We don't have to go anywhere." His tone is unreadable. I can't figure out if he's upset with me, or if he just doesn't care about telling anyone.

I nod, not wanting to start a fight. Every time he mentions me leaving, I want to tell him that I'd consider staying if he'd just ask. Or we could figure something else out. I could do this semester in person and then look into virtual classes. I'd do anything if it meant whatever is happening between us didn't have to expire the day I move away.

I swallow the emotions that are threatening to spill over. I don't want to ruin our night together talking about this so I have to find a way to keep it together. This is supposed to be one of the best nights of my life, I just have to steer our conversation to something safer.

"I don't need a public date anyway. I like spending time with you here."

Cade watches me carefully. Whatever is going through his head, he keeps it to himself. He makes me anxious with his brooding stare as he watches me carefully turn the burner down before the boiling water overflows.

He doesn't utter a word as I cook the macaroni noodles, and not when I strain the water out and mix the artificial cheese packet with milk and butter.

In fact, he doesn't say anything until I place a bowl of steaming boxed mac and cheese in front of him. And only to say thank you. I take a seat across from him, suddenly not very hungry thanks to the lingering tension in the air.

I spin the noodles around in my bowl with my spoon, never committing to actually taking a bite. I continue the pattern for a minute or two before Cade clears his throat.

"What are you expecting to happen to us when you leave?"

His words catch me off guard. I'd kind of figured we'd switch the conversation to something inconsequential like the weather or how the trails were today. Not about the future—not about what's going to happen between us.

I shrug because I don't really have an answer for that. It

seems like all of our lives lead up to this summer, to us finally accepting the fact that there's a connection between us that's undeniable. It's both terrible and perfect timing for us to come together like this after all this time. But there's still the giant *what-if* at the end of this.

"We figure it out?" I ask hesitantly.

Cade nods, scooping up a large bite of mac and cheese and taking a bite. He chews slowly, his eyebrows furrowed as he thinks about my answer. "And what does figure it out mean exactly?"

I push my bowl out from in front of me. I'm not hungry. I don't want to think about what happens when I leave. I want to think about tonight with Cade. It's too painful, filled with too many unknowns, to think about the future.

"It means that I don't want to ruin what's happening between us at this moment with questions about what happens next. Because I don't know what will happen next. All I know is that I want you."

Two lines form in between his eyebrows as he stares back at me. He gives no indication on what direction his mind is going in. I don't even know what his plans are for when I leave. Does he even want to try and keep this up—whatever this is to begin with?

His silence makes me anxious. I pull my lip from my teeth before I worry it so hard it bleeds. I swallow all the anxious nerves bubbling up in my throat to get out my next question. "Do you want me?"

A loud growl rips from Cade's throat. He stands up so quickly that the chair hits the wall behind him with a thud. My mouth opens at the shock from the noise before he's dropping to his knees in front of me, pulling me against his chest.

He holds me by the back of the neck, angling my head to look back at him. "Do you really not know the answer to that question?"

"I don't know," I whisper.

His eyes soften as he looks at me with such a powerful look, it's the first time I wonder if he may love me back. And not the kind of love that comes with growing up with someone. The kind of love that's all consuming. The kind of love that's like a brand to the soul, one that lingers in the deepest depths of your heart for the rest of your life. The kind that goes from *I love you* to *I'm in love with you*.

"It doesn't feel right to say I want you," he begins. My stomach plummets at his words, coldness washing over my body as I worry that this is him ending something we've barely begun.

He must sense the dread overtaking my body because he pulls me to the edge of the chair, and my legs wrap around his middle as our chests brush up against one another. "It doesn't feel right to say I want you because it's so much more than that. Saying I want you makes it seem like it's just a choice. What I feel for you—how bad I need you—doesn't just feel like a choice. It feels undeniable. Like fate."

Cade leans in, trapping my lips between his before I can get out any kind of answer for him. It's best that way, I was about to tell him that loving him never felt like a choice to me—it feels embedded in my soul. It just is. No choice, no accident. But that would've been me confessing I've fallen for him, and I don't know if we're ready for that yet.

Not for the first time, we let our bodies do the talking. Words don't come as we get lost in the kiss in the middle of my childhood home's tiny kitchen.

When my lips feel raw, our bodies finally parting slightly, a smile lifts both corners of my lips.

"Should we go to my room?"

Chapter 34
CADE
age twenty-two

HAVEN'T SEEN Mare's room in years. The last time I saw it I'm pretty sure she still had silly boy band posters covering every inch of her walls. It wasn't often that I even visited the cabin she shared with her father, let alone came up to her room in the loft.

Mare closes the door behind me, her bare feet stopping on a fluffy white rug next to her bed. She looks nervous to have me in her space. I've never thought about the fact that she's been in my room so many times and probably could describe it in vivid detail to anyone who asked about it. Until now, if someone had asked for me to tell them about her room, I'd bring up the Anticipation Rising posters that had been thumb tacked into her walls. I would've said I thought she had an animal print comforter and that's all I'd be able to recall. It's just now occurring to me how much she knows about my personal space and how little I know about hers.

Now there isn't a single poster in sight. Her comforter is a pale pink. She has abstract prints on her walls and shelves lined with books and personal items. None of that really catches my attention. Not when I notice the boxes lined up on one of the walls.

It feels like a punch to the gut, another reminder of how much she wants to get away from this small town.

I have to immediately look away from the moving boxes

before I let it ruin our night together. I already ran my mouth when we were in the kitchen when I shouldn't have. It feels like we're walking on thin ice now. I can't take my words back. I can't un-ask what happens to us when she leaves.

What I *can* do is make the most of the time we have together until then.

"What are you thinking?" Mare asks, taking a seat at the edge of her bed.

"I was thinking how you've been in my room—in my bed—so many times, but I hadn't stepped foot in yours in years."

Her eyes scan the room as if she's looking at her own space with new eyes. I look to the side of the room that's caught her eye. Letting out a breath, I walk to the spot that's captured her attention. Right next to a stack of papers that look like what might be pages of whatever she's currently writing, there's a picture frame with a photo of Mare, Pippa, and me. Except Pippa isn't really in it. Her face is blurry and half of her body is cut out of it.

It's mostly a photo of just Mare and me. We're riding the ski lift at one of our local slopes. She'd pulled out her phone wanting a selfie but Pippa had been too busy complaining about how cold her cheeks were so she'd missed the photo. I'd been caught off guard by Mare pulling out her phone. I think if I remember correctly, I'd also been scolding her that she was going to drop it. It doesn't matter. In the photo Mare stares at the camera, her cheeks bright red from the wind with a huge smile on her face. My eyes aren't on the camera, they're on her. My smile is as wide as hers.

It's weird to look back at some of our memories together and see them with fresh eyes. Even though the picture was taken close to two years ago, I wonder if I felt something more for her back then and I just didn't know it. The way I look at her in this picture, it's hard to imagine I didn't. Maybe something has always been there, it just needed time to come to the forefront of my mind and heart.

Mare wraps her hands around my middle, squeezing me from the back as she tucks her head underneath my arm. "It's one of my favorite pictures."

"I didn't even remember that you took it." I'm struck by an overwhelming feeling that I can't describe. It's like that photo helped me realize how deep the feelings I have for her really run and how long they've been there, just waiting to be addressed.

"I forgot about it at first, but one night I was flipping through my phone's camera roll when I saw it. I knew I wanted to frame it immediately."

"I'm shocked Pippa hasn't complained about not really being in it."

Mare shrugs underneath my arm. "Oh, she hasn't noticed. She'd be pissed if I framed anything that didn't have her as the center of attention."

I chuckle. That's my sister. She demands all the attention and doesn't want to accept anything less. It's always worked out well for us. She wants all the attention when I want none of it. We were a perfect pair, even with the few years of an age difference between us.

Turning around, I grab Mare's arms and wrap them around my neck. I pull her small frame into me, wrapping mine around her back.

"I like your room, Goldie. Want to show me your bed?"

Her cheeks turn pink. She nods enthusiastically, backing up as she keeps a firm grip on my hand.

When the back of her thighs hit the mattress, I pick her up and toss her onto the bed. She squeals, a bright smile on her face. Quickly, I slip out of my shoes and leave them on the rug. Mare props herself up by her elbows, her hair spilling down her shoulders, as she watches me closely.

I crawl along the bed until my body hovers over hers. Holding myself up, I look down at her, running my fingers along her cheeks. "Has anyone ever told you how beautiful you are?"

Her teeth dig into her bottom lip as she does her best to fight a smile. It doesn't work for long. "No one," she lies. I've told her countless times, but I don't mind telling her again.

"You're beautiful," I declare, kissing the new freckles on her face softly. She laughs with each press of my lips to her skin.

I kiss every single inch of her face except for her lips before I pull away. My hair hangs off my forehead, obstructing my perfect view of her. I'm wondering how I'll ever survive having her leave this town when she smiles up at me with so much affection it makes my heart constrict in my chest.

"Say it again," she whispers.

What I want to tell her is that I think I've fallen in love with her.

"You're beautiful," I repeat.

"I'm yours," she responds.

There goes my heart again, squeezing inside my chest with the terrifying pain of loving her with the knowledge there's a great chance I don't get to keep her. She says she's mine, but I can't help but wonder for how long.

It'll break my heart to have her anything less than forever.

Mare's hands drift underneath my jacket and T-shirt. Her hands are cold against my warm skin as she tentatively explores my abdomen.

"Cade?"

"Yes, Goldie?"

"Are you mine?"

I flinch because I don't understand how she doesn't know the answer to this already. That photo she has framed should tell her everything she needs to know. I've always been hers, before I even knew it. It seems obvious now that Goldie has always been my world. I'd do anything for her. It's why I opened my bedroom door to comfort her each and every night—even when I knew I shouldn't.

I separate our bodies enough that I can unzip my jacket. It falls to the ground with a soft thud as I throw it to the side, my T-shirt following in its path. Mare's eyes go wide as she watches my every move. Her breaths get heavier, her chest rising and falling rapidly.

With the top half of me undressed, I climb on top of her body again. I grab her hand, pressing it against my chest. There's no way she doesn't feel the intensity of my rapid heartbeat against her palm. "You feel that?"

She nods. "I do."

"Ask me again if I'm yours."

"Are you mine?"

"My heart only beats like that for you." I press her hand against my chest, proving to her that no one controls my heartbeats like she does. I don't think anyone will ever be able to, even if she and I don't work out the way I hope. I don't see any kind of love that can compare to the love I have for the woman gazing up at me.

Mare pulls her hand from my chest. For a brief moment, I wonder if I've said too much, if there's a chance that I've scared her. Before I can try and take back my words, she's guiding my hands underneath her shirt. My fingers brush the sides of her breasts, bringing my attention to the fact she isn't wearing any sort of bra.

Our hands, with our fingers interlocked, come to a stop on her chest. Her heartbeat matches mine. It beats strong against my skin, the erratic rhythm in perfect sync with mine.

"For my entire life, my heart has only beat for one person. That's you, Cade Jennings. Even without knowing if you'd ever be mine, I knew I was yours."

"I like the sound of that, Goldie." When she arches into me, I can't help but let my fingers drift a bit lower. My fingertips trace the swell of her breasts.

"I like being yours and you being mine. I want to be yours in every way." Her voice is timid but sure as she arches deeper into my touch.

My head comes forward until my forehead presses against hers. I suck in air, unable to come up with reasons why we should wait. I want her in every way possible—physically and emotionally. I just didn't want to do anything she wasn't ready for.

"Goldie..."

Her hands are firm against my cheeks as she rests them on either side of my face. "I'm ready, Cade. Please, I want to feel what it's like to be yours."

"I'm yours no matter what."

She nods and fuck if I wasn't already madly in love with her, I know that this moment would be the reason I fell. It's the way she tenderly rubs my cheekbone before her hands travel down my bare chest that does me in. I don't stop her when her slender fingers play with the waistband of my pants.

"I'm yours and you're mine. Now can we be us?"

My cock strains so hard against my briefs and cotton sweatpants. I've never been touched by her but fuck I'm ready for it. "If that's what you want," I mutter against her lips. Before she can answer me, I kiss her. I know I can take my time with her, but I'm so used to our kisses being rushed that this one is no different. This time, the rush is fueled by passion. By the desperate need from both of us to finally feel what it's like to go all the way together.

"You know it's what I want, Cade. I just don't know if it's what you want."

I move my hips until the outline of my cock presses against her palm. I'm hard as fuck, my dick aching to feel her touch. "Feel how hard this is for you, Goldie?" I guide her hand until her fingers slip underneath the pieces of fabric shielding me from her. "I'm sorry if I've ever made you think anything other than the fact that I'm fucking wrecked by the thought of feeling you touch my cock, of burying myself inside you."

"Oh," she whispers as her fingertips brush along my shaft.

"I'm fucking crazy about you. And if you're sure you're ready, I want this just as bad as you do."

Mare takes the lead, her fingers wrapping around my dick

inside my joggers. She's slow at first, taking her time at memorizing the feel of me in her grasp. "I don't know what I'm supposed to do," she whispers.

My head falls backward. Her hand moves up and down slowly as she applies the smallest of pressure, but fuck it already feels too fucking good. "Grip me tighter. Don't be shy as you get to know my cock."

Chapter 35
MARE
age nineteen

MY THIGHS clench together from Cade's filthy words. He's never spoken this dirty to me, but I hope that it's something he doesn't stop doing. Getting braver, I tighten my fingers around his thick length. I don't know what I expected when I first got to see him, but I hadn't expected him to be as big as he is. I'm scared at even attempting to fit him inside me, but at the same time I'm thrilled by the thought of him stretching me, forcing me to fit him.

I stroke up and down, watching every single reaction from him. I make sure to watch him closely to figure out if I'm doing this right. His eyes flutter closed as he swallows slowly. His prominent Adam's apple bobs up and down. Judging by the low groan coming from his throat, I must be doing something right.

As I move my hand up and down his hard, thick length, I begin to twist a little. Air hisses through his teeth as his hips come forward slightly.

"Teach me how to touch someone. I want to learn to do it right."

His body shudders. "I'll teach you to touch *me*. You won't be touching anyone else."

"Teach me how to touch *you*."

"Goddamn, Goldie."

"Is this what I'm supposed to do?"

Cade shifts his body so he lays next to me, his body pressing against mine. I'm so busy making sure I'm making him feel good that I don't notice him snaking his hand into the lace fabric of my panties.

"You're doing perfect," Cade says, his jaw clenching. "So perfect. Let me make you feel good, too."

I moan when one of his fingers lightly drifts over my sensitive clit.

"Does stroking my cock make you wet?"

My hand slows on him for the briefest of moments as I'm too caught up in his filthy words and his fingers teasing me between my thighs.

"I haven't even touched you and you're already soaking wet. Was it feeling how fucking hard I was for you that did it?" One finger slides in. I moan loudly, thankful that no one is around to hear. I don't want to hold back. Not tonight. Not with him.

"You going to answer me, Goldie?" He slowly slides his finger out. I take it as a threat. If I don't answer what has me turned on, then he'll just stop.

"I don't know," I confess. I've never felt this way about anyone. He's the only person to ever touch me intimately. Just being around him turns me on. Every little thing he does makes me feel things all over. The clench of his jaw, the muscles that ripple on his arms, the heat of his stare, all of it has me in a constant state of wanting all of him.

My hands hook into either side of his joggers. I've felt him, but I want to see him. I want everything.

Cade lifts his hips, allowing me to pull the joggers and boxers down his muscular thighs.

I sit back for a moment, missing the feeling of his fingers inside me, but I want to soak in this moment. I've laid in my bed so many nights, dreaming of what it would be like to be the object of his desire.

Now I have him. His copper eyes stare right at me, his irises black and filled with lust.

Cade grabs his cock, his long fingers wrap around his length as he strokes himself up and down.

Not only is Cade naked in my bed—he's looking up at me with so much want and need that for a moment, I can't move.

His eyes move from mine and head south. He licks his lips as his gaze focuses between my legs. Feeling bold, I strip myself of my own clothes. We're both completely naked, and I'm ready to find out what happens next.

Slowly, I push my knees apart so he can see all of me like I see all of him.

The two of us touch ourselves, intently watching the other. As he strokes himself up and down, I imagine how he felt in my hand. He's bigger than I imagined in every single way. In the thickness of his dick, making it hard for my fingertips to even touch as I held him. In how long it took me to go from the tip of his length to the base. I still don't know how it'll ever fit inside me, but I'm eager to try.

Two of my own fingers slip inside myself. These two fingers are nowhere near the size of his cock, and yet they stretch me.

"Are you making yourself ready to take me, Goldie?" His voice is gruff and filled with lust. The scratchiness of it is like a touch to intimate parts of me.

"I'm trying."

His smile takes me so off guard that I hadn't even noticed that he'd stopped touching himself. Before I know what's happening, he's grabbing me by the hips and throwing me down onto my comforter. Cade hovers above me. He still smiles, and it does so much to me. It isn't a sweet smile. It's almost predatory how he looks down at me.

"You did good getting yourself ready for me, baby." His thumb brushes my clit. My hips buck at his touch. "But I think you need more. Do you need my help to make you ready to take me?"

All I can do is nod. My senses are overloaded. His smell

surrounds me, his touch disarms me. But his dirty words, they undo me.

"Don't worry, I'll get you ready to take me." His words are uttered against my inner thigh. His breath is hot, the air caressing my clit. He pushes one finger inside me. Once I'm accustomed to it, he sticks in another.

I moan, my head rocking back and forth at feeling so full of him. "God, Goldie, you're so wet. Your pussy is just begging to take me."

My eyes squeeze shut. Before I can respond, a third finger joins in. It's too much. He's too much. I can barely take three of his fingers, there's no way I'll be able to take his cock.

"Cade." I moan, my fingers grasping the fabric of my comforter.

"Yes, baby?"

"I can't…"

"You can do it," he encourages. His tongue glides against my clit. He's mixing pleasure with the pain, totally overwhelming my senses.

Cade has made me come many times before. I've shouted his name in pleasure more times than I could keep track of, but I've never been this unglued for him. My moans ricochet through the room. I don't hold back. I *can't* hold back. He's stretching me and licking me and it's all too much.

"Good girl," he praises. I manage to open my eyes and look down at him. Our eyes connect immediately. He watches me with fervent passion. There's wetness all around his mouth that I think is *me*.

I'm so turned on right now. But I want more. I want more of him.

"Cade," I plead, pushing up on my elbows.

"Yes?"

My eyes flick to his cock, my tongue peeking out to wet my lips. "Can I…"

His fingers slide out of me before he runs his palm up and down his length. "You want to suck my dick, baby?"

His gaze settles on my mouth. "I'm so fucking hard at the thought of you taking my cock in your mouth, Goldie."

That's all the encouragement I need. I push up, my clit throbbing in protest at the loss of his fingers and mouth. He had me so close to an orgasm, but I couldn't wait another second before learning what it feels like to push him down my throat. I want to see him unravel under my mouth the same way I do under his.

Cade lets me push his broad shoulders into the mattress. His eyes are hooded as he watches me closely. His dick stands at attention, ready for me to take it. Before I can put it in my mouth, Cade's hands are falling to either side of my waist. He pins me down, not allowing me to lean forward and do what I've been dreaming about.

"We have one slight problem."

"What?"

"I'm so fucking ready to feel your mouth try to take all of me, but I'm still not done getting you ready to take me in your pussy."

"So..."

His teeth rake over his lip. "So what's going to happen is you're going to ride my face while you suck my cock, Goldie."

"How does that even..."

Cade takes control. He spins me around, guiding my hips up his body. I don't know why, but I feel so much more shy now that I'm hovering over him. Cade's hands push my knees out, making my body lower until I'm lined up perfectly with his mouth.

"Fuck my face while I fuck your mouth," he demands, his warm palms running down my ass.

I brace my body with one hand next to his hip. My other one grabs the base of his shaft. It jerks in my hand.

"Just like that. Get familiar with it. I'm going to bury my face in your pussy now, Goldie. Take your time with my cock. Fuck, I know I could spend forever getting to know this sweet cunt of yours."

Every single one of my firsts have been with Cade Jennings, and riding his face while he licks and laps at me is no different. I look at his dick hungrily, ready for Cade to take another first from me.

My hair falls around me, dusting the tops of his thighs as I lean in close. There's already so much pressure where Cade licks me. In this position it feels like his tongue goes so much deeper.

Not having any idea what I'm doing but wanting to make Cade feel as good as I do, I take the tip of him in my mouth. My tongue flattens against my teeth as I coax him in. I don't make it far down his length before I gag. I ignore my body's way of telling me it's too much and go even deeper.

Cade's finger circles around my clit as his tongue plunges into me. He's not using words, but I know he's encouraging me to keep going. The way his other hand grips me so tightly, I know that I must be doing something right. It must feel good because one of his hands digs so deep into my hip that I think I might have bruises from his fingertips tomorrow.

I take my time getting familiar with him—just like he told me to. I bob up and down, attempting to take him deeper down my throat each time. No matter how hard I try, I can't fit all of him. I use my hand to stroke the part of him I can't.

I don't even realize my hips are rocking against his face until he pulls away slightly. "You're so fucking hot, riding my face, taking what you want from my mouth baby, as you choke on my cock."

I moan around him. Tears prickle my eyelids from my attempts to take him as much as possible.

Cade licks me up and down. He hums against my clit. "You're dripping onto my face. Such a good girl."

My hips buck at his words combined with the feeling of his fingers and tongue caressing me. I had no idea it'd feel *this* good. That I could busy myself with taking his cock down my throat while also relishing in the feeling of him bringing me close to a release.

"I'm going to come," I tell Cade, trying to pull myself away from him. He doesn't let me, he pulls my body to his face, sealing his mouth to my clit.

"Come all over my face while you suck my cock."

Chapter 36
CADE
age twenty-two

MARE'S THIGHS shake in my hold. I pin her to my mouth, wanting to feel every single rock of her hips and spasm of her orgasm as she comes against my tongue. I can tell by her moans that she's close. Her attempts to get away from me are futile. I'm going to taste every single moment of her orgasm.

My fingers dig into her hips as she shoves my length down her throat. She's taking me deeper than I thought she could. She gags every time my head hits the back of her throat. It does nothing to stop her. If anything, she seems turned on by the feel of me testing her limits.

If she keeps up at it, I'll be coming down her throat. As tempting as that sounds, now that I'm confident she wants to go all the way, I want to come while my cock is buried inside her.

"Cade." Her moans are the sexiest thing I've ever heard. They're so loud and untamed. She isn't embarrassed to let me know how good it feels.

She rocks back and forth against my face, taking what she wants from me as she's sent over the edge. I feel her pussy greedily wrap around my fingers as she comes. Wetness coats my tongue as she screams out in ecstasy, the sounds muffled due to my shaft being shoved down her throat.

Mare does exactly as she's told. She chokes on my cock as her pussy shutters with pleasure against my tongue. I let her ride out the orgasm, not allowing my tongue to let up until I'm confident she's enjoyed every second of the release.

I stop at the same moment she pulls her mouth off me. My cock throbs, already missing her mouth wrapped around it. It jolts at the thought of going from her warm mouth to her sweet pussy.

"Oh my god," Mare pants. She slides to my side, her head falling next to mine on the pillow.

Our sides press against one another as I inch my mouth closer to hers. "Did you like fucking my face, baby?"

She bites her lip and nods. "I didn't know I'd like it so much."

My thumb brushes over her cheekbone. Her lips are red and puffy from stretching around me. It's the hottest fucking sight mixed with the flush to her cheeks from her orgasm.

"Which part? My face buried in your pussy or you gagging on my cock? Taking me as deep as you can?"

"Taking you," she answers, pressing a kiss to my lips. "Or maybe both."

I laugh. "Good answer."

"Cade?"

"Yeah, baby?"

"I'm ready."

"Ready for what?"

"Ready for you to fuck me."

She sounds so innocent, saying such filthy words.

I slide off the bed for a moment, fishing a condom out of my wallet. I hadn't expected for things to happen tonight, but with how much Mare has been saying she wants me to be the one to take her virginity, I wanted to be ready just in case.

Using my teeth, I rip open the wrapper and pull out the condom. We make eye contact as I slide it on. She watches me hungrily. Her breaths are heavy as her thighs rub together for some relief.

She's the most beautiful thing I've ever seen. I don't take it lightly that somehow she's chosen me for her first time. I don't think I'll ever deserve it, but fuck, I rage with jealousy at the thought of anyone else ever seeing her like this.

Climbing onto the bed, I settle between her legs. She's so wet that there's paths of wetness down her inner thighs where she's dripped with pleasure.

Mare watches closely as I pump up and down on my shaft, making sure the condom is well-fitted.

"You sure about this?" I'm desperate for her, to know that I'm the only man to ever do this, but I'd wait forever if she needed me to. I want her to be confident in giving me this.

"I've always wanted it to be you. I've never been more sure."

I hold eye contact with her, wanting to gauge her reaction to make sure she's telling the truth.

She looks back at me with so much want and desperation— something I'm sure she sees mirrored in my own features—that I know she wants this.

I glide the tip of my cock through her wetness. She moans even though I haven't pushed inside her in the slightest.

I pause, catching Mare's attention. "Why are you stopping?"

"I'm scared of hurting you."

"No physical pain could compare to the hurt of not having this moment with you. Fuck me, Cade. Make love to me and let me give you this. Let me have this. Hurt me because I promise it'll be the best pain of my life."

Her words unravel me. I haven't even inched inside her yet, and I know no one else could ever compare to her. She's my everything. My ruining, and I want everything she'll give me.

Before I push inside, I lean down and trap her lips between mine. Our hips rock against one another as we lose ourselves in a kiss. The kiss seems to say so much. Neither one of us has ever uttered the three words that will change everything, but the kiss seems to say it for the two of us.

I am hers. I'd do anything to keep her as mine.

At least I can hold onto this moment forever, knowing for

however fleeting this thing between us is, for a moment I was enough for her to give me everything.

"Tell me if it's too much, Goldie."

"Too much would never be enough with you."

She grabs my cock and lines me up perfectly with her pussy. It's all I need to take this all the way.

"Even so, tell me if you need me to stop." And then I coax myself into her, feeling her pussy mold around me perfectly.

Chapter 37
MARE
age nineteen

ALWAYS KNEW my first time would hurt. I wasn't quite expecting the intensity of it. But I also hadn't expected to like it so much, for there to be so much pleasure mixed with the pain.

"Breathe," Cade whispers. He feathers kisses along my forehead, my cheeks, my jaw as he coaxes himself inside me slowly.

My legs shake as I worry that I won't be able to take him. I look between us, seeing there's still so much of him left.

"Say the word and I'll stop."

I shake my head, my eyes burning from tears forming in my eyes. The tears might be from the pain, but I think it's also knowing that I finally get this with the man I've loved for what seems like my entire life.

"No, please, don't stop. Keep going."

One of his hands drifts down my body until his thumb brushes over my clit. It sends ripples of pleasure down my body, distracting me from the pain of him fitting himself inside me.

"This next part might hurt, baby," Cade starts, his thumb picking up pace against my clit. "But I promise to make you feel good, okay? It'll hurt, but I'm going to worship that pretty pussy of yours the way it deserves."

My hands find his back, my nails digging into the taut muscles. I'm ready, so ready. I grind my hips, a silent plea for him to do it.

Cade's lips move from my mouth to my neck. He kisses my neck roughly, his teeth grazing my throat.

"You're so fucking tight, baby," he mutters. "Your pussy is molding so perfectly to my cock. It knows my body belongs to yours and yours belongs to mine."

He uses dirty words and the slight pain of his teeth on my skin to try and distract me from him breaking the last barrier between us.

Pain erupts through my body as he pushes through, breaking through the last thing that kept me from fully being his.

Now, I'm his in every single way.

I can't help the tears that fall from my eyes as he slowly pushes all the way in. I don't think they're from the sting of him inside me. They're from the sweet way he distracts me by switching between muttering sweet and dirty things in my ear.

"That's it. God, you're doing so good. You feel too fucking good, too fucking perfect for me."

He moves his hips, pulling out before slowly pushing back inside.

"Faster," I plead, my back slightly arching to try and fit him deeper.

The pain hasn't gone away, it's still there, but the thing I feel most is the pleasure from his thumb against my clit and the intimate way his lips travel over the hollow of my throat.

"Can you handle it?"

"Anything for you."

He picks up pace, doing as I asked. I can feel myself stretch around him, my body doing its best to take as much of him as possible. I've never felt so connected with somebody in my entire life. I want to memorize the feel of his body in mine, to never forget what it feels like to join our bodies as one.

Cade props himself up with one hand, but the other cups my face gently. His fingers drift to the base of my neck as he rocks in and out of me. His face is so close I can't see anything but him.

"You're so tight." He groans, his hips hitting my inner thighs as he thrusts inside me. "You doing okay, baby?"

"I'm perfect."

"So goddamn perfect."

I moan at his words. His hips still after he's pushed as deep as he can go. He lets my body adjust to him.

Cade's fingertips thread in the strands of my hair as he pulls our faces close together. I breathe in his air as he breathes in mine. "You're so fucking perfect," he mutters against my lips. We don't kiss, but the way his lips move against mine with his words, it almost feels like we are. "You're so perfect that you've ruined me for anyone else, Goldie."

He thrusts in and out of me, his hips moving slowly but pushing deep.

"Cade." I moan and he steals the sound from my lips. His tongue thrusts inside my mouth at the same time he buries his cock inside me. It's like he's trying to get back at me for ruining him. If he only knew it wasn't necessary. I've been ruined for anyone else except Cade Jennings for as long as I can remember.

"Say my name like that again and I won't be able to keep being gentle." His forehead collapses against mine. I can tell that his entire body is coiled tight. He's holding back. He doesn't want to hurt me.

"I don't want gentle." I wiggle my hips to show him that the last thing I want is for him to hold back.

Cade groans. He pushes in and out of me once—hard. He watches me closely. The moan that comes from my lips isn't one in agony, it's from pure ecstasy.

This is the version of Cade I want. I don't want the soft, muddled down version. I want the raw and unhinged one.

My hands find either side of his face, cupping his cheeks tenderly. "Please," I beg.

He holds onto my face for dear life. His mouth fuses to mine, and then he does just as I ask. He sets a punishing rhythm with his hips. It isn't fast, but it isn't slow. It's somewhere in the middle, a pace that makes my toes curl against my comforter. Cade grabs my thighs, wrapping my legs around his waist. It allows him deeper, the sensations driving me wild.

The kiss is wild. It's lips and tongues and teeth, both of us trying to get as much as we can from each other. I didn't know if it'd feel good enough for an orgasm to build, but he pushes inside so perfectly that pressure begins to build between my legs.

"You going to come for me, baby?"

I moan against his mouth. I can't form words as he brings me to the brink of an orgasm.

"Your pussy fits me so perfectly, takes me so greedily, that I'm going to come. But not until I feel your perfect cunt squeezing me. Not until I know I made you come first."

His words send me over the edge. I scream, my hips bucking back and forth as the strongest orgasm rips through me. It feels like my entire body is lit with bliss as I ride out the orgasm.

"Fuck, yes, baby. Good girl, coming so hard you're going to make me come."

I'm breathless from the orgasm he gave me. My chest hits his as his tongue plunges into mine. I love that I can taste every single one of his moans as he unravels. His body tightens against mine as he rides out the waves of his release.

It takes both of us a moment to regain ourselves. We clutch each other, our bodies so intertwined I don't know where his begins and where mine ends.

Cade sighs and pulls his face away from mine just enough to look me in the eyes. "Tell me it was as perfect for you as it was for me."

Chapter 38
CADE
age twenty-two

"CADE," Mare says breathlessly. "I didn't know it could be so perfect."

My heart hammers against my chest from her words. I don't know how to feel in this moment. My senses are on overload as I try to process what just happened between us.

Perfection feels like such an overused word to describe what just happened.

I pull out of her slowly, trying my best not to hurt her with the movement.

"Are you feeling okay?"

Mare nods, pushing hair out of her face. Her nipples are hard, her breasts heavy. If I didn't know how sore she must be, the sight of her tits so heavy and desperate to be tasted and teased would have me playing with them. I'd give them ample attention until she was ready to take me again.

"Did I hurt you?"

Her smile is breathtaking. It's like a punch to the gut to have a woman like Mare look at you like that. It's something you want to keep and cherish forever, but terrifying when you know you nowhere near deserve it. She runs her thumb along my jawline. There's so much affection in her eyes. "You didn't do anything I didn't ask you to do."

"You aren't answering my question."

"Is it that or is it that you aren't listening to my answer?"

I laugh. Fuck. I love her. I love her so goddamn much my heart hurts.

The only thing I can think to do at the moment is to kiss her. I don't want to tell her I've fallen in love with her weeks before she's supposed to leave. I don't want to make her feel guilty for wanting to leave. But fuck, the words are on the tip of my tongue. I kiss her instead of confessing my love to her.

Maybe I still do that, with the fervent way my lips press against hers—desperate and hungry for anything she'll give me.

Eventually, I have to stop the kiss before it gets too heated.

Pulling away, I nip at her lips playfully. I want to take care of her after what just happened between us. "It's time to get up."

She pushes up on her elbows, giving me a confused look. I turn slightly, obstructing her view as I pull the condom off and toss it into a small trash can under her desk.

"Why do we need to get up?"

Climbing back on the bed, I pull her body against mine until I'm cradling her body to me. One hand supports her weight underneath the backs of her knees while the other goes underneath one of her arms. "We're getting up because I want to take care of you."

"And giving me the best orgasm of my life wasn't taking care of me?"

Her comment catches me off guard. I laugh, shaking my head at her. "Technically, I think it was two orgasms. That counts too, but I know you must be sore and I want to help with that."

I carry her into her small bathroom. I couldn't remember if there was a bath in here or not, but I'm happy to find an old claw-foot tub nestled into the corner. I set Mare down on the corner of the tub before reaching forward and turning the water on. As it begins to run, I turn to face her.

"Do you want bubbles or something in there?" My eyes rake over her bathroom, wondering if she even has any in here or not.

Mare smiles. "I'd love bubbles." She points to a little basket that sits on top of a small table. I reach for it, finding multiple bottles inside. I pull them out until I find the one labeled as bubble bath and pour it in until bubbles develop.

The water fills the tub enough for Mare to get in. I stick my hand in the water, testing the temperature. "Ready to get in?"

She steps toward me. I reach out, grabbing her hand to help steady her as she lifts a leg and steps inside. Bubbles gather around her body as she takes a seat.

"How's the temperature?"

"You tell me."

"I'm not the one taking a bath."

"But you should be. Get in here with me." Mare reaches over the edge of the tub, water droplets falling to the floor with the movement.

"This bath was for you, not me."

"I don't want to take a bath alone." She attempts to keep her hair out of the water, but it's no use. Eventually she gives up trying to pile it on top of her hair and lets the ends fall into the bubbly water.

I know her well enough to know how persistent she is. I could stand here and argue with her, or I could just get in because the thought of feeling her naked body next to mine is too hard to resist.

"Why do I never find myself saying no to you, Goldie?"

"I have my theories." She bites her lip playfully as I step into the water. It's hot, but not too much. It's the perfect temperature. Mare leans forward, giving me room to squeeze behind her. The bathtub isn't that big, so fitting my large body even with her small one is difficult. We make it work.

Peace settles over my body as her head falls to my chest. Her legs are on top of mine, her toes sticking out of the bubbles slightly. She uses her foot to turn off the water once the bath is almost filled to the brim.

I lazily draw shapes on the tops of her forearms. "So, are you going to tell me your theories?"

She giggles. It's the most perfect sound. I can feel it up against my chest. "I think I'll keep them to myself...for now."

I grunt, once again fighting the urge to tell her that I'm madly in love with her. It's one of those things that once you see it, you can't unsee it. That's my love for her. I think it's been there all along. I just hadn't known until she forced me to confront it.

Reaching over my shoulder, I grab the little basket of bath items. I grab a bottle of soap and a washcloth. I dip the washcloth in the warm water and squeeze soap onto it. Mare doesn't say anything. She keeps her back pressed to mine, her eyes trained ahead as I swipe the washcloth across her skin.

"How are you feeling?"

"Happy."

My hand stills. That wasn't what I meant when I asked her that, but her words still steal my attention.

Because I've never felt happier. But I've also never felt more sad—more scared. Because happiness can be fleeting, and if she brings this much happiness, what happens when she leaves? Her leaving is inevitable. The date of her move is looming.

I'll lose her and Pippa at the same time.

It's not something I want to think about.

"Are you happy, Cade?"

"Yeah, Goldie," I manage to get out. "I am."

She pulls her knees to her chest and rests her cheek on her knee. Her smile is wide and bright. "Then I don't just feel happy. I feel perfect. Now stop worrying about me."

Chapter 39
MARE
present

NERVES COURSE through my body as I get off the bed and tiptoe to my bedroom door, my mind fixed on making my way to Cade. I know I shouldn't be doing this. Before anything else happens between us, we need to have a long talk about what we are, about what's happening between us. But I doubt that'll happen.

We're like magnets. Unable to deny the temptation between us, no matter how hard we fight it.

I stop in front of my door, wondering if maybe I shouldn't go to him. Even Pippa could tell something was wrong with me when we had dinner tonight. She kept asking me why I was acting weird and I couldn't answer her. Her questions were just another reminder of something else Cade and I need to talk about.

If we're going to keep doing this, we need to tell Pippa.

I'm second guessing everything that's happening between Cade and I when my door is pushed open.

"I couldn't wait a second longer," he growls out. Before I can respond, he grabs me by the hips and pulls me into his body. The door slams shut, making my heart race.

"Cade," I scold, "Pippa could've heard that."

He grabs both sides of my face and backs me into the closed door. God, why does he have to look so good in the moonlight shining through my window? "I really don't care if Pippa hears. What I do care about is the fact I had to come find you."

I melt into his touch as he tilts my head sideways, giving himself better access to my throat. He kisses along my jaw, his lips caressing the tender spot underneath my ear.

"I was seconds away from showing up at your door," I confess.

"About fucking time."

"You had to give me time to let Pippa go to bed. Plus, you put me in the room farthest away from anything in the house."

"I didn't trust myself around you, Goldie. For good reason, look at us."

My eyes flutter shut as he nips at my skin. A moan falls from my lips when his tongue caresses away the pain from the bite. "What do you mean?"

"You'll probably break my fucking heart again, yet here I am, unable to resist you."

"Cade." My hands find his chest. I mean to push him away, but I end up pulling him closer instead.

"I don't want to do it again." He presses his hips against me —hard—keeping me pinned to the door. I wouldn't move even if he gave me the space to do it.

"Do what?"

"Hate you."

I arch into him as his teeth rake against my tender skin. "You've already told me you didn't hate me."

"I wanted to."

"I wanted to hate you, too."

He pulls his face close to mine. It's like he's searching for every little secret of mine when he stares into mine. "And did you?"

My heart feels heavy in my chest. It aches at the memory of the last time I saw him. I remember sobbing in the airport; strangers stood around and gawked at me as I walked away from him. The truth was, I didn't want to leave his arms, but he left me no choice. He didn't love me, and I couldn't fight for us alone. He made me walk away from *us* when I thought we'd be more than just one summer.

"Goldie." He towers over me, his body caging mine in as he stares into my soul. "Answer me."

"I don't know," I whisper. "I don't know if I actually hated you or if I hated what you did to us. Does it matter?"

"Why wouldn't it matter?"

"Because either way, things ended up the way they did. Whether I hated you or not, you hurt me. You were supposed to be the person who didn't hurt me. And you ended up being the person who hurt me the most."

Cade grabs the fabric of my shorts, sliding them down the tips of my thighs. I let him do it because I'm not strong enough to deny him. "I'd let you hurt me time and time again if it meant you'd eventually find your way back to me."

He holds me steady as I step out of my shorts. I don't pay attention to where he discards them. I'm too caught up in how he looks at me to pay attention to anything else. Cade stares at me hungrily. His gaze is possessive. He falls to his knees as his hands skim the sides of my hips.

"I didn't mean to hurt you. I didn't think you'd care," I confess.

"Are these more lies you tell yourself to forgive yourself?"

Before I can get any words out, he lifts one of my legs and drapes it over his shoulder. He nibbles and bites against the inside of my knee. I moan, my hands finding his shoulders to keep myself upright. "If I knew you felt the same, I would've been on the first flight back."

His tongue moves up my inner thigh. His breath is hot against my skin. He's so close to where I ache for his touch, yet it feels like he's so far away. "That's why I didn't want to tell you. I didn't want you to risk your dreams for me."

"Don't you know you've always been my biggest dream?"

He sighs, his face incredibly close to my throbbing clit. If he just leaned a little closer, I'd feel his touch. I'd feel relief. He doesn't give it to me. He makes me wait, drawing it out in pure torture. "I didn't believe it back then."

Cade presses a kiss right next to my clit. My knees shake in anticipation. His lips are too gentle against me. I want them rough and wild, unrelenting until I'm coming apart at the seams for him. "I won't make the same mistake again."

"What mistake?"

"Letting you leave me." His tongue presses against my clit, circling it slowly. He must not want an answer from me because he becomes unhinged. He forces his head between my legs, his tongue plunging deep inside me.

My head hits the door behind me with a loud thud. I'm too caught up in the way he makes me feel to be worried about who could hear us.

It's the effect he has on me. I stop seeing reason around him. I forget how much hurt we've caused each other, how long it took to try and get over him. My heel digs into his back in an attempt to pull him closer even though his face is buried inside me.

Cade proves a point with his tongue. He proves that I have no hope of being anyone's other than his. My heart, body—my entire being—is his. At one point, I may have actually hated him. Or maybe I hated how much I was his, even when I thought he didn't want to be mine.

He's making things clear as ever now. I'm his, and he's mine, but there's still so much we have to figure out.

Right now, it doesn't matter. Everything could blow up in our faces tomorrow, and it probably will, but for tonight, we can pretend. My hips buck as pressure begins to build. I know my fingers aren't gentle as they rake across his scalp, but he doesn't seem to mind. He licks and laps at me, a loud growl of pleasure coming from his lips. His fingertips dig into my skin as he keeps one hand on my inner thigh, keeping me wide open for him. The position allows his tongue to go so deep, hitting the spot that sends me over the edge.

I moan as an orgasm ricochets through my body. I bite down on my lips, trying to stay quiet as he doesn't let up. He makes no attempts to slow his tongue, to keep me quiet. He works my clit, milking the orgasm for everything I've got. He pulls his face from between my thighs, his mouth glistening from my cum. I'm seconds away from my knees giving out beneath me.

As if he could read my mind, Cade stands up and lifts me by my hips. My legs wrap around him as he walks us to the bed. He lays me down gently. His smell surrounds me, from his body hovering above me and from the sheets below me. I can't escape it, and I don't want to.

His hands are warm as they drift underneath the T-shirt I'd worn to bed. I let him pull the fabric off my body slowly. I'm expecting him to say something. The room is silent except for our rushed, heavy breaths. Cade slides off the bed, keeping eye contact with me as he slides his pajama pants off. He wears nothing beneath. I'm met with this sight of his hard, thick cock. It stands at attention, the tip wet with precum that glistens from the moonlight that drifts through the window.

His chest pulls in, his muscles taut with the movement. He's so fucking perfect, his hard, chiseled muscles exactly what a romance novelist's dreams are made of. My eyes are traveling over his rippling ab muscles when Cade finally breaks the silence.

"Do you see this?"

"See what?"

"How hard I am for you?"

Heat pools in my cheeks and between my legs. My arousal still coats his face, and yet I'm blushing from his words, unable to look where he wants me to.

"Look at my cock, Goldie."

My eyes meet his. They're dark and clouded, his pupils so wide I can barely see his amber-colored irises anymore. He stares right back at me, challenging me to listen to him. I can't help it, there's so much desire in his features that I have to do as I'm told.

I want to see how much he wants me. I want to know I'm not the only one feeling this way.

I take my time, memorizing every single muscle on his body before my gaze focuses on where he wants me to.

His fingers wrap around the base of his shaft. He pumps up and down, keeping my attention.

"Do you see what you do to me?"

I think about the wetness between my legs, the proof still coating his face of what he also does to me.

He lets go, his dick still pointing toward the ceiling with how hard it is. Cade climbs onto the bed, settling himself between my legs.

"You can't hide what I do to you," he notes, running the tip of his cock against my clit. "I can see how wet you are for me, baby. I can still taste it." He pushes in a little deeper, making me moan in pleasure. "Our bodies can't lie to each other. I'm wrecked for you, and despite you fighting it every chance you get, I know you're wrecked for me, too."

My eyes squeeze shut. His words, his touch, the feelings between us, are just too much for me to handle.

"Look at me," he demands, his voice closer this time.

I close my eyes even tighter. I can't look at him, not with the overwhelming sense of passion I'm feeling. If I look at him, I might not ever leave this bed. I might stay here forever, never writing another word, just to keep things like this and I know I can't do that. I know I can't lose myself, I can't lose the parts of me I'm proud of that've developed since the moment I left this town—since he told me to leave.

I've laid in his bed so many nights of my life. He's always been my comfort, my safe space. I was young and naïve to think that I'd ever find this same feeling with anyone else. The problem is, I did leave this town. I did leave him. I followed my dreams and I'm happy, despite the missing piece of me that had always stayed behind with him.

Now I'm faced with the catastrophic realization that the dream I thought I had—the big city, the busy lifestyle—might not have been my dream at all.

He roughly grabs me by the chin. It takes me by surprise so much that my eyes pop open.

Cade's quiet at first, letting our bodies do the talking. He slides deeper inside me. His actions are slow but powerful. I feel him everywhere, my body gladly stretching to fit him, to connect our bodies. He rocks in and out of me as a moan falls from my lips.

"I'm yours." One thrust. "I love you." Another thrust. "I won't survive if I lose you again."

Chapter 40
CADE
present

I KNEW I was making the mistake of a lifetime when I watched Mare get on that plane. Every part of me wanted to chase her, to beg her to stay in Sutten and find a way to make her dreams come true from our familiar small town.

I couldn't do it. I couldn't ask her to sacrifice her dreams to stay with me.

Every day after that day, I've wondered what would've happened between us if I risked telling her how I felt.

I told myself if she ever came back that I wouldn't hide it anymore. But year after year, she didn't come back.

All I felt when she first returned to Sutten was anger. Trapped behind all of the anger was hurt, and behind that hurt was the love I've always had for her.

You don't stop loving someone even after they break your heart. You can't stop loving them, no matter what damage was done. I can only hope the same can be said for her. I know I broke her heart, I'm ready to plead with her and hope I kept her love.

Mare's legs shake against my sides, her entire body trembling as I push my way in.

"I love you," I repeat. "My love for you won't go down without a fight this time." I plunge in and out of her. No part of me wants to be gentle but I want to leave my mark all over her. I want her to feel me with everything she does, to be reminded of who owns her. She can fight us all she wants—I've done the same—but it's no use.

Marigold and I are undeniable. We'll always come back to each other. It's just how we work.

"Cade." She moans, her hands grabbing at the sheets to give herself something to hold on to.

I push off the bed, grabbing one of her legs and draping it over my shoulder. The position allows me even deeper inside her. Her pussy clenches around me, her moans filling the space between us.

I let my hand drift down her body, loving the view I have of her beneath me. From up here, I can see every reaction as I pound into her. Each time I push all the way in, her head leans back and her back arches. It gives me the perfect view of her round tits. They bounce up and down with each thrust, her hard, pink nipples begging to be played with.

My hand drifts across her skin until I get a handful of her perky tit. I brush my thumb over her nipple, my cock twitching inside her at the sound of her moans. I pinch, moving the peaked bud between my thumb and pointer finger.

I push deeper, testing her limits. I hold her leg in one hand, my fingers anything but gentle as they dig into her calf muscles. Pushing her leg into her chest, I do whatever it takes to make sure she feels me everywhere. I tug at her nipple, soaking in the way she moans at the same time her pussy hugs me tighter.

"You're it for me," I whisper into the dark. "You've *always* been it for me."

"It's always been you," she responds, her voice strained from the way she greedily takes my cock.

My words are soft and full of my love. My thrusts are angry and full of desperation. By the end of tonight, I want her to be fully aware that I won't let us end again. I'll do whatever it takes to have the chance to love her forever.

I look down, watching my cock push in and out of her. She's

so wet, the evidence all over both of us. Moving on from her perfect nipples, I trace all the way down her sculpted stomach until I'm brushing over her clit.

Her hands immediately find her tits. She palms them, her fingers pinching her perfect, peaked nipples.

"I'm ruined by this pretty pussy of yours."

"Oh god." I press my thumb into her clit, feeling myself move in and out of her.

"Tell me your cunt is ruined for me."

"I—" Her words break off as my thumb begins to do circles against her clit.

"I know, baby," I tell her, captivated by watching my cock push in and out of her. She's so pink and swollen, her pussy just begging to be fucked by me. "You're so goddamn wet that your cum drips down my cock. Your pussy gives you away, Goldie. I know I own it. I know you're all fucking mine."

"I'm yours. You're mine."

"Damn fucking straight. Now scream my name and come around my cock."

She plays with her tits as I play with her clit. Her moans get louder and louder. She pants as I claim her pussy. My thumb speeds up when I know she's close. It sends her over the edge.

Her moans are so loud that it even takes me by surprise. She chants my name over and over again, her hips rocking up and down as I don't stop my pace. Her breath is hot against my palm as I shove my hand against her mouth to keep her quiet.

Fuck, her moans are so powerfully enthusiastic that I could come at any fucking moment.

I slow slightly, knowing I'm not done with her yet. I know I can take more from her, and that's what I plan on doing. I don't plan on *ever* being done with her.

"Fuck, baby." I look down between us. "Look at you being such a good fucking girl, coating my cock in your cum. You're doing so fucking good at making sure my cock is nice and wet, making it easier to slide into your perfect pussy."

Her eyes squeeze shut as she moans. I've always loved how much my words drove her wild.

Goldie doesn't want me to be quiet. She goes fucking wild for every single one of my filthy words.

I'm generous and give her a few seconds to recover. Once her time is up, I'm leaning down and lifting her off the mattress. I lift her knees over my thighs, sitting her on my lap. We're face to face. I can see the flush to her cheeks as I lean in and plunge my tongue into her mouth.

I taste every single one of her moans. Grabbing her by the hips, I lift her up and down, making her ride my dick.

"Fuck," I groan against her lips. Her ass hits my thighs each time I lower her, making a slapping sound through the room. "You feel too fucking perfect."

"You're so big," she moans, clutching my shoulders. "So deep," she pants. Her hips rock against me. Her movements mixed with the way I bounce her up and down on my cock, feels way too fucking good. My balls tighten, and I know it won't be long until I can't fight the orgasm any longer.

"Take my cock as deep as you can, baby. It's time for you to come again." I slow my pace, being more mindful of how deep she takes me. I force her hips down as I plunge myself even deeper into that perfect cunt of hers.

Her thighs shake. Tendrils of her long, blonde hair hit the mattress as her head falls backward with an untamed moan. I want to fucking wrap my fingers in the strands, but I can't let go of her hips. I can't stop pounding into her. Not until my cum is mixed with hers and is leaking from between her thighs.

"Kiss me," I grunt. "Let me taste your fucking screams while I fill your pussy."

Mare opens her mouth, and I don't hesitate. Our teeth hit as we ravish each other's mouths. I moan into her mouth and she moans into mine as we're both sent into pure bliss.

Chapter 41
MARE
age nineteen

"I CAN'T BELIEVE we're actually doing this."

I plop down next to Pippa on her bed, joining her in staring at the ceiling. "I can't believe you're moving in to the dorms first. I know you're going to pick out the better bed."

Pippa turns her head to face me, a wide grin on her face. "I was going to pick the better bed to begin with."

I laugh. "I'm still a little jealous that you're arriving a few days earlier than me."

I'm lying. I'm not jealous in the slightest that Pippa is leaving Sutten early. If anything, I wish I could stay here a little longer. The idea of leaving Cade is getting harder and harder. I want to see the world with Pippa, I just wish I didn't have this feeling that doing that will be the end of Cade and me.

"What if I don't get the job?" Pippa chews on her bottom lip anxiously.

Sighing, I push off my elbows and turn to face her. Everyone that meets Pippa instantly falls in love with her. It's hard not to love Pippa. "You're going to get the job. They'd be stupid not to hire you."

Pippa mimics my position, the two of us lying on her bed facing each other. She traces the floral pattern of her comforter with her finger. "I know it's just a barista position, but I'm hoping they'll want me. And then eventually, maybe they'll even let me into the kitchen."

"You'll steamroll your way into the kitchen. I have no doubts." While I'm going to college to get a liberal arts degree in creative writing, Pippa is going for business management. Her dream is to one day open a bakery here in Sutten, and with her determination and a personality that everyone falls in love with, I have no doubt she'll achieve it. Her interview with our college town bakery and coffee shop is definitely a way for her to get a foot in the door in her industry.

I'm a little sad to not have her here with me these last few days before I join her at school. Both of her parents are going down with her to help her move. We were all supposed to go together, but Pippa got the interview at the last minute, and with Cade having to stay behind to hold down the ranch, I had to make up an excuse to be able to stay, too.

I want these last days with him. I want to broach the subject of what happens when I leave. I'm sad to see my best friend go, but happy about the extra time with Cade.

Most of all, I want us to make it long distance. But first, I have to make sure there even is an us.

Pippa flips to her stomach, her legs kicking at the air as she stares ahead of her. "My room looks a little sad all packed up."

I sit up, looking around her room. Two large suitcases sit near her door. "If you think your room looks sad, you should see mine."

Most of my belongings fit into my own two suitcases. There are some things packed into a few boxes that dad will have to store somewhere, but for the most part, I was able to fit every-thing into the bags the airline allows me to check.

"We'll have to get new stuff anyway. *First* we need to feel out the vibe of the campus. Is it normal to dress up every day for classes or can we just rock our leggings and hoodies and call it good?"

"You'll wear whatever you want."

Pippa winks at me. "Obviously."

Something catches her attention over my shoulder. She smiles, popping off the bed. I turn around to find Cade stepping into her room.

He looks good in a Jennings Ranch T-shirt with the sleeves cutoff, bringing way too much attention to his muscles. He holds a plaid shirt, one I'm hoping he's going to put on so I'm not so distracted by how much I want to jump his bones. His jeans are worn and faded, molding to his sculpted thighs and ass perfectly.

Damn. He really has no business looking this good when I can't do anything but smile awkwardly at him since Pippa is here to witness any interaction between us.

"Mom sent me up here to grab you," Cade explains. He risks a glance over at me, but quickly focuses back on Pippa.

I bite back a smile, remembering all the places on me his lips caressed last night.

Pippa whines, turning to face me with her bottom lip jutting out. She rushes toward me and leaps onto the bed before landing on top of me.

I scream, laughing, as Pippa envelopes me in the biggest hug. "I'm not ready to say goodbye."

We squeeze each other, a tangle of hair and limbs on her bed. "You'll see me in a few days," I encourage her. The words are meant to soothe me as well. Pippa and I aren't used to being away from each other like this. And even though I'm looking forward to spending my last days with Cade under the guise of not wanting to leave my dad too early, I'm going to miss Pippa like crazy.

"That's a few days too long. Why don't you just come with me?"

"You know I can't leave my dad yet."

She groans, clutching me tightly. "Maybe I don't need to do the interview."

I roll my eyes, pushing her off me so I can look her in the eye.

"Pippa, you can't cancel the interview. It's your first step at taking the bakery world by storm. Plus, this is your chance to have all the fun before your boring, responsible, friend comes to ruin the party." I reach out and rub a tear from her cheek.

She nods, looking up at her ceiling for a moment.

Cade clears his throat, catching both of our attention. He fixes the hat on his head, looking between the two of us. "What if Mare comes with us? I can bring her back. It could give the two of you more time together..."

"Yes!" Pippa squeals, tackling me to the bed all over again.

"You're choking her," Cade points out, humor in his voice as Pippa squeezes me with all her might.

I laugh when she finally pulls away, brushing pieces of hair out of my face.

"What do you say, Goldie? Keep me company on the drive back from the airport?"

My heart pounds against my chest when I meet Cade's eyes. I can't look away from him. He's being so obvious right in front of his sister, but I can't seem to care. I love the thought of riding back with him.

Cade and I have never been off the ranch together. This is our chance. After we drop Jasper, Linda, and Pippa off at the airport, we can do whatever we want.

"It'll be fun," Pippa interjects, wrapping an arm around my shoulder. "You'll survive the car ride home with Cade. Please see me off at the airport."

I bite my lip to try and hide how excited I am to ride back with Cade. The two of us share a look. His eyebrows rise to his hairline as he challenges me to give her an answer.

"Yeah, I *guess* I'll survive."

Chapter 42
MARE
age nineteen

"WHY ARE YOU SO QUIET?" I ask, plucking at a strand of my fraying cutoff shorts. Cade hasn't said a word to me since we said our goodbyes to his family.

I had all these visions for what it'd be like to finally go out in public with Cade. None of them included having him ignore me.

We both sit in the truck, idling on the side of the curb as people rush around us.

"Cade?" I press. Nerves settle in my stomach. He won't even look at me. His body is eerily still as he stares straight ahead.

He doesn't answer me. Instead, he shifts the car into drive and pulls away from the curb. I look in the mirror, watching the airport disappear behind us as I wonder what's going through his head.

Cade doesn't make me wait for long. As we're pulling onto the highway, he glances over at me.

"What are we doing?"

"It doesn't matter to me. I'm good going wherever you want to."

He shakes his head. "No. What are we doing with us, Goldie? You're leaving in two days. What the hell are we thinking?"

I try to get him to look at me again, but he's too focused on the road. His grip is so tight on the steering wheel that his knuckles are turning white. My mind races with so many answers, but he's caught me so off guard that I don't even know what to say.

"I don't think we were thinking. I think we were feeling, and I don't see anything wrong with that."

He laughs. It's bitter and cold, not the one I've fallen in love with. "That makes one of us. There's so many things I see wrong with it."

A pit forms in my stomach. I wish we weren't driving so he could look at me. I wish I didn't know him well enough to know that he's shutting down. He's shutting me out. "Like what?"

I know I shouldn't ask it. I know I don't want to hear whatever answer he gives me, but I can't help myself. I'm a masochist and I want to know every detail going through his head, even if his sudden change in demeanor is bound to cause me hurt.

"Like you're leaving. You're leaving and I'm staying and there's no way we can make this work with the distance between us."

"People do long distance all the time."

"People *try* long distance all the time," he corrects, pulling the car off at an unfamiliar exit. Wherever he's taking us, it isn't home. I don't even ask him where, I'm too caught up in the way he's breaking my heart. "People don't survive long distance all the time."

My bottom lip quivers as I try my best to not cry. I will *not* cry over him. I will not cry like this. Most of all, I won't let him do this to us.

Cade and I are different. We can survive this. I know my love for him is enough to survive anything. The problem is, I don't know if he feels the same.

"Don't do this," I beg. "This was supposed to be our first real date. Don't ruin it."

He lets out an angry sigh, pinching the bridge of his nose between his thumb and pointer finger. "God, I've fucked this up so bad," he mutters under his breath. His jaw clenches so tight I can hear his teeth grind against each other in the quiet cab of the truck.

"What does that mean?"

He pulls into the parking lot of a retail shopping center. Angrily, he shifts the car into park and finally faces me. The look in his eyes makes my heart stop. He looks at me cold and unattached. You'd have no idea that last night I was staring into those copper eyes as he looked at me in what I swore was love.

"It means I should've never let this happen between us. Do you hear yourself? I took your virginity and I haven't even taken you on a real date. That's so fucked up. I've fucked up."

I jolt at his last words, at the regret in his tone. Tears spill down my cheeks, no matter how much I fight them. "I don't care. Every single one of our moments together have been perfect. I didn't need a date. I just need you."

He rakes his hands over his face. "Being at the airport made things real. In two days you'll be getting on that plane, and you'll say goodbye to Sutten."

"You make it sound like it's final."

"Isn't it? How often do you plan to come back?"

I shrug, quickly wiping the tears off my cheeks in hopes that he doesn't catch them. "I don't know. A lot? There's breaks, and summer, and I can even try to transfer at the end of the semester and move back."

"You don't want to move back."

"I can think for myself." My words are cold, but he made me this way. His sudden mood change has me feeling all sorts of emotions, most of all rage and despair. "Stop telling me what I do and don't want."

Cade stares at me. I'd give anything to know what runs through his head, but his walls have gone back up. His defenses are high, and he's retreating back to the Cade I knew before this summer. The one who was quiet and didn't tell me what he was thinking.

The Cade that looked at me like Pippa's friend, the person he grew up with, and not the girl he had feelings for.

Sighing, he opens his car door. I stare at him, my mouth hanging open as I try to piece together what's happening. My door swings open. He takes a step back, his arms folding across his chest.

"Follow me."

Chapter 43
CADE
age twenty-two

My boots scratch loud against the pavement as I rush toward the front doors of the building. I don't have to look behind me to know that Mare is following closely behind.

"I don't understand what we're doing here," she says at my back.

I ignore her, pulling the door open and ushering her inside.

She stops. "Answer me," she demands, her eyes roaming over the store.

Instead of answering her question, I grab her hand and tug on it. I pull her through the aisles until I find what we're looking for. Mare looks at the shelf hesitantly, looking at it, to me, and then back.

"Cade," she presses.

I read the words on a little plaque hanging on the shelf: *Fiction Bestsellers*. I point to it. "One day, you're going to be on this shelf, Goldie."

Her eyes soften slightly. When she tries to take a step closer to me, I take a step backward. I can't be this close to her right now. Not with what I'm about to say. Not with what I have to do. I have to do what's best for her.

I swallow past the lump in my throat. Since it hit me in the airport that she's days away from leaving, I've thought about what I want to say to her a lot. It's all I've thought about since the moment I hugged my family goodbye.

Mare is leaving too. Mare has to leave to follow her dreams. And I can't be the guy sending her off in the airport begging her to come back. I can't be the guy to hold her back.

"Tell me what's happening," Mare mutters, glancing over her shoulder at people that shop for books around us.

I sigh, tracing the top of the plaque. "You're going to make it on these shelves one day. Your books will be everywhere, and you're going to be this phenomenon. People will fall in love with you and your words because it's hard not to."

"Maybe."

"No. Not maybe. I know it'll happen. I know you. I know your talent. You're going to get there, Goldie. You're capable of achieving every single one of your dreams. But you can't do that from a small town like Sutten." My words break with the last sentence. I hate knowing that our lives are on different paths.

I hate knowing the best thing I can do for the woman I'm hopelessly in love with is to let her go.

Mare won't be the one to end it. It has to be me, and it fucking sucks to know that I have to hurt her.

"Cade, you're scaring me," Mare admits. This time, when she takes a step closer to me, I let her. I'm not strong enough to let her go completely. Not yet, not now. "This feels like the end."

When her arms wrap around my middle, I break. I pull her into me and clutch her to my chest. "You're going to do the biggest things. Everyone will know your name, and I can't wait to cheer you on."

"Be there with me," she says against my chest.

My eyes close. We're probably a show for those around us, just innocent bystanders trying to buy books. They don't know that I'm breaking inside or how much it hurts me to know I can't be the best for someone who is everything to me.

"You're meant to go, and I'm meant to stay."

I grab the back of her head, running my fingers through her hair as she softly cries into my chest. There's not much I can do but comfort her. I won't back down on this. I won't let her sacrifice her dreams for me. And there's no reality where I can leave the ranch, the one bearing my last name—the one that's been passed down in my family. So it leaves us with a heartbreaking conclusion.

No matter how perfect this summer was. No matter how perfect *we* are. A future for the two of us just isn't possible at the moment.

"It won't be long until your book sits on this shelf. I can't fucking wait to read it."

"No," she argues. "I don't care about that. I care about you. About us."

She pulls away and I cradle her face between my hands. "Remember me when you're famous?"

Her laugh is sad. Mine is too.

I press my lips to her forehead. "One day you'll thank me for this, Goldie."

Mare shakes her head, her hands fisting my T-shirt as she clutches me to her. "We're not done talking about this. I'm not giving up on us."

My eyes track over her. There are so many new freckles on her cheeks from the summer sun. I've kissed every single one of them. It's sad to know that any new ones on her face won't get a greeting from me.

It's sad to think she'll have a whole new life that won't include me in it.

"How about I get you home?" I grab her hand, not able to lose her completely just yet. "You need to finish packing."

DAD TAPS the tailgate of the Jennings Ranch work truck. He turns to face me, puffing his cheeks out with a large sigh. "Got everything you need?"

I give him a nod as I peer over his shoulder, searching for a familiar face.

My heart sinks when I don't see anyone else in sight. It's just me and my dad.

Sadness washes over me.

He's really going to do this. Cade isn't even going to say goodbye to me after everything that happened between us.

"Mare," my dad says cautiously. "You ready to go?"

"Yes," I lie. I'm nowhere near ready to leave. Not until I speak with Cade. Since we got back from dropping off his family at the airport, he hasn't spoken to me. I've tried multiple times, but he's been avoiding me. And with a ranch like this one, it hasn't been hard for him to do so.

During a fit of rage in the middle of the night last night, I stomped from the cabin all the way to the main house. I was ready to give Cade a piece of my mind, but when I went to open his door, it was locked.

That door is never locked.

I was too shocked by his clear line in the sand that I turned around. I cried the entire walk back to my house.

It was hard accepting he was doing this to us.

I'd hardly slept last night, but part of me thought he'd eventually show up to say goodbye.

Dad gets into the truck as I fight back tears. I'm seconds away from asking my dad if we can stop by the stables so I can try to find Cade one last time when I hear the familiar sound of an engine.

My heart skips seconds before Cade comes into view. He stops his truck behind Dad's. The truck's barely in park when Cade jumps out of it, his boots making a thumping sound on the gravel as he lands.

"Cade?" Dad asks, getting out of the truck. He scratches his head. "What are you doing here?"

Cade looks at me. There's so much pain in his eyes. The bags under his eyes rival mine.

Does he know I came to see him last night? Has this been as hard on him as it has been me?

He tears his eyes from mine, his broad shoulders rising with a large sigh. "I was looking for you, sir."

"What for?"

"What is it?"

"Rhett is looking for you. I asked him if there was something I could do, but he said he needed to speak with you since my dad is gone."

Dad sighs, his hands finding his hips. "Don't they know I have to drop Mare off at the airport?"

"How about I do it?"

My stomach drops at his words. I don't know if it's in fear or excitement. Now with Cade near, I don't know what to do. I don't know if I want him to be the one to take me to the airport.

Dad gives me a hesitant look. I can tell by his demeanor he'd much rather go help with something on the ranch than drive me the two hours to the airport. It stings a little, to see it so clearly written on his face.

"What do you think?" Dad watches me closely. I feel numb

staring into his eyes. I should want my dad, my only living parent, to be the one to take me to the airport. We should have some grand goodbye where he instills some kind of wisdom into me like...*don't get pregnant* or *remember to keep the bear spray handy!* I think Momma's death has done a number on both of us. Goodbyes seem final, and no matter the complicated relationship Dad and I share, it's hard to say goodbye to him.

"Mare?" Dad prods, breaking me from my thoughts.

I jolt. "If you're needed here, I'm fine with Cade taking me."

I don't look at Cade, instead I keep my focus on my dad. He watches me carefully. His lips turn down in a frown as he walks toward me. "I've never been very good at goodbyes," Dad mumbles, pulling me into his chest.

I breathe in, relishing in the familiar scent of him. Our history is complicated and not the typical one you see between a father and daughter, but he still smells like home. He smells the same way he did when I was a child. When Momma was alive and we were all happy.

I wrap my arms around his middle and squeeze. "It won't be goodbye for long. I'm expecting you to come visit me. It's time you get a little city in you."

Dad laughs in my hold. He kisses the top of my hair. "Only for you."

We're silent for a few more minutes as we hold each other tight. I'm the one to pull away first, but only far enough to look him in the eyes.

"I love you." My throat feels tight. It's harder to say goodbye to him than I thought it'd be.

"I love you, kid," he responds. His voice is gruff and there's tears welling up in his eyes. I squeeze one more time before pulling away. I know Dad wouldn't want to cry in front of us, so I stop the goodbye before it happens.

Turning my head, I find Cade putting my second suitcase in his truck. I was so locked in the moment with Dad that I didn't notice what Cade was doing.

"I'll get her there safely," Cade assures my dad.

Dad nods, looking at me. "Don't forget to tell me when you land."

I nod my head. "Love you."

Cade doesn't say anything to me. He just rounds the back of the truck and opens the passenger door for me.

"Thank you," I whisper, trying to catch his gaze. He doesn't give it to me. As soon as I'm safe in the front seat, he softly shuts the door.

In the time it takes for him to come around the front and slide in on his side, I wonder if this was a good idea after all.

Chapter 45
MARE
age nineteen

CADE BARELY LOOKS AT ME. With each minute that ticks by, I expect him to say something, but he doesn't. He's silent, and I'm so upset that he'd go to such great lengths to take me to the airport without planning to say a damn thing to me.

Neither of us say a word.

Not on the long drive to the airport.

Not when he parks the car in the unloading zone.

He doesn't even look at me until he's handing me one of my suitcases.

I've had two days to get angry. I've had two hours to get angrier and angrier.

How dare he downplay us? How dare he pretend that we weren't happy together a week ago?

How dare he let me leave without even fighting for me —for *us*.

"So that's it, huh?" My words are angry and untamed. He's given me a long time to think about what I want to say to him, and I won't hold back.

Clearly he has no intention of fighting for us, so I might as well say everything I'm feeling. I might as well get every single thing off my chest.

"Don't do this." His voice is rough. He looks rough. There are bags under his eyes, and there's no color in his cheeks. There should be color in them. He's been working from sunrise to well after sunset the past few nights.

"Don't do what? Try to understand what the fuck is happening between us?"

"You're leaving, that's what's happening. There's nothing else to understand."

I laugh sarcastically, catching the attention of people around us. I don't care if they see me lose control or not. The boy I've loved my entire life is slipping through my fingers, and there's nothing I can do about it. I can't keep it together. Not anymore.

Cade is doing what everyone else has done before. He's fading away from me. My Mom did. My Dad did. And now he is, too.

He attempts to roll my bags toward the entrance, but I yank them from him. It's awkward and one keeps bumping into my ankles, but I roll them toward the doors. I don't need his help. Not with him acting like this.

He only allows me to get them a few feet before one is ripped from my grip. It doesn't take him long to grab the other one as well. He keeps walking, not looking back at me.

I run after him, grabbing a fistful of his T-shirt to stop him.

When he turns around, there's a split second where I see the hurt etched into his face. He hides it almost immediately, but for a moment, he falters. I saw it and the look confuses me more than ever.

He's the one doing this to us. I haven't hurt him. He shouldn't be hurt, and if he is, then he doesn't have to go through with letting this be the end of us.

"Talk to me," I beg, my fingers clutching his shirt.

Cade looks down. He takes his hand from the suitcase handle and wraps his fingers around my wrist. "I don't know what else to say," he answers, his voice low.

"Anything."

Someone bumps into me, knocking my body into Cade's.

Two lines appear on his forehead as he frowns. "I can't wait to watch you make your dreams come true."

"That's a cop out, Cade. I'm not going to let you send me away with a speech about my dreams and let you avoid talking about what the hell has changed in the last few days."

"I guess reality hit me." He looks around at the airport. "I hadn't let myself think too hard about the fact you were leaving. But you are leaving, and I really, truly, am happy for you."

"That isn't fair. You always knew I was leaving. I've suggested us doing long distance, me coming home more, me taking classes online to keep us going. You've shot down every single suggestion. You kissed me, told me all these things about how we're ruined for each other, and now you're just what…done with me?"

His jaw tenses, the muscles in his cheeks flex angrily. "Yeah. I guess I'm done."

His words feel like a punch to the gut. I take a step back from the impact from them. My head rocks back and forth in disbelief. I can't fight the tears that stream down my cheeks. "I don't believe you."

"You should."

My eyes squeeze shut. My mind rushes with all of our memories from this summer. We were happy. I loved him, and there were times he had me believing he loved me too. Our moments together weren't one-sided. I was convinced he felt something too.

When I open my eyes, my vision is blurry from the tears that won't stop falling. "I love you. I've been in love with you my entire life, Cade Jennings. This summer was the best summer of my life because of you. And if you felt anything close to what I feel for you, you wouldn't let us end this way."

"Goldie…" His voice is laced with anguish, but his features are masked into a stone cold mask that I don't recognize. He's not the man I've come to know, and it hurts to wonder if I really ever knew him at all.

I close the distance between us once again. I look up, not bothering to hide my wet, tear-stained cheeks from him. "Look me in the eye," I say, my words coming out choked from the devastation wreaking havoc on me. "Look me in the eye and tell me you don't love me."

Our chests hit one another with our heavy breaths. To anyone walking by, we probably look like quite the scene. It doesn't matter. I don't care what we look like. I'm breaking down because of him. Worrying about what people think of my current state is the least of my worries.

I jab a finger into his chest, feeling his racing heart up against my fingertip. "Do it, Cade."

"Stop it," he says through gritted teeth.

I push against his chest. He stands steady, letting me take out my anger but not budging an inch.

My head rocks side to side. "You don't get to tell me what to do. I'm the one in charge right now. And if you want to end us, If you want to demolish the most perfect thing I've ever felt to nothing, then you're going to do it to my face."

I push again. He grabs my wrists, pinning my hands to his chest. His heart beats wildly against my palms, like it's trying to prove he cares, no matter how much his words contradict it.

The way he looks back at me breaks my heart. His eyes are void of any emotion. There's nothing written on his face when I desperately want there to be something, *anything*.

I'm devastated to lose him. He seems fine with losing me.

Chapter 46
CADE
age twenty-two

"Don't be a coward," Mare spits. Her lips tremble as she tries to push against me again. "Say it to my face, Cade. Tell me right now you don't love me, and you'll never have to worry about me again."

It'd be easy to tell the truth. I'm so in love with her that I already can't breathe at the thought of losing her. I don't want to go back to the ranch without her. Sadness courses through me when I think about returning to all the places we've made memories together without her. But it's something I have to do.

I sigh, wishing I could be honest and tell her I think she'll be the only person I love my entire life. I think the ghost of our memories will haunt me on the ranch. It'll be bittersweet to watch her make every single one of her dreams come true without me in her life.

Her fingers wrap in the fabric of my T-shirt once again. She clutches them so tightly I fear that her grip is the only thing keeping her upright.

"You can't," Mare sobs. "You can't tell me you don't love me because I know this isn't all in my head. Love like this doesn't have to be talked about. It's so much more powerful than words. It can be felt and I feel that you love me like I love y—"

"I don't love you," I interrupt. The words taste vile coming from my mouth.

Her head rears back like I've hit her. "No," she whispers. Fuck, there's so much anguish in her voice. I hate myself for doing this to her. I hate myself for being weak and letting anything happen between us. I fucking hate that I'm having to lie to the woman that owns my entire fucking heart.

"I'm sorry. I just don't love you the way you want me to," I lie.

She sobs, the sound is loud and obliterates my bruised and broken heart. I want to hold her, comfort her, and apologize for having to do this to us. My feet stay planted. I know the comfort from me won't do anything. Not if I won't take back the worst lie I've ever told.

Her falling tears soak the collar of her shirt. She attempts to wipe under her eyes, but the moment she pulls her hands down her tears fall again.

"I'm so sorry. I wish I could've been it for you. That I could've felt that way..."

She lets out a choking sound, and the noise has me way too close to giving up the charade. I'm seconds away from telling her I'll risk her hating me later if it meant she didn't hate me now.

I'm in too deep. I've broken her. I can see it in her eyes. There's no coming back from this. I've ruined us. If I just remind myself that one day, when her books are sold in every store and her name is known to thousands, that she'll thank me. She'll appreciate the fact that she didn't let a man hold her back.

It doesn't make it hurt any fucking less.

Mare's chest shakes as she tries to suck in air. She hiccups, looking at her two suitcases at my sides. "I think it's time I go."

"Yeah," I answer sadly.

Her eyes search my face one final time. I'll never forgive myself for what I've done. But I wouldn't be able to live with myself if I held her back and asked her to stay.

"I think you'll regret this," she says, attempting to keep her shaky words steady. "One day, I think you'll realize that what we had together was the realest thing you ever had, but you were too scared to fight for it. I won't be waiting around for that moment."

I can't help it. I pull her body into mine, needing to feel her pressed against me one last time. My arms cling to her desperately. I want to keep her in my grasp forever and never let go.

She's the first one to pull away. I let her, afraid of things I'll confess if she stays in my hold much longer. Before she's fully out of reach, I lean down and press a kiss to her forehead. My eyes close, my mind filling with all the things I wish we could be.

"One day you'll forget all about me," I tell her. "I'll just be a boy you thought you loved once."

Mare grabs both her suitcases and backs away from me. I think that'll be the end of it—the end of us—but she meets my eyes one final time. "You're not just a boy to me, Cade Jennings. You never will be."

Then she leaves.

I tell myself that if she looks back, if she still has that same devastated look on her face that I'll come clean.

I'll tell her that she owns me. That I'm hers in every way, and that I'll do anything to be the one she comes home to at the end of the day. I'm ready to unleash everything…if she'd just look back.

She never looks back.

Chapter 47
MARE
present

I WAKE up surrounded by warmth, and it's not from the sun that beats through the bedroom window.

It's because Cade lays next to me, his arms firm around my middle. I look up, shocked to find him awake.

He smiles, reaching to cup my cheek. "Good morning," he says, his voice gravelly.

"I like waking up with you." I snuggle deeper into his chest.

Cade trails his fingers through my hair. "I was just thinking the same thing."

"You sleep okay?"

His chest shakes from his deep, throaty laugh. "Do you even have to ask that?"

I run my hand over his chest, loving the feel of the warmth and the way the light splatter of dark chest hair feels against my palm. "It wouldn't hurt for you to tell me…"

Cade pulls me into his chest. My chin hits his sternum as he holds me in place. "Goldie," he starts, letting his thumb brush over my cheekbone. "I've laid awake so many nights remembering what it felt like to wake up with your body against mine. There's something about you being next to me that just calms my head. Last night was one of the only nights since Mom left that I wasn't haunted by the last time I saw her."

"I always found it harder to sleep without you," I confess. "It's probably why I was in your bed more than I was in mine."

"I preferred it that way."

I stare into Cade's copper eyes, relishing in the moment with him. It seems like the easiest decision to wake up every day in his arms. There's nothing that feels better than having him look at me like this as the early morning rays illuminate the room.

Absentmindedly, I begin to trace the tattoo on his chest. I still remember when he first got it at eighteen. He thought Linda would be so mad about it, but she actually thought the details were cool. I vividly remember her making some remark like maybe now he'll wear sunscreen to protect the fresh ink or something like that. She'd always been on him to wear sunscreen when working long days outside.

"What are you thinking?" Cade asks, allowing me to trace every curve of the ink.

"That you've added some new tattoos since I was here last."

"Want to see my favorite?"

I push off his chest, my interest piqued. The knowing smirk on his lips only fuels my curiosity. He bites his lip playfully. I watch closely as he hooks his fingers into the waistband of his boxer briefs.

I gasp, my eyes catching the small tattoo permanently etched low on his hips.

"Cade," I whisper, reaching out to trace the delicate lines. "It's..."

"A marigold," he finishes.

I can't look away. It's the size of my thumb and nestled so far down his hip that it wouldn't be noticeable unless he points it out or he's naked. It must've been too dark for me to see last night, and there was too much heated passion happening in the tack room for me to pay any attention.

"When?"

He tucks a stray strand of my hair behind my ear. The look on his face is so loving that it takes my breath away. Everything about this moment has me reeling. The longer I spend in Sutten and the more time I spend with Cade, the more I realize how different things really were from what I believed at nineteen.

"I got it about a month after you left. To be honest, I wasn't in a good place. I kept telling myself I did what was best for you, but I was so fucking lost after you left. For the first time in my life, I didn't have you. It hit me hard and all at once that I didn't know how to live without you."

My eyes burn with unshed tears from the reminder of how unbelievably hard that time of my life was. It felt like everything was going wrong and I couldn't tell a soul—not even Pippa—what was happening. Nobody knew that I'd had my heart broken by a man who was my entire world.

"I thought I was alone with my pain," I confess, feeling the need to be vulnerable with him. I still have no idea what we're going to do now, but I'm tired of the lies between us. If Cade and I have any shot at a future, we both have to be honest.

"You were never alone," he says. "I was so fucked up over losing you. I truly didn't know how to go on without you with me."

"If only you would've told me. We could've saved us both years of pain." An overwhelming sense of sadness washes over me. I was so angry at him that I never imagined him being hurt. I thought he'd been honest when he told me he didn't love me. But now, I realize that maybe everything I felt, he felt too. I ache from thinking about how hard it must've been for him because I know how hard it was for me.

I was able to move on—at least partially—because I was out of Sutten. But Cade didn't have the luxury of leaving, and now I can't help but wonder about the toll it took on him to have to live in a place full of some of our best and worst memories.

"The marigold was my own way of keeping you close to me. I know I did some things that really hurt you, and I hate that I did that, but I never stopped loving you, Goldie. Not for a single second."

I drape a leg over him, adjusting my body until I'm strad-dling him. I lean down, letting my hair create a little barrier from the world around us. "I tried so hard not to love you. I was in denial for a long time before I finally accepted that there would always be a part of me that loved you. And there was nothing that was going to change that, even though that drove me crazy at times."

"Sometimes I wonder what would've happened if we'd waited until we were a little older," he says, grabbing either side of my neck.

"I don't want to dwell on it. Let's focus on us. Right here. Right now."

I trail kisses along his neck, my hips grinding against him of their own accord.

Cade grips either side of my hips, pinning me so I'm lined up perfect with his eager, long, thick cock. "I want to focus on you right now, on the way your hips move against me in a way that has my cock eager to feel you. But…"

"But?" I push, trying to sway my hips.

"But I don't want to just focus on right here and right now, Goldie. I want to focus on forever."

My desperate need for him overtakes my body. Before I can really think about the impact of his words on my heart, I lean down and kiss him. It seems like I've wasted so many mornings not kissing him during the time we've spent apart. I want to make up for lost time.

Cade kisses me back with matched passion. His tongue claims me, plunging deep into my mouth as if he's staking his claim.

His fingers thread through my hair as he gives me free rein to move my body against his however I please. I'm lost in kissing him, in the dream of keeping him forever, when the door flies open.

Chapter 48
CADE
present

"MY EYES!" Pippa screams dramatically, holding her hands over her face.

"Pippa!" Mare yells, sliding off my body. She tries to get off the bed but the discarded sheets tangle between her legs.

"Did I just walk in on my best friend dry humping my brother?" Pippa gawks, spinning so her back is to us.

Mare finally gets herself untangled from the sheets just before Pippa attempts to flee out the open door.

"Pippa, wait," Mare pleads, looking to me for help. I grab one of the pillows from the bed and arrange it over the proof of how close I was to taking things past dry humping with Mare.

Pippa spreads the fingers of her hands covering her face just enough to see through the gaps. She looks between the both of us, probably making sure we're decent before she decides to stay and listen.

"This was not how I expected to start my morning," Pippa quips, letting her hands drop to her sides.

"We were going to tell you," I explain. "We just hadn't had the chance."

Mare shoots me a look. Technically, we hadn't talked about telling Pippa at all, but it was only a matter of time before we would've had to broach the subject.

I meant it when I said I wasn't going to lose her again. I'm all in, and that means getting Pippa on board with Mare and me.

Pippa narrows her dark eyebrows. She gives me an inquisitive look. "You were going to tell me what, exactly?"

"Things between Cade and I have...changed."

Pippa stares at Mare for a few moments before her gaze pops back to me. "This isn't the first time is it?"

I shake my head at the same time Mare sighs.

"Are you mad?" Mare asks nervously.

Pippa is my sister. I know her well enough to know that I don't think she'd ever be mad about something like this. She knows how to mind her own business. She's not exactly a meddler, but I do think a part of her could be hurt that Mare and I kept a secret from her.

"No, I'm not mad. I just need a minute to process things, and we're supposed to be leaving in"—she pulls her phone out from her pocket to check the time—"five minutes for a wedding delivery."

Mare's eyes widen in surprise. "Oh my god, I forgot."

Pippa grimaces for a moment. "Please give me no details on how you were so busy that you forgot."

Mare combs her fingers through her hair, trying to tame her wild locks as she looks around the room. Probably for some clothes.

"Look. Apparently the three of us have a lot to talk about, and I have a lot of fucking questions, but I have to get this order out, and Mare, you're the only one that can help me so I need you ready in five."

Pippa gives me a look before turning around and gunning it out of the room. I sigh, jumping out of the bed and quickly pulling my sweats up my legs. I want to catch my sister before she and Mare leave.

"What are you doing?" Mare asks, pulling a T-shirt over her head.

"I'm going to go check on Pip real quick before you leave," I say, wrapping my arms around her shoulders and pulling her into my body.

I cup both sides of her face, angling her chin so she looks up at me. "Pippa finding us changes nothing about how I feel about you. You know that, right?"

She nods, leaning into my palm. "I do."

My thumb skirts along her cheeks, loving the sight of the fresh freckles on her face. They're new and have just popped up in her time here in Sutten. I make a mental note that I need to give them a proper welcome to her face later on today.

"I love you." I press a kiss to her forehead.

"I love you too," she whispers as I walk out of the room to leave her to finish getting ready.

Ambling down the hallway and then the large staircase, I search the house until I find Pippa waiting in the kitchen.

She opens up a box of cereal, reaching her hand into the box and popping a handful of the sugary cereal in her mouth. She pins me with a serious look. "You know I didn't have it on my BINGO card to find out my best friend and my brother were hooking up—especially since I felt like a buffer between the two of you when you first arrived."

I sigh, running my hands through the hair at the top of my head. "There's a lot you don't know about Mare and I."

"I gathered," she fires back.

"What do you want to know?"

Pippa ignores my question. She shoves a few more handfuls of cereal in her mouth before she closes the box and puts it back in the pantry. "You know, it's funny because I think I always suspected something might be happening between the two of you. I mean I knew the way she looked at you. She thought I didn't see her doodle your name in her notebooks but I'm nosy, and I always saw them."

"She was doodling my name in her notebooks?"

Pippa rolls her eyes. "I guess I always thought it was one-sided. That you were just kind of this elusive crush to her. There were times before we went to college that I wondered if maybe you looked at her in that way too, but I just really thought one of you—or both—would tell me."

"Yeah, well, things didn't end great for us when both of you left for college."

Pippa stares at me for a while, her elbows leaning against the stone countertop as she watches me carefully. "I think it makes sense now."

"What?"

"One night during my fall semester I was talking to mom, and I was going on and on about how Mare was acting weird and I didn't know why. Mom told me that maybe Mare was just having a hard time being away from Sutten, and I just couldn't really imagine why. I was there with her. I didn't really think about what Mare was missing in Sutten but it turns out what she was missing was…you."

Pippa's admission makes regret wash through me all over again. I don't want to think about how Mare spent her time at college. She was supposed to go there and forget about me. Her heartbreak wasn't supposed to spill into Chicago, too.

"Mom also mentioned that you weren't doing well. She kept telling me that I needed to come and bring Mare and I didn't understand why you'd be so upset. To me, you didn't spend that much time with Mare and I anymore, but I listened." She pauses, her eyes flicking to the stairs when she hears something. "And I tried getting Mare to come back, but she wouldn't and it didn't make sense why, but now it does."

"Yeah…" I let out a long breath, wondering where I should even begin in telling Pippa about us.

"And you. I get what Mom meant. I came back and you were so sad. You weren't yourself. Yeah, you were quiet and broody which is normal for you, but you still weren't Cade. That was because of Mare?" Pippa looks at me and the hurt in her face takes me by surprise. I hadn't given any consideration as to what others thought of the person I became when Mare left. I couldn't really think about anyone but her. I barely even took time to think about myself—and clearly more people noticed than I realized.

"Everything okay down here?" Mare comes downstairs, looking between Pippa and me.

Pippa holds my stare for a few moments longer before she pops off the counter and heads toward the door.

"Follow me, Mare. We've got a lot to talk about."

Chapter 49
MARE
present

"ARE you giving me the silent treatment?" I ask hesitantly. Pippa could talk to a brick wall, so the fact that she hasn't said a word to me during this car ride is unnerving.

She grips both sides of her bakery van's steering wheel, her stare focused directly ahead. I'm wondering if we're going to spend the entire ride in silence when she finally makes a noise. Albeit, it's a loud, dramatic sigh, but it is *something*.

"Maybe if you just start from the beginning I can understand. I'm not trying to give you the silent treatment, I'm just trying to figure out the relationship between the two of you."

I let out a sarcastic laugh. "That makes two of us."

Pippa looks at me from the corner of her eye. She hits a bump in the country road a little too quickly, making both of us bounce in our seats. "Oops," she says under her breath. She slows down a bit, sitting straighter in her seat. "Look, I'm not the one to give relationship advice, my dating history is filled with mistake after mistake, and my type seems to be assholes with a side of commitment issues, but don't you find it a little off that you can't answer my question?"

"What happened with Chase at Slopes? The two of you looked cozy."

Pippa gives me a look to tell me she knows I'm trying to divert the conversation. The raise of her dark eyebrows tells me she sees right through me, and she won't fully let me get away with avoiding the looming conversation.

"He's nice and fun, and we've flirted plenty of times before, and I want there to be chemistry because he might actually be a good guy, but there isn't a spark. He might be *too* nice. Which makes me go back to my earlier point. For some reason my type is assholes."

"You guys looked like you were into each other. Do you think that spark could happen over time?"

Pippa shakes her head. "I've tried. *Trust me*, I was really trying the other night. But I seemed to have more chemistry with some rich asshole I accidentally bumped into that night."

"*Rich asshole*? Tell me more. Any possibilities there?"

She makes a fake gagging noise. "First, he screamed tourist, so absolutely not. Second, I meant it like I had more of a spark with some douche yelling at me more than I do with Chase. Neither is a good choice, obviously. The dude at the bar wasn't the good kind of asshole that's kind of hot. He was just a straight up dick."

I nod because I don't know what else to say. I get what she's saying. There are many times I've tried liking guys I knew were good for me. You can't force it, no matter how much you want to.

"Tell me more about this rich asshole," I tease.

"I know what you're trying to do." She flicks the blinker to turn onto the main highway in Sutten. "You can't avoid talking about what's happening between you and Cade forever."

"Just humor me with this last question."

She sighs. "After you ran off, which I'm assuming now that I'm thinking about it had to do with my brother, I was still ready to party. I was having fun, despite everything that's happened recently. So I bought the table a pitcher of beer, and on my way to bring it to the table, I accidentally ran into some guy who was wearing fucking slacks to Slopes. Like who does that?"

"Yeah, that's unusual." I laugh. Due to its touristy nature, most people go to Slopes dressed up in full country attire. The corny kind of country type of outfits that locals never *actually* wear. What isn't typical in Slopes is people wearing business attire.

"So I accidentally ran into him, and I apologized because beer did get everywhere. His button up was soaked, but it was an accident."

"And he was a dick about it?"

Pippa whistles. "He was more than a dick about it. I tried buying him a new shirt because I felt so bad and was wondering if he was just having a bad night. He was still an enormous dick after the new shirt."

"Yikes."

"Now back to you because you're not getting out of this, and we're getting close to the Livingston Estate where the wedding is."

I sigh, thinking about everything that's happened between Cade and I over the years. "I don't really know where to start."

"From the beginning," Pippa offers.

So I do. I start from the very beginning. From the first night I ever crawled into Cade's bed and all the nights after that. To the birthdays we spent together and the first time we kissed. I skim over a few parts I don't want to tell her because Cade is her brother, and there's some lines I won't cross with her. I tell her about the few months when he was my everything. And then I get to the part where he broke my heart and what's happened between the two of us since I've been back.

I take a deep breath. "So that covers it."

"Your book makes a whole lot more sense now."

I keep my mouth shut. When people in interviews would ask me how I could weave so much angst and hurt into the story, I lied and said I had a vivid imagination.

That wasn't the truth. I could pour myself into the book because it was *my* hurt and heartbreak in those pages. It was my anguish. It was *my* story. Well, *our* story.

Pippa pulls into the long driveway that leads to the Livingston Estate. We went to high school with some of the Livingston boys. Their family owns so much of Sutten that they have multiple houses and estates in the town. They're rich enough to rent one of their many properties out for weddings and events.

"Okay, you don't have to tell me the book is about you and Cade. I can make my own assumptions, which is kind of gross because I've read your *sex* scenes."

My cheeks heat with embarrassment. "Next question," I plead.

Pippa parks the van in the driveway. She immediately opens her door and hops out, giving me no choice but to follow. When I come around back, she has the back doors open and is bending inside grabbing boxes.

She looks over at me. "What are you going to do when you leave?"

I chew on my lip because I really don't know what happens when I leave. Soon, I'll have to go back to Chicago and pitch the new story and ending I've created for this duet. Rudy keeps calling me to remind me that I have to at least come back for those meetings and the ones we'll have when finishing the book, but I've been avoiding his calls. I don't want to think about leaving yet. Everything is still so new.

"I don't know if we've thought that far ahead yet," I answer. I don't want to leave things the same way I did last time I left Sutten, but I also can't give up everything I've worked for in the years since leaving. There's a lot we have to figure out, and I can't give Pippa the answers because I don't know them myself.

Pippa lets out an annoyed sigh. She starts scooting boxes to the edge of the van, lining them up so she can unload them easier. "You have to think about these things, Mare. I'm not blind. I've known there's been something between the two of you for a long time. But you really, really hurt him. I don't want to see him go through that again. Especially after Mom."

I'm silent, thinking of all the times Pippa probably caught on to what was happening between Cade and me. We tried keeping it a secret, but looking back, I can see where she would've had her suspicions.

The last thing I want to do is hurt Cade. Back then, I wasn't aware of how much he was hurting. But I know now. I don't want to hurt him again. I don't want to be hurt by him again either. I have faith that this time around, Cade and I can figure things out together. But we need *time* to do that. I don't have much time until I have to go back to Chicago.

"We're adults, Pippa," I tell her, hoping that we will be able to figure it out. Pippa begins to stack boxes in her hands, the tower getting higher and higher. I'm worried it may topple over if she adds any more. "Here let me help you," I demand, taking a step closer to her.

"I've got it," she gets out, her voice straining under the stack of boxes. "I'm not trying to get involved in any business that involves my brother and my best friend. But you need to really think about what's going to happen when you leave."

Pippa's words make me pause. She has a point. Cade is steadfast in saying that he won't let us fall apart again, and I believe him, but we also need to have a long conversation about what happens next.

Pippa shoots me a warning look over the stack of boxes before she turns toward the large house.

The next chain of events play out in slow motion. I try to pull Pippa backward, but it's no use.

Pippa runs straight into a man in a suit, sending boxes flying in different directions.

"Fuck," the man yells.

"Oh fuck," Pippa screeches, her arms flailing as she tries to catch some of the boxes.

I lunge forward, trying to catch something, but it isn't any use. There's a group of us all attempting to save even one box, but none of us are able to.

Pink boxes tumble to the ground. Pippa looks down at them, defeated, a string of curse words falling from her mouth.

Pippa looks up, meeting the eyes of the man she ran into. She looks like she's about to apologize, but recognition takes over her features. Except, this doesn't seem like the *good* kind of recognition. Her face gets red with anger. "*You* again? You've got to be kidding me!" Pippa yells.

"Oh my god, Pippa," I rush to get out, crouching down as I attempt to find boxes that can be salvaged.

I'm busy trying to save the cupcakes that haven't hit the pavement when the man clears his throat loudly. "Do you just not look where you're going, or do you just enjoy running into me?" His voice is scathing. My eyes immediately snap to him, wondering why this guy is being such a dick for something that was clearly an accident.

My eyes bounce to Pippa. She stares daggers at him. The look she gives him makes me nervous. She's normally happy go lucky. Whatever history she has with this guy must be bad.

It dawns on me that this must be the guy from Slopes. It'd make sense. If he's here for a wedding, he probably did go to our tourist bar. And his comment about them running into each other again makes sense now.

The asshole in a suit stares back at Pippa, completely undeterred by the dirty look she gives him. If looks could kill, he'd be a goner.

"You know you're supposed to actually *look* where you're going when walking," he chastises.

A girl in a bridesmaid's dress hits the guy in the arm. She looks at him like he's grown a third head because she reaches down to help me with the boxes.

"Don't worry, he's really an asshole to everyone," the girl says under her breath.

"You're friends with him, why?" I ask, wondering if he really can be this much of a dick all the time.

"His asshole personality is kind of endearing after a while. It's a defense mechanism for him."

I nod, still wondering why anyone would want to associate with somebody like that. He's a total grump. Maybe even past grump and into straight up douchebag territory.

The bridesmaid and I are busy picking up the last of the boxes when Pippa squats down next to us and starts to pick up the cupcakes. "You know you're supposed to actually have a big dick if you're going to be this big of an asshole," Pippa mutters under her breath, making a point to aim her eyes at his groin.

The douche in a suit's jaw snaps shut. "I think you just ruined a thousand dollar suit," he growls.

"Oh I get it," Pippa barks. "You use expensive suits to cover up the fact that you've got the worst fucking personality on the planet. Not to mention, *you* just ruined hours of hard work." Pippa points to the colorful globs of icing lining the pavement.

A woman in white—who I'm guessing must be the bride—steps forward. "We'll see what we can salvage," she offers. "It really only looks like a few things got ruined."

"Oh my God, you're the bride and I just—well, this asshole—just ruined your desserts! I'm Pippa, the owner, and I'm so sorry." Pippa looks at the van, her eyes connecting with mine for a moment. I feel bad, she looks flustered, and I know what she walked in on this morning between Cade and me probably doesn't help things. "If I leave right now, I can replace the damages and bring them back in time…"

The bride shakes her head. "It's fine. Don't worry about it. I think I severely over-ordered anyway."

Pippa frowns as I hand over a box of cupcakes that don't look like the best presentation wise, but they're edible since they didn't topple over on the ground.

"The strawberry ones are my favorite," Pippa whines.

"I never really liked strawberry anyway," the bride answers.

"You really should replace the cupcakes," the asshole interjects.

The bride glares at him. Surely this can't be the groom. The girl looks too nice to be marrying such an ass. "Camden, stop," she says low.

The guy—Camden—doesn't break eye contact with Pippa, the two of them locked in a heated stare.

Pippa takes a deep breath, her eyes glancing at me for a split second before she glares back at Camden. She smirks and the sight makes me nervous. "You know, *Camden*," she begins, venom laced in her words. "I'm having a really, really bad day, and I'm just not in the mood to deal with a rich, entitled asshole."

"Your bad day matters to me, why?"

Pippa throws her hands up in the air and turns to face the back of the van. She looks at the boxes that didn't get ruined in the whole incident. Pippa takes a long, dramatic deep breath. "Other than the fact that I found out my brother and best friend are fucking *again* and quite literally ran into the same dick from the bar the other night who doesn't give two shits that he ruined something I worked *really* hard on in the process? I don't actually give a damn if my bad day matters to your not."

"Pipp—" I interrupt, wanting to apologize for the part I played in the way her day has gone. I start to reach out to her, but I realize I have icing all over my hands so I wipe my hands on my jeans.

"Not right now, Mare," Pippa interrupts. Not only does this Camden guy get a dirty look, but I do too.

"How about I take a load in?" The bridesmaid offers, obviously trying to ease the tension in the air.

Pippa's eyes soften slightly as she takes a deep breath. She grabs a few boxes, and without saying anything, she follows the bridesmaid inside. I'm left watching her walk away, having no choice but to help bring things in.

The Camden guy steps next to me, and despite his obvious anger, he starts helping by grabbing some of the boxes.

He looks over, catching me looking at him. "What?" he asks, stacking one box over the other.

My eyes go wide as I turn back to my own task. "Nothing," I say under my breath. "I just really thought you were such an asshole that you kind of surprised me by helping with the boxes."

He grunts, creating a stack far larger than mine. "Your boss have a habit of spilling shit on people?"

I laugh, his question taking me by surprise. "She's not my boss, she's my friend. But no, apparently it's just you."

His dark, gelled hair doesn't budge an inch as he shakes his head. "Lucky me."

Chapter 50
CADE
present

I'M PLACING bales of hay into the bed of one of the work trucks when Mare comes into view. I toss the bale I was holding into the truck bed before closing the distance to her.

The look on her face makes me nervous. She chews her lip as she keeps smoothing out the fabric of her cotton sundress. I don't know how long she's been back from helping Pippa, but apparently long enough to change her clothes.

"Hi," she says softly, looking up at me.

"How was it?"

Mare shrugs. "It was good, I guess."

My heartbeat picks up because of her demeanor. She's too quiet, too in her head. I can't help but wonder what direction her conversation with Pippa went with the way she's acting.

"Good?" I press, grabbing her by either side of the face. She immediately leans into the touch, calming some of the nerves coursing through me.

"Yeah. I know she was hurt by us keeping a secret from her, but I also don't think it was fully a surprise to her either. She was cool about it though. The biggest thing was that she asked a lot of questions about what our plans were…"

"Your plans are my plans, Goldie," I assure her.

Her eyes trail over my face. I hate that they turn down slowly, that there's a sadness in her expression that I can't take away. She lets out a slow, defeated sigh. "I think we're faced with the same problem again. You're meant to be here and my job is somewhere else."

"I don't care. We'll make it work." I slide my hands down her neck and shoulders until I'm grabbing her waist and pulling her body to mine.

"Pippa told me not to hurt you again. She said she didn't want to see either of us hurting at the end of all of this."

"There is no end to this."

"What does that mean?"

"It means I agree with her. I don't want either of us to end up like last time. For neither one of us to get hurt, we can't end. I *won't* let us end."

Mare snuggles into me, pressing her cheek against my heartbeat. She clutches me tightly, like she's afraid that I could disappear at any moment. She must not be listening to me because there's nothing that will stop me from keeping her forever. I'll do whatever it takes, no matter the distance between us, for us to never give up on each other again.

"I love you, Cade," Mare says, her words muffled by the fabric of my shirt. "I've loved you my entire life. I don't plan on stopping anytime soon. I just don't know what happens when our real lives catch up to us."

I grab the back of her head, keeping her against me as I press a kiss to her hair. "I love you. I don't plan on letting *anything* stop me from loving you this time."

The moment she tilts her head up to look at me, I'm pressing my mouth to hers. I need to feel her lips against mine. I need to taste her, to caress her tongue with mine and use our bodies to promise how I plan on loving her forever.

I don't know how much time passes as we stay locked in the kiss. I take my time with her, not wanting to rush things between us. It isn't until she pulls away, a whisper of a smile on her pink lips, that I speak up.

"Can I show you something?"

Mare tilts her head, looking at me with curiosity in her eyes. "Show me what?"

"If I told you it wouldn't exactly be a surprise."

"You never said it was a surprise. You just asked if you could show me something."

I roll my eyes, wrapping an arm around her and pulling her into my side. "Okay let me rephrase this, can I show you something? It's a *surprise*."

"A surprise?" she says in mock shock. "I'm intrigued."

I open the passenger side door of the Jennings Ranch work truck and help her climb into it. As soon as she's comfortable, I close the door and round the front to get inside.

Once I'm seated in the driver's seat, Mare slides across the bench seat until her body presses into mine. I love the feeling of her head against my shoulder as I put the truck into gear. I could get used to her riding around with me. For it to become something mundane to us. Something we do forever.

She's silent at first, peacefully looking out the windshield as I head toward our destination. I was expecting her to ask questions, but she doesn't. She's quiet the entire ride, not saying anything until I pull down the driveway of the house I've spent years planning.

Mare sits up in the seat, leaning forward to get a better look at the framed out house coming into view. "It looks so different in the sunlight."

I look over at her, trying to get a read on her emotions. "Good different or bad different?"

The truck comes to a stop. Once it's in park, I sit back and run my hand over my mouth, soaking in the moment of watching her look at the house I've worked tirelessly on.

I didn't bring her here to show her the home I want to spend forever with her in, but I'm caught up in the way she's looking at it. The other night she looked at the house like she feared it. There was something so heartbreaking and haunting in the way she looked at the house we'd dreamed of together. It was like she didn't want it to even exist, like she hated me for bringing it to fruition. That night I was terrified that things were so damaged between us that we wouldn't be able to repair them.

Watching her now, I know that isn't true. She looks at the house now with hope. Before I can say anything, she's opening the passenger door and hopping down to the gravel. She doesn't wait for me as she walks toward the house.

I stay in the truck, letting her take it in with fresh eyes. Hopefully now she can see through her hurt. Maybe now she'll be able to understand what I've been trying to tell her.

I've loved her this entire time. While she was making her dreams come true, I was doing everything to build a house she could call home once she'd achieved every single one of her wildest dreams.

Mare disappears into the house. I grab something from the bed of the truck and follow after her, feeling like she's had enough time to take it in on her own.

The gravel crunches underneath my boots as I climb the driveway. I can't hear her, but my eyes land on Mare in the open floor plan almost as soon as I walk in.

It's a lot easier to see the details of the house in the daylight. My headlights could only illuminate so much the other night, but now with the sun shining high above us, everything can be seen.

I stop in the kitchen, watching Mare trail her hand over the framing of the living room. She lets her eyes travel the space slowly, like she doesn't want to forget a single detail of the house.

My heartbeat picks up when she takes a step closer to the kitchen. Soon she'll be close to the nook she'd always told me she dreamt about.

Soon, the real reason I brought her here in the first place will come into view.

Chapter 51
MARE
present

WHEN CADE BROUGHT me to this house the other day, I wasn't ready to see it. My heart couldn't take knowing he'd been here in Sutten building a life for himself—a life he hoped I'd be in—while I was miles and miles away believing he never loved me.

I'd been in denial when he first confessed that he loved me. That he'd loved me all along. I'd gone so long believing I was the only one who left heartbroken after our summer together. It was hard for me to wrap my head around the fact that I left this town to avoid him because I couldn't face him not loving me back, when all along he was here, unable to let us go.

Building a house for us.

I look around the kitchen, at the corner where Cade vividly described a breakfast nook would go. I can easily imagine myself writing there.

It's weird to feel so happy and sad all at once.

I'm happy because the only man who has ever owned my heart wants to spend forever with me.

I'm sad because I worked so hard at creating a life that didn't involve Sutten—that didn't involve him—that now I don't know how to intertwine our lives so we can have our happily ever after together.

But I want to try. I *have* to try. In the years since, I've spent so much time comparing every other man to him. Cade slipped through my fingers once before, but now that I have him and he's made it clear how much he wants us, we'll just have to figure out the rest.

I'm opening my mouth to tell him that when my eyes drift to the back of the house and what I imagine is going to be a back door leading to an expansive back porch.

Orange and yellow hues catch my attention. I take a step closer, my pulse humming in my ears as my heartbeat picks up.

"Cade," I whisper, emotion clogging my throat.

His silence has me tearing my eyes from the scene in front of me to make sure he's still there.

Of course he is. I knew he was because I could still feel him, like I always have.

He stares back at me, a hint of a smile on his full lips. In his hands he holds a large, folded blanket. He clutches it to his chest.

"How about you go check it out?" His voice is low and rough as he speaks through his own emotions.

I nod, not fighting the tears that fall down my cheeks. Ripping my gaze from his, I run from the kitchen and down a small slope. My feet don't stop until I'm standing at the edge of the most breathtaking of views.

In front of me is a sprawling field of marigolds.

My vision blurs with new tears at the vivid shades of orange and yellow in front of me. The field is large and beautifully kept. The colors are so vibrant that I can't look away.

I feel Cade before I see him. I turn to him, my tears hot against my cheeks as they stream down my face. "What is this?" My words come out hoarse.

"A reminder of you," he answers honestly. His gaze doesn't falter from mine. His amber eyes stare back at me with an immense amount of love and adoration. "A heartbroken man's attempt to cling to the love he'd lost."

"I don't understand."

"There's one more thing I haven't told you," Cade confesses.

Chapter 52
CADE
age twenty-six

"WHAT ARE you doing out here so late, honey?" My mom's voice catches me by surprise.

Dolly lets out a sigh as she waits for me to dig another peppermint out of my pocket. I laugh, pulling out one for her and one for me.

"Couldn't sleep so I ended up out here."

Mom nods, stopping next to me as she lovingly scratches the horse's chin. "She seems in good spirits."

I finish unwrapping Dolly's peppermint. Holding my hand out flat, I wait for the tickle of the horse's lips against my palm as she takes the peppermint from me. "She was being moody earlier today, so I thought I'd stop by and spoil her a little extra."

"I know it's been years, but sometimes I wonder if she still misses Mare. If the reason for all her little outbursts is because she hasn't seen Mare."

I grunt. I don't blame the horse. Mare should've been back by now to give attention to the horse she's had since she was a teenager. Dolly is only getting older. She deserves to see the one person she really loved.

Feeling bad for the horse, I unwrap the last peppermint in my pocket, the one I was about to eat, and feed it to the horse. "I've got bad news for you, Dolly. I don't think she's coming back."

Mom straightens the purse on her shoulder. It catches my attention. Propping an elbow on the stall door, I give my mom a look. "Where have you been tonight?"

With how high and bright the moon is in the sky, I know it's late. Mom isn't normally one to stay out late. Most nights she's home at the ranch before the sun even sets.

"It was book club night with The Sutten Mountain Book Exchange ladies. Lotty tried out this new recipe for fresh blueberry mojitos. We were having a blast and lost track of time."

I laugh. "Lotty is always trying something new, isn't she?"

Mom sets her purse down. She runs her fingers through Dolly's mane. "We read a fantastic book this month." She watches me closely—too closely.

"I'm happy for you," I quip. I know exactly what book they read this month. More importantly, *whose* book they were reading. Mare's debut novel has been the talk of the town since it was released. You walk in anywhere, and it's all anyone can talk about.

Even Buck at Bucky's can't seem to shut up about how proud he is of Mare for publishing the book. The memories of her already haunt this small town enough. She had to pour salt in the wound by publishing a book that sent this entire town into a tizzy.

"Are you going to ask what book?" Mom asks after some time, letting me have time with my thoughts before she prods.

I turn to face her, finding her already watching me closely. She's got that look, the one that makes me feel like she can read me like a goddamn book. I try to be closed off, to not let anyone know what I'm thinking because it's really none of their business, but none of that works with Mom. She can easily tell when something is bothering me.

And right now what's bothering me is Goldie and the fucking book everyone in this town is fawning over.

"I already know what book," I clip, giving Dolly one final pet before backing away from the stall door.

My mom follows closely behind as I walk out of the barn, stopping in front of an old porch swing Dad built for her years ago.

"Cade, wait." Her voice raises an octave with concern.

I stop, pinching the bridge of my nose. I've had enough reminders of Mare to last a lifetime. I don't need my mom bringing her, or this book, up, too.

I turn to face her, taking a deep breath so I don't take my hurt out on her.

I wasn't expecting her to look so concerned. Her eyes track over my face as she takes in my sad expression. Mom sighs softly. "You know you can talk about her with me."

I shake my head. "I can't talk about her with anyone, Mom. I just can't."

Her eyes soften. She places her small hand against my cheek. I lean into it and allow a little bit of comfort from my mom. I've kept all these feelings bottled up for so long, maybe it's time that I let some of them go and face them.

"I know how you feel about her," Mom whispers. Her amber eyes, the same color as mine, roam over my face.

"I don't know what you're talking about," I lie.

Mom lets out a sad laugh. She lets her hand drop to her side before she backs away. Her hand smooths out the fabric of her dress as she takes a seat on the swing. She pats the spot next to her, silently inviting me to join her.

I sigh but follow her direction. The swing groans underneath my added weight. When Dad built it years ago, I think it was mostly a spot for Mom to sit with us while he did chores in the stables. It's old and has withstood many Colorado winters, its sturdiness not the same as it used to be.

"From when Mare was little, I knew she had a crush on you."

My heart sinks at Mom's words. I look back at all my child-hood memories, and it's obvious to me Mare felt that way, but it isn't something I like to think back on. It hurts too much. All I can think about in the end is how bad I hurt her. She spent all those years idolizing me, loving me, only for me to break her with a few words at the airport.

I left her standing in that airport four years ago, and it still hurts to think about. It's like a bruise that won't heal, one that throbs and aches no matter how much time passes. I rub my chest, trying to soothe the pain.

Realizing I have nothing to say to her comment, Mom keeps going. "She always looked at you like you were her hero. You could do no wrong in her eyes. As she got older, I'd wondered if she'd stop looking at you like that. I thought maybe she'd grow out of it and look at somebody else that way."

A pit forms in my stomach at the thought of her ever looking at somebody else the way she used to look at me before I broke her heart. I shake my head, trying to rid myself of any thoughts about what she's doing now or *who* she's looking at now.

I made sure I have no right to care about who she's looking at and in what way. It doesn't stop the dull ache in my heart at the thought. It's burned in my memory how special it felt to be looked at by her like I was the world. I hate whoever has the honor now.

"Things never changed," Mom continued, ripping me back from my jealousy. "And then one day, you were looking at her the same way."

"Mom—"

"I don't need any details. I know my son enough, and I know Mare well enough, to know that something happened between the two of you. I never said anything because I figured if one of you wanted me to know you would've told me. But still, I knew."

"Nothing ever…" I sigh because I don't want to lie to her. I'm tired of hiding that Mare was everything to me, and even though it's been years, that wound still hasn't healed.

"You haven't been the same since she left. I know you've got to be hurting, but I can't help but wonder if you've read Mare's book. If you know how she feels…"

I clear my throat, feeling uncomfortable with the emotions running through me. "Why would I want to read it? I'm happy for her, Mom, truly I am. But I can't read that. All I've ever wanted for her is to achieve every single one of her dreams, but I can't read the words she's written. It's too much."

"I think a lot of things would make more sense if you just read it." She leans forward, grabbing the book and softly putting it in my lap.

I try to hand it back to her, but she doesn't let me. "Have you ever really thought about her dreams?"

My head rears back at her silly question. Of course I've thought about her dreams. They're all I thought about in the days leading up to her leaving, in the days after when I wondered if I should just drop everything at the ranch and fly to her and confess how fucking gone I was for her.

Her dreams were the only reason I never told her that I've spent many nights worrying that I'll never be able to love somebody like I loved her.

Mom runs her fingers over the front cover. "Read the dedication. Read the *book*. I think you might find out that while she has many dreams, her biggest one was always *you*."

I look at my mom in disbelief, my head spinning from her words. There seems to be some hidden meaning laced within her sentences, but she seems hesitant to tell me more until I read the book.

Mom sighs before she grabs my hand and interlocks our fingers. The book falls in the space between us, and I'm relieved to no longer have it teasing me. I'm afraid at what I'll find between the pages, at what I could discover in Mare's words.

"I think the two of you have a lot to figure out. After reading her words, after seeing you be the shell of a person I know you to be since she left, I think there's still a lot left unsaid. I'd hate to see a love story as beautiful as the two of yours end before it was meant to."

"Mom," I argue, wanting to tell her I'm incapable of getting my hopes up when it comes to Mare. I can't have hope to have her again. I selfishly held onto it for days, months, years after she left. I'd tell myself that when she came back, I'd tell her everything. I wouldn't hold back. She'd finally know how much I loved her. But she never came back. Eventually I had to come to terms with that. Some fictional book that Mare has published isn't going to change things. It *can't*. Because I can't have hope of having her again and lose her. I won't survive it.

"Cade Jasper Jennings, do as you're told and read this book. I'm going to book you a flight for the morning because I can tell you after reading what she's written, you'll want a flight. You can go or refuse, and I promise to not say another word about it either way. But I'll only make that promise if you promise me to read the book."

"I don't know if I can." My voice breaks. I'd be embarrassed if it was anyone but my mom sitting next to me.

"You can and you will," Mom says, her voice assured. She places the book back in my lap.

"I don't want to steal your copy," I say as one last pathetic excuse.

Mom smiles. "I bought all the ones for sale at Bluebird Books. I've got some to spare."

Unable to find another argument other than the fact I'm terrified at what I'll find between the pages of this book, I concede and tuck it to my chest.

"Bring our Marigold home," Mom says, her voice hopeful. She leaves me alone with my thoughts, the Colorado night, and the book.

Sighing, I open it, anxious at what I'll find.

MARE STARES BACK at me with wide eyes as I tell her how Mom encouraged me to read her book despite my many arguments. "Did you read it?" she whispers.

I unfold the blanket I was holding and spread it out on the ground. Mare and I are both quiet as I lay it out in the middle of the marigolds.

Taking Mare's hand, I pull her down until she rests against my chest. We used to lie together in this position all the time, staring up at the moon. It feels good to be doing it again, this time the sun shining down on us.

We aren't hiding anything; we aren't sneaking around, we're just us.

"I read the book," I confess. My fingers play with the hair that spills down her back.

"And?"

"And I think that *Our Story* seems a lot like *our* story."

I think back to the night my mom handed me the book. I didn't even make it past the dedication before having to take a break. The title and the dedication made everything click for me.

"What makes you say that?" she asks.

"To the one that got away," I recite from memory. "I'll always love you, even from a distance."

Mare turns her body so she can meet my eyes. "That could be about anyone."

"But it's not about anyone."

"No. It's about you. It's only ever been you."

"Goldie, if you'd just told me I didn't ruin it all. I would've..."

Mare runs her hands along my cheeks. She presses her palm against my stubble, letting it scratch against her skin. "I wrote the book thinking if I just told our story, every beautiful and heartbreaking moment, that by the end of the duet, I'd be putting our love story to rest, too. That if I could give them a happily ever after, if I could change the ending, that I'd get over you."

"Did it work?"

"I haven't written the ending yet."

"Is it working?"

"I thought it was," she confesses, tucking her hand underneath my T-shirt. Her hand is warm, and the way she trails it along the waistband of my jeans is doing things to me. "Before I came back, I was hoping it would work, but now I know that was hopeless."

"I read the book in one night. I couldn't stop, even at times when reading so many of our moments together felt too heavy. The sun had come up by the time I made it to the ending. If you could even call it an ending."

"That's the way we ended...or so I thought."

The ending of the first book ended with an airport scene similar to the one shared between Mare and me. The hero told the heroine he didn't love her, and the last words were the heroine wondering how she could ever love again.

"As soon as I read it, I wanted to change the ending."

"What does that mean?"

"I went to Chicago the day that I finished the book. Mom booked me a plane ticket, even gave me her personal copy of *Our Story* with tons of tab things in it because she wanted you to sign it, and I flew to Chicago. I had nothing but a change of clothes thrown into a bag and the hope of winning you back."

Mare looks at me, stunned. "You did what?"

"I went to Chicago. I went to win you back."

Her eyes dart across my face as she tries to understand my words. "You were in Chicago?"

My eyes close for a minute, remembering the day so clearly. It was over a year ago now, but it's still burned in my memory.

I remember it being shockingly warm as I stepped out of the airport. In my mind, Chicago was always cold and cloudy. It wasn't cold or cloudy that day. The sun was beating down on my skin as I waited for my Uber to pick me up.

"Yeah," I finally get out. "I came to tell you everything I should've said the day that you left Sutten."

"But you never…"

Our surroundings are calm and still as we both get lost in the silence. I think back on the hopefulness I felt in my chest that day. The thought of finally having my girl back in my arms had me asking the Uber driver to speed to the address Mom had given me for Mare.

I remember anxiously tapping my thigh as that twenty minute car ride felt like two hours. Time moved slow as I waited to reunite with the woman who owned my heart.

"It was early in the morning. I had no idea what your schedule looked like, but I was hoping you'd be home. My driver dropped me off in front of this apartment complex. The building was so tall, and everything was so crowded," I add, remembering how out of place I felt. I was used to wide open spaces and being on a first name basis with most of the people I saw day to day. It wasn't like that in Chicago. People were bumping into you, people refused to make eye contact, and the only reason my driver knew my name was because he had to double check he was picking up the correct passenger.

"I don't understand," Mare says under her breath. Her palm lays flat against my chest, her chin resting on top of her hand.

Her hair fans down her back, some of the long pieces trailing along the blanket with her small movements. "How could I not know you were there?"

Pain courses through me at remembering how quickly my excitement and hopefulness turned into regret and despair. "I was waiting outside the building. I thought about having the front desk call you and tell you I was there, but I was hesitant. I didn't know if you'd believe them. So, I figured I'd wait and if you didn't show up, then I'd think of something different."

The mountain breeze picks up. The marigolds rustle against one another, swaying in the breeze as I tell Mare about the second time my heart broke for her—for us. "I was just about to ask the front desk to call you when you walked out. You looked so stunningly the same, but so painfully different. Seeing you again, it caught me off guard. I couldn't move—couldn't breathe —for a few moments. All I could do was stare at you and try to figure out if it was really you."

She'd been so breathtaking in a fancy dark green dress with some sort of sweater over it. It wasn't what I was used to seeing her in, but she was beautiful nonetheless.

"You looked busy, like you were running late to something," I continue. My fingers find her cheeks, trailing across her sun-kissed cheekbones. "During the few moments it took me to work up the courage to talk to you, someone else came into view."

I pause for a moment, remembering the exact moment I realized that I missed my chance to apologize and confess to her how I really felt. "This man came into view. He had a nice suit on, he looked older, and you smiled widely at him. It was a familiar kind of smile—one that broke my fucking heart. He asked you something, and you nodded. He reached out and fixed the collar of your sweater, and it was at that moment it hit me that while I was still clinging to my love for you, maybe you'd let your love for me go. Maybe you'd moved on."

"I've never—"

"I don't want to know who it was—what it was. I'm not

telling you this to blame you for trying to find happiness, Goldie. Now that I've let the anger of losing you go, I've realized I can't be upset with you for doing what I told you to do. But it still didn't make it hurt any fucking less."

"So you came all that way and never said anything?"

I nod. "I couldn't do that to you. You looked happy. You were with someone who obviously fit in the life you'd created for yourself. I didn't fit there, and it really hit me watching the two of you together. I wanted you back, but I still couldn't give you everything. There was no way I could drop everything and move out there with you, and you'd just published that book and were killing it. It felt selfish of me to ask you to drop all of that and come back to Sutten with me."

Mare sits up. "I think you saw Rudy, my agent." She cradles her knees to her chest and wraps her arms around them. Her chin rests on her knees as she stares at the marigolds. "Are you going to ask me to drop Chicago and move back to Sutten this time?"

I push off the blanket and position my body next to hers. Reaching out, I grab her hand and wrap her fingers in mine. "To be honest, Goldie, the only thing I care to ask you is if you'll be mine forever. Where forever is spent doesn't seem to matter as much as it used to. I want you—wherever that will be."

"Rudy called this morning. I have to go back to Chicago to meet with my publishing house to sell them the new ending for the book."

I let go of her hand only to trace the bare skin of her leg. My fingertip traces over the soft skin of her knee. "Do you plan on coming back?" I ask hoarsely. Before she can say something else, I add, "Or am I getting a second shot at seeing you in Chicago?"

My finger drifts higher up, caressing her inner thigh. Her eyes flutter shut at the touch—or maybe it's from my words— either way, it doesn't matter. We aren't falling apart at the thought of a little distance between us. That's what matters.

"I don't know what to do next."

"You know what I know?" I ask, tracing along the edge of her dress. It'd be so easy for me to let my hand drift underneath and feel her. We were interrupted this morning before anything could happen and I'm desperate to be inside her again.

"What?"

"I know that I'll stop at nothing to figure this out. I'll talk to my dad about the ranch once a little more time has passed since Mom. I'll find new people to hire. Whatever it takes, Goldie. I'm not fucking up a second time. I'm not losing us again."

"So I'll go back to Chicago and you'll stay here?"

Leaning forward, I press my lips to her shoulder. I slip my fingers underneath her dress, letting my hand drift slowly up her thigh. "If that's what we have to do for right now, yes. You finish that book and do what you need to do in Chicago. I can't fucking wait to read it."

"Cade," she moans as my lips hit the hollow of her throat. Her back arches. The sound makes me lose the last bit of control I had. Grabbing her hips, I pull her on top of me.

"Goldie," I respond.

"What happened to *long distance relationships never work*?" To tease me, she grinds her hips up and down, grinding right over the denim covering my length. I smile, loving how she's giving me shit for something I said long ago.

"I was wrong, baby. I'll make anything work to keep you. To keep us."

I cover her mouth with mine, needing to taste her. She eagerly slips her tongue in my mouth, taunting and teasing me with the slow rhythm of her hips.

"But if you have to leave, I'm going to give you something to remember me by."

CADE'S MOUTH isn't gentle as he seals it to mine once again. His kiss is a claim. He won't back down at the thought of me leaving. The possessive way his tongue slides into my mouth tells me everything I need to know.

This time is different.

I will leave Sutten to finish what I've started, but he'll be here waiting. My chest feels heavy, but it's with happiness. I never knew I could feel this way again. Sometimes in the middle of the night, I'd hoped and wished that maybe one day Cade and I would find our way to each other again, but by morning I always made sure to not let that hope live.

But things feel different this time. We have no clear plan, and maybe that's okay. Maybe just the knowledge of how we feel about each other is enough.

Cade slips his finger underneath one of the thin straps of my dress. The strap falls off my shoulder, allowing him free reign of my exposed skin. He doesn't hesitate for a second. He kisses a trail around my neck. They aren't soft. He nips at my collar bone, easing the pain with his warm tongue.

"I want you," he rasps. "Right here. Right now."

I moan, bucking my hips when his fingers drift across the front of my panties.

"Out here?"

"Yes. I've had you under the moon before, let me claim you under the sun, in our field of marigolds."

He begins to slip my underwear down my legs. I help him by sliding off and pulling them the rest of the way off.

Cade licks his lips next to me, staring at where my dress bunches at my hips. "Fuck. One glimpse of your soaking wet cunt and I'm ready to bury myself in you."

Keeping his focus, I reach down to grab the hem of my dress. Slowly, I pull it up and over my body.

I'd feel bashful having the sun beat down on every bare inch of me if it was with anyone but Cade. I should feel exposed, being completely naked outside. But it isn't awkward at all. It feels perfect having his hungry gaze focused on me.

His cock strains in his jeans. I can't look away. Excitedly, I close the distance between us, letting my hand drift along the tented denim. "I wonder how ready I'll be if I put my mouth right…" my fingers skirt along the top of his jeans, "here…"

Cade sucks in a long breath. I stare at the muscle feathering at his jaw. I trace the outline of him once again. His hard length twitches against my touch, beckoning me to pull it out.

I bite my lip in excitement. It's time he loses all his clothes like I have. We sit in front of one another, our bodies brushing against each other's. "You're driving me fucking crazy, Goldie," he growls.

His words send me into action. My fingers begin to undo his jeans while he strips out of his shirt. If I wasn't so excited to take him in my mouth again, I'd take a second to appreciate the slopes and planes of his muscles. I'd take my time licking every inch of him, paying extra attention to the marigold flower he has permanently inked on his hip.

With his jeans now undone, I can see the tip of him peeking out from the waistband of his boxer briefs. It already glistens with the slightest hint of precum. My tongue wets my lips in anticipation. I look up, smiling.

"Lie down," I whisper, feeling brave and taking control.

Cade's dark eyebrows raise. The smirk he gives me elicits a rush of pleasure through me. Without any kind of argument, Cade lowers his body to the blanket and lays down. He lifts his hips for me as I pull the denim down his legs, throwing them off to the side because knowing Cade, clothes won't be needed for a long time.

Now that we're both completely stripped, I'm ready to fully feel his thick, hard length in my grip—in my mouth.

I crawl between his legs, crouching down until my mouth hovers above him.

"I love the way you stare at my cock," he says, his eyes hot on me.

I push my hair to my back, getting it out of the way so I can look at his every reaction as I take him as far as my throat will allow. Slowly, I coax him into my mouth, positioning my tongue flat against my teeth as I push him deeper and deeper.

He hasn't even hit the back of my throat and his fingers are twisting in my hair, gently guiding me as I take him as far as I can go. I stay there for a moment, fighting my body's urge to gag. It's so freaking hot to watch him as I do this.

He grunts, his fingers grasp at my hair firmly. "Goddamn, Goldie."

I bob up and down, twirling my tongue along the tip. When I shove him down my throat again, he helps me take him even farther by lifting his hips at the same time. My eyes burn with unshed tears at the force of taking him so far, but I want to do more. I try to swallow his length as he applies more pressure to my head to get him even deeper.

The look on his face encourages me. Cade stares right back at me. There's so much lust in his eyes, it has me speeding up my movements and reaching down to massage his balls, just to see what other reactions I can get from him.

"Fuck, baby." His eyes flutter shut momentarily as I continue to suck his dick enthusiastically. I use my tongue to flutter around his head, and continue massaging his balls with one hand and stroking his length with the other. "You're so fucking sexy. Do you see what you do to me? Feel what you do to me? I'm so fucking gone for you."

My clit throbs from his words, at the sight of him losing control from what I'm doing to him.

Before I can have any more fun, Cade is sitting up and sliding his cock from my mouth. He lines his face up with mine, his breath hot against my cheeks.

For a moment, we just stare at one another. Our inhales and exhales matching up. Cade's eyes flick to my lips. He reaches out, drifting his finger over my bottom lip.

"Look at your lips all red and raw from taking my cock so well."

I squeeze my thighs together, incredibly turned on by his words. "If I was doing so well, why did you stop me?"

He picks me up like I weigh nothing. Gently, he lies me down on the blanket. His cock brushes against my inner thigh as he settles himself between my legs. It's a tease, making my hips buck at the prospect of having him inside me again.

He pushes my legs open. The breeze hits my wetness, making me feel exposed and vulnerable. The feeling turns me on even more. Or maybe it's just the way he hungrily stares between my legs. "I stopped you because I wanted to taste this pretty pussy of yours. There's so much I have to do to remind you that even though soon there might be distance between us again, this pussy is all mine." His thumb brushes against my clit.

"It's yours," I repeat.

He slides two fingers inside me, not bothering to ease me into it. "That's right, baby. This pussy is mine. Always has been, always will be."

My eyes squeeze shut with how good it feels. He knows just the right things to say to me, just the right ways to touch me, to drive me to the brink of pleasure. "My tongue is going to remind you of how no matter where you are, you belong to me. And then once my cock is buried deep inside you, I'm going to show you that I belong to you."

His tongue circles my clit, leaving no more room for discussion. He licks and sucks as my moans get louder and louder. His two fingers work inside me, moving so expertly that it doesn't take long for pressure to build. When he uses his other hand to reach up and pinch my nipples, I know I'll be coming against his mouth in no time.

Cade doesn't falter once. His mouth works diligently against my clit while his fingers push in and out of me. His calloused fingers roughly squeeze my breast before he pinches my nipples over and over again.

There are too many feelings happening. I moan, shouting his name as a powerful orgasm rips through me. He doesn't relent. His tongue milks the orgasm for everything it is. He doesn't stop until my nails scratch at the hair on top of his head as I try to pull him up.

"Cade," I pant. I didn't have to do anything, yet I feel exhausted by the intensity of the orgasm.

His mouth moves from between my legs, but not far. He kisses the inside of my thigh, my hip bone, close to my belly button.

"What are you doing?"

He laughs, his breath tickling my ribcage. "Kissing every inch of you, branding you, loving you."

"Keep it up and maybe you'll make it into this next book."

He comes face to face with me, kissing around my lips but never right on them. "Something tells me there's going to be a lot about me in this book...just like the first one."

I arch when he strokes his cock against me. "Maybe," I tease.

He pushes in slightly, taunting me by not seating himself fully inside me. "It better be about me." He pushes in just a little further. "Fuck, I'm so turned on by the thought of you thinking of me while writing those dirty scenes of yours."

Even though he was inside me yesterday, I still feel myself

stretch around him as I get used to his thickness. He's slow as he works his way deeper and deeper. It's so achingly slow that my hips buck to try and speed him up.

"I'm going to take my time with you," he says, proving his point by the pace he keeps while rocking in and out of me.

I forcefully grab his neck, pulling him down so I can taste his lips again. He tastes like me, and I love it. His tongue slides into my mouth at the same time he fully pushes himself inside me, stopping for a moment to give me time to adjust.

I moan. He steals it from my mouth, responding with his own sound of pleasure. It feels too good—too perfect—as he pushes in and out. It feels so good that I don't know how I'm going to leave Sutten, how I'm going to leave this.

He has a way of fucking me and making love to me at the same time. His hips pick up pace but his tongue takes its time.

It's just the two of us, the house he built, and the marigolds he planted. Everything is too perfect. I never want to leave this moment.

I moan when he circles his hips. He just made me come and I feel like I could come again. If it weren't for him, I'd think multiple orgasms are meant for romance novels. He knows my body so perfectly that he knows how to steal one after another from me. Making sure my body is completely spent by the time he's done with me.

Cade's lips move from my mouth. He finds my neck, nipping at the sensitive skin enough to leave a mark. He does it again, and I don't have to say anything to know he's marking me on purpose.

I love it. I want to be branded by him. He eases the sting of his bites with his tongue, distracting me from the pain by reaching between us and brushing his thumb along my clit.

It doesn't take long for another orgasm to build and rip through me. This time, I moan against his mouth. My fingers dig into the muscles of his back as he pushes in and out of me.

As I come down from the orgasm, he pulls away. His lips are

now red, too. I'm sure my cheeks and mouth are red from the scratch of his facial hair. They feel raw.

I lift my hips slightly, trying to let Cade deeper in. "Your turn," I say, my words coming out more like a plea.

He gives me a cocky smirk. "Maybe. But I'm not coming until I get one more out of you."

"I don't know..." My words trail off but he seems to know exactly what I mean.

He pulls out of me suddenly, taking me by surprise. Before I can argue, he's pressing his front to my back and turning me to my side. He lifts my leg and drapes it over his hip. It's a position we haven't been in before, but when he slides inside me again, it feels totally different.

The position feels too good. His lips press to the back of my neck as he pushes in and out of me.

"Cade." His name comes out as a moan. The arm wrapped under me reaches to play with one nipple before it moves to the other. His other hand works against my clit, stroking me furiously, as he moves in and out of me.

His rhythm is achingly slow, but he goes so deep that the slow thrusts feel better than I could've ever imagined. I'm so sensitive from the orgasms he's already given me. With every slow, deep thrust of his, I get closer and closer to another orgasm.

"I'm going to come inside you, Goldie. I better feel you come too as my cum fills you."

My head falls backward with a powerful moan. I want to kiss him, but this position feels too good. I don't care that I can't reach his mouth. My teeth dig into my lip with each moan that falls from my lips.

I feel an orgasm build and despite my doubts, I know I'm going to come again. He pounds into me slowly, stopping for a short moment when he's all the way in, before he repeats the cycle.

He moans and it's the hottest thing I've ever heard. His

mouth presses to my ear as he moans with so much pleasure it fuels my own orgasm. He squeezes my breast, like he needs something to hold onto with the power of his own release.

His cum spills out of me, hitting my inner thigh with his continued thrusts. It feels like the orgasm builds for forever, until I'm finally pushed off the ledge I was waiting on.

I scream, not having to care about how loud I am in the middle of this field. I chant his name over and over between each scream as the orgasm takes everything from me.

My body goes limp as the last bits of the release courses through me. Cade presses a soft kiss to my shoulder. He slides out of me. My leg falls from his hip, my thighs pressing together. He keeps our bodies pressed against one another.

His fingers are featherlight as he traces them along my skin. "I'm going to be thinking about that for days even after you're gone."

"I wanted to talk to you first, but I think they're booking my flight for tomorrow, so technically...we have time to do that one more time before I go."

He nestles closer to me. "One? Oh, if you're leaving tomorrow morning, we're doing this a lot more than one more time..."

I look at the flowers in front of me, a question popping into my mind. "When did you plant these?"

His finger continues to trail along my skin. "This year or last year?"

This catches my attention. I turn to face him. "What do you mean this year or last year?"

Cade cups my cheek. "It means they need to be replanted each year. The first time I planted them was when I got back from Chicago. I needed something more than just the house to remind me of you. It was a way for me to distract myself. Maybe if I could take perfect care of these marigolds, in my fucked up head, I thought it meant that maybe you'd come back."

"Cade..." I try to comprehend the meaning behind his

words. It's still hard to imagine, knowing all the things he did while I was left believing he never loved me at all.

"This year, I planted them a little more angry. It really hit me that you weren't planning on ever returning and yet I felt this need to plant them just in case. I put it off for weeks, but eventually, I was out there delicately taking care of each seed, the smallest part of me hoping that one day you'd see them. That you'd see the house and the flowers and me and know that despite my fuck ups, I really have always loved you."

I press a soft kiss to his lips. "I love you, Cade Jennings."

"I love you, my Goldie."

I laugh. "I love my marigolds, too. They're so beautiful."

Cade pulls me into his chest. "That's the thing about marigolds, they're all beautiful."

Chapter 55
CADE
present

"I'm sorry I have to go." Mare looks up at me with the smallest frown. I hate the sad look in her eyes. I swipe my thumbs along her cheeks, not caring that we're standing in the middle of the airport while people hustle around us.

"Stop apologizing," I demand, pressing a kiss to her hairline. "Don't apologize for having to work, for working toward your dream."

"I just…" Her eyes look at the crowded airport around us. It's far more busy than I was expecting, but with summer coming close to an end, it makes sense that more people may be out traveling.

"Things aren't like last time, Goldie." I hate how nervous she looks. I hate knowing that the last time we stood together in this position made her feel this way. "Last time we were here, we were both far younger. I was stupid and didn't know how to deal with my feelings. I didn't know how to keep you and let you have your dreams. But this is different. My love for you won't falter. I'm in it, baby. No matter where you are. No matter how long we're apart."

She nods, reaching up to grab both my forearms. My hands cradle her cheeks as we stare at each other for a few moments.

"I know you have to go finish the book and you'll be busy, but don't forget about me here in Sutten, okay?"

She laughs. "Pippa has made me swear to call her every day."

"I don't need every day. Texts would be nice. Hearing your voice, maybe seeing your face on FaceTime now and then, but I respect your job. Do what you need to do to finish this book so we can be back together again."

"When will that be?"

I shrug. We don't have everything figured out. There's still a lot I have to do at the ranch since Mom's death. We're slowly catching up on work and getting more customers again, but it's a slow process. "I'll try and come out to Chicago as soon as I can."

"And I'll try to finish the book so I can come back to Sutten as soon as possible."

"I love you," I say, just needing to say the words. I want to repeat them over and over again. I know I can't erase the damage that was done last time we were in this position, but maybe if I tell her I love her enough this time, the old memory will become a little less prominent in her mind.

"I love you, too."

When her bottom lip trembles slightly, I pull her body into mine. My arms wrap around her, caging her in and pressing her to my heartbeat. Her tears don't hurt the way they did last time. They still hurt, but it's different. Last time it was so heart-breaking to see her cry it felt like a piece of my soul died having to hurt her. This time, it feels like a piece of my heart is leaving, but I have the comfort and assurance to know that it'll return.

"I don't want to go." Her words are muffled as she talks into my T-shirt.

"You have to, baby."

"I know. It doesn't suck any less." Her shoulders shake as she cries. I just hold her. She cried while saying goodbye to Pippa before she left for the airport. She bawled when my dad hugged her goodbye and told her Linda would be so happy to know Mare finally came back. I comforted her both times, and I do the same right now. I hate the thought of her leaving, but it's something I'm at peace with. We won't be apart forever. Either I'll visit her soon or she'll come see me. Being apart will be fucking hard, but we'll do it. We'll make it through this.

"Promise me this won't be the end of us?" The look on her face is so vulnerable. The shakiness to her words about kill me.

"I can survive being away from you—even though I don't want to—I won't fucking survive losing you again. This isn't the end of us."

"Okay." She lifts to her tiptoes and presses a kiss to my lips.

We stand there, using our lips to say everything we can't put into words.

I don't know how many people pass us or how long we stand there, but we kiss and kiss some more until both our mouths are rubbed raw.

A voice comes over the intercom, telling us that Mare's flight will begin boarding soon.

"Rudy will be picking me up as soon as I land to go into meetings, but I promise to keep in touch."

My forehead presses into hers. "Don't worry about me. I can't wait to hear all about what they think."

"I love you," Mare whispers. Tears now fall from her eyes. I wipe them away, wishing they weren't there.

"I love you with everything that I am. We'll make it through this, you hear me?"

She nods, rubbing her tear-soaked lips together. The sight of her crying makes my throat swell with emotion.

"I know we will."

I grab her arm and walk her toward security. The line isn't terrible so she should still have enough time to make it to her gate before they finish boarding.

"I love you, Goldie. Good—"

"Don't say goodbye," she says immediately. "I don't want it to feel final."

I nod, pulling her to me for one final kiss. "Hi," I whisper against her lips.

She laughs, a sob coming from her throat right after. "Hi," she responds back.

"I love you," I repeat, making good on the promise I made to myself that I'd make sure she knew how much I loved her.

"The kind of love that lasts forever."

"The kind of love that lasts *past* forever."

I kiss her, letting the feeling of it brand into my mind forever. I don't want to forget the way her lips feel against mine. I have to keep it in my head—in my heart—to hold onto until we're together again.

"Until next time," I say against her forehead.

"Until next time," she repeats.

We share one last kiss before she reluctantly peels herself from me. Neither one of us look away from one another until she gets swallowed in the line of people waiting at security.

It hurts like a bitch to see her go. It already feels like a piece of myself is missing, but this time I have the luxury of knowing it won't be long until we're together again.

I know that this time, this won't be the ending to our story.

Chapter 56
MARE
present

> **MARE**
> They love the idea.

CADE
Of course they do. It's our story. It's perfect.

CADE
Dolly has become an escape artist in your absence. I think she's throwing a fit that you've left.

> **MARE**
> That's my girl!
> I really do miss Sutten.

CADE
Sutten misses you.

I miss you.

But I'm so proud of you.

CADE

Checking in to make sure you've eaten.

Goldie?

I know you're writing, but I want to make sure you're taken care of.

If you don't answer me in the next ten minutes I'm going to order food to be delivered to your door.

I told the delivery driver to knock and hand it to you. You're going to have to take ten minutes to eat.

MARE

I'm sending a photo of me and the pizza for proof of eating. The food is delicious, and the book is coming along. I love you 🤍

MARE

I wish I didn't suck at being productive during the day. I feel like we're on opposite schedules, and I miss you.

CADE

I'm still here Goldie. 🦋

MARE

Tell me your favorite part of your day.

CADE

In about five seconds.

MY HEAD COCKS to the side. Before I can question what he means, his picture pops up on my phone. I swipe to answer immediately, comforted by seeing him.

Cade smiles. "There's my girl."

I tuck my feet underneath me, snuggling deeper into my writing chair as I hold the phone out in front of me. "You're up late."

As if on cue, he yawns. "To you it's early."

"I'm trying to write two chapters tonight so I'll probably be up until you wake up for chores in the morning."

"How's it coming?" His voice sounds tired and his eyelids are heavy. I pick up my glass of wine with my free hand, taking a sip as I appreciate the man on the other side of the screen.

Even though I know he'd typically be asleep by now, he's staying up just to talk to me. To see my face. My heart thumps in my chest with love. I can't believe he's mine.

"I'm so happy with the direction of the story. I think people will love it."

"Of course they will." His voice is sleepy. His eyes get heavier and heavier with each minute that passes by.

"How's everything on the ranch?"

He pulls the blanket close to his face, getting more comfortable. "Busy. *So* busy."

This time when his eyes drift shut, they don't open again. His breaths even out, and he's fallen asleep. I watch him for a few moments, wishing I was lying in bed next to him. I wish I could reach out and play with his overgrown hair. That I could feel the scratch of his facial hair against my palm.

"I love you," I whisper. He doesn't respond but he doesn't have to. I can feel his love. I feel it all the time, even though we aren't with each other.

Sighing, I end the call. I want to rifle through my suitcase that I still haven't unpacked from Sutten and pull out one of his shirts I stole and brought home. I packed as many as possible, wanting to have things that smell like him while we were apart.

Tonight, as I write, it hits a little harder that I'm not with him. I use the pain of missing him to my advantage. I write three chapters quickly, knowing the more I can give to my editor, the closer I am to finishing the book—which means the closer I am to seeing him.

CADE

Sending a picture of your marigolds.

They look beautiful this morning.

MARE

I wish I were there with you.

CADE

I love you.

MARE

I love you, too.

MARE

You haven't answered me all day, and I know you're busy getting ready for the fall.

Send me a picture of you all sweaty from working outside. Don't be shy, get that marigold in there. 😌

CADE

I'll send you a picture of whatever you want, Goldie.

But fair is fair.

I'll show you mine if you show me yours.

MARE

This book is officially halfway done!

CADE

Proud of you baby!

I love you.

MARE

I love you, Cade Jennings.

MARE

If I wasn't writing all night and sleeping and attending meetings all day I'd be a little offended that both you and Pippa aren't answering my calls...

"Hi, Goldie." Cade's voice is raspy. Even through the phone screen I can tell that he's sunburnt.

"Finally," I tease, snuggling into my bed. It feels cold and lonely without him next to me. I wish I could finish the book in Sutten, but I have meeting after meeting with people at my publishing house about this book. We have movie deals in the works and all these things where they want me here until the conclusion of the duet.

I like being here, but I hate being away from him.

Cade sets the phone down on his bathroom counter. I smirk when he steps away and I can see every perfect inch of the top half of his body.

"I see you staring," he says.

"I wasn't trying to hide it."

I bite my lip, suddenly turned on by watching the ripple of his abs. If only I could reach out and run my hands along them, feeling them harden underneath my touch.

"If you keep looking at me like that, I'll be late to morning debrief with our employees."

I smile, despite how exhausted I am. "You can't be late," I tease, letting my eyes roam over him. Despite the summer months turning to fall, he still has a perfect, golden tan to his skin. It's all the long days he's been putting in at the ranch.

Cade groans. It's sexy and rough. His forearms find the counter as he stares down at the phone. "I'll call you before I go to bed tonight? I want to talk more but I can't be late this morn-ing…" His words drift as he looks back at me, a heated look to his eyes.

"Of course. I should be up. Hey, have you talked to Pippa recently?"

Cade shrugs. "Here and there obviously but I've barely had time to think for myself recently I've been so busy. Why?" He turns his back to me as he reaches inside his shower and turns it on.

"I just haven't really heard from her much, that's all."

Cade pushes his pajama pants down, stripping to everything but his boxer briefs. "Dad is keeping everyone busy, and the cafe has been packed recently too, so maybe that's why?"

I chew on my lip a little. It isn't like Pippa to not be good about responding, but I don't say anything else.

"Guess what?" I ask.

"What?"

"They've loved everything up to the halfway mark. I don't have to do any rewrites which means I can start writing the second half."

"Maybe it's time I try to come out there soon?" he offers. "Once things die down a little bit here and I can give Dad a break, I'll come see you. It's been too fucking long."

I nod. The longer I'm here, the more I realize that I want to be able to write books, but I'm not sure I always want to write them here. "I'd love to have you come visit. I'd love to just see you. It's been almost two months."

"I'll be there," he says, with conviction in his voice.

"Guess what?" he asks, repeating the question I just asked him.

"What?"

"I love you. Nothing will change that. No matter how much I miss you."

"I love you, too."

M<small>Y PHONE VIBRATES</small> on the other side of the room. I hid it over there on purpose so I would get some work done. The book is close to being done, and I don't want anything to distract me.

After realizing I went down a rabbit hole for over an hour looking at puppy videos that somehow turned into watching other people organize their house while my apartment was a disaster, I had to resort to drastic measures.

But my phone vibrates again, and I can't help but wonder if it's Cade. It's late and normally he's asleep. We'd said goodnight to each other earlier…but I just have to check.

Annoyed by my lack of willpower to stay focused while finishing the last ten chapters of the book, I set my laptop aside and walk over to my phone.

I smile when I do see the messages are, in fact, from Cade.

CADE

I miss you.

At night is when it really hits. When I think about how I used to be able to reach across the bed and pull your soft body against mine.

I can't stop thinking about you.

> **MARE**
> You need to sleep.

> **CADE**
> It's getting harder and harder to sleep without you.

> **MARE**
> What if you pretend I'm there?

The bubbles pop up like he's typing something, but then they disappear. I frown for a moment, wondering if he isn't going to say anything back. Just when I'm feeling disappointed, they pop up again.

> **CADE**
> Only if you pretend I'm right there with you.

> **MARE**
> If you were next to me, what would you do?

I bite my lip. Heat passes over my body. There are so many nights I've had to touch myself thinking of him. I can't stop thinking about the possessive way he fucked me in the tack room. Or the way he loved me in the field of marigolds. Or the multiple times he claimed my body in the bedroom. All I want is to feel his touch again, to taste his lips, and finally start a forever with him.

> **CADE**
> Settle in, Goldie. There are so many things I'd do...

First, I'd pull your perfect body against mine. It's been too goddamn long since I've felt you pressed against me.

MARE

I miss having your arms around me.

CADE

It's been so long that I'd run my hands along your body, needing to memorize every perfect curve of you before I do anything else.

I walk to my bed, crawling over the pile of blankets on my mattress until I can get comfortable. When I look back at my phone, I see that Cade has sent another text.

CADE

I'm hard from the thought of even touching you. Fuck, I would barely be able to control myself if you were next to me.

Wetness pools between my thighs. I try to rub them together to get some friction and relief, but it isn't enough.

MARE

Tell me more.

It feels naughty to be having this conversation with him, but it feels so right. I've always loved the filthy things that come out of

Cade's mouth. He's always so quiet, so careful with his words and thoughts. But when he says something dirty, I can't help but come apart.

CADE

Touch yourself.

And then I'll tell you more.

MARE

I can't...

CADE

Imagine it's me.

If I were with you, I'd let my fingers trail right above the line of your panties. I'd tease you before touching you.

Tease yourself a little, then touch what belongs to me.

I close my eyes for a moment, wondering if I'm really going to do this. I've touched myself plenty of times in my life imagining Cade. But never have I had phone sex. Never have I texted all my dirty thoughts about him.

Turning to face the moonlight that drifts through my apartment window, I snap a photo of myself. I'm wearing a T-shirt—his T-shirt that still smells like him. You can see my nipples peeking through the faded white fabric. My cheeks are red in the photo. I send it anyway, wanting him to know exactly how I'm feeling.

MARE

I don't know how to do this.

CADE

Pretend you're doing research.

You're writing one of those dirty scenes in your books that make me fucking crazy.

It only makes sense you need to experience what it feels like to come just by my words and pictures while we're miles away from one another.

MARE

I do need to write a sex scene tonight.

CADE

My girl shouldn't have to write a sex scene while she's hot and horny for me.

Let me take care of you.

Feeling brave, I slide my T-shirt up and expose the boring cotton pair of underwear I put on. I dip my fingers into the top of them a fraction of an inch. My thighs fall open, showing off a small wet spot on the light pink fabric. I hold my phone up, taking a photo and immediately sending it before I chicken out.

My phone lights up immediately, Cade's photo illuminating on my screen. My eyes go wide, imagining what this would be like if we do this over FaceTime.

I swipe to answer, keeping the camera on my face instead of the same angle I just gave him between my legs.

"Hi," I whisper, suddenly feeling so much more shy seeing his face on the screen.

Cade holds the phone out, letting me see his upper half. He wears no shirt, giving me an unobstructed view of his perfect abs.

"Are you touching yourself yet?" His voice is rough and lust-filled. My clit throbs at the sound of it.

I shake my head. "Not yet."

Cade turns the phone, taking me by surprise when I see his large hand wrapped around his length. He pumps up and down, running his thumb along the tip each time. "I'm touching myself thinking about you. Fuck, I wish I could slip my fingers inside you. Feel how wet you are."

I let out a sound that is a mix between a squeak and a moan. I'm not brave enough to show myself slipping my fingers into my panties, but I do as I'm told. I tease myself, letting them drift into the cotton but not touching the spot where I need relief quite yet.

"Touch yourself and tell me how wet you are for me. Use your words."

I moan. Normally he's the one that says all the dirty things between us, not me. Somehow I can write them, but I can't say them out loud. Right now, I want to, though. I want to do this with him—to feel intimate no matter the distance between us.

"Okay," I whisper, my fingertips trailing low. I'm met with my arousal. "I'm wet," I continue, "so wet..."

He grunts. He's got the camera on his upper half again, but I can see the ripple of his bicep as he works himself up and down. "I'm here, baby," he growls. "Pretend it's me touching you, pleasing you."

"I am." I moan, imagining what it'd feel like to have his thick fingers pushing inside me. "I have to do two of mine to imagine it's you."

"Push them inside you, hook them to hit the spot you like, baby."

"It feels too good. Do you feel good, too?"

He sighs, flexing his jaw as his head falls backward to his pillow. "It feels so fucking good. I'm so fucking hard right now imagining you playing with your perfect pussy."

I rock my hips back and forth, grinding against my hand as I pick up pace. It feels so hot to be doing this with him, to have this conversation knowing what both of us are doing.

"Show me," he presses, holding the phone out so I can see both his face and his cock. It's like I forgot how big and thick he is as his hand pumps up and down. It takes a good amount of time for his hand to travel the entire length of his shaft. "Let me watch you touch yourself, baby."

I let out a loud moan, one I know he heard. I set my phone on the other side of the bed, propping it against a pillow so he can see what I'm doing. With a tentative sigh, I push his T-shirt up my body until one of my peaked nipples pops out.

He sighs. "God, I wish I could run my tongue along that pretty pink nipple. Imagine how good it'd feel if I pulled it into my mouth, sucking it until your back arches in pleasure."

I grab and tug at my nipple, pretending it's him in bed with me. Pretending that this long distance was over and he could ravish my body any time he wanted.

Once I feel like my nipple has had enough attention, I slide my hand down my hips and pull my panties all the way off.

"That's my girl. Show me my pussy. I'm fucking starving for it."

Another loud moan ricochets through my body. I turn my hips slightly, bringing all of me into view.

I can hear his deep inhale through the phone. He curses under his breath. I watch him squeeze his cock, his hand picking up pace in pleasure.

"Now go back to what you were doing, Goldie. Slip those fingers inside you. Not just one…not just two…but maybe three. Maybe that'll be thick enough so you can pretend it's my cock."

I do as I'm told but it isn't the same. God, I wish he was here so much. I want to wrap my legs around his strong body and let him have his way with me. My fingers aren't enough. I don't know if anything will be enough until we're together again.

"Wait," I pant, an idea forming in my head.

"What is it, baby? Did I say you could stop?"

I turn to face him, biting my lip because I can't believe I'm about to say this out loud. "I have an idea..." I begin, feeling so incredibly turned on.

"Whatever you want," he growls. "You're in control now. Tell me what you'd imagine I'd be doing to you and that'll happen."

My eyes focus on my bedside table. I reach over the phone, opening the drawer and pulling out a recent purchase. I bring it into the camera's view, heat spreading throughout my cheeks as Cade focuses on what I have in my hand.

"What if I used this to pretend it was you. It's still not as big as you, but..."

Air hisses through Cade's teeth. It's so loud and obvious, even through the speaker of the phone.

"Have you gotten yourself off with that vibrator thinking of me, Goldie?" His voice is tense, like he's so turned on he can barely speak.

I nod, thinking of all the times I'd come undone with the toy inside me, Cade's name falling from my lips.

"Fuckkkk. Why are you so fucking sexy?"

"Is this okay?" I ask tentatively, turning it on at its lowest setting.

Cade's hand pumps up and down his cock so quickly that a vein appears on his bicep, trailing all the way down his arm with the exertion. "Fuck yeah it's okay. I'm so fucking hard at the thought of you using that to get yourself off. Show me what you do. Show me how you fuck yourself while pretending it's my cock."

I moan, pressing the button two more times until it's at the setting I prefer. I have to shut my eyes to be able to do this in front of him. Somehow I just know—I can feel—him watching my every move.

The toy vibrates in my hand as I guide it in the direction where I want it most. I adjust my position, letting my thighs slide open so he can see even more of me.

At first, I slide only the top of the vibrator inside me, needing to adjust to the feel of it. It's almost too much, having Cade's heated gaze on me through the screen and feeling the pulsing vibrator inside me.

"God, you're so fucking hot. So goddamn perfect." Cade's words encourage me.

I watch him fist his cock, totally swept up in watching him touch himself. I shove the vibrator even deeper inside me, imagining it's his cock stretching me.

"Cade," I moan, pushing it as far as it can go. It feels way too good, I know it won't be long until I come. I angle it, the pulsing head of the vibrator hitting the perfect spot.

"Look at you taking that so fucking well. God, your pussy is so greedy for it."

I palm my breast, feeling goosebumps pop up on my body everywhere knowing I'm close to coming. "I'm close," I pant, needing to know that when I come, he will too.

Cade lets out a sound of approval. "When you come, you imagine that's my cock. I'm going to come too, baby, pretending that I'm wrapped up in your sweet, perfect pussy, imagining it holding me tight as I make my girl scream my name."

"Oh my God," I moan, feeling the buildup of the orgasm.

"Watch me, Goldie," he demands, his voice stern and leaving no room for argument. "We come together, watching each other. You got it?"

I nod because that's all I can do. I'm seconds away from being sent over the edge. I buck my hips slightly, allowing the vibrator in a little farther. Suddenly, I'm coming, my vision getting blurry with the intensity of the orgasm.

It seems to last forever, the orgasm ripping through my body as I watch Cade come.

It's the hottest thing I've ever seen. Even through the screen, I can see the cum leaking down his hand. I can see it shoot onto his skin, the evidence of his orgasm everywhere for me to see.

Most of the time he'd come inside me. It's a totally different experience to see it all over him, to watch it keep coming out as he pants my name over and over.

I meet his eyes through the screen, finding his eyes already on me.

He grabs the phone with the hand not coated in his come. I grab mine, following his lead. We both catch our breaths for a moment, staring into the heated gaze of the other.

"Goldie," Cade finally says, his voice low.

"Yeah?"

"I don't fucking care how we make it happen, but soon, you'll be in my arms again. You hear me?"

I nod because I couldn't agree more.

Chapter 58
CADE
present

My feet ache in my boots as I walk up the stairs to the main house. Every night before going back to the cabin, I come by and check on Dad. I know he's got to be lonely in this big, empty house. Even though we spend a lot of time together during the day, I can't help but want to check in on him before I go to bed for the night.

Today was hard. It's been a week since Goldie and I watched each other get ourselves off over the phone, and it's been getting harder and harder to be away from each other. I think it's in part due to the fact that we're both so busy right now it's hard to make time for one another.

She's almost done with the book, and I've been helping Dad prepare for winter. Even though it's only early fall, there's still a lot we have to do before the first frost. I want to make sure I help Dad as much as possible, to shoulder what I can of the ranch so he can take some time for himself, to heal from Mom.

It's been months since Mom died, and Dad is still a shell of the person that he used to be. It's not as bad as it first was when she passed over the summer, but he still doesn't smile the way he used to.

I don't know what else to do but be here and show up for him. But it also hurts because the duty to the ranch is getting in the way of me being able to fly out to Mare.

It's a fucking mess, and I don't know how to fix it. Mare and I are good, we're strong, and I know we'll make it through this. But it doesn't mean I don't fucking miss her like crazy.

My boots thump against the hardwood floor as I walk through the main room.

"Dad?" I yell, not finding him in the kitchen.

"In here," Dad responds from down the hall. I walk the house until I find him in his office.

It's weird seeing him sitting at his desk, hunched over a calculator that's ancient and a laptop that probably needed to be replaced five years ago. After Mom died, he avoided his office like crazy. Even though it was technically *his* office, it was where they spent most of their time together. Her sitting in her chair in the corner keeping herself busy as he worked.

"You just getting done?" Dad asks, typing something into the calculator before looking up at me.

I nod, taking a seat in the recliner in the corner of the room. "Yeah." I groan, my body melding into the recliner Mom used to sit in and read her books.

"You know you can take a break," Dad says, pulling a pair of reading glasses from his face.

"I'm not the one still working."

He gives me his typical warning look that I got plenty of times as a child.

I shrug. "You can't tell me I don't have a point."

He lets out an annoyed sigh. "I'm old. Without your mother here, work is kind of my life, son. But it doesn't have to be that way for you."

My heart feels heavy at the mention of Mom. Of knowing how hard it still probably is for him to be without her. I can't fucking imagine not having Mare. Even the years we spent apart I could tolerate because I knew she was somewhere else, following her dreams. I knew she was happy.

But I can't fucking think about what it'd be like if she was just...gone.

I shake my head, trying to rid myself of the thought. There's no fucking way I can approach thinking of that. I've really got to find time to go to her, to go to Mare and see her. Hug her. Touch her. Remind her that I'm hers however long our forever will be.

"I'll take more time for myself once winter sets in."

Sutten Mountain becomes crazy around ski season. Tourists descend upon our small town, all of them wanting to take their winter vacations here. Things slow down for us at that time. We can't do trail rides in the snow, so we don't have to worry about catering to any clients. It's just making sure the ranch stays running and the horses stay happy and healthy.

Dad taps his knuckles against his desk. "No."

My head rears back. "What?"

"I'm not going to let you work yourself ragged because you feel like you have to for me."

My mouth snaps shut. I think through my words, not knowing what to say back to Dad. He's caught me off guard. "I'm not doing anything because of you. This ranch will be mine one day. I want to hold my own."

"Why haven't you gone to Chicago yet?"

"Because you've needed help."

"I'm not asking for help now."

I sigh, running my hands over my thighs. "We're not even close to bailing enough hay to last us through the winter. There are four more pastures that need to be turned. I've got to update some of the—"

"Yes, there are things that have to be done. And while I appreciate you working yourself to death to help me, I'm better now. I'm present. As present as I can be. I can do this. You held this ranch together when your mother left us, but it's time for you to take a break."

I swallow, not knowing what else to do at the impact of his words. They do something to me, making emotions I've tried to stifle in this time away from Mare bubble up to the surface. "I miss Mare like crazy, Dad. I want to go see her, but I don't want you to have to do everything on your own."

"Do you know Linda used to go on and on about you two?"

"Pippa and me?"

Dad grunts. "No. You and Marigold. As soon as Mare became a teenager, she was always watching you. Your mom knew that girl was wild about you."

"It seems like everyone noticed that but me."

"She noticed the *moment* things changed between you and Marigold. I can hear her voice so clearly in my head. *'Did you see the way they looked at one another at dinner, Jasper? Our son is crazy about Marigold. I don't know if I've ever seen two people as in love as those two.'* It was all she wanted to talk about at night," he says. "It made her so happy to see the two of you happy. It hurt her fragile heart when it was clear things had changed between you and Marigold."

"Dad," I croak. My eyes sting from the memories. At the knowledge that she so clearly knew everything happening between Mare and me.

"Your mom couldn't wait for the day the two of you would find each other again. She was devastated when Mare left and didn't come back. But she *always* had hope that the two of you would find each other again."

Guilt seeps into my bones. If I would've handled that summer years ago better, maybe my mom would've been able to see Mare more.

"Now you're with her, and you both are happy, but I can tell you're not truly happy, son. You need to go to Marigold."

"Who will help you?"

He swats at the air. "We've hired two new people in the last month. What are we paying them for if they're not helping?"

"You know what I mean."

"I do. You feel a responsibility not only to this ranch, but to me, and while I love you for it, son, I need you to make a different decision."

I open my mouth to argue, but he holds his calloused hand up to stop me. "Your mother would want you to be with Marigold. It was *all* she ever wanted. And I think if you stopped and thought about it for a moment, you'd give this ranch up in a heartbeat if you had to choose between Marigold and it."

"I don't have to choose. I love her with an intensity that scares the hell out of me, but we're good this time. We can make it. I can help you and she can finish her story and then we can figure it out."

Dad swallows. For some reason, his eyes get a little misty, and it makes my throat swell. I don't see him like this, not ever. He lets out a shaky breath. "If someone came to me today and told me I could see your mother again, even just for a minute, but I'd have to give up the ranch, I'd do it. I'd give it up in a fucking heartbeat, son. All the work my dad, my grandfather, and I put into it is nothing compared to the love I felt for your mother."

I shake my head, trying not to break down in front of my dad. "Dad..." I croak, knowing if I had to choose, I'd do the same thing. Making my dad proud—keeping this ranch in the family—is one of the things I want most in this world. But what I want the *most*, is Mare. My Goldie.

"I'm not blind. I know the way you look at the girl. I remember looking at your mother the same way. Like she hung the damn moon and all the stars around it." He sighs, his shoulders becoming shaky with the exhale. "There's nothing I can do to get your mother back, but I'd give up just about anything to be given the chance. I won't let you miss out on a love as powerful as I shared with your mother because you feel like you owe it to me or this ranch. You get your girl, Cade."

"What if she doesn't want to move back to Sutten?" I ask, finally voicing my deepest concern. I know we talked about making this work for now, but we never talked about where we'd settle down. I don't know where her head is at, if she'd want to move here forever or if she truly sees herself living in the city for good.

"Then you'll tell your old man and your sister goodbye and you'll follow her anywhere."

I stare at him for a few moments at a total loss for words. I don't know what to say. There's no clear answer on what to do here except for one thing—I need to go to Mare. We'll figure everything else out, and knowing that I won't be letting my dad down—this ranch down—if I leave is all I needed.

"You sure about this?" I ask, standing up. I fix the hat on my head, already thinking about if there'll be any flights available tonight. I'll probably have to wait until tomorrow, but it's still sooner than I was expecting.

Maybe I could even surprise her. Do a redo of the last time I went to Chicago.

Dad stands up, rounding his desk until he puts his hands on my shoulders. "I've never been more sure of anything in my life. Follow your heart, son. All the rest of life's bullshit we'll figure out later, okay?"

Breaking down, I cry. I cry because for the first time since Mom died, I feel like I have my dad back. My arms wrap around him. For a few seconds we hug, not needing any further words.

I pull away, taking a deep breath and getting my shit back together.

Dad pats me on the shoulder a final time. "Let me know if you need a ride to the airport tomorrow."

Chapter 59
MARE
present

MY EYES ARE BURNING from staring at a computer screen for so long. I'm so close to the end, to finishing this book that I can't stop. My fingers ache and I can't remember the last time that I ate, but none of it matters because the words won't stop flowing.

I take a deep breath, blinking a few times to try and get my eyes to focus. I'm at the ending of the book, writing the second to last chapter before the epilogue. I've been staring at a screen so long that tears burn at my eyes from the brightness of the screen.

This story is taking everything out of me in the best possible way. I type and type until I feel like I need a five minute break to collect myself before continuing.

I look around my room, wincing at how messy it is. I haven't cleaned it in God knows how long. There are protein bar wrappers on the floor from when I've tried giving my body some kind of sustenance. My eyes land on my suitcase. It's been a couple of months since I've been in Sutten yet I still haven't fully unpacked. I thought if I kept it shut, only opening the suitcase to grab another one of Cade's shirts, that I'd preserve the smell of him longer.

I slide off my bed, my knees cracking from sitting in the same position writing for hours. Crouching to my knees, I unzip the suitcase and open it slightly, trying to find another one of Cade's shirts.

I don't see anything in the tiny hole I've created. So I unzip it a little farther. There's no way I've already made it through the entire stock I stole from Cade.

Or maybe I have.

My stomach drops at the thought. I just have a few more chapters. Probably only days until I can go back to Sutten to see Cade after finishing this book. I just need one more shirt—a few more days with his scent—before we'll be together again.

Not caring about being careful anymore, I unzip the suitcase fully and throw it open. I sigh in relief when I find one final T-shirt left. It's an old one from a 5K that Cade did one year while in Sutten. It's worn and has the perfect softness. My hands reach for the fabric, pulling it out of the suitcase and to my nose.

Inhaling, I relish in the smell of him. It surrounds me, allowing me to pretend, if only for a few moments, that he was here in this room with me. When my eyes finally flutter open, I find an old copy of *Our Story* in the bag.

I set the T-shirt aside and reach for the book. It's worn and well-loved. Like it had been read cover to cover many times.

I open to the first page. Stamped neatly is a line that says *Sutten Mountain Book Exchange If Lost Please Return To...* My fingers run over the neatly printed name on the line.

Linda Jennings.

Tears well in my eyes from the sight of her familiar handwriting. It's not lost on me how worn this book is. It's clear she read it a lot. There are tabs hanging out the side and pages that look to be dog-eared. I turn through the pages, tears falling down my cheeks as I read the little notes she'd left in the book.

I shift, bringing the book to my chest as I get comfortable. An envelope slips from between the pages, falling into my lap with a soft *thud*.

My breath catches when I see my name printed across the front.

"Oh my God," I whisper, staring at my name in Linda's handwriting.

My heartbeat picks up as I slide my finger under the flap of the envelope. There's a small tearing sound as I open it as carefully as I can. I don't know what's inside, or when it was written, but I want to preserve anything I can from Linda.

A piece of paper is nicely folded inside. I carefully unfold it, a lump forming in my throat when I realize it's a letter from Linda to me.

My darling Marigold,

There's nothing I want more in this world than for you to be reading these words. If you're reading this, it means Cade found you and gave you this book like I asked. I may have lied and told him that I wanted your signature, which I do want, but I gave the book to Cade with an ulterior motive.

I needed you to know from a mother's point of view how much my son loves you. For years, I've watched him grieve you leaving. I've watched him mourn the loss of you all alone because he's too stubborn to tell any of his family about the two of you.

But I've known. I've always known about the love you share for each other. You've always looked at my boy like he was your entire world. And I noticed the moment he started looking at you like that, too. I love you like my own daughter,

Marigold, and I know you. I know you've always loved him. And I know my boy loves you more than anything else in this world.

I don't know everything that happened between the two of you. One moment you both were happy and the next moment you wouldn't come home, and Cade shut down. I'm not telling you this to make you feel bad, please know that, I'm telling you this next part because you need to know that whatever my sweet, quiet, stubborn son has done in the past, he loves you with his entire being. He hasn't stopped loving you in the time you've been away.

Cade hasn't been the same since you left. I thought maybe time would heal his wounds. Maybe you'd come back, maybe he'd laugh more, maybe you two would find each other again. But that didn't happen. At least it hasn't yet—until tonight. Tonight I looked in my son's eyes, and I saw hope. I told him to read your book, I hope you don't mind since I suspect most of Wade and Daisy's story is reminiscent of yours and Cade's. I think Cade has been under the assumption that there's no hope for the two of you. But I can't help but read the words you've written in these pages and think that there somehow still is hope. For the both of you, I hope that love can overcome anything that's happened between the two of you.

From the moment your momma died, I've

always wanted to take care of you, Marigold. I love you like I love my own children. I want what's best for you. And from what I've observed over the years, what's best for the both of you, is each other. The two of you have always been like magnets. It's always been like you can sense each other. It's something special that I don't think comes around often.

You may not know this, but I know you used to sneak into his room late at night. I could hear your soft footsteps through the house. I wanted to scold you as a child for doing it, but I couldn't. I'd open the door in the mornings and find you and Cade sleeping so peacefully. Your pinkies would be touching across the pillows, and I could tell that no matter the fact you had just lost a mother and your father was distant, that you were going to be okay.

Because of my baby boy, you were going to be okay.

I know this is long but I have a small request for you, Marigold. I know Cade held you together all those years—and he may not know it—but you were holding him together too. I ask that maybe this one last time, you help hold him together.

Please believe him when he tells you he loves you.

Please look in your heart...because maybe you still love him too.

After reading this beautiful story, I'm hopeful that you do.

So many beautiful love stories have endings. I hope that isn't the case for you and Cade. I hope maybe the two of you can rewrite your story.

Whatever you decide, I will support you. I love you. I love my son. I will be there for both of you no matter what happens.

I'm proud of you. I'm proud to call you mine.

All my love forever,
Linda

P.S. Maybe I could watch you sign the book in person when you come back to Sutten? When you come back home?

Powerful sobs overtake my body. I can't see a thing through the tears. I set the letter down, not wanting to ruin the paper from the tears streaming down my face. The letter must be from when Cade came to Chicago last year after he'd read *Our Story*.

I can't believe the letter had been sitting in my suitcase all along. That it'd been in Cade's possessions all along, and we didn't know it existed. He must've slipped the book in my suitcase before I left. He couldn't have known what waited for me in the pages of Linda's book.

My shoulders shake as I try to take a deep breath. It's a useless attempt, the more I try not to cry, the harder I cry. There's so many feelings coursing through me that I don't know what to think or how to feel.

I feel guilty for never coming back to Sutten knowing what waited for me there. I feel so sad that I can't tell Linda to her face that Cade and I have found each other again.

And then I feel clarity.

Because nothing has ever been more clear in my life.

Sutten has always been my home. It always will be. And no matter what living in Chicago has done for me, I don't want to be here forever.

And I can't go another minute without being with the man I fell in love with as a teenager when he remembered my birthday and told me to make a wish.

Everything falls into place. I know the ending of my book. I know what I need to do.

There's only one thing left to do.

"I FEEL this is really poor planning on your part," Pippa chides from the other line of the phone.

I sigh, taking a seat on one of Linda's front porch rockers. "I understand that now. However"—I say dramatically—"you lecturing me doesn't help whatsoever. Are you going to come pick me up or not?"

Pippa sighs. "I'm just saying that *maybe* if you and Cade had just texted one another that you were planning on doing these big, elaborate gestures, that the two of you wouldn't have literally missed each other at the airport by a couple of hours."

"I wanted to surprise him in Sutten, Pip. Not once did I think Cade would be planning on flying all the way to Chicago at the same time."

"You know if you would've just told me you were coming back, or called me when you landed instead of hiring a driver, I could've told you he was planning on surprising you."

"Yes. I should've told you. For once in my life, I'm sorry I kept a secret from you."

She laughs nervously. "Technically, it's not the first. I'm on my way, but there's just one little thing…"

"Wait to tell me when you get here. Focus on driving. Speed a little. Sheriff Phillips will understand."

"Miss Betty is a huge fan of yours."

I turn pink thinking about trying to talk Pippa out of a speeding ticket by offering up a signed book to our sheriff's wife.

"No more talking," I instruct. "Get here so we can hopefully catch Cade at the airport."

"You've got to be kidding me," I mutter under my breath, gawking at the man sitting in the passenger seat of Pippa's work van.

Pippa leans forward, her hands gripping the steering wheel as she stares at me with wide eyes. "Mare," she begins, looking from the man to me and back again. "You *might* remember Camden."

My mouth hangs open as my eyes bounce between the two of them. Yes. I remember Camden. It's hard not to remember the asshole of a man sitting shotgun in Pippa's work van.

He stares back at me, an unreadable look on his face. I don't know why on Earth he's willingly sitting in Pippa's van. And why she's letting him.

"Oh my God, Pippa, did you abduct the asshole tourist?" I try to whisper inconspicuously.

Pippa laughs uncomfortably. "*Technically*, no."

Camden shoots her a look. His jet-black eyebrows rise to his hairline. "Abduct might not be the best use of words. Blackmail? Maybe that's better..."

Pippa rolls her eyes. "Don't be so dramatic."

"The last time you talked about him you said, and I quote, '*There's no way that man has a big enough dick to be that big of a dick.*' And then I think you said something that his terrible attitude is his way of compensating for his 'small dick' and 'lackluster looks.'"

Pippa squeaks as Camden aims a menacing look her way. It's so cold and intimidating that I get goosebumps just from witnessing it. Camden is quiet for a moment, running his finger over his lip. When he turns to face me, there's a fake, cold smile on his lips. "Pippa didn't seem to think my cock was small when she was trying to fit it in her mouth when you so *rudely* interrupted us with your rather desperate call for help."

Pippa's forehead falls to the steering wheel. The van lets out the tiniest squeal of a honk.

I stare between the two of them, wondering what in the actual hell is going on.

Pippa is hooking up with a tourist? This tourist?

Apparently more has happened in my absence than I was expecting.

"Pippa, it appears we have *much* to catch up on," I say, still completely shocked about what's transpiring before my eyes.

"Pippa," Camden begins, copying me. His voice is low as he turns to look at her. "You'll be paying for those little comments of yours later."

I try not to grimace when my best friend looks excited by the words coming from Camden's mouth. A weird sound comes from my mouth as my lips flap open and shut like a fish because I can't comprehend what's going on in front of me.

Camden sighs, aiming an annoyed look in my direction. "Are you going to get in or are we just going to keep gossiping?"

I narrow my eyebrows at him. "I've known Pippa longer, so I get the front seat." My eyes pop to the back of the van. There's one tiny little seat, the rest of the van meant to hold deliveries and not another person.

Camden clicks his tongue. "I'm not sitting in the back."

Pippa pats him on the shoulder. "In all fairness, we're doing the whole dramatic rush to the airport scene for Mare. She should get the front seat."

Camden looks appalled at Pippa's words. Pippa doesn't look apologetic in the slightest. His menacing glare doesn't seem to deter her. "You're the one who *insisted* on coming. Get in the back. And hurry, we've got to go!"

He lets out a low growl, shocking me by getting out of the front seat.

Oh my God. *He just listened to Pippa?*

There's way more to this story I'm dying to find out. But first, we've got to get to the airport.

Camden gets in the back of the van, a few curse words coming from his mouth as he squeezes his tall body into the narrow space.

I hop in next to Pippa. She takes off immediately. The van shakes along the bumpy gravel driveway.

Pippa sighs. "You know, we could just call Cade and tell him not to get on the plane. Or to come back here."

"That would be the logical thing to do," Camden pipes up from the back of the van.

I shoot him a look. "I write romance novels for a living. That isn't romantic and I wanted it to be a surprise that I'm back."

"We could make up an excuse?" Pippa offers. "Come up with some reason to make him not get on the plane and come back home?"

My heart beats in my chest when I think about reuniting with him again. I shake my head at her suggestion. "No. I want to meet him at the airport."

Before I can say anything else, Pippa slams on her breaks, sending Camden roughly against my seat. "What the fuck!" he shouts, his large hand grabbing the head rest of my seat to right himself.

Pippa laughs, undeterred by his harsh words. "Sorry!"

"Tell me, why couldn't you just drive yourself?" Camden asks.

I chew on my lip. "I haven't really driven a car in years. I haven't had to."

"We're going on a little mini road trip to win Mare her man! Think of it as fun, Camden. You need more fun in your life."

"My idea of fun was watching you choke on my—"

"Okay then!" Pippa yells, talking over Camden. She turns up the radio, and a country song blares from the speakers.

I look between the two of them, trying to piece together what has happened with Pippa in the months I've been gone. I keep my questions to myself—for now. Soon I'll ask her what's going on. I have to know how she apparently started hooking up with *him* of all people.

For now, I focus on getting to Cade. On making sure we get there before he boards.

I've got one question I need to ask Cade.

Chapter 61
CADE
present

I STARE AT MY PHONE, wondering why Mare isn't answering any of my texts. I've been trying to get a hold of her all morning and haven't heard a thing. I keep reminding myself that it's possible she's just locked away finishing this book, but I can't help but be a little worried.

Hopefully she's taking care of herself. At least in a few short hours, I'll be there with her to help however she needs. I'll cook for her, clean for her, do anything while she finishes the book just as long as I'm with her.

I look at the text I'd sent Pippa earlier, wondering why it's also gone unread.

I'm about to go through security when I get this feeling. It's the same one I used to get late at night when Mare would show up at my door. I don't know why I do it, but I look over my shoulder, halfway hoping to see the love of my life.

She isn't there. It's just my mind playing tricks on me.

The line moves again, but only by a few steps. I let my eyes wander around the crowded airport, wondering why I can't seem to shake the feeling that she's here. I've always been able to feel her, and I've never been wrong about it, except for apparently right now.

We've spent too much time apart. My heart—and mind—are playing tricks on themselves with how much they miss her.

I'm following the businessman in front of me when I hear my name called from behind me.

I freeze. I could be in the most crowded of rooms and I'd recognize the voice anywhere. My heart feels like it could beat right out of my chest with excitement. I turn slowly, wondering if it's been so long since I've seen Mare that I'm now hearing things.

Everything around me fades away when my eyes land on her.

My Goldie.

She looks so beautiful. Her blonde hair falls down her shoulders in waves. There isn't a lick of makeup on her face, and I can already tell that her eyes have misted over.

"Goldie?" I ask hesitantly, stepping out of the line. It seems like I might not be getting on the plane after all. At least not yet.

I can't believe my eyes. She's here. My intuition wasn't wrong. I could still feel her anywhere, even when I wasn't expecting it.

"Cade," she whispers. For a moment everything seems to be frozen in time. There's nothing but the two of us. The world around us fades to black as our bodies collide.

Mare lets out a sob as her arms wrap around my neck. I don't know who clings to the other tighter. Her legs wrap around my middle as she hoists herself up. She tucks her face against my chest as she lets out another cry.

"What are you doing here?" I ask, my lips pressed to her forehead. We're probably making a scene, but I don't give a shit.

"I could ask you the same question." Her words are muffled against my shirt. She pulls away, her eyes puffy and cheeks red with emotion.

I lean in, unable to wait another second. Our lips press against one another and it's like everything falls into place. You would never know we've spent time apart. We kiss like a couple of teenagers, unable to keep our hands off one another. Her hands cling to my face, holding my cheeks so tightly it's like she's afraid if she lets go that I'll fade away.

I keep her pinned against me with one hand. The other hand travels up and down her back as I relish in the feeling of holding her again.

"We're never spending that long apart again," I demand, talking into her hair. I breathe in, wondering how I've gone so long without her comforting scent.

Mare laughs as I wipe the tears from her cheeks. These tears I can handle. They're happy tears. They're proof of our love—of us being together again.

"What is it about us and airports?" she jokes, wrapping her arms around my neck once again.

I set her down slowly but don't let go of her. "What are you doing here, Goldie?" I had all of these plans about going to Chicago and telling her that I was ready and willing to do whatever it took to *actually* be with her.

"I came to Sutten to ask you a question." She bites her lip to try and hide a smile. It's the most stunningly beautiful thing I've ever seen. *She's* the most breathtakingly beautiful thing I've ever seen. She's my Goldie. My sunshine. The light of my life.

And fuck, am I so incredibly happy to have her with me again.

"You came to ask me a question?" I ask, remembering her earlier answer.

Mare steps away, just far enough to reach into a purse I hadn't realized she'd dropped to the ground when her body collided with mine.

"Yes," she answers, reaching into her bag. "A *very* important question."

I cock my head to the side, confused. A flight attendant calls over the intercom for the next group of people to board my flight. If Mare is here, I have no intention of getting on that plane.

"Ask me anything."

Mare pushes a stack of papers into my chest. They're held together by a large binder clip at the top. Her smile is so bright as she holds it against my chest, waiting for me to take it. "How about you tell me the ending?"

"What?"

She carefully guides my arms to take the stack of papers. She shifts it in my grip until she can fan through all of the pages. Mare stops when she reaches the very last page. At the top it says *EPILOGUE* in big, bold letters, but the rest of the page is blank.

"If I were writing an end to Wade and Daisy's story"—she uses the fictional names as if this isn't exactly *our* story—"then I see Daisy realizing that she has a lot of big dreams she wants to come true, but her biggest dream was always Wade."

I swallow because I remember my mom saying a line almost exactly like that one. It isn't lost on me.

"Are we really talking about Daisy?"

Mare shakes her head. "I have a lot of dreams, Cade Jennings. But none of them compare to the best dream come true of all. Loving you. Being loved by you. It's the most special and real feeling I've ever experienced. I think I'm in a place now where the whole author thing can be done from anywhere—from Sutten—as long as it's somewhere with you."

I stare at her because I don't know what to say. She's everything I could've ever wanted in my life. There's a thread that ties us together that is unexplainable, but also something so rare and precious that I'd put anything on the line to keep it—even if it meant moving wherever she wanted me to. Giving up whatever I had to in order to be with her.

"You're not going to say anything?" she asks.

I run my hands along her cheekbones, needing to touch her. "All I want is you. With me. Wherever you want, Goldie. I can't be without you."

"I think it'd be a poetic ending if Daisy made her dreams come true from the small town she left in the first place."

"You'd move back to Sutten? What about being an author?"

Mare leans into my touch. "I hear the man I'm in love with is building me a house with a breakfast nook I'd love to write at."

"I'll build you ten," I say through the emotion clogging my throat.

"So what's the ending going to be?"

I pull Mare's forehead to mine, speaking against her lips. "An ending together in Sutten seems fucking perfect to me."

Mare smiles. "That's what I was hoping you'd say."

Our next kiss is full of the promise of forever.

Epilogue
MARE *eight months later*

pull at the piece of fabric over my eyes. "Cade, I can't see a thing underneath this," I complain. I try to feel around me to find my surroundings, but all I can feel is his warm chest underneath my touch.

"It's a blindfold, Goldie. That's the point."

I let out an aggravated sigh. He's been hush hush all day about what we're going to do for my birthday surprise. I'd tried getting it out of him, but the man never faltered.

The door to his truck shuts. I'm left in silence for a few moments. I fight the urge to use the time to my advantage and push the blindfold off my eyes so I can sneak a peek.

Somehow I'm able to resist the urge. Or maybe it's the fact that Cade doesn't take long to open the passenger door of his truck. His warm hands slide up my thighs, sending shivers of excitement down my spine.

"You ready for your surprise?" His voice is close. So close that I can feel the tickle of his breath against my cheeks.

"Is that even a question?"

He laughs. It's low and comes from deep in his chest. It's almost been a year since Linda left us, and eight months since I moved back to Sutten. I've found him laughing more and more. All of us have laughed more, time taking part in healing our wounds.

Cade takes my hand. He tugs on my arm slightly before he lets go. My hand tumbles to my lap as his lips crash against mine. I eagerly kiss him back, despite him catching me by surprise.

My thighs rub together, loving the feel of his strong fingers digging into the soft skin. I moan into his mouth when they dance against my inner thigh.

"Fuck," Cade growls. "We may have to use this blindfold again, baby. I have so many ideas of what I could do to you while you wear this…"

I arch my back into him, already turned on by the idea of letting him have his way with me while I couldn't see a thing.

Cade groans, laying one last chaste kiss against my lips before he pulls away. I miss his warmth immediately. "As much as I love the idea of you naked underneath me, wearing nothing but the blindfold, I have big plans for you tonight, Goldie."

My bottom lip juts out. "It's my birthday, what if I want that as my birthday gift?"

He chuckles. "That can be your gift later, baby. I've got other plans first."

His strong arms wrap around me and pull me out of the front passenger seat. Then, he helps me plant my feet on the ground. There's concrete underneath my boots, but there's not many sounds around us. We can't be somewhere too public or too busy or I'd be able to hear more.

When I breathe in, I'm hit with the smell of fresh, mountain air.

Cade interlocks our fingers, tugging on my hand a little to get me to walk. I step forward, letting him guide me wherever he wants.

It's silent, the only sound is our boots scuffing against pavement as he guides us. I fix my purse strap on my shoulder, wondering if bringing it was even necessary. It may be my birthday, but I have one little surprise for Cade as well.

Finally, we stop. Cade's hands find my shoulders. He

massages the tender muscles at my neck for a moment. I lean into it, my muscles sore from spending days in front of my laptop plotting a new book.

"You ready?" Cade asks, his lips right next to my ear.

I nod, goosebumps popping up on my bare arms from the excitement.

Cade's fingers brush against the back of my head as he unties the blindfold. He slips it off. I blink a few times, letting my eyes adjust to the sight in front of me.

My hands come to my mouth as I stare at the house in front of me.

Our home.

It's finished.

I turn to him, tears welling in my eyes. "You said there was a hold up with the flooring?"

Cade shrugs, wrapping an arm around me and pulling me into his chest. "I may have told a little lie. The contractor's guys have been working real hard to have everything completed by your birthday."

I shake my head in disbelief. We've been doing our best at getting the house built, but there's been delay after delay since I moved back. It hasn't bothered me too much, but I've been eagerly waiting for Cade and me to finally finish the house we've dreamt about since I was a teenager.

"I can't believe this," I whisper, staring at the finished house. It looks so different from the last time we were up here. I've been trying to get Cade to bring me to the house for over a month now, but he kept saying nothing has changed.

Turns out, *everything* has changed since then. There's now landscaping in the front. Our front porch has two brand new rockers facing where the sun will set every night. It's so perfect.

It's ours.

I rise to my tiptoes, pressing a kiss to Cade's lips. "It's perfect," I whisper.

His hands find my cheeks. He cups them tenderly. "This isn't the end of the surprise."

I wrap my fingers around his wrists, holding his hands in place. "There's more?"

"Much more. Follow me?"

He leads us through the front door and into the house. I'm stunned speechless when I look at the completed house. It's empty, no furniture or decor in the house yet, but it already feels like home.

Cade lets me look around for a moment before he cocks his head toward the kitchen. The patio doors are open, candles lining a walkway out the door.

Before I can ask what's happening, Cade takes my hand and guides me toward the candles. When we step back into the evening air, I gasp.

There's a trail of candles in glass jars all the way to the start of the marigold field. My feet stop. I'm in too much shock to even remember how to walk.

Cade stops with me, letting me soak in the moment.

It's the most stunning view I've ever seen. The sky's the perfect orange color, matching the blooming field of marigolds. It's summer, meaning the marigolds and the sky are both showing off for the night. All of the lit candles add to the magical ambience.

Cade gently nudges me forward. We walk down the pathway until Cade stops us in front of a mass of candles. They're arranged in a semi-circle, with us standing right in the middle of them.

There's a quilt laid out—one made by Linda. On top of the quilt there's a picnic basket and additional candles.

"What is this?" I ask breathlessly. I don't know where to look, what to focus on.

I turn to focus on him. His eyes crinkle at the sides in adoration as he gestures for me to sit. I'm left with no choice but to do as I'm told. I'm too stunned to think for myself.

"This is your birthday gift."

Cade lends me a hand as we both lower to the quilt. I smooth my hand over the familiar stitches, remembering the nights Linda sat by the fire stitching it together.

"I can't believe you did all of this for my birthday."

"I've always loved celebrating birthdays with you."

Emotion swells through me from the memory of us nine years ago. I thought it was the best thing in the world, to spend my sixteenth birthday with Cade Jennings. If only I'd known how many more I'd get to spend loving him—with him loving me.

I look at my surroundings, taking in the beauty of what he's laid out. "This must've taken forever to set up."

Cade smirks. "I had some help."

It's silent for a moment as we both look out at the setting sun. I don't know if he realizes he does it, but Cade reaches out and grabs my hand. He places it in his lap, brushing his fingers along my palm.

His amber eyes focus on me, and I have an overwhelming sense of gratitude knowing he's mine.

"Hey, Goldie?" Cade asks, letting go of my hand to reach for something in his pocket.

My heartbeat speeds up. His voice is hoarse and vulnerable. Something about the moment feels different. It feels special.

"Yes?" I whisper.

"I know it's not midnight, but I was hoping we could break the rules and have you make a wish now?" He pulls out a black lighter. One that looks exactly like the one from all those years ago.

He flicks it on, the flame illuminating the space between us. "Make a wish."

My eyes flutter shut as I pretend to make a wish. There isn't anything I could wish for that I don't already have. Year after year, I wished for Cade Jennings. All I wanted was for him to love me. And now I have that. I've never been happier. He completes me in a way that I thought was only meant for romance novels.

He's my everything. My every wish. My dream come true. The only wish I could make was for things to stay like this forever.

When I open my eyes, I find Cade staring back at me. The flame reflects off the gold flecks in his eyes.

"Did you make your wish?" he whispers.

"My wish came true. I have *you*." I lean forward and blow out the flame, missing seeing the reflection of the dancing flame on his cheeks.

Cade slides the lighter back into his pocket, but he doesn't come out empty handed.

Between us he holds a red velvet box.

"Cade," I whisper, wondering if I'm seeing things correctly.

Cade moves, shifting his body onto one knee in front of me.

A choked sob comes from my throat as I figure out what's happening.

I've dreamt of this day since I was a little girl. He's on one knee in front of me, looking at me with so much love.

He opens the box. I gasp at the brilliant, beautiful solitaire ring nestled safely in the box. "Nine years ago you made a wish, and I desperately wanted to know what you'd wished for. I wanted it to be for me—for us. I want to spend every birthday with you, be your every birthday wish, Goldie. Because you'll always be mine. I want to be your forever. There isn't a version of my future that doesn't have you in it." He taps his chest, hitting against his heart. "You're my entire heart. My entire world. I love you so much that it feels like I live and breathe you. Marry me, Goldie? Make me the luckiest man in the world and become my wife?"

I blink through the stream of tears falling from my eyes. Everything is blurry and it feels like my throat is clogged with too much emotion. All I can do is nod. My body falls forward as I wrap my arms around his neck.

"Yes," I say against his skin. "Yes. A *million* times yes."

"God, I'm so fucking happy to hear that."

I laugh, letting go of him enough to meet his eyes. "Of course I'd say yes. I love you."

We kiss, lost in the touch and taste of one another.

I can't believe I'm going to be his wife.

He grabs my left hand. Both of our hands shake as he tries to slide the ring onto my finger. We're both so shaky he has to line it up a few times before it works.

The moment he slides the ring down my finger, an overpowering sense of peace washes over me. Cade sucks a breath in at the same time as me, like we both feel it.

The wind picks up, caressing my cheeks.

In the same way I can always sense him, I can sense her. I can sense *them*.

My eyes flutter shut as the wind delicately caresses my cheeks.

Hi Mom. Hi Linda.

In the middle of the marigolds, with Cade clinging to me, I know that Mom and Linda somehow, some way are here with us. They're sharing the most special moment of my life with me. With both of us. Mom kept true to her promise. I may not be able to see her, but I *feel* her.

And I know that in this breeze, in the middle of the mountains surrounded by marigolds, she's giving her approval.

A sob ricochets through my body. They're here. They're with us.

Cade and I soak in the moment. Then, I remember the surprise I brought for him.

I part from him only long enough to reach into my bag. My fingers wrap around the book softly. I pull it out, setting it down between us. The wind picks up again, rustling the marigolds around us.

I turn the book so Cade can read the title. He traces it with his finger. "*Rewrite Our Story*. I love it." I look at his forearm, at the ink permanently etched on his skin. A line from Linda's letter to me.

"It's the first official copy of it," I tell him. "I can't believe it will be released later this year."

Cade pulls me against his chest. My back presses to his front as he positions us to look out at the setting sun. "I'm so proud of you, Goldie."

"I love you. I can't wait to be your wife."

Cade lets out a satisfied sigh. "Marigold Jennings sounds perfect."

I nod. There was a time that I thought I'd never get the man I love back. But I did. And as we stare out in front of us, the marigolds blowing in the wind, I think about everything that happened to lead us to this moment.

Our story is nowhere near perfect. We had bumps and bruises along the way that took ages to heal. But the imperfections make it ours. And to me, it's the best love story that's ever been told.

And as the man who I love holds me tight to his chest, his ring on my finger, I have this overwhelming feeling that it wasn't fate that brought me back home. It was my mom and Linda who helped Cade and me rewrite our story.

WANT MORE
Sutten Mountain?

Make sure to preorder Pippa and Camden's story—an enemies to lovers romance that releases September 21st.

PREORDER HERE: https://amzn.to/44uNJsZ

Want more Cade and Mare? Sign up for my newsletter to receive an extended epilogue to *Rewrite Our Story*. The extended epilogue will be sent out at the end of May.

SIGN UP HERE: https://bit.ly/3pgnbM1

Acknowledgments

There are so many people who cheered me on every step of the way while writing this book and I'll never be able to put into words how much I appreciate them, but I'm going to try my best.

First, to *you*, the reader. I wish I could effectively put into words how much I appreciate you, but every thing I've typed doesn't even begin to share how much I love and appreciate you. It is you who is the lifeblood of this community. It is you that shows me endless support. You're the reason I get to wake up every single day and work my dream job, and for that, I'm so freaking grateful. Thank you for choosing my words to read. Thank you for supporting me. You've given me the greatest gift by choosing *my* book to read. I love you so much.

To my husband, AKA Kat Singleton's husband (iykyk), A-A-ron. You do so much to help make my dreams come true and I'll never be able to tell you how thankful I am for the endless hours you put into all things Kat Singleton. Being an author was never your dream, but you support the hell out of mine and I love you so much for that. I wouldn't be able to do what I do if it wasn't for you. Thank you for the countless late nights you spent helping me when there were so many other things you could be doing that are way more fun. I'm the luckiest girl in the world to call you mine. Now stop being so perfect so people will stop googling 'Kat Singleton's Husband'. I'm supposed to be the talent here. I love you so much.

Erica, wtf would I do without you? I know neither of us could've ever expected how busy you'd get with all things Kat Singleton. Thank you for loving me anyway and keeping me in line. I love you so much and am forever grateful that books brought us together.

Ashlee, you consistently create the most beautiful and epic aesthetics for my books and this book was no different. Thank you for not only being the best designer I could ask for, but the best friend I could ask for. You were my first friend in this industry and I'm so thankful for everything you've done for me over the years. I love you. Thank you for sticking with me even when I annoy the shit out of you.

Maren, Monty, and Trilina—thank you for the late nights and early mornings you spent with me while writing this book. You guys were the sounding boards for everything that is Rewrite Our Story. Thank you for all your words of encouragement and for telling me to write even when I didn't want to. I'm so lucky to have friends like you and I cherish each of you so much. Here's to many more sprint sessions that turn into therapy sessions. I love you three so much and have no idea what I'd do without you.

To Salma and Victoria, thank you both for helping me make this book perfect. Cade and Mare wouldn't have the epic love story that they have if it weren't for the two of you. Thank you for everything you did to make this book ready to be released into the wild. Your feedback and notes is so vital to me. I love you both so freaking much.

To my alphas. You ladies were the first people to read this book and you got it in its most raw and real form and you loved it anyway. Thank you for helping make this book what it is. Thank you for believing in me and encouraging me when writing felt hard and I wanted to scrap the entire story. I'm so fortunate to have you ladies in my life. Please never leave me. I love you.

To my betas. Thank you for all of your vital feedback that made this book what it is. I wouldn't be able to do this without you and I appreciate your help in making Rewrite Our Story as perfect as possible. I love you forever.

To the content creators and people in this community that share my books, I'm so eternally grateful for you. I've connected with so many amazing people since I started this author adventure and it means the world to me to have all of you to connect with. I'm appreciative of the fact that you take the time to talk about my stories on your platform. I notice every single one of your posts, videos, pictures, etc. It means the world to me that you share about my characters and stories. You make this community such a special place. Thank you for everything you do.

To Valentine PR, thank you for everything you do to keep me in check. It's not a secret that I'm a constant hot mess and all of you are the reason I'm able to function. Thank you for making all things Kat Singleton run smoothly and amazing. I'm so thankful to call VPR home and for your help in getting Rewrite Our Story out to the world.

I have the privilege of having a growing group of people I can run to on Facebook for anything—Kat Singleton's Sweethearts. The members there are always there for me and I'm so fortunate to have them in my corner. I owe all of them so much gratitude for being there on the hard days and on the good days. Sweethearts, y'all are my people.

Lastly, to *me*. Cade and Mare weren't the easiest couple to write at times, but damn I'm so glad I stuck with them. They're my favorite couple I've ever written and I'm proud of myself for finishing their book no matter how hard the imposter syndrome and self-doubt sunk in. I'm so fucking proud of this book and so proud of myself for being brave enough to release it.

ABOUT THE
author

Kat Singleton is an Amazon top 5 bestselling author best known for writing *Black Ties and White Lies*. She specializes in writing elite banter and angst mixed with a heavy dose of spice. Kat strives to write an authentically raw love story for her characters and feels that no book is complete without some emotional turmoil before a happily ever after.

She lives in Kansas with her husband, her two kids, and her two doodles. In her spare time, you can find her surviving off iced coffee and sneaking in a few pages of her current read.

facebook.com/authorkatsingleton
twitter.com/authorkatsingle
instagram.com/authorkatsingleton
bookbub.com/profile/kat-singleton
goodreads.com/authorkatsingleton
tiktok.com/authorkatsingleton

ALSO BY
Kat Singleton

STANDALONE
Black Ties and White Lies: https://amzn.to/40POdqu

THE MIXTAPE SERIES
Read the completed series of interconnected stand-alones free in KU!
Entire Series: https://amzn.to/40Tzvid

Track 1: *Founded on Goodbye*
https://amzn.to/3nkbovl
Track 2: *Founded on Temptation*
https://amzn.to/3HpSudl
Track 3: *Founded on Deception*
https://amzn.to/3nbppvs
Track 4: *Founded on Rejection*
https://amzn.to/44cYVKz

THE AFTERSHOCK SERIES

Volume 1: *The Consequence of Loving Me*
https://amzn.to/44d4jgK
Volume 2: *The Road to Finding Us*
https://amzn.to/44eIs8E

WANT MORE
Kat Singleton?

Sign up for Kat's newsletter and receive a bonus epilogue for *Rewrite Our Story* at the end of May. Keep reading for the first chapter of *Black Ties and White Lies.*

Chapter 1
MARGO

"Margo, Margo, Margo."

A familiar voice startles me from my computer screen. Spinning in my office chair I find my best friend, Emma, hunched over the wall of my cubicle. Her painted red lips form a teasing grin.

Pulling the pen I was chewing on out of my mouth, I narrow my eyes at her suspiciously. "What?"

She licks her teeth, flicking the head of the Nash Pierce bobblehead she bought me ages ago. "Who did you piss off this time?"

My stomach drops, and I don't even know what she's talking about. "Are you still drunk?" I accuse, thinking about the wine we consumed last night. We downed two bottles of cheap pinot grigio with our roommate and best friend, Winnie. Split between the three of us, there's no way she's still tipsy, but it's the best I could come up with.

She scoffs, her face scrunching in annoyance. "Obviously not. I was refilling my coffee in the lounge when *Darla* had asked if I'd seen you."

I stifle an eye roll. Darla knew I'd be at one of two places. I'm always either at my desk or huddled in front of the coffee maker trying to get the nectar of the gods to keep me awake.

Darla knew *exactly* where to find me.

She just didn't want to.

You accidentally put water in the coffee bean receptacle instead of the carafe and suddenly the office receptionist hates you. It's not like I meant to break it. It's not my fault it wasn't made clear on the machine what went where. I was just *trying* to help.

"I haven't heard from her," I comment, my eyes flicking to Darla's desk. She's not there, but her phone lights up with an incoming call. Darla rarely leaves her desk. It isn't a good sign that she's nowhere in sight. The sky could be falling, and I'm not sure Darla would leave her perch.

Emma rounds the wall of my cubicle, planting her ass on my desk like she's done a million times before, even though I've asked her not to just as many times.

"I'm working." Reaching out, I smack her black stiletto, forcing her foot off the armrest of my chair.

She laughs, playfully digging her heel into my thigh. "Well, Darla, that *amazing woman*, told me the boss wants to see you."

"I thought Marty was out for meetings all day today?"

Emma bites her lip, shaking her head at me. "No, like the *boss*, boss. The head honcho. Bossman. I think it's somebody new."

She opens her mouth to say something else, but I cut her off. "That can't be right."

"Margo!" Darla barks from the doors of our conference room. I almost jump out of my chair from the shrill tone of her voice.

Emma's eyes are wide as saucers as she looks from Darla back to me. "Seriously, Mar, what did you do?"

I slide my feet into my discarded heels underneath my desk. Standing up, I wipe my hands down the front of my skirt. I hate that my palms are already clammy from nerves. "I didn't do anything," I hiss, apparently forgetting how to walk in heels as I almost face-plant before I'm even out of the security of my cubicle.

She annoyingly clicks her tongue, giving me a look that tells me she doesn't believe me. "Obviously, I knew we had people higher up than Marty, they're just never *here*. I wonder what could be so *serious...*"

"You aren't helping."

There's no time for me to go back and forth with my best friend since college any longer. Darla has her arms crossed over her chest in a way that tells me if I don't haul ass across this office and meet her at the door in the next thirty seconds, she's going to make me regret it.

I come to a stop in front of the five-foot woman who scares me way more than I'd care to admit. She frowns, her jowls pronounced as she glares at me.

Despite the dirty look, I smile sweetly at her, knowing my mama told me to always kill them with kindness. "Good morning, Darla," I say, my voice sickeningly sweet.

Her frown lines get deeper. "I don't even want to know what you did to warrant his visit today," she clips.

Your guess is as good as mine, Darla.

"Who?" I try to look into the conference room behind her, but the door is shut.

Weird. That door is never closed.

"Why don't you find out for yourself?" Grabbing the handle, she opens the door. Her body partially blocks the doorway, making me squeeze past her to be able to get in.

Whoever this *he* is, doesn't grant me the luxury of showing me his face. He stands in front of the floor-to-ceiling windows, his hands in the pockets of the perfectly tailored suit that molds to his body effortlessly. I haven't even seen the guy's face but everything about him screams wealth. Even having only seen him from behind, I can tell that he exudes confidence. It's in his stance—the way he carries his shoulders, his feet slightly apart as he stares out the window. Everything about his posture screams *business*. I'm just terrified why *his* business is *my* business.

When they said boss, they really meant it. *Oh boy.*

What have I done?

Even the sound of the door shutting behind me doesn't elicit movement from him. It gives me time to look him up and down from the back. If I wasn't already terrified that I was in trouble for something I don't even remember doing, I'd take a moment to appreciate the view.

I mean *damn*. I didn't know that suit pants could fit an ass so perfectly.

I risk another step into the conference room. Looking around, I confirm it's just me and the mystery man with a nice ass in the empty space.

Shaking my head, I attempt to stop thinking of the way he fills the navy suit out flawlessly. From what I've been told, he's my boss. The thoughts running through my head are *anything* but work appropriate.

"Uh, hello?" I ask cautiously. My feet awkwardly stop on the other side of the large table from him. I don't know what to do. If I'm about to be fired, do I sit down first or just keep standing and get it over with?

I wonder if they'll give me a box to put my stuff in.

His back stiffens. Slowly, he turns around.

When I finally catch a glimpse of his face, I almost keel over in shock.

Because the man standing in front of me—my apparent boss —is also my ex-boyfriend's *very* attractive older brother.

KEEP READING HERE: https://amzn.to/40POdqu

Links

SPOTIFY PLAYLIST:
spoti.fi/3H6Stef

PINTEREST BOARD:
https://pin.it/4O5z5AE

Made in the USA
Columbia, SC
01 June 2023

17593456R00228